THE GARDENER IN THE GRAVEYARD

A gripping cozy murder mystery full of twists

LIS HOWELL

Suzy Spencer Mystery Series Book 5

JOFFE BOOKS

Joffe Books, London
www.joffebooks.com

First published in Great Britain in 2023

Cover art by Dee Dee Books Covers

ISBN: 978-1-83526-146-0

CHAPTER ONE

See! The winter is past; the rains are over and gone.
Song of Songs 2:11

The woman stepped gingerly from the road, on to the path which wound uphill through the long grass. She could smell summer for the first time that year. She heard pigeons making that sad, rueful cooing noise. The sound always depressed her in the city. But here they seemed to be welcoming her, and she felt her spirit lift.

She was about to do something she should have done years ago, and put something right. She repeated that thought with each step. She looked down at her brown ankles and the salmon-pink Capri pants she had chosen for the occasion. She looked good for her age and her confidence was strengthened by her sense of purpose. She tucked her stylish bag closer under her arm and felt its reassuring weight. She had come a long way, but hoped to get back home that evening, and the bag held everything she needed. Vital material.

Of course, traipsing uphill in the first heat of summer would make her perspire, and she had to keep her cool, so she paused for a moment. She hadn't anticipated ploughing through vegetation, and hoped the dirty path wouldn't spoil her trainers. They'd cost a packet. She had gone into town to buy them, the old-fashioned way. She liked the shops. She was a city girl, and out here in the country, she found the proximity of the long grassy stalks and thick green weeds overwhelming. This wasn't the sort of walk she liked.

Then suddenly she saw the daisies ahead, a big, beautiful clump of them, white with bright yellow centres, almost shiny in the sunlight. Despite having forced herself to forget, she couldn't help remembering: *Come away my love. The flowers appear on the earth, the time of the singing of birds is come, and the sound of the dove is heard in our land.*

Ahead she could see the building she was making for, a squat stone church. An odd venue for a meeting. But very quiet. The last thing they wanted was to be overheard, so perhaps it made sense. She could still hear the noise of the road nearby and it wasn't far to the church now. Safe enough. Anyway, she wasn't the one with anything to fear.

The blow on the back of her neck was so sudden, she didn't register it before she died.

* * *

Pat Jones felt the hot door of her car. It was parked outside her terraced cottage, in an attractive little cul-de-sac. She had been a widow for six years and had lived in Norbridge for nearly five of them. But it still felt odd, especially when the seasons changed, and she was reminded of the passage of time.

She shut her eyes and breathed in, then tentatively allowed the warmth to wrap around her. It stayed. No sudden cold wind or cloud shadow. This was how summer felt. You forgot it could ever be like this. She had an urge to take off her cardigan, but wasn't ready for something so dramatic. *Ne'er cast a clout till May be out.* Good advice in Cumbria. There had been intimations of summer, brief hints that it might once again be hot, but this was the first reliable day of consistent sunshine, with the promise of more tomorrow. She opened the hatchback, sucked in the smell of warm upholstery, and stuck the bag of gardening tools in the back.

First, she was going into the centre of Norbridge to meet her friend Lorna and the other gardening volunteers, for coffee at The Pantry. It was Lorna's favourite coffee shop. Pat planned to be early, so she could order a slice of chocolate cake without Lorna telling her to watch her weight.

Then they would drive out and have a big clearing session at the Lesser Friary. They had already tidied some ground near the church, around the old gravestones, but the bottom bit of the ancient burial place was still a mess, especially as passing motorists tossed cans and wrappers into the long grass of the Lesser Friary's land. The gardening volunteers had cleared a lot of litter. Crisp packets and plastic bags were their most successful crop so far.

Not that there would be any other crops.

Lorna didn't agree with planting vegetables or herbs. She was obsessed with rewilding and wanted a meadow sprinkled with highly coloured flowers. Pat had her doubts. She thought a disused graveyard with medieval origins, on the edge of an ancient highway, should be planted with grasses and herbs. It had originally been a cemetery for a group of friars, formally tended for centuries before the dissolution of the monasteries. Pat sometimes imagined ox carts and pilgrims winding their way towards the shrines of St Bega and St Columba on the coast, or towards the huge abbeys of Yorkshire and Northumbria in the east.

There was still traffic on the old road although the new bypass had taken a lot of it. Pat thought that a neat stone wall, plots and a tidy vista might be more likely to dissuade them from littering than a messy mass of wildflowers.

But Lorna would have none of it. It was to be a meadow and that was that. Lorna was wonderful, of course. A force of nature who ignored opposition. Pat had known her since their school days in Liverpool and often reminded herself that Lorna hadn't always been so confident. But now, there was no stopping her.

3

Pat sighed. She was genuinely fond of Lorna but sometimes felt a little bit railroaded by her friend. It had been her own idea that they should volunteer for gardening at the Lesser Friary. After all, they had both, coincidentally, ended up in Norbridge, at a loose end, when they had suddenly bumped into each other in Marks & Spencer. They'd not been so friendly at school, but Lorna would have fallen on Pat like a long lost relative in the bra department if it hadn't been for social distancing.

Pat suspected that Lorna, like herself, hadn't many old school friends. Or many friends at all. They had that in common. Pat had found herself alone after her husband's long terminal illness, whereas Lorna had been a dedicated executive secretary, money rich and time poor. Now, though, she and Lorna had each other. They met several times a week, including every Saturday at The Pantry coffee shop.

Talking of which, Pat needed to get a move on, or her new best friend would arrive, and comment on the size of her hips before Pat had taken her first bite of Mississippi Mud Cake.

* * *

Along the old main road east, a few miles past the Lesser Friary in the village of Tarnfield, media producer and local podcaster Suzy Spencer was having coffee with her husband, Robert Clark. It was the Saturday before the start of the May reading week at the University of Mid Cumbria, where Robert worked as a senior lecturer. He was perusing a heavy theology book while sipping absent-mindedly.

Suzy said again, louder, '. . . and you could take advantage of the good weather 'cos it's supposed to last a few days and paint it while it's not raining. Robert, are you listening to me?'

'Yes.' Robert didn't look up.

'No, you're not. I said you could paint the front door. It looks awful.'

Robert levered his eyes up from the page and took off his specs.

'You never used to fuss about things like that,' he commented. He spoke gently, knowing she could fly off the handle. They laughed about it now, but Suzy had wanted to dye purple streaks in her dark blonde hair when she was stir-crazy during lockdown. Robert had said tactlessly that purple streaks might look good on some people but not on her. Suzy had been furious and flown into a sudden, rare rage of hurt, wounded vanity and insecurity. Since then, he'd trodden more carefully, but he missed their old easy relationship.

There was no doubt that Suzy had been touchy lately. It didn't help that she had been 'working from home' full-time for a while. Suzy was a development executive for an independent TV company three days a week, but in the pandemic she had worked exclusively from The Briars, their house. She had also expanded her local podcast-making, but most of that had been done online. She had missed the company of her co-workers.

He said, 'I think the front door's OK. What's wrong with being shabby genteel?'

'Because we are not genteel. We are just shabby. I hate that front door. Bits are flaking off it like giant dandruff and in the sun it looks like it's got a disease.'

'I'll do it before the end of the week. Just not today. OK?'

Suzy sighed noisily and stood up. She didn't know why she was so obsessed with the house. Of course, she was more aware of it, being based there all the time, so she was intolerant of leaking taps and flaking paintwork. But there was something deeper and more disturbing going on. The past few years had given her a sense of age and decay, and of herself getting older, which was new and disturbing.

Of course, the pandemic had changed everybody, and cast a long shadow. But like many shadows, the details were blurred and confused. It was hard to remember exactly what had happened when. Things looked different . . . and Suzy herself had changed.

There were times when she didn't like what she had become. She was so crabby these days. It didn't help that her daughter, Molly, had gone to the Arts University in York the previous September, so The Briars seemed emptier and dustier. Her son, Jake, was in his twenties and had been away from home for a few years now, though he came back for high days and holidays. But Suzy missed Molly painfully, and then blamed herself for being so weak. She had thought of herself as strong and capable — a bit disorganized sometimes, but independent. After all, she had been a single mum when she'd met Robert. Nigel, the children's father, had defected to the bright lights of Newcastle after one winter in Tarnfield and Suzy had needed to work full-time to buy him out of the house. She had gone on to have a successful career with some TV hits to her name. But recently she felt she was becoming increasingly dull and useless. Her brain wasn't sparking. And there were the hot flushes too . . .

She banged around at the sink.

Robert said, 'Is it home or away today?' He meant would she be closeted in the attic working for the Manchester TV company — which he classified as 'away' — or working on her local community podcasts at the kitchen table, which he called 'home'. He hoped it was 'home'. He knew that Suzy was stressed out about her latest TV pitch for 'away'. The show had the working title of *Lockdown Life Change*. It was about people whose lives had been surprisingly transformed not by the disease but by the social constraints — men who had been secretly running two families and had had to make a choice; people who had found themselves with unwanted guests leading to unexpected outcomes; or those who'd had surprise successes, like meeting the love of their life on Zoom or getting a book published. But it was research-intensive, needing to find all the right participants, and Suzy was worried that the show wouldn't make it into production. She didn't want to think about it and knew she was shelving it, taking refuge in her local podcast work.

'It's home today,' she said tetchily. 'My community pod-cast. But when you say 'home' you make it sound more boring and that isn't fair. Just because it's local—'

'OK, sorry,' Robert said, and swallowed a sigh. 'So, what's the subject?'

'It's a local gardening group.'

'Really?' He was surprised. It didn't sound like one of Suzy's usual topics.

'I knew you wouldn't find it very interesting on the face of it,' Suzy retorted. 'But actually, it's fascinating. I found out about it when the council asked for volunteers. Becky Dixon, Molly's friend, is one. They're clearing up the old graveyard at the back of the Lesser Friary.'

'Over in East Norbridge?'

'Yes.'

'And what's especially interesting about it?'

'Well, it's controversial because the Friary was suppos-edly abandoned at the time of the Reformation. But the new church retained a graveyard at the top, and the bottom area was supposed to be for grazing. But it soon became waste-land where the villagers dumped their nightsoil. Too lush for sheep and too hillocky for cattle. Maybe the locals were a bit superstitious as well.'

'So, bodies and body waste for six hundred years. Yuk.'

'Yes, and now it's a giant litter bin.'

'But how are they going to restore it?' Robert was begin-ning to feel intrigued.

'Ah well, that's what makes it even more interesting. The woman running the group, Lorna Duxford, is formida-ble. She's one of these rewilding enthusiasts and she wants it to be a meadow, but that means they need to clear all the mess and get rid of the alien incomer plants.'

'Except that some people might like them . . .'

'Exactly. There are big overgrown rhododendron bushes, which are superficially attractive, but they'll have to go, and there's even one of those "trees of heaven", which are

7

hellish and can grow to thirty feet. Lorna Duxford's plan isn't universally accepted, but she's got a celebrity on her side.'

'In the shape of?'

'Hiram King,' Suzy said significantly.

'Who?'

'Oh, for goodness' sake, Robert, even you must have heard of Hiram King! He's a national treasure.'

'Sorry. Is he a footballer?' Robert was hopeless on sport.

'No, idiot, he's a celebrity gardener. He had a big show on broadcast TV, then left in a huff and started his own YouTube channel. He's massive in the homes and gardens genre. He's got a Scottish baronial pile just across the border. Anyway, he is big on rewilding and he's giving grants out to community groups who can restore the natural environment. He's Lorna Duxford's guru.'

'Now you're talking. I can see this being something that gets people interested.' Robert knew that Suzy had a knack for finding stories that piqued the public's curiosity. 'So will you be interviewing Bill Gibson?'

'Who's he?'

'Aha, now that's something *you* don't know! Bill's the vicar of St Michael and All Angels, the big church on the edge of Norbridge. He has responsibility for the Lesser Friary as well. He is also chaplain for Norbridge Hospice — a busy bloke.'

But Suzy wasn't really listening. She was thinking that she should take advantage of the weather and get over to the graveyard. 'Well, this isn't about the church, Robert. It's an independent group. The volunteers meet on a Saturday morning, so I thought I'd drive over there. It's such a nice day, so hot and sunny — though of course that just makes my heat spikes worse . . .'

For a minute Suzy drooped over the sink. 'For the first time in my life I really understand about ageing. I can see an end, one day, to my energy. It's a funny feeling.'

Robert got up and walked over to her. He put his arm around her shoulders, hoping she wouldn't shrug him off.

Suzy said quietly, 'I'm sorry, Rob. I'm not stupid. I expected the moods and the hot flushes. But I've always been a healthy type, you know, getting through most things. I didn't expect to feel, well, as if I'm not me anymore.'

'A lot of that is lockdown. And you certainly are you. Even more so. You've done some of your best work in the last few years. You've got two kids safely launched. And you've been involved in some pretty grim scenarios round here. Of course, we all get old, but that's not necessarily bad. And you still look gorgeous, though maybe a few purple hair streaks . . .'

'Oh, for heaven's sake! Don't remind me.' But Suzy smiled. It was good that she could laugh about it now. Yes, he was right. The last few years had been tough. The so-called 'new normal', which wasn't normal at all, seemed to mean lurching from one nasty surprise to another. It had led to some philosophical, and occasionally pessimistic, thoughts. But maybe that was inevitable when you had time to think. Too much reflection had been a new experience for Suzy.

'And what about painting the front door?' she said. 'No, Robert, only joking.'

'Well, you might come home and find it's got purple streaks. You're not the only one to get stupid ideas.'

Suzy threw the dishcloth at him, but it missed.

* * *

In The Pantry coffee shop on a Saturday morning, customers were enjoying the coffee and the people-watching. It was packed.

Lorna Duxford was holding forth. 'And then there's the disgusting dog mess. People let their dogs roam over the end of the graveyard where it slopes to the road. Of course, dog mess on the pavements in Norbridge is bad enough, but in that corner of the graveyard there's a fresh pile every day.'

Pat suddenly couldn't face her chocolate cake. She pushed her plate away. Lorna was totally unaware of the effect of her graphic comments and was still ranting when two more of the gardening volunteers, Tim Markham and Becky Dixon, threaded their way between the busy tables of Saturday shoppers.

As always, Becky Dixon said nothing, but nodded at Pat and ignored Lorna. Becky was a strange, androgenous young creature, but Pat had never spoken to her about the tricky subject of gender and, as Becky didn't talk much, the issue had never come up. Somehow Pat had come to understand that Becky was on a gap year before going to a prestigious university to read medieval history (Cambridge, was it? Pat hadn't wanted to pry), which explained Becky's interest in the graveyard. Pat suspected that Becky thought the rewilded meadow idea was ridiculous. She had mentioned briefly that the space had never been a meadow — it had been rough fell land enclosed by the small band of Dominicans based at the Lesser Friary in the twelfth century.

Pat didn't doubt her. Becky was probably a lot more knowledgeable than Lorna, but wise enough to keep her mouth shut.

Tim Markham, following Becky, was one of those men whose age was hard to assess. He had a good head of dark hair with a touch of grey, and he seemed fit, but he had an unhappy face etched with wrinkles. He had recently retired as a paramedic. Lorna told Pat that Tim had been through a bitter divorce, but he never mentioned it. Lorna had heard about it from their fifth volunteer, Seth Beddoes, who was yet to arrive. That was probably a good thing. Seth Beddoes was a huge, hairy man in messy clothing sprouting scarves and ponchos. The idea of Seth manoeuvring between the crowded spindly tables of The Pantry made Pat shudder.

These two new arrivals were unassuming. Like Becky Dixon, Tim Markham didn't say much. Pat wondered if it was quiet types who volunteered to do gardening. But that certainly wasn't true of Seth Beddoes, who rambled all the time, mainly about himself and his wife, who was some sort of fancy therapist with a local fanbase. As well as being enormous and clumsy, Seth was a tattooed old hippy type with a big mouth, always making crass comments. Pat had the horrible thought that he would probably strip off to the waist now it was warm, and she would have to pretend not to be repulsed by his wrinkly tats and grizzled chest hair. If Pat wore a vest top and showed her cleavage Seth would be the first to make some snide remark about her age.

Lorna nodded at Becky and Tim and moved her piles of bags and tools off the seats she had been saving despite the glare of waiting customers. She carried on without drawing breath. 'And that brings me on to the issue of those old wheelie bins near the layby. They're in completely the wrong place and never get used. I've enquired and they don't belong to the council. And they're locked.'

'Are they anything to do with the church?' Pat asked tentatively.

'They might have been once, but they haven't been touched for years. I'm going to ask Father Bill about them. They're an eyesore. We need to open them, clear them out and get them removed. There's a key for them, which I've found, hanging in the church!' she added triumphantly.

Lorna was right. The group put their gardening waste in big hessian bags up by the Lesser Friary church on the crest of the hill, where the suburban top road ran. The council emptied them every week.

Lorna went on, getting louder, 'I think we should see if we can get the council to remove the bins and give us something more ecological. I suggest we have a look this afternoon. I know it will be a smelly job, but we all need to get stuck in.'

Oh dear, Pat thought, *Lorna will make us three stooges do all the dirty work. Seth Beddoes will find something to hack at on the other side of the site while we delve inside the bins and Lorna supervises.* But Lorna was right, as usual. No one ever dealt with the rusting metal wheelie bins next to the underused layby on the old road. They needed tackling.

But what Pat didn't know was that, for once, Lorna was wrong. At the graveyard it was hot, still and deserted. But someone had been there earlier, and one of the bins was already full. Not with ordinary litter, though. The flies were already starting to buzz.

CHAPTER TWO

I went down to the grove of nut trees, to look at the new growth in the valley.

Song of Songs 6:11

The gardening volunteers finished their drinks and set off for the Lesser Friary. They worked with a mixture of cheap gardening tools bought with start-up funds from the council and their own implements.

Without a car it was difficult to get to the Friary, especially with bags of equipment. Lorna sorted out who was travelling with whom. Pat Jones was to drive Tim Markham, as his Range Rover was at the garage for its MOT. Becky Dixon went on her bike. Lorna drove the last volunteer, Seth Beddoes, who had caught up with them outside The Pantry with some complicated story about the septic tank at their cottage. He was always doing something up, or building or refurbing, usually rather too quickly.

As Pat drove to the graveyard, she chatted to Tim Markham. They had rarely spoken before. 'Dealing with these bins is going to be a mucky job,' Pat said to break the silence. 'Not really what we signed up for.'

Tim sighed. 'I'm not sure what I signed up for, to be honest.'

'You aren't a great gardener then?'

'Not really. My wife did all that. But I needed something to do after my divorce.'

Pat said nothing.

After a minute Tim said, 'We split up at this time of year. Just when the garden was looking nice. I liked plants and she liked garden furniture. We'd been doing barbecues in the summer and a firepit in winter with the neighbours. Then one weekend she said she was leaving with the man next door. Just like that. It had been going on under my nose for months.' He stared out of the passenger window.

'When was that?' Pat asked, to keep the conversation going.

'The May before the pandemic. I was starting to get my life back together when Covid came. Then I was worked off my feet. I took early retirement last Christmas. I think that's when it all really hit me.'

'Are you on your own now? Do you have any children?'

'One. My son's in his thirties. He lives down south. He took his mother's part anyway. He was right, I was to blame for working too hard and not listening to her. Not that we were ever compatible, to be honest.' He sounded bitter, and surprised at his own loquacity.

Pat filled the awkward silence. 'You always blame yourself. My husband died of cancer. When he'd gone, there were so many things I wished I'd done for him.'

'I'm sorry for your loss.'

'So am I — still. But you sort of get used to it. I've got one child as well. She's a teacher like I was, but in Norbridge. That's why I moved here from Cheshire. To help with my grandchild. We were a bubble in the lockdowns. But now he's at school.' Pat paused to negotiate a difficult bend in the road and was pleased that Tim didn't give her any advice. 'When I met Lorna again, I had just seen the notice in the library saying the council wanted to start a gardening group and I suggested we both join. Lorna got her teeth into it straight away. She was the driving force.'

'But you started her off.' Tim turned to look at her. 'Are you and Lorna old friends?'

'Well, we knew each other at secondary school in Liverpool. Lorna came to Norbridge after she retired. We were never that close, though, as teenagers. Lorna was quite timid at school, but you'd never believe it now.'

Tim said nothing. Pat was worried that she might be blathering, but as Tim was still looking at her, rather than out of the window, she went on, 'We're planning to go to an old school reunion next weekend. I would never have dreamed of doing such a thing without Lorna. But she's rather forceful, as you know. And anyway, as you get older, you relate more to the past.'

'Really? I don't know about that.'

'Maybe you're too young.' Pat glanced at his profile. Late fifties, maybe? Younger than she was, certainly.

Tim laughed rather harshly. 'It's more that my past is ever-present. I've never moved anywhere. My family were Cumbrian farm workers. Norbridge was my limit.'

'Did you come here to work for the ambulance service?'

'That's right. My wife was a nurse and we met at the infirmary. We were just like everyone else, wanting a nice semi and holidays in Spain. But I always wanted to have a smallholding. Then it turned out that her idea of a bit of land was a lemon grove in Majorca. She's got that now. Lover boy next door inherited his father's garage business, so money is no object.'

'I hope you're not getting your MOT done at his place!'

Tim laughed. 'No way! He sells BMWs. And he wouldn't dream of working over a weekend. I'm picking up my motor tomorrow. It's pretty ancient now. I got a good deal at a local workshop.' He was still smiling as Pat pulled up and she felt gratified. She couldn't remember seeing him look cheerful before, and he had a nice face when he wasn't brooding.

She parked in the rarely used layby on the old road not far from the bins, glad to see that Lorna was already there, striding up the path. Lorna was tall, and no heavier now than when they had been at school. She was an attractive woman, Pat thought. She had presence. Pat had put on more than a stone in the last forty years and had never been slim. She had thought her weight was OK for her age, but Lorna constantly nagged her about it.

Yet despite Lorna's forthrightness, Pat was very fond of her. As she had said to Tim, shared memories meant a lot. And occasionally Pat wondered whether her friend's life had really been the triumph she implied. Lorna had never had a partner, though she often mentioned affairs. She had hinted archly that the men concerned were significant players. But Pat wondered if the reality was that Lorna had failed to catch someone important enough to marry. She had moved around a lot for work and had always established a prestigious, if short-term, place in local society wherever she lived. It helped that Lorna was a churchgoer. In Norbridge she was a parishioner at St Michael and All Angels, where she did everything from flower arranging to reading the lesson.

Lorna stopped on the path and gathered the group around her. 'This is exactly right!' she said exultantly. 'Look at these glorious daisies. A tapestry of wildflowers like this is what we want.'

Becky Dixon snorted. Pat glanced at her.

Becky mumbled, looking down. 'These are marguerites. *Chrysanthemum frutescens*, from the Canary Islands originally. I looked them up. They were probably seeded from someone's garden. They're not medieval meadow flowers. We need mugwort, borage, caraway, rue, sage, stuff like that. Not pretty enough for Lorna.'

Pat said nothing. Lorna hadn't heard Becky's remark and went on, 'We'll go up to the chapel and get our hands dirty rooting up the ivy on the stonework and then we'll have a break before going back to the road to tackle the bins.'

The little group followed her up the 'people's path' created through the old graveyard, peaceful in the sunshine now after the drama it had seen that morning.

* * *

Down at the dusty layby, Suzy Spencer pulled up. Her equipment — a multi-track recorder, three mics and several cables — was in a bag which she would have to lug with her, but she couldn't afford to miss the right time to record. She needed to catch the sweet moment when people relaxed and exposed the differences which made community groups so interesting — people of opposing political views jointly raising money for charity, people of different religions uniting to save an old church building — it was all about constructive tension. Her podcast was honest but sympathetic. And every episode had some new local information.

Suzy looked up the path at the group of volunteers. She had spoken to Lorna Duxford on the phone and assumed she was the tall woman talking animatedly to the others. Suzy recognized Tim Markham, the paramedic who used to live in Suzy's own village until his glamorous wife had left him. Their split had been the talk of the Spar, the artisan bakery, the pub on the green, and the tiny nail parlour on Tarnfield's high street.

Suzy also knew Seth Beddoes by sight. His huge body and bohemian image made him hard to miss in Norbridge. His wife, Tranquillity, had built up quite a clientele, in a short time, as a New Age 'spiritual therapist'. Suzy had toyed with the idea of a podcast feature on Tranquillity, but somehow it hadn't happened. She had mentioned to Robert that she was put off because Tranquillity sounded like a made-up name.

'Wow, Tranquillity! That's some claim!' Robert had said. 'Stick to Suzy. Tranquillity wouldn't suit you.'

That time Suzy had hurled the dishcloth at him without missing. But later they'd had a longer chat about Tranquillity

Beddoes. Robert rarely took a dislike to someone, but he was dismissive of the 'spiritual therapist'.

'Is it because you want a monopoly on spirituality?' Suzy had said jokingly.

'No . . . Well, in a way maybe . . . but it's not that. I've nothing against people setting up with any sort of feel-good stuff if it helps — meditation, mediation, even medication. Especially medication, if I'm honest. And a lot of HR stuff has a therapy base. But I think Tranquillity Beddoes is something different.'

'You mean a fraud?'

'No, not that. She's highly qualified.'

'Oh, so you do know about her. Tell me more.'

Robert had paused. 'OK, but this is just my feeling. She approached the university last year to offer counselling, particularly for young people with eating disorders. She went straight to the Dean. He's had a lot of trouble with one of his daughters and her eating. Anyway, I thought it was a bit too much of a coincidence.'

'You mean Tranquillity Beddoes knew the Dean had this problem and was pushing his buttons.'

'Maybe. The Dean talked to me about working with Tranquillity because I've been dealing with students and mental health in the pandemic. But we have a good student counselling service, so it came to nothing.'

Interesting, Suzy had thought.

She pulled her thoughts back to the gardening volunteers. Watching the group on the path, Suzy also recognized Becky Dixon, who was a friend of her daughter Molly, although Becky looked thinner and more elfin than ever. That left a small, stocky elderly woman in a mushroom-coloured cardigan and unflattering baggy jeans.

Slowly, Suzy walked up the path towards the group.

* * *

Back in Tarnfield, Robert Clark was enjoying his book. It took a moment for him to register the knocking at the front door and to remember that the bell didn't work, another of Suzy's moans. It didn't matter, as they usually heard cars draw up. Theirs was the only house at the bottom of a lane, where Suzy had famously — to her children anyway — run into Robert's fence many years ago, leading to their unlikely romance. Robert had been a widower and traditionalist, prepared to live the rest of his life alone after a demanding marriage. But he had discovered he was a family man, and he loved Suzy's children, Jake and Molly, not as if they were his own, but for themselves. And Suzy, who laughed a lot, had brought out his own repressed sense of humour. Despite — or perhaps because of — her frenetic lifestyle, she had given him the chance to relax.

But the last two years hadn't been easy. On top of the lockdowns, he could see the menopause was tough, though of course he could only sympathize rather than empathize. Years ago, it could be ignored or joked about but now it was talked about all the time. Trying to understand that it was life-changing, disturbing, and as much of a surprise to Suzy as to him was challenging. But it shouldn't be demeaning, and although Suzy was more irritable and sometimes dejected, she was no less effective, and sometimes more so. He appreciated her frustrations and loved her more because she was coping with them, though she was definitely more irascible. And of course, men had their mid-life problems too.

He was musing about this when he heard the knock at the door. Putting his book down, he stood up slowly and went to answer. It was his friend Neil Clifford, the Area Dean. Robert was a churchwarden at All Saints, Tarnfield, and a member of the Deanery Synod. He'd been involved in church affairs for decades. But it was rare for Neil to turn up at The Briars unannounced.

'Coffee?' Robert asked. 'It's fairly fresh.'

'Thanks.' Neil seemed unusually distracted and awkward. He was a good man and a good priest, but he looked tired that morning. He followed Robert into the kitchen.

Robert said, 'Seems like the first day of summer, doesn't it? Might have to water the garden this week. Talking of gardening, Suzy's gone to do a podcast episode about the gardening volunteers at the Lesser Friary.'

Neil looked relieved. He'd been given a helpful conversational opening. 'That's a coincidence. I've come to talk to you about Bill Gibson at St Michael and All Angels.'

'The vicar who looks after the Lesser Friary too?'

'Yes. He's been overworking, with that, and the parish, and the hospice. And what I say must be in the strictest confidence, Robert.'

'Fine.' Although Neil must know that Robert tended to share everything with Suzy and vice versa.

Neil pushed his coffee mug around a bit and absently took one of the biscuits out of the tin but didn't eat it. 'I knew this was bound to crop up at some point with some vicar. I've been dreading it. But I didn't expect it to be Bill Gibson.'

'What's the problem?'

'I've had an anonymous letter accusing him of historical sexual abuse.'

'Bill Gibson? Good grief!'

'That's what I thought.'

'Male or female?'

'Interesting you should ask that, but it's a female. It accuses Bill of inappropriate touching when the victim was a teenager, over thirty years ago. It's not clear whether it's the victim who is writing, or someone on their behalf. They want Bill to confess and apologize. And, of course, they want compensation. I went to see Bill. He's been very stressed anyway and now he's beside himself. He categorically denies it.'

'So, he's going to fight the allegations?'

'No. He says he can never prove it so we should pay up. End of story.'

'That's an odd position to take.'

'Yes. Of course, I'm going to the bishop about this, but I don't think it's straightforward. It would help if I could find out why Bill is being so obdurate. Either it's a tissue of lies, in which case we should deny it and fight, or he really was giving a pubescent girl religious instruction by himself in the vestry. That would have been colossally stupid. And uncharacteristic. I've got a meeting with the bishop on Tuesday — she's away till then.'

'When did you find out about this?'

'Yesterday. I went straight over to see Bill. It was hopeless. I'm sure there's something in the back story but he won't say any more to me.' Neil paused; then he went on, 'I wondered if in the meantime you could talk to Bill. I did mention to him that you've been very helpful in the past and he didn't say he wouldn't see you. I know you've dealt with similar issues at the university.'

Robert nodded. 'These things are very serious. You can't afford to waste any time. You probably want me to go over to Bill's now . . .'

'I was rather hoping you would.'

'Does Bill's wife know?'

'Ruth? No, I'm pretty sure she doesn't. And she needn't at this stage. Maybe you could take Bill for a pint over at The Partridge.'

'OK. I'll do what I can,' said Robert.

But he could do without this, in the university's reading week. He wouldn't get much reading done now. He and Suzy had been saying only that morning that they still needed time to readjust to a new world of crises with one unexpected jolt after another. Since the pandemic everything seemed to be out of kilter. Unlike Suzy, sometimes Robert wanted to retreat behind closed doors, away from the rigours of the real world. He had laughed and said they needed to be reintroduced to the wild.

It was phrase which was going to rebound on Robert in the days ahead. But for now, he had enough to worry about.

CHAPTER THREE

Awake, north wind, and come, south wind! Blow on my
garden, that its fragrance may spread abroad.

Song of Songs 4:16

Suzy walked through the old graveyard in the heat. It wasn't
quite noon, but it was already hot.

'Hi!' she said. 'You're Lorna? It's Suzy Spencer here from
Neighbourhood Norbridge. We spoke last week.'

'Yes, of course,' Lorna said graciously. Pat, standing next
to Lorna, was embarrassed by her friend's imperious tone,
but she could tell that Lorna was secretly delighted.

Lorna turned to the group. 'I hadn't mentioned this
because our visitor wasn't sure she could come. Welcome,
Suzy. Guys, this is Suzy Spencer, who makes the podcast
which so many local people love. I didn't say anything in case
you all got too excited.'

Becky snorted again, and Pat smiled at Suzy Spencer,
trying to look friendly in contrast to Lorna's grand manner.

'We're the core volunteers,' Lorna went on. 'As you
know, I'm Lorna Duxford and here we have Tim Markham
and Seth Beddoes.' Despite all her protestations about
equality, Pat had noticed that Lorna always gave the men

precedence. 'And we have my friend, Pat Jones, and our young enthusiast, Becky Dixon.'

'Hi, Suzy,' Becky said, with the slightest eye roll in Lorna's direction.

Suzy smiled. 'Nice to see you again, Bex. Becky is a friend of my daughter,' Suzy explained, 'and it's great to meet you all. How about if you start doing exactly what you were going to do, and I come and join you and chat to you all in turn?'

'So do we have any control over what you put in the podcast?' Lorna asked, wrinkling her brow.

'Well, I won't record anything you don't want to say, and I'll record far more than I'll use. I can't let you edit it — that's my job — but you all know my style. I'll give you my phone number, so if you have second thoughts or want to add anything, just phone me.'

The group seemed to nod, but not enthusiastically. No one said anything, but Suzy felt they needed added reassurance. 'This is not about catching you out, or making you look silly, but I need to get a sense of talking to you naturally, as you're working. Starting with Lorna of course,' she added quickly.

'Ace. Fantastic. Groovy, I can hack it,' boomed Seth Beddoes. 'Hey, Suzy, I'm sure you've heard of my wife, Tranquillity. She's a fantastic spiritual therapist. She'd be a great subject for your pod—'

'Thanks, Seth,' Lorna butted in sharply. 'We all admire Tranquillity's work, but Suzy's here to talk about the graveyard. I'll give you the background, Suzy, and then you can speak to all the volunteers individually. You know the party line, guys — we're clearing the land and seeding it with wildflowers to replicate an English meadow. It's called rewilding, Suzy.'

Suzy nodded, trying not to smile. Rewilding was the latest gardening trend and hardly unique to the Lesser Friary. But this strange bumpy rise wasn't what she thought of as meadow. It was stony and tussocky, more like the foothills of the fells.

She glanced in turn at the members of the group. Becky was staring at the path and kicking up a bit of earth. Seth was grinning, not at all upset at being told off by Lorna, hacking lazily at a big thistle with a dangerous pair of shears. Tim Markham was staring into the distance, shielding his eyes from the sun, while Pat Jones was holding a hoe, looking at Lorna with a sort of anxious affection.

'OK, Suzy, come with me while I unlock the chapel and dig out — no pun intended — our tools.' Lorna laughed brightly.

'We blokes bring our tools with us, Lorna. No pun intended there either, eh, Tim?' Seth Beddoes roared, but Tim Markham ignored him and turned away.

Pat felt sorry for Tim and hoped Seth wouldn't make smutty remarks on the recording. Seth shook out his long grey hair and Pat felt sure a blob of sweat splashed on to her cardy. But she wouldn't take it off yet in case Seth made jokes about her bingo wings.

Tim had turned back to the group. 'Lorna, d'you still want to investigate the bins, now we're being recorded?' Tim sounded serious, but he caught Pat's eye, and she knew he was being mischievous. She bit back a smile.

Lorna looked cross. Bins were an unappealing aspect of their work. But Suzy jumped in. 'Oh yes!' she said quickly. 'Please do. That would be a nice realistic touch.'

Lorna capitulated gracefully. 'Why not? Follow me, Suzy.'

They all climbed the final hilly bit of the ground to the Lesser Friary church, where Lorna produced an iron door key from her gardening bag. The others sat in the shade on the ivy-clad stonework parapets while Lorna opened up.

Inside, the church was cool and smelled damp. The walls were whitewashed. There was a small altar under one of the big east-facing windows, but no seats. At the back, which looked like an Edwardian extension, there was a screen with a door leading to a loo and kitchenette.

'Do they ever have services here now?' Suzy asked.

'Oh, I don't think so,' said Lorna, who clearly wasn't very interested in the interior. Some of it seemed medieval to Suzy. She had heard of the Lesser Friary and passed it many times but had never been inside.

Lorna went on, 'As Seth said, we bring our own tools, and of course I understood his silly innuendo. He can be annoying, but he and his wife have quite a local following. Good for awareness of our work.' She tugged out a large plastic bucket. 'We have secateurs and trowels in here. I discourage people from bringing their own secateurs because they get lost so easily in the ivy. These have bright pink handles so we can see them, and as we're attacking the ivy first today, we'll start with them.'

'Do you mind if I record you, Lorna?'

Lorna was leaning over the bucket and stood up swiftly, composing herself for an interview.

'No, please,' said Suzy. 'Go on rummaging.'

Lorna frowned but went back to rattling the secateurs. She said rather stiffly, 'So far, we've sourced the equipment ourselves spending the council start-up grant wisely. If we are lucky enough to get a further grant from Hiram King's Back to Nature fund, we can buy more tools and wildflower seeds from Hiram's own range, which is top quality of course. He's offering several hundred pounds separately to ten local community groups interested in rewilding. You do know who I mean, of course? Everyone has heard of Hiram King.'

Except Robert Clark, thought Suzy, and smiled to herself.

Lorna continued, 'What Hiram is doing is marvellous. He is helping public gardens break free from the formal Victorian park idea which took such a hold in the nineteenth century. We are so lucky that Hiram has moved in just over the Border.'

'So where are you from originally, Lorna?'

Lorna Duxford made throat-cutting signs to tell Suzy to switch off the recorder. 'I really don't want to go into that,' she snapped. 'I'm from Liverpool, and so is Pat, but we don't want to give the impression that this isn't a genuine local initiative. Tim, Seth and Becky are all Cumbrian born and bred, though Seth did move down to London for a while.'

'In the swinging sixties?' Suzy suggested.

'I suppose so. He talks about the King's Road sometimes.'

I bet, thought Suzy. 'But Hiram King's a Scouser like you, isn't he?' she added. 'That might help you get ahead in the race for the grants he's giving out.'

For a minute Lorna looked caught off guard. 'I, well . . . er, I wouldn't dream of mentioning that,' she said sharply. 'Liverpool's a big place and frankly I don't have any contacts there anymore. That's why I was so pleased to meet up with Pat again and it's nice to share memories, but we are both committed to life in Norbridge now.'

'OK.' Suzy sighed. It was not going to be easy to get Lorna to relax. 'Now tell me about your ideas for the grave-yard. And after I've talked to each member of your group, we'll walk down to the old bins and get some sound effects.'

Flies were buzzing round the bins. But they weren't the sound effects Suzy was thinking of.

* * *

Robert had driven off towards the vicarage of St Michael and All Angels. He had no idea how he was going to approach Bill Gibson. As always, he thought, honesty was the best pol-icy. Although perhaps not with Suzy's purple hair idea. He laughed aloud. She had been like her old self this morning, throwing the dishcloth at him.

But he needed to be serious. He would tell Bill Gibson the truth about why he was there, and if the vicar told him to get lost, he would leave him be. But Robert knew that most of the time, people needed to talk, which meant having someone to listen.

He was in luck. When Robert pulled up outside, Bill Gibson was mowing the vicarage front lawn for the first trim of summer. Gibson was a tall elderly man, with thick eye-brows and a thinning close-cropped fuzz of iron-grey hair.

He was quite stooped now and Robert guessed he was into his late sixties. He had a bit of a paunch and wore sunglasses clipped to his spectacles, which he flipped up when he saw Robert and walked towards him. He was wearing an orange-and-black striped polo shirt, and he had a jumper tied around his waist with the sleeves flapping as he walked. The effect was of a grumpy giant wasp making its way across the garden.

'Did Neil Clifford send you?' he said peremptorily.

Robert nodded. 'Neil told me you wouldn't mind meeting with me. Neil's worried. He's told me about this awful allegation. I'm sorry about this, Bill.'

'I bet you are. It's going to be a big nuisance for the precious diocese *team*.'

'It's not just that. Neil is worried about you too. He thinks you're not telling him everything.'

'So, the idea is that I tell you and you tell him, is that it? You both must think I'm stupid.'

'Well, Neil thinks you're holding back but might talk to someone who isn't in your management hierarchy. We might be able to work on a version to tell Neil. These things are pretty nuanced.'

'Nuanced!' Bill Gibson scoffed. 'Another trendy word meaning nothing, like "meme" and "trope" and "optic". In my day, an "optic" was hanging up in the pub.'

'Talking of which, why don't we go over to The Partridge? Unless Ruth is expecting you in for lunch?'

'Ruth's down at our daughter's in Skipton. To be honest, on a hot day like this a pint of real ale would go down well.' Then in a sarcastic tone he went on, 'And before you ask, I'm all organized for tomorrow. Tea rota sorted, sermon recycled, children's worker briefed. Everything tickety-boo. Bit short on the Holy Spirit, but you can't have everything. I'll just put the mower in the shed, then you can drive, and I can relax.'

But then Bill Gibson softened. 'I'm sorry for shooting the messenger, Robert. It's good of you to come. When this business breaks, a lot of people won't touch me with a barge-pole. And the funny thing is, they'll be barking up the wrong tree. Now there's a mixed metaphor for you. Just wait, and I'll be with you.'

Robert watched him stomping over the lawn. He was a while in the shed, then he came back and climbed into the car without saying anything. They set off for The Partridge, the country pub just opposite the Lesser Friary on the top road.

In the pub, Bill Gibson ordered a pint with a scotch egg and chips. 'Ruth has vetoed meat unless she can track it from cradle to abattoir, and chips have been off the agenda for years. I've put on a few pounds since she's been obsessed with the daughter's pregnancy. Is there any ketchup? Salt?'

Robert had a smoked salmon platter and salad. He knew Suzy was planning an early supper. As he was driving, he had half a pint of the delicious local beer. He would have liked more. A pint would have helped him relax with Bill, who looked sulky and difficult. Even the vicar's defiant ordering of the least healthy food on the menu had been an angry gesture.

Robert said, 'You know what this is about, obviously. Neil tells me that he's had an anonymous letter accusing you of historic sexual abuse with a teenage girl. You categorically deny it, but you don't want the Church to fight the allegations on your behalf. But let's face it, thirty years ago a lot of people touched others in a way they wouldn't do now.'

'But I didn't do it.'

'So why should the Area Dean advise the bishop to settle with the accuser?'

'I've got my reasons.'

'But why not deny it and let this liar do their worst? They need to specify time and place. If there was no time and no place, there's no case to answer.'

Even as he said it Robert knew, from similar cases at the university, that if there was even the slightest chance that offence or hurt or damage had been caused, however inadvertently, the guilty party had to 'fess up.

'Do you have any idea who wrote the letter, Bill? Was it the victim — the alleged victim — or someone acting for her? I haven't seen it.'

In answer, Bill Gibson groped in his pockets and pulled out a sheet of paper. 'Neil gave me a copy,' he said. 'That's why I was so long in the shed. I'd put the copy in there because that's the only place where Ruth never goes. Read it for yourself.'

The letter was handwritten:

To the Area Dean:
Dear Mr Clifford,

You have a child abuser on your team. Thirty-three years ago this month, one Tuesday evening on the hottest day of that year so far, Rev Bill Gibson was preparing a young teenager for confirmation. He was a new vicar at St Michael's in East Norbridge. Quite handsome then.

He took her into the vestry, and they sat on chairs opposite each other. He led the conversation to sex before marriage. Sounds so archaic now, doesn't it? But it still mattered then. The vicar said he understood the temptation. He leaned forward and put his hand on her knee. She leaped up and ran away. And she gave up any thought of ever being confirmed after that.

Mr Clifford, you need to go to your superiors in the Church and get advice about how this girl, now a middle-aged woman, can be supported. She needs counselling and therapy. That's not cheap. But the Church should pay. In two weeks, we'll come back to you to find out what you're going to do.

If you do nothing, we will. She needs support and she needs closure.

Help for the Abused

Robert was surprised by the letter. 'This is quite specific. And you say it's completely untrue?'

'Yes. I would never hold a class for a teenage girl, or boy for that matter, one-to-one in the vestry and anyway . . .'

'Anyway what?'

'Nothing.'

'Bill, you must explain why you're so adamant this never happened but you're not prepared to fight your corner. And what makes the writer think that you're going to cave in if you both know that the whole thing is a pack of lies?' On a hunch he said, 'Do you know who's written this?'

Bill Gibson's head shot up. 'What makes you say that?'

'Because if it were pure fiction, you could survive it. Your wife and your churchwardens and PCC members and the other kids from your church, now in their forties or fifties, would back you up. Wouldn't they?'

Bill said grumpily, 'I suppose so.'

'But you want to make some compromise with this person, even though you say you are completely innocent. That makes no sense unless you want to placate them for another reason.'

Bill stared into his second pint. There was a long silence.

'Yes. You're shrewd, Robert,' Gibson almost whispered. 'But I honestly can't tell you anything. You see, you're right. I may have to confess to something I never did. But the most important thing is that the real truth never comes out and Ruth never gets to hear of it. Do you understand?'

Not really, Robert thought. *What truth could be worse than confessing to abusing an underage girl?*

CHAPTER FOUR

You who dwell in the gardens with friends in attendance, let me hear your voice.

Song of Songs 8:13

At the graveyard, after talking to Lorna about her hopes for a grant from the Hiram King Foundation, Suzy went to find Seth Beddoes. He was sawing at a huge ivy root. Suzy asked if she could record his efforts. He grunted and pulled till the root broke off. Great actuality.

Seth muttered, 'It takes muscle doing this. Feel that. Solid. Yes, I've still got what it takes, baby. You should have seen me back in the day.'

She would have to edit that out. Seth Beddoes had a pleasant Cumbrian accent but his speech was overloaded with dated slang. And he mumbled as well. Suzy couldn't imagine why he was in the gardening group. He should be running a country and western club in a cellar somewhere. 'And are you excited about the rewilding idea? The wildflower meadow?'

'I get excited very easily.' Seth Beddoes roared with laughter and Suzy's recorder hit the red. She backed off.

'Hey!' Seth shouted, misunderstanding. 'Don't do that. I'm just a gentle giant kinda guy.'

'I had to move back. The sound was distorted. Too loud suddenly.'

'Gotcha. I'll keep my voice down.'

'So, seriously, how do you feel about the rewilding?'

'Oh, it'll never happen,' Seth muttered, and laughed. He sounded more country and less western now. 'When this meadow idea goes tits up, this could be a nice little mountain-biking track. It needs clearing either way.'

'Do you want me to quote you on that?'

'Shit no. Mustn't upset Lady Lorna.'

'And what do you do when you're not here, Seth?'

'Me? I'm a retiree. I do a bit of this and that, and I look after my missus — who's truly amazing.'

'And before you retired?'

'You're pretty nebbie, eh? Google me. Nah, I'll tell you. Vintage. Vinyl. That was my thing. I had a shop. And mail order . . . down in the Smoke. I trade a bit now as well. But not so much since I shacked up with the lovely Tranquillity. You should be interviewing her, darlin'. She's the business. Say no more.'

Suzy didn't. She doubted Seth had anything perceptive to offer about the historic graveyard. On the other hand, Becky Dixon always took everything very seriously. 'Hi again, Bex. So, is this one of the things you're doing in your gap year? I know you've been down to York to see Molly once or twice.'

'Yep. It's good. I think she made the right choice.'

'And you? Cambridge, isn't it?'

'Yes, but I'm not sure. It's a long way. Different culture. I can hack the course, but the people . . .'

'I think you'll be fine. They need to adapt to you, not you to them. Anyway, tell me about the graveyard. Can I record?'

'Yes sure.' Becky stood up. 'It's very interesting. I've been to look around the Lesser Friary once or twice before. It's the sister church of the main house of the Blackfriars, the Dominicans, up on the Solway.'

This was better stuff. Suzy smiled encouragingly.

Becky said enthusiastically, 'In 1335 there were twenty friars there. Their graveyard was properly excavated. This place was much less important and was probably like a sort of hostel on the way into Norbridge.'

'So is the church of historical importance?'

'There's not much left that's medieval. But the original Friary was never deconsecrated because it served the locals here as a parish church before St Michael's, East Norbridge, was built.'

Suzy nodded. Becky went on, 'In the eighteenth century they tidied it up and made it into a little church, so that's why it looks rather squat. But sweet. Of course, once they'd messed about with it, it lost its authenticity, but the chancel is from the fourteenth century.' Becky paused, and then added scornfully: 'And obviously, this was never a meadow.'

'So, what was it?'

'I think it was what they used to call a wilderness. The friars cleared enough land to have a garden at the top, where the eighteenth and nineteenth-century gravestones are now. The shallower medieval graves were in what might have been a terraced arrangement, going down to the road. There would have been a few pilgrims who died on their way to St Bee's. Friars were quite tolerant and buried women and children as well as their own followers.'

'But doesn't that mean you might dig up bones?'

'Very unlikely,' said Becky. 'They would have decomposed or been rooted up centuries ago. It's a myth that bones last for ever. And these bodies weren't protected by anything. They only used coffins for the best people, or to move corpses about. The people here would have been buried in their winding sheets.'

'Thanks, Becky. That's really interesting.'

'Yes, but don't quote me on anything that might upset Lorna. She's a pain, but at least she's getting the land cleared. Her meadow idea is rubbish — there were never carpets of brightly coloured wildflowers here. But if it's what she wants, it doesn't matter. You can never recreate the past, anyway.'

Becky was wise for her years, Suzy thought. She moved on towards Tim Markham, but when he saw her coming, he became absorbed with some particularly stubborn ivy. *He doesn't want to speak to me*, Suzy thought. He was probably embarrassed because his divorce was the talk of Tarnfield.

Suzy approached the dumpy little woman still wearing her cardigan despite the heat. 'Pat?'

'Yes.'

'I hear that it was you who started the venture after you saw an advert in the library for volunteers, after the lockdown eased. It was a council initiative, wasn't it?'

'Yes, that's right. Then I met Lorna again after more than fifty years. We'd both moved to Norbridge, we were both on our own, and I thought this might be a nice project for us.'

'And Lorna is running it now, right?'

Pat laughed. 'Yes! I didn't realize Lorna would be so enthusiastic. But that's her way.'

'And what do you think about the rewilding idea?'

Pat paused for a minute. 'I think rewilding can be brilliant. I'm a fan. I enjoy the Britain Rewilding website though I don't agree with all of it. Hiram King is a great rewilding champion, and now he's almost local. And there have been some wonderful roadside verges planted with wildflowers.'

'But this isn't a roadside verge, is it? It's a graveyard. Do you think a meadow is in keeping with the history of the place?'

Pat sighed. Suzy's questions might be hard to answer but she didn't suck up to interviewees and trick them into talking. Pat had heard some *Neighbourhood Norbridge* editions and admired the way Suzy managed to include different points of view, then pull them together into something positive. And Suzy's engaging way of waiting patiently for her to speak made her want to confide. She had no one to talk to about how she really felt.

'Turn off your machine,' said Pat. 'Look, Suzy, to be honest Lorna is a huge fan of Hiram King's. A lot of people who have never even had a potted plant love gardening on TV, and Lorna is one of them. She's had a successful career and lived in modern flats with only a balcony for most of her working life. This is an exciting change for her. I'm willing to support whatever she wants.'

'And what about you? What brought you to Norbridge?'

'Me?' Pat looked surprised. 'Oh, I moved here to help my daughter after my grandson was born. Then we were in a lockdown bubble, so I didn't get to know many people. This group is great for me. You can record this bit.'

Suzy switched on her machine.

'I want to say that at this stage none of us here are experts. The really experienced local gardeners weren't interested in the Lesser Friary. Too complicated a proposition, I think, and too much heavy lifting. Not enough work with plants. I think this project is more about clearing and tidying than horticulture. Getting rid of the rubbish.'

As if on cue, Lorna came striding towards them. 'I want to tackle the bins now,' she said. 'We need to find out what's in them, if anything. I suspect they haven't been opened for years.'

The little band moved down the path towards the bins on the edge of the layby. Lorna was right: they were a mess. Suzy dropped behind but turned on her recorder. A few feet in front of her, Tim Markham stopped suddenly.

'I think we should be careful, Lorna. There are a lot of flies around the bin and there's also a rather odd smell.'

'I can't smell anything but car fumes,' Lorna barked. 'It's not going to be a nice job, Tim, but don't put people off.'

Tim looked worried. His experience as a paramedic was making him apprehensive. Flies were not a good sign and they appeared very quickly when there was flesh involved. 'I think there might be something decomposing in that bin, Lorna.'

'A dead cat? Or a fox? But how could they possibly get in? I told you — they're locked. But I've got the key here, from the church. Look — it's this triangular little metal shaft with a handle. You put the shaft into the lock like this and just twist it. Really easy. And then lift the lid like this—'

'Lorna, don't!' Tim shouted.

But the big bin lid had swung open. For the next few seconds there was silence, with Lorna peering into the bin and Tim pulling at her arm. Lorna made some gurgling, indistinct noises. Then, leaving the lid open, she backed away, screaming hysterically.

Tim pushed her aside, looked, and slammed the lid down at what was in the bin. A small cloud of fresh flies flew lazily upwards.

'All right!' he shouted. 'Pat, get Lorna to sit down, take deep breaths and put her head between her knees.'

Pat had put her arms around Lorna, who was shaking violently and had started to retch. 'The rest of you, back off. Becky, call the police.'

'Hey, Tim, mate, what gives?' Seth Beddoes had caught up with them from the other direction. Clearing out bins wasn't his scene.

'There's a woman's body in there. I'd say she's not been there long. We all need to stay here. I'll call the ambulance service. It might be a long wait but none of us should go anywhere until the police have arrived. They'll want to talk to us.'

Lorna started to wail, a strange, animal sound which shocked them all.

* * *

It was a hot, tedious Saturday for Hiram King, once known as Kevin McMurran until he'd changed his name. Our Kevin. He had hated that name. So ordinary.

Hiram sat in the big drawing room of his Scottish baronial-style castle and looked out of the mullioned window to where his lawn dropped to real meadow. It was already a mass of colour. Wild grasses fringed the edges but there were big heads of cow parsley the size of cauliflowers, red campion with its frilly petals of pale purple, bird's-foot trefoil like butter smeared on the grasses, bright meadow buttercup, pale lemon cowslip and dusty purple clover.

The flowers came from his own wildflower seed brand, Hiram's Sweet Meadow, available online and in shops at the designer end of the homes and gardens market. The issue now was whether to wait to mow till September, leaving the seeds to germinate, or mow in July, like they did at Highgrove, bringing sheep in to trample the fallen seeds into the ground. But maybe sheep weren't a good idea. There had been those sheep-worrying incidents down in Cumbria. Plus, there were other good reasons for not having sheep on the place. Hiram was moving on from flora into fauna and sheep might be a problem. And if his ambitious plans came off, he might be able to teach them a thing or two at Highgrove one day.

He stopped dreaming and pulled himself back to the present. Beyond the meadow was his wood, a dense mix of deciduous and evergreen. Past that was a sliver of purple fell before the land went on rolling towards Hadrian's Wall and England. Hiram loved the place for its isolation and sense of wildness. He often said that the lockdown at Kirkaber Castle had made 'f— all difference' to him. Maggie, his annoying but indispensable PA, had worn a mask throughout and had insisted he did too on the rare occasions he went out.

Maggie came sidling into the big drawing room in that obsequious way which both irritated and flattered him. She was, as always, carrying her laptop. In days gone by it had been a clipboard. Both were passive-aggressive devices to keep him under control.

'What?' he said grumpily.

'Hiram, I need to confirm with the dentist in Norbridge. He closes on Saturday afternoon. You need special arrangements for the car. Your appointment is on Tuesday afternoon. And I'm catching a train from Norbridge today at three o'clock, remember?'

'Of course, I remember, you silly moo. You've gone on about it often enough.'

Maggie was going back to London for a cherished forty-eight-hour break. She would check on her Kensington flat and do a few chores for Hiram. It was typical that Maggie's leave would mean being on his own, Hiram thought sulkily. His driver had the weekend off too, something to do with his mother. But there you go. Hiram was susceptible to mums and the staff always beat you down. Ironic, wasn't it, when he was the celeb.

'The dentist needs confirming, Hiram.'

'OK, OK, obviously I'm going to go. I've paid enough for this treatment.' Hiram hated the dentist. It cost a fortune to see the one in Norbridge whom Maggie had sourced and who had claimed he could use hypnotherapy. Hiram needed to get out of the car when he went there, which was a downer. You couldn't make the dentist do his stuff in the back of the motor.

Hiram hated the thought of being seen in the town. Even in the lockdown there had been people around, and he didn't like people. But he disliked his bad teeth even more. They had been a problem since childhood, caused by sugar butties for tea in winter and bright fluorescent lolly ices at the slightest hint of warm weather.

Hiram didn't like the heat. He had fair skin, which burned, and he got headaches easily. His adult holidays had been on cruises in the Med, giving talks in darkened lecture theatres, and smearing himself all over with sun cream. Discovering the temperate beauty of the Border country had been a revelation.

Today was the first day of the year with any significant warmth. Scotland was cooler than England, but around Kirkaber Castle there was a little microclimate. It was always warmer here than in the open country or on the fells, but never hot — the castle even had a functioning icehouse dug under a man-made hillock in the garden at the back. His castle was more like a mini chateau, a fairy-tale building, with just enough pointy towers and Gothic windows to look the part. Hiram wished his mum could have lived to see it, but she was long dead now. At only sixty-three. Poor diet, poor lifestyle, poor everything. But Hiram wasn't going to let the poor Scouse genes get him.

'OK, just give me some peace,' Hiram said. Maggie was hovering edgily, lest there was any petty task he could think of to delay her preparations for departure to her spiritual home.

Hiram mooched over to the Steinway and played a few notes. He still had the touch. He had always been a performer. Before he had become one of Britain's favourite TV gardeners, Hiram had already honed his broadcasting skills as a musician. But he had never been an Elton John. His skill was as a session player. That was how he had met his inspiration, mentor and, ultimately, best mate, Sol Temple. Sol was a real celebrity. He had been a brilliant guitarist and composer, and had flown high, crashed and burned in ten glorious years. Those were the days. After that it had just been Abba and Fleetwood Mac. So commercial. What a comedown.

Hey, that was then, this was now. And now he was nationally famous, doing something he loved, making meg-abucks and living in Kirkaber Castle. He suddenly flashed Maggie a brilliant and charming smile. 'Enjoy London!'

Pink with relief, she smiled back. 'Thanks, Hiram, I'll say bye-bye now. I'll be back soon.'

Hiram felt better. On reflection, he quite liked the idea of being alone, monarch of all he surveyed. Monarch of the Glen, in fact. Buying the castle was the most brilliant thing he had ever done, apart from taking up gardening. Who would have thought it? Little Hiram King, Sol Temple's bag carrier, making it in his own right and living like royalty.

It hadn't been easy, but he'd made it. Against the odds — and no one knew how high they had been. Maybe the chancer in him was spurring him on to his next venture. Now, that was going to be really something. National fame was great, but Hiram wanted to be internationally renowned. And do something which would change the world. Maybe one day Highgrove would come to him.

CHAPTER FIVE

Do not stare at me because I am dark, because I am dark-
ened by the sun.

Song of Songs 1:6

In The Partridge, Bill Gibson still hadn't said much. Robert
had been thinking during Bill's moody silences. He had been
wondering if the priest might have been having an affair
when the alleged abuse had taken place and was terrified his
wife would find out. But Bill could still confess, confiden-
tially, to Neil Clifford. An affair was bad news, but it would
clear him of the sexual abuse charges. The allegation was so
specific — a Tuesday night in May thirty-three years ago —
that if Bill had been somewhere else, the serious charge could
be countered.

'If you're prepared to make a false confession now, why
didn't you when Neil told you?' Robert asked.

'Because Neil didn't give me chapter and verse. He just
said someone had accused me of — what do they call it now?
— "inappropriate touching". And before he went on, I said,
"No, not me, not in any circumstances." So, when I saw the
letter, I could hardly say, "Oh, gosh, I made a mistake, yes,
there was this girl one Tuesday night thirty years ago."'

'Doesn't it bother you that the Church might have to make a settlement with someone who is lying?'

'Well, there've been enough genuine complaints.'

'But the person who wrote this is targeting you, Bill. They must have a reason for doing this.' Robert took a breath — and then a risk. 'I think you know exactly what this is about.'

Bill Gibson said nothing for a moment. 'OK, Robert, you win. I do know. Or I think I know. But it's complicated and difficult. And I'd rather die than let anyone find out. Do you hear that? I'd rather die.'

Robert thought he had better leave it. He got up to settle the bill, noticing that Bill made no attempt to pay for his meal but sat there, pale and angry, head down, eyebrows furrowed.

Then, as Robert put his card back in his wallet, one of The Partridge regulars came dashing in and made for the bar. 'Have you heard?' he said breathlessly to the barman. 'They've found a body in a bin over at the Friary—'

Robert stopped to take in what the man said. After a moment he went back to the truculent figure at the table. 'Bill, you need to hear this.'

He pulled out his phone and punched in Suzy's number.

* * *

At the Lesser Friary, the volunteers were sitting on the low wall outside the church. Tim was down at the layby with the paramedics and the police. A flurry of other police cars arrived. Officers were putting on scene-of-crime overalls. The volunteers, plus Suzy, were going to be stuck here a long time.

Lorna Duxford was still crying. Since finding the body, she had been shaking and silent for half an hour, incapable of talking except in monosyllables.

Pat had put her cardigan around her. 'She's cold and she's not really responding to me. It must be shock.'

Suzy was berating herself for not knowing more about first aid. Then she saw Tim striding back up the path.

'They'll be taking the body away as soon as Forensics and the pathologist have done their stuff,' he said. 'Then the police will come to talk to you.'

Lorna started to moan, and Pat put her arms around her.

'Lorna looks in a bad way,' Suzy said to Tim. 'I'm just googling what to do when someone's in shock.'

'It's not shock in the clinical sense, more an adrenalin rush. Flight or fight. Keep her as warm as you can and try to soothe her.' Tim was authoritative.

Seth Beddoes jumped off the low wall. 'Jeez, mate, whaddya mean? Of course, she's in shock, you can see it.' He had been sitting, kicking repeatedly at a clump of nettles. They were being mashed under his huge boot. Becky Dixon was also sitting on the wall, but with a clear space between them. She was scrolling on her phone and didn't look up.

'Shock's a medical term for heart failure, or an allergic reaction,' Tim said. 'That's not what is happening to Lorna. But she should see the paramedics.' He turned to Lorna. 'Come down with me, Lorna, and let them check you over. You've had a terrible experience.'

Lorna flung out her hands to ward him off and almost screamed, 'No, I'm not going down there. I don't want to see her again!'

'No one's asking you to do that, Lorna, of course they aren't,' said Pat.

Tim said, 'She's probably disoriented. That happens with this sort of reaction. Lorna, we need to wait for the police, and it may take a while, but then you can go. I think Pat needs to drive you home. Or maybe Suzy could take you both.'

He was called by one of his former medical colleagues and went back down the path. It seemed to be an eternity before the police came to talk to the volunteers.

In the meantime, Suzy took a call from Robert and told him the bare facts. She had no idea when she would be back at The Briars. She didn't feel like talking, and she couldn't sit and play on her mobile like Becky. She just waited. She was aware suddenly that the ambulance had gone, and another unmarked van had arrived to take the body to the pathology lab. There was blue-and-white tape around the layby. Two police officers were coming up the path.

Lorna was still crying softly, while Pat sat next to her on the wall, alternately putting her arms around her friend or stroking her arms. Lorna seemed oblivious.

Pat left her and came up to Suzy. 'I've never seen her like this. She's usually very much in control, of herself and everyone else. But she's really shaken.'

The police officers questioned them all in turn. Lorna managed to answer the questions very briefly, saying she would be all right and refusing offers of support. Tim took the lead and explained succinctly how the body had been discovered. When they were allowed to go, Suzy did as Tim suggested, driving Lorna and Pat back to Pat's little terraced cottage. Lorna didn't argue or ask to go to her own smart flat in a converted mill in the Norbridge Old Quarter.

Suzy and Pat settled her on the sofa. Pat made strong tea and put sugar in without asking. Lorna started to gain some colour in her pallid face.

'I'm so sorry, Pat,' she whispered. 'I really lost it. I do feel awful. But it was ghastly. Really ghastly. You don't know how terrible—' She started to cry with big hacking sobs.

'Would you like to stay here?' Pat said. 'Should I try and get hold of your GP?'

The sobs stopped. 'You must be joking.' For a moment there was a touch of the old Lorna. 'It's Saturday. You can't get an appointment, even on a weekday, without waiting on the phone for an hour, and having to go through triage. Triage!' She spat out the word, but then seemed deflated and empty, like a shell of herself. She shut her eyes.

Pat saw Suzy to the door. 'I'm really worried about her. What if she needs to be interviewed again? After all, she was the one who found the body.'

'Well, yes. But then Tim took over, and he dealt with the police.'

Pat nodded. 'He was good, wasn't he? Goodness knows what we would have done if he hadn't been there. As it was, none of the rest of us saw it, thankfully.'

'Tim made sure we didn't look.'

'Except Lorna. I think she needs medical help. I'd suggest Tim, but he went off with the police. I don't know where Seth disappeared to, and Becky left on her bike. To be honest, Suzy, I don't know how to cope with this.'

Suzy thought for a moment. 'I've got a friend who's a Police Community Support Officer. Her name's Ro Watson. It might be a bit unorthodox, but I'm going to phone her. Someone with professional understanding might be the right person to talk to Lorna.'

'Thank you,' said Pat. 'In the meantime, I'll keep the hot tea coming.'

In the car, Suzy phoned Ro. 'I know it's an imposition, but I'd like you to come and see this woman,' she said. 'She's in a bad state. And then why don't you come over to The Briars and give me and Robert the gen on the body in the bin?'

The phrase was so trite, Suzy shuddered at her own insensitivity. Someone had treated a woman like rubbish. It was pure chance that the volunteers had opened the bin. The body could have lain there undiscovered for months. Hardly any cars stopped in the narrow, dirty little layby other than to pull in and chuck out litter. No animals could have found their way into the locked bin and the area already stank. Suzy wondered if the person who had dumped the woman thought that she might just decompose in there, forgotten. But she had been found — surely not what the killer had intended. The police should be able to find out who she was and where she had come from.

* * *

Much later, Suzy was sitting in the big kitchen at The Briars. Ro Watson had just come back from her visit to Lorna and Pat. It had been only a qualified success.

Ro said drily, 'Yes, well, me being a Liverpudlian too went down like a bucket of cold sick with Ms Duxford.'

'I thought it would help that you were all Scousers. Anyway, tell me what happened.'

'Pat Jones had done a good job of calming Lorna Duxford down and had even managed to feed her some soup. And Lorna was happy to see me — I look harmless when I'm not in my uniform. I told her that the coroner might want to speak to her, but the police will probably leave her alone now. The big issue is identifying the dead woman. Jed Jackson is in the loop.'

DS Jed Jackson was a police officer based in Workhaven who knew Suzy and Robert. He was a friend and colleague of Ro's too.

Ro went on, 'Jed told me that the dead woman was middle-aged and black, which means she's likely to have been noticed if she came through Norbridge, but despite an appeal no one has come forward.'

'So, she wasn't local?'

'No. There's a handful of black families around here, and no one recognizes a description of her. There's no way of identifying her. No handbag or anything. They had an emergency post-mortem this afternoon and she'd only been dead for a couple of hours, so she must have been in the district early this morning, but no one seems to have seen her. Our boss keeps insisting it's some sort of gangland killing. He desperately wants it not to be local.'

Suzy raised a sceptical eyebrow.

'I know.' Ro rolled her eyes. 'Anyway, the Norbridge force is already busy with the terrible business of the sheep.'

'What's that?'

'Some psychopath has been worrying and killing sheep. Phil Dixon was the first to lose some of his flock.' Ro coloured slightly. Years ago, when she had been caught up in the investigation of a local teacher's death, she had been attracted to Phil. She thought Suzy might have suspected. Since then she had been careful never to mention him. Phil

Dixon was a local hobby farmer and Becky Dixon's grandfather, and farmed near the small town of Pelliter towards the west coast.

Ro went on quickly, 'But the other farmers who lost animals were north of here. The perp kills the sheep and butchers them and takes the meat but leaves the other bits. The rest of the flock panics and runs everywhere. It's sadistic. Local farmers are in a heck of a state about it. It's a bit much for the local force, with this murder as well.'

'So, it was definitely murder?' Suzy asked.

'Yep. The dead woman had suffered a neat blow to the back of her head. It happened in the graveyard. There were grasses on the back of her clothes. But seeing any dead body in a wheelie bin is going to have been traumatic.'

Suzy pondered. 'Don't get me wrong, obviously it was awful. But Lorna kept on and on about how ghastly it was. How was she when you left?'

'Still in a state but not crying anymore. And she was getting visitors.'

'Really? Who?'

'Oh, a pickup arrived. This great big giant haystack bloke with tats and earrings got out. Pat knew him, so I decided I'd better skedaddle. And I'd better leave here too. I've got a date tomorrow, but I'm going to have to reorganize my schedule. It might be a busy Sunday.'

Suzy said goodbye rather distractedly. The giant haystack guy must have been Seth Beddoes. He hadn't seemed the slightest bit concerned about Lorna Duxford when they'd been waiting in the graveyard for the police. So why was he turning up at Pat's?

* * *

Later, Suzy and Robert sat in the kitchen with a small whisky each. Robert listened to Suzy describing her disturbing afternoon. She was about to suggest they went up to bed and read some easy fiction till they fell asleep when her mobile rang.

'Suzy, it's Pat Jones. From the gardening group. I'm sorry to ring you at this time of night. I've tried Tim but there's no answer.'

'Are you OK? What's wrong?'

'Well, I'm not sure. But Lorna's gone.'

'Gone? Gone where? Home?'

'No. She left my house with Seth Beddoes.'

Suzy was surprised. Seth visiting was strange enough, but Lorna leaving with him was news.

Pat was still speaking. 'I hope you don't mind me calling you, but I'm quite stunned. Please don't think I'm upset just because my nose is out of joint. But it doesn't make sense. Lorna hardly even said goodbye to me. I went into the kitchen to get Seth a glass of water and when I came back he just mumbled in that half-baked way of his that they were leaving. I feel as if I've been dismissed.'

Suzy could see that it was an odd way for Lorna to behave, and hurtful to Pat. But if Lorna were still in a state of shock, maybe the thought of going home with Seth to his therapist wife had seemed attractive.

'She'd seemed to be getting better,' Pat said. 'She'd talked about going to church tomorrow. We were just about to go to bed. This came out of the blue.'

Suzy said gently, 'I can see it must be upsetting. But there's nothing we can do tonight.' Then she had a thought. 'I might call on the Beddoes tomorrow. I can go round on the pretext of wanting to feature Tranquillity in one of my recordings.'

'Would you? That would be very kind. I'd just like to know why Lorna went off like that, without any real explanation. I don't want to pester her myself. Seth made it clear I was unwanted.'

There was certainly something intrusive about Seth's behaviour, Suzy thought. Maybe Tranquillity Beddoes wanted a piece of the action, and her dopey husband was happy to oblige. Robert had said that the psychotherapist fed off local dramas, and they didn't come much more dramatic than this.

46

Or did they? Later, when they were in bed, with the window open and the smell of fresh grass and convolvulus drifting in, it was her turn to listen to Robert's account of his Saturday.

When he had finished, Suzy said, 'What a day! My gardeners found a body and your vicar chap has been accused of historic sexual abuse.'

'And clearly he was up to something else at the time. He said he'd rather die than tell the real truth, and he meant it.'

'It would have to be really bad. I mean what's worse than that? Murder?'

The word fell heavily into the quiet warmth of the bedroom. Suzy wished she hadn't said it.

CHAPTER SIX

There he stands behind our wall, gazing through the windows.
Song of Songs 2:9

Saturday night in May, in Norbridge, post-pandemic, could go one of two ways. Usually, the city centre would be dead after half past ten, with a few people still drinking, but after the pub kitchens closed at nine, most folk would have gone home out of the cold wind. Or the wind might drop, and the temperature might be a few degrees higher, and the streets would fill with girls in tiny skirts, eyelashes like yard brushes, and huge high heels, tottering about in search of fun. Slightly later the lads would appear in tight trousers showing their ankles, ready to provide it.

The students weren't back in force yet after the pandemic, and on top of that it was reading week, so Norbridge was mainly the province of the locals. There was a bit of a town-and-gown divide, but students at the University of Mid Cumbria were often local kids anyway. There were some postgraduate degrees like Robert Clark's MA course in English Literature. This had gained attention because of his work on locations featured in the classics. His course was small but popular with international academics or students who wanted to know more about the shivering sands or the wuthering heights, from *The Moonstone* to *Moonfleet*. Robert had partnered with other small-town universities to ensure his students saw the length and breadth of Britain. Not only was his course respected, it was also a bit of a money spinner.

But the mature students weren't in evidence tonight, and this warm Saturday had brought out the youth in force. It wasn't necessarily the obvious types. In the Crown and Thistle, Becky Dixon and her small group of friends were drinking lager and having a heated conversation about cancel culture.

'I don't necessarily agree that we should cancel celebs who deny our right to decide our own destiny. I sort of get the free speech thing.' Roxy was small and thin, dressed in a vest top with dungarees. They should have been shivering but seemed oblivious to the climate, in and out of the pub. Roxy was a final-year undergraduate who had been stuck at home and had arrived back in Norbridge after the Easter holidays.

Becky really liked Roxy and felt guilty for being slightly preoccupied. She kept thinking about the body in the bin, but she wanted to try and forget it. Going out with her mates, who were uninterested in local news, had seemed the best way. In about five months she was due to go down south to university and she wasn't at all sure how that would be. In Norbridge, even though she broke the mould, most people knew her and her gang, and although they got the odd insult after the pubs closed at weekends, it was all familiar. And her mates, like Roxy, were there for her. Of course, there could be hate in Norbridge, like anywhere else, but she was never far from home. She knew no one in Cambridge. It was hundreds of miles away and she couldn't just pop back for weekends. She loved medieval history, but how would it be, studying it with a load of southerners from private schools? In Norbridge, there were very few schools like that. Dodsworth House was the only one Becky knew of.

Becky stood up to go to the ladies. That was an existential decision, according to Roxy. But looking out of the pub window into the street, she was aware of a harsher reality. She had a sensation like a dream. No — a nightmare. She saw someone out there she thought she knew. Maybe she'd only clocked him because she had been thinking of Dodsworth House. Or had that made her imagine him? He was the only person she knew who had gone to the private school. Someone she never wanted to see again in her life.

But it was true. Jonty McFadden, local psychopath, bad boy, and Norbridge's main exponent of knife crime was walking jauntily along the pavement outside. He was supposed to have gone to Spain, never to return. He had been implicated in the death of one of their primary school teachers and before that had been one of Becky's tormentors at school.

Becky had always been unusual. As they had approached puberty Jonty had persecuted her. He'd seemed to be drawn to her yet he'd treated her with contempt and bullied her. It was as if they spent the whole of Year Six circling each other, drawn together by a strange fascination, which had led Becky into terrible danger.

Then after the death of their teacher, Jonty had gone to a different school and the thread had been . . . not broken, but stretched, until Becky rarely thought of him and their strange connection. But the danger of her world unravelling had always been there, if Jonty ever decided to come back to Norbridge.

Suddenly, Cambridge being so far away from home seemed like a very good idea.

* * *

Thirty miles to the north on Saturday night, Hiram King was musing about his life. Maggie had gone to London and the other staff were, as usual, rarely seen and never heard. He didn't want to watch telly or listen to music. He needed to think. He did that quite a lot these days. That was what a pandemic did to you, even if you were as insulated from it as he had been.

Sometimes he couldn't believe his luck, and sometimes he thought it was richly deserved. In the soft candlelit early evening, he sat with a glass of Lagavulin, the twenty-six-year-old special, a tribute to his newfound Scottish connection. It felt right to reflect.

He thought about his mum. After Sol died, Hiram had gone home to live with her in her corporation flat in Liverpool. She had an allotment, which she loved. His grandad had worked for the corporation parks department. And his great-grandfather too, so she'd told him.

In fact it was on the stage, erected in the park in the summer, that Hiram had first felt the exultation — no other word for it — of performing. He had stood up there and sung 'Que sera, sera' at the top of his voice, aged six. He had known then he wanted to be an entertainer. In that performance zone. That was the oxygen he needed.

Mum had paid for his music lessons. She loved dancing. She had got married too young, to a factory worker with a quiff in his hair and drainpipe trousers, and the marriage had been short. He was killed in a car crash on a night out with the lads. No seat belts and they'd been drinking. It was the sixties and Mum got a new corporation high-rise flat. She was happy just with Kevin. They got on well. They had a nice old upright piano, though his mum preferred to play the radiogram. Kevin was better on the keyboard than on the guitar, though the guitar was universal with boys of his age. On piano he wasn't a prodigy, but he got to grade eight — his 'cap and gown' as his mum had said proudly. But the whole Mersey Sound, Cavern thing had passed him by because he was born just a bit too late.

One day after he'd done his CSEs, aged sixteen, his mum had said, 'Let's go to London. Your Auntie Myrtle will let us rent her upstairs. We can try it for a few weeks in the summer and come back if it doesn't work out.'

It didn't work out for his mum. She came back to a smaller flat and smaller world, but Kevin didn't. He stayed and found his own London life on the fringe of the BBC music scene, hanging round television studios at first, then getting his Musicians' Union card and playing in sessions.

And he'd met Sol Temple. Kevin had been on the edges of the big time. He had never expected to see Liverpool again, but then Sol had died, and he had needed a bolthole. But he was a different person by then. Not 'Our Kevin' anymore. No way. He was Hiram King from the Smoke. *Que sera, sera.*

But he was also a chip off the old block, and while he was lying low, he had taken to gardening. It had given him some peace. He'd walked round the park and seen it with different eyes. He'd decided to give up on the celeb thing for a while, and work with plants. A more reliable audience. And like his forebears, he got a job with the corporation. But soon it was time to get back in with the rich and famous.

His second big chance came when one of the music producers he had worked with started his own indie company making inserts for the new daytime TV programmes. Hiram had seen the guy's name on some credits for a 'shed show'. He went back to London and blagged himself a job as a researcher, and he was back in the game.

Within a year he'd done a fantastic screen test and was on the way as a TV gardener on a morning magazine show. Hiram was a good gardener, but his expertise was no greater than that of many others. His talent lay in communicating it. He had ideas, and he wasn't bland and boring. Perky, northern, making cracks about music, which made him seem trendy, and he was not unattractive, in a slightly camp way. Hiram King was a hit with the daytime audience. And his mum had lived to see it, though not for long. Ten good years followed, culminating in his own show, *Hiram's Hedge*.

Then, suddenly, he didn't want anything more to do with conventional homes and gardens. It was all getting too plastic. The crunch came when he was asked to feature false lawns. Nylograss, it was called. There had to be more to his life than getting people to buy fake turf. He felt emasculated, over-domesticated, controlled. Producers treated him like a puppet and the audience thought he was a sweetie. But there was more to Hiram King. He had flounced out and started looking for a new USP.

He had come across the idea of rewilding in the very early days when the first books came out. Ironically, Hiram had rarely been into the real countryside, and his knowledge of farming was limited to Old Macdonald, so he was easily seduced. And when he took advantage of a sponsored break in the Lake District, he felt as if his head had been blown open. So much space. So much nature. In Britain! It was awesome. His producer mate offered him a YouTube channel. Though rewilding was taking off, there was no broadcaster behind it. Rewilding became Hiram's new USP and made him another fortune.

But as he often told himself, money wasn't everything. There was an element of therapy in his rewilding ideas. And now he'd done the wildflowers and the woodlands, he wanted to go further. He had read about the heroes who wanted to bring back the lynx, and there was the polecat, reintroduced so successfully in neighbouring Dumfriesshire. There was even a colony of marsupials — wallabies, was it? — on an island in a Scottish loch, and if they could survive, then how much better was the outlook for indigenous species? He knew that this had to be his next step. Except he would do something even bigger.

Sometimes, though, like those hunted predators, he was pursued by old demons. Well, you couldn't live the life he had lived and not have a few of those. He still needed counselling sessions. But finding a good counsellor was tough. He had worked through everyone in London. He had felt penned in by the city and ripped off by the celebrity therapists. He had needed a break.

When the castle came up for sale, with acres of woodland and fellside, it was perfect. He took Maggie, his PA, with him, kicking and screaming about leaving her flat in Kensington, and he had collected a small number of local staff. But there was something, or someone, missing. He needed a fixer.

* * *

53

The next day, Sunday, Suzy chose not to go to church with Robert. She was going to see the Beddoes and find out how Lorna was getting on. Her excuse would be that she needed another podcast edition.

A few months ago, Tranquillity had sent a marketing pitch to Suzy. Since the podcast had become popular, a lot of people had contacted Suzy trying to get a slice of the publicity. Tranquillity's letter had been beautifully composed, in a handwritten envelope, saying that for more information there was also Tranquillity's website, just google. There was an address at the top:

Dear Suzy,
We haven't met but I have heard a lot about you. I am sure you are interested in mental health — your own and that of those around you, your loved ones, friends and family. The stress of the Covid-19 pandemic is causing more anxiety than ever before. We all know someone who needs help, it might even be you. And I could provide it . . .

There was short paragraph about Tranquillity's qualifications, but it was the next section that had stood out.

There's a need for us all to examine our spiritual nature, the special something which makes us, as human beings, act unconditionally to do good. Whatever our religious views, finding our inner saint can help us come to terms with the sinners we may have been.
*   If examining yourself in this way resonates with you, or if you know someone who might find this unique, positive and spiritual form of therapy useful, don't hesitate to contact me. There will be no pressure to go any further. But even one conversation might help change your life . . .*

What's more, Tranquillity wrote, any suggestion of spiritual context or religious relevance had been abandoned by a secular profession. Her website used the phrase 'find your inner saint' several times. Whatever your beliefs, or if you had no beliefs, Tranquillity could help you by deconstructing and analyzing your problems in the context of a loving god, however you envisaged that entity. And more importantly, there was the attractive certainty that everyone was capable of great goodness. Fees could be arranged on a bespoke basis and a series of ten one-hour sessions was recommended.

It was very clever, Suzy thought. The modern obsession with 'being yourself', 'being the best you', mindfulness, self-actualization, peak experiences and all those other mantras, had been neatly encompassed by Tranquillity's assertion that whoever you were and whatever you had done, you were a good and deserving person, and she would prove it to you. No need for remorse or forgiveness. What a relief!

Tranquillity had finished her letter saying she knew it was unusual for a therapist to write on spec but, because she was striking out as an independent operator, she had chosen this unconventional method, post-pandemic. She was originally from Norbridge and wanted to bring her skills home. She would help people of any age with any problems, especially Covid-related stress and trauma.

Suzy reckoned most people would have put the letter straight into the recycling. But anyone worried, grieving or suffering alone might find it appealing. Suzy didn't necessarily think the notion of a touting psychotherapist distasteful. But the idea of young people like Molly and her friends finding their 'inner saint' without acknowledging their moral obligations was disturbing.

Anyway, as a result Suzy had Tranquillity's address. Her consulting room was next door to her home, which was whimsically called Camomile Cottage. There were some pictures on the website showing a bucolic idyll. Robert had said that Camomile Cottage had been numbers 4 and 6 Lower Farm Lane when he had come to Norbridge. Now the building was festooned with various creepers, and crusty with exterior stonework. One image showed candles in the garden giving haloes of light in the dusk of evening, while another showed a herb garden, dappled with raindrops that caught the early morning sun. The shots of the interior were also appealing — a pleasant sitting room with two modern leather chairs either side of a large black-leaded fireplace, and a picture of Tranquillity at her desk.

She looked very delicate, almost tiny, with a heart-shaped face framed by thick blonde hair pulled into a pony-tail, and large dark eyes. Another picture showed her in the garden, in typical outdoorsy gear — waxed jacket, wellies, big scarf around her delicate frame — leaning on a fork with a caption saying, *Tranquillity is a keen gardener, growing herbs she uses in her therapy.*

Suzy knew where Camomile Cottage was. The morning was fresh and clear, a little bit chilly before the sun got into its stride. She started on the road.

CHAPTER SEVEN

I have taken off my robe — must I put it on again?
Song of Songs 5:3

On Sunday, Tim Markham rose late. He felt emotionally exhausted and physically shattered, with his arms and legs aching. He knew it was psychosomatic. The events of yesterday had plunged him back into the world of work after six months of trying to forget. Old habits had kicked in, and he had spent a lot of time with the police. As always, these days, the ambulance service was too stretched, and he had found himself helping at the mortuary in Norbridge and even waiting for the post-mortem results. He had been interviewed there by a detective, who had clearly seen him as a confederate, another member of the services which swung into action when there was a suspicious death.

It had been nine o'clock at night when Tim arrived back at his flat in one of Norbridge's few Victorian red-brick squares. It was fairly basic. His ex-wife had taken possession of their 'executive home', which he'd been paying for on a massive mortgage. Then she had sold the house anyway, and somehow managed to give him less than half the equity.

Their divorce had been granted because of 'irretrievable breakdown'. But at first, Tim's wife had alleged 'unreasonable behaviour', citing his long working hours, and the rows about Tim's desire to retire to a smallholding. She saw this as a sort of bullying, accusing him of unthinking assumption and lack of consultation which amounted to coercion. He had never discussed it with her, she said, and had sprung it on her one day, announcing they would be selling up and moving in a year's time. Her next-door neighbour had identified Tim's selfish behaviour and had rescued her. At least, that was her story and it had caused gossip, rancour and partiality, with everyone in Tarnfield having a view on the Markham break-up. In fact, Tim seemed to be the only person in the village who wasn't interested anymore. He was too tired and depressed to argue — besides, what did he need the money for? He would never get a place in the country now.

The divorce process had taken a few years, and with the Covid epidemic and his overworking on top, they had passed in a blur. He had gone from being a good dad, valued colleague, happy husband and good provider to being a bit of a pariah.

He had taken up the gardening in the graveyard to get him out of the flat. There had been a flyer about it on the noticeboard at the supermarket. He hardly considered the other volunteers, but when he did, he thought Lorna was all right, despite her bossy manner. It was easy to follow her lead. He had been quite amused by Becky and admired her originality. Pat was pretty in a faded way and seemed pleasant if a bit dull. He couldn't stand Seth Beddoes, and had as little to do with him as possible.

In the middle of his divorce, he had received a letter from Tranquillity Beddoes, offering her services 'after the traumas you have been through'. Tranquillity had said that a friend of Tim's had suggested she might help. Tim thought it unprofessional for a therapist to approach a potential client. The friend — an acquaintance from the pub — was embarrassed when Tim challenged him. He said Tranquillity had been counselling his sister after a break-up. Everyone knew

Tim was going through a grim time. And maybe Tranquillity might be helpful.

'No, she wouldn't. Back off,' Tim had said.

On an ordinary weekend the gardeners would meet on Saturday in The Pantry and on Sunday in the afternoon at the graveyard. Lorna was fond of telling everyone about her morning at St Michael and All Angels Church. She made the coffee and in return she picked up gossip — or 'local intelligence', as she called it.

She rated Tranquillity Beddoes highly and often mentioned Tranquillity's wonderful work and how she had counselled various parishioners from St Michael's. 'Father Bill thinks she's very caring and helpful,' Lorna had said when Tim had asked her why Tranquillity was so valued. 'She's been wonderful with the MacPhees' daughter, and so good to old Mrs Wallace, not to mention what she did for Myra Smith after her husband died.'

Tim had thought these people wouldn't want their problems aired. Who'd been talking? Tranquillity, probably. And Lorna had lapped it up.

That Sunday morning, Tim had been out to pick up his car from the garage. It was basically a lock-up round the corner. The old black Range Rover had passed its MOT, just. Tim hadn't shaved and was wearing an ancient sweatshirt and shorts. As if it mattered. He might as well go to the pub again.

He was thinking about the Beddoes when his mobile rang. He didn't recognize the number.

'Tim,' said a rather hesitant female voice, 'I'm sorry to bother you, but it's Pat.' He was slow to catch on, so the voice added hurriedly, 'Pat Jones. From the gardening group. I tried you twice last night but you were out.'

Tim recalled two missed calls from a number he hadn't recognized. 'Yeah. I popped out to the pub last night. It was rather a heavy day for me, as it turned out.'

'Without you, I don't know what we would have done. Lorna came back with me as you suggested, but then Seth came and took her off.'

'Seth Beddoes?'

'I don't know any other Seths, do you?' Pat said sharply and Tim paid her more attention. 'Lorna has gone off to stay with them.'

'Really? With the Beddoes? Crikey, I would have thought Lorna was far too self-reliant to need Tranquillity.'

'I'm so glad you said that, Tim. It seemed very odd to me too. Lorna's a fan of Tranquillity, but that's because of her vicar, who seems to admire the woman a lot. But Lorna doesn't usually have much time for Seth.'

'Who does? That's very strange.' But this was clearly not all Pat had to say. Tim wondered why she'd called him. He could almost hear her struggling to get to the point.

'But you see, Tim, another uncharacteristic thing is that I don't remember Lorna locking up the Friary or collecting up the tools. Of course, we were all a bit shocked and flustered. And later, she went off so suddenly with Seth that she left her gardening bag here at my house, with the Lesser Friary key in it. So — I was wondering if you might give me a lift to the graveyard and we can tidy up. That is, if your car passed its MOT.'

'Which it did . . .'

'My car's still parked there, and I need to go and get it. And I could leave a message for Becky too. She might join us.'

'Of course, I'll give you a lift. Tell me where you live. I'll come round.'

'Oh.' Pat sounded startled. 'Are you sure?'

'Yes, I'm sure.' He was amazed at how his mood had lifted. 'I'd like to do that, Pat. To be honest I'm at a loose end today, and I spend too much time in the pub as it is.'

'Right, shall we say eleven o'clock?' Pat told him her address though she still sounded rather stunned.

Tim thought he ought to have a shower and shave. Suddenly there was a point to his day. 'Great. Looking forward to it.' And he was.

* * *

'Oh go on, Tee.' Seth Beddoes rolled over in their king-size bed and pushed the patchwork quilt away. 'She won't hear. Not through the walls in this place. Anyway, the knockout pills you gave her mean she should be zonked for another few hours.'

'They're *not* knockout pills, Seth.' Tranquillity sat up. 'I wouldn't dream of drugging someone in her state, you know that. It was just valerian.'

'OK, darlin'. Whatever you say. You know it really gets me going when you go all demure and strict like that.'

Her long, thick, very blonde hair cascaded over her shoulders and rippled onto her pure white, genuine antique Victorian nightdress. Her skin was honey coloured and very smooth. Her buoyant breasts rose and fell under the lacy yoke. The bedroom was dim, with a thick Roman blind in a heavy floral print keeping out the early morning sun.

Tranquillity knew her look was a turn-on. The thick tresses of hair covered the slight stringiness of her neck, and the etched lines on her tanned face could not be made out in the shadowy room. She needed work doing again on her face, but funds were an issue. She sighed. The musky scent of last night's candle, burning long after Seth had collapsed, snoring, was still in the air around the old brass bedstead. 'Lay lady lay' he would croon when he was in the mood, which was usually at night after some wine, but then he was often overtaken by sleep. Still, the morning demands weren't that unusual, and he would sulk if she didn't give in.

Five minutes later she hitched down her nightie and said, 'That was lovely. I'm going to get up and make some coffee.'

'Yeah, fine, Teeena,' Seth drawled, but he was already closing his eyes.

Tranquillity hated it when he called her Tina. She had gone through several iterations with her name, and Tranquillity was the best. But she had been Tina to Seth when they got together twenty years ago. She'd been in London on a mind-blowing course. She had heard about it at the destination church she attended, which attracted like-minded people with challenging views acquired though their trendy professional backgrounds. They were psycho-therapists, artists, designers, homeopathic practitioners and yoga teachers, self-consciously off the wall, who enjoyed being different from the average parish church Anglicans.

Tranquillity was already a qualified therapist and had been interested in spiritual counselling. The Westminster Pastoral Group and the Christian Therapy Association hadn't done anything for her, but the tiny collection of ther-apists from her church, who called themselves Soul Search, had given her the basis of the psychotherapy system that became unique to her. It had brought her tranquillity, hence the name. And it had brought her to Seth.

One evening, she had gone to a party with some of the fringe members of the group. She was tired, wasn't close to any of them and didn't really want to go. At the party, wait-ing for the loo, she had seen Seth and made a beeline for him. He was ten years older than she was, and he had made a lot of money in the retro and vinyl record world. But he had sold his business, and had a coke habit to sustain.

Six months later she had cured him of the latter and given him a substitute for the former.

'Jeez, I'm like your manager,' Seth had said, glassy-eyed and slack-jawed after an afternoon of sex and business plans.

Tranquillity had smiled. Seth was a sharp operator when it came to assessing EPs or old hi-fi sets. The drugs or the drink or the exhausting lifestyle seemed to have blunted his brain, but he was still smart enough to be an asset and aimless enough to be controllable. Most importantly, he adored her. Tranquillity needed to be adored.

So, they had made a go of it for nearly fifteen years in London until Seth's capital ran out, and then Tranquillity had decided they would go home. They had arrived in Norbridge five years ago on a grey, wet February night, Seth looking like a huge bedraggled teddy bear as they waited in pouring rain outside the station for a taxi. They'd rented, unseen, a modern, bleak, bungalow on a farm in the middle of nowhere, and had looked around for the perfect premises for Tranquillity's consulting room. Seth could do the maintenance and DIY, and maybe discover some hidden bargains in the junk shops and jumble sales of this remote part of northern England. And when they found the cottage, or rather the two farmworkers' houses, Seth had thrown himself into the refurbing, while Tranquillity found clients through the local church and her medical contacts.

But attracting people hadn't been as easy as she'd thought. She went back to London to dredge up old contacts and had been on the verge of suggesting they went back down south for good. But when she returned to Norbridge, Seth had done the kitchen and it was wonderful. She couldn't break his heart by saying they needed to return to London. And it would have been awful, of course, sofa surfing, then renting something scuzzy, though she needed the work and the punters in Norbridge were just too few.

They'd got by since then and she had hoped that the post-Covid trauma would see a fresh crop of clients. But people seemed to have become more wary. Her Zoom sessions hadn't worked nearly as well — she knew that a lot of her attraction was personal and that a video link somehow reduced and flattened her.

Then they'd had one great stroke of luck. And, unbelievably, now it looked as if she was on a roll. She just had to play her cards right and stop Seth blundering in and messing it up.

Tranquillity climbed into her thick fleecy dressing gown and put on her fluffy slipper boots. She was changing from sexy nineteenth-century housemaid to cute snuggly dormouse. That look would work with Lorna. She tiptoed along the corridor so as not to wake Seth again and tapped on the guest bedroom door.

* * *

Pat Jones went into her bedroom at the back of the cottage to get dressed. She had been unsure what Tim Markham would say when she phoned, and had been strangely nervous about asking him to give her a lift to the graveyard.

Or maybe it wasn't so strange. Since her husband Derek had died Pat had had little interaction with men, and none where she had taken the lead. Her son-in-law always treated her with affectionate contempt, even though he and his wife were completely dependent on Pat for childcare. Pat's daughter Katie had declared that she was never going through another pregnancy, having waited until her late thirties for this one. Bobby was a lovely little boy, adored by all of them. But Steve, Pat's son-in-law, treated her as if she were an idiot. 'Oh no, Mum,' he would say, 'do it like this.' And whatever it was, Pat would comply. Anything rather than a row.

Since Bobby had gone to school and Pat had joined the gardening group, things had changed. She had her own hobby now, though she still took care of Bobby after school two nights a week. Steve had been made redundant when the furlough scheme came to an end, so he looked after Bobby for the other three evenings while searching for a new job.

Her bedroom was warm. Glancing in the mirror as she took off her dressing gown, Pat was surprised. Maybe she had changed in other ways too, thanks to the gardening. Her arms, for a long time a cause of embarrassment with their fleshy flaps, looked a little firmer. It could be all that work hacking at ivy and collecting litter. She was a little slimmer — not helping Bobby eat up his dinner had probably helped. And because it was so warm, she fished out a denim skirt rather than her routine loose trousers, plus a baggy T-shirt with short sleeves. She was more tanned than usual, too, thanks to the outdoor work.

When Tim came to pick her up, her first thought was how awful he looked. He seemed ten years older. His face was pale and haggard. But he smiled to see her, and when she climbed into the car he said with unconscious surprise, 'You know, you look different.'

Pat bit back the obvious reply of 'So do you', because she couldn't tell him he looked much worse.

Tim said, 'Any news of Lorna?'

'Not yet. I'm hurt that Lorna hasn't contacted me. We've become such close friends. At her instigation.'

Why had she added that, Pat wondered? It was because she wanted Tim to know that she wasn't just an also-ran. It looked as though Lorna was the stronger partner in their friendship, but Lorna had needed her. If she could, she would have corralled Pat on to the flower and coffee rotas at St Michael and All Angels, but since Derek's death Pat wanted nothing to do with the church.

Tim was quiet until they reached the Friary, deliberately going along the top road and avoiding the layby. He parked outside the Lesser Friary.

'Oh look, there's Becky's bike!' Pat said. It was chained to the railings.

'I'm surprised Becky's here,' said Tim.

Becky was surprised to be there herself. After the nightmare of seeing Jonty McFadden saunter past the Crown and Thistle, she had hardly slept. Normally she and some of the gang would spend Sunday afternoon on a pub crawl punctuated by aggressive debate with Norbridge drinkers about what she considered their backward ideas on identity and self-expression. But today she wanted to keep out of the town centre in case she saw him again.

She was hoping and praying that either she had been mistaken, or that he had just been passing through and was now gone. If Jonty McFadden was back in the area, then she wanted to be somewhere else. Staying at home that day was not an option because Jonty knew where she lived. Pat's tentative invitation to join them in the graveyard had been a godsend.

Becky came out of the shadows as Pat and Tim climbed out of the car.

'Oh, you look nice,' she said to Pat.

'It's just gardening gear. But a bit more summery. Should we see what state the church is in?'

They all looked at one another warily. This death had nothing to do with them. The police seemed to have already made up their minds and discounted the gardeners.

Except that the bin had been locked, and their key had been hanging up in the church. Obviously there had been another key used by whoever dumped the body. Old metal wheelie bins like that were hardly high tech. You could probably buy the keys online.

But Pat found that her heart was hammering. She was an agnostic but that didn't mean she couldn't pray. *Please, let us find all our tools present and correct. And unstained by the dead woman's blood.*

CHAPTER EIGHT

Who is this that appears like the dawn, fair as the moon, bright as the sun?

Song of Songs 6:10

The three of them opened the door. It had been unlocked all night. Inside, the church was untouched. No one, it seemed, had been near it since the body had been found. The boxes and buckets for the gardening tools were still out.

'There's a pair of shears missing,' said Pat, 'and maybe two pairs of secateurs.'

Becky said, 'I was using some secateurs on the ivy. I'm sorry, I might have dropped them down by the bins in all the fuss.'

'I think I dropped mine too, in all the commotion,' Tim added.

'OK,' said Pat. 'The first thing is to try and find the missing tools. And then we can have a chat about what we're going to do next. I think we can assume that Lorna's out of action and I'm not sure about Seth.'

They trooped out of the church, Becky brandishing a hoe. Pat smiled. Lorna had been rather bossy when it came to who had the hoes and spades, which she tended to reserve for the men.

Without speaking again, the three of them fanned out. Before long Becky called that she had found the shears, taking them back up to the church. Tim found a pair of pink-handled secateurs in the grass near the layby but there was no sign of the other pair.

A few minutes later Becky shouted, 'I can see them!' But instead of picking up the secateurs, she stood still.

'What's wrong?' Pat said.

'It's something pink . . .' Becky scrambled forwards. 'It's not the secateurs,' she said. 'It's the straps of a pink hand-bag, practically covered by the rhododendrons.' She picked the handbag up with the end of her hoe — then stopped, horrified.

'Put the bag on the grass.' Tim suddenly asserted the authority he had assumed so naturally the day before. 'I think this is the dead woman's bag. She was dressed in pink. Even pink trainers. Drop it, Becky. We need to call the police.'

'But it's just a dumped bag. We'll look stupid getting the police out here. Anyway, it's open and completely empty.' Becky didn't want any more to do with the police. Not after last time. She didn't mean the day before and the body in the bin, but that terrible time when one of their primary school teachers had been murdered, and she and Molly had known too much and been too frightened to tell. 'I don't want to call the police,' she said, a note of panic in her voice.

Pat looked quizzically at Tim, who shrugged. 'OK. So, what should we do? We need to report this somehow.'

'I don't know.' Becky sounded desperate. For the first time the two older volunteers heard her voice quaver.

'Tell you what,' said Pat, 'a friend of Suzy the podcast woman came to see me and Lorna last night. She's a Police Community Support Officer. I took her number. It's in my phone. Here it is. Ro Watson. Why don't I call her and ask her to come over?'

Becky's face crumpled with relief. 'Yeah, Ro Watson. She's OK. I know her son, Ben.'

'Great solution,' said Tim.

Pat took out her phone and made the call.

Ro was surprised but answered briskly. She said she would be there in fifteen minutes. Leaving a note for her sleeping lover, she got into her car to drive to the Friary.

* * *

Tranquillity Beddoes left Lorna sipping coffee in the conservatory at the back of Camomile Cottage and shuffled in her big fluffy slippers to open the front door. It stuck slightly. Seth had done an amazing job of stone-cladding the red brickwork to make the cottage look more rustic, but he had been a bit heavy-handed. Some parts didn't bear a close inspection.

She expected to see one of the delivery drivers who brought daily packages from eBay to Seth — usually vinyl records, but sometimes bits of retro kit, from hi-fi parts to artwork, all of which he stored in the garage, which never saw a car. Or Tranquillity either. It was a tip, she thought. Seth called it his man cave, but she called it a mess.

Standing on the doorstep was a blonde woman with short spiky hair. She was wearing jeans, a bright mustard T-shirt and a quilted navy-blue gilet. She looked hot.

Tranquillity took it all in, processed it like crazy, smiled gently and said, 'Hi?'

'Hello. I do hope you don't mind me calling out of the blue like this. I'm Suzy Spencer from *Neighbourhood Norbridge*.'

'Oh yes!' Tranquillity broadened her smile. 'Do come in, Suzy.' She opened the door wide and Suzy followed her in. 'It's so nice to meet you. I suppose Seth has been telling you tales of my amazing therapy?' She rolled her eyes self-deprecatingly.

'Well, yes, he's very supportive of your work.'

Tranquillity laughed, looking embarrassed. 'Oh, honestly, he's such a love, but he does make a big thing out of my practice. I expect he tried to get you to feature me on one of your brilliant podcast episodes.'

All this was said rather breathlessly as Tranquillity walked Suzy down a long narrow hall and into a fabulous kitchen extension. Suzy couldn't help saying 'Wow' and Tranquillity laughed again, this time a surprisingly open, throaty sound.

'Yes, this is the result of Seth's ill-gotten gains in the wheeler-dealer world of retro.' She stopped at an enormous marble-topped island, which was slightly out of alignment with the real slate floor tiles, but still impressive. 'When we came back to Norbridge we blew everything on making this cottage the best it could be. Seth is an enthusiastic DIY man. I love him to bits, except when he overdoes the husbandly pride in my achievements. I'm a straightforward psychotherapist, basically. I can show you all my certificates in the consulting room. I just happen to have hit on a therapy which works for a lot of people.'

'Yes, so I hear,' said Suzy, awkwardly.

'And obviously I've listened to your podcast.' Tranquillity gave another of her warm, slightly conspiratorial smiles. 'They're excellent. I'm a big fan of *Grounded* and *Fi and Jane* but you've got flair. You make the oddest groups sound fascinating and it's always so positive.'

'Thank you,' said Suzy, who was too surprised at what sounded like genuine, well-informed praise, to think of anything more to say.

Tranquillity shook some homemade biscuits out of a genuine 1950s tin onto a china plate. 'But actually, Suzy, I can't see my work making anything for you, if I'm honest. You specialize in groups, not individuals. And every wellbeing practitioner in Norbridge would be after you if you featured just one of us.'

This was so close to Suzy's own thoughts that she found herself unable to add anything.

'I'm so sorry if you felt pestered by Seth,' Tranquillity went on. 'He's just an enthusiast. Would you like a coffee?' She paused to put the biscuits on a pretty tray, with three cups and saucers. 'I expect you've really come to see how Lorna's getting on,' and smiled.

Suzy felt she had been sussed out. 'Well, that would be good if she's in a fit state. But that wasn't the only reason why I came.'

Tranquillity turned back and smiled. 'It's OK, I completely understand. Pat probably sent you to check up. Don't worry about it. It must have seemed very odd, us abducting Lorna like that.'

'Well, it was rather sudden,' Suzy said weakly. Tranquillity was certainly perceptive.

The psychotherapist looked more serious now. 'But I do know Lorna through St Michael's Church. I think she really needed to talk over her trauma with a professional counsellor. And someone with an understanding of her religious outlook. She's much better now. Come and see for yourself.'

Tranquillity pushed through the connecting glass door into a beautiful miniature Victorian orangery with a fanciful cast-iron roof frame. It was so different from most of the conservatories in the area that Suzy gasped. She did notice that some of the ironwork seemed out of kilter, but it added to the antique charm.

'Another of Seth's wonderful efforts,' Tranquillity said. 'I think he was at rather a loose end when we ran out of projects, which is why he took up with the gardening volunteers. He's a wonderful workman. You wouldn't expect it, would you? He looks as if he lives under a rock listening to Waylon Jennings. Here's Lorna.' She waved in the direction of a huge wicker chair. 'Lorna, see who's here. Suzy Spencer the podcast producer has popped by.'

Lorna Duxford was sitting curled up with her feet underneath her, sipping coffee from a big bright mug. She was less pale, but her eyes were dull and glassy. She looked very tired, Suzy thought.

Tranquillity pulled up another chair and put Suzy's coffee on a little table between them. In the morning sun, with the big plants and the garden view, it was an idyllic setting.

'How are you, Lorna?' Suzy asked. 'I wanted to meet Tranquillity, so I thought I'd pop by and see you too.' It sounded so pathetic, Suzy thought. She was used to being able to size up situations and get the best out of them. Now her mission of spying out the land for Pat seemed rather childish.

'I'm feeling much better,' said Lorna. 'Tranquillity and Seth have been marvellous.'

'And Father Bill is coming over later to see Lorna,' Tranquillity added. 'I'm one of his regular parishioners. I've had a few people from his congregation come to me, thank goodness. It's not that easy getting clients these days.'

Suzy eyes widened. Tranquillity was also frank.

'If Father Bill thinks Lorna is recovered, mentally and spiritually, I reckon we can let her go home tonight,' she went on.

'I hope so,' said Lorna. 'I do feel I've been rather an idiot. But it really was such a terrible thing to see. Do they have any idea who that poor woman was?' Lorna looked enquiringly at Suzy.

'I don't know a great deal about it,' Suzy said.

'So, they don't know where she came from, or what she was doing there? Was she brought there in a car?' Lorna asked.

'I don't know.' Suzy had a strong urge to escape. But before she left, she needed to say something. 'Pat has been very worried about you, Lorna. I think she was concerned because you disappeared so quickly with Seth.'

'Ah yes,' Tranquillity interrupted. 'I think that might have been our fault. But you know what Seth's like. He doesn't hang about. He was so keen to help, and he always thinks I can work wonders.'

'And you have, you really have,' Lorna added quickly.

Tranquillity said, 'Well, I hope talking it all through last night was useful, but maybe Pat felt snubbed. That's not good and I'm sorry.'

'But Pat couldn't have helped me like you did, Tranquillity.'

'Thank you. But you know what? I'll call Pat and apologize for whisking you away.'

'I'm sure she'd appreciate that.' Tranquillity was always one step ahead, Suzy thought.

Tranquillity turned to Lorna. 'And you should call Pat yourself this morning. There's no time like the present. Or would Pat be at church?'

'Pat? You're kidding!' The old scornful note creeped back into Lorna's voice. 'Pat wouldn't darken the door of a church. She's an agnostic. She won't discuss it because she hates arguments. But she wouldn't have anything to do with St Michael's when I asked her to help.'

'Oh well,' said Tranquillity. 'Each to their own. More coffee, Suzy?'

'No thanks. I should go. I see how busy you must be, Tranquillity. And I'm glad to have met you.'

Suzy felt distinctly uncomfortable. Tranquillity had been gracious about letting her off the hook over the podcast. She thought perhaps she should offer something in return. 'Now I know you, I'm sure you would be a great interviewee, perhaps about Norbridge's alternative medicine scene?' As she said it, Suzy could suddenly envisage it — a review of the non-mainstream medical options in the town. There was the dentist who did hypnotherapy, and the homeopathic chemist, and the reflexologist. It could be fascinating.

'Mmm, worth a thought!' Tranquillity murmured. 'Perhaps we should meet again to talk it over? I'll see you out.'

She walked Suzy into the hall. 'Lorna's much better now,' she said, 'but of course I mustn't talk about patients with you. I suppose you think I'm indiscreet because I sent you one of my letters about the practice. But it's difficult to get clients here.' She leaned forward confidentiality. 'When we first came back to Norbridge I was worried, and I actually went back to London for a while. But I couldn't disappoint Seth so I came home. And I know there's a need out there, since the pandemic. People have suffered so much.

The lockdowns weren't just an extended holiday. Many will never get over them. I think we're only just realizing how serious it's been.'

Suzy thought about *Lockdown Life Change*. Could that be seen as making light of the lockdowns? Had she got it wrong? She felt her self-confidence ebbing. Tranquillity was obviously far more in tune with the zeitgeist.

'And it's not unprofessional to publicize a psycho-therapy practice,' Tranquillity went on. 'But maybe you thought it was a bit iffy? Would it help if you knew I had one VIP local client? I can't disclose of course . . .' She smiled at Suzy, as one professional woman confiding in another. 'And I like your idea of a podcast about Norbridge's medical scene, though some of those people are rather wacky. I'm not strictly alternative, so much as complementary. My basic ideology is Jungian, but I use some philosophical elements in my work. I did look at the Westminster Pastoral Foundation. You know, Christian therapy. But I felt that was too prescriptive. Strangely enough I'm a fan of Iris Murdoch and *The Sovereignty of Good*. I'm sure you know what I mean.'

Suzy didn't, but she nodded.

'Anyway, no worries,' Tranquillity smiled. 'Just contact me if you want to interview me. And call in any time if you fancy a general natter.'

Suzy found herself outside on the path in the sunshine feeling slightly dazed, as if she had opened a Mills and Boon novel and found it was George Eliot.

Behind her, Tranquillity shut the door. She'd got it right as usual. The Iris Murdoch reference had been a stroke of genius. She hadn't read *The Sovereignty of Good*, but the online synopsis was attractive, and she had taken the risk that Suzy Spencer wouldn't know what she was talking about, though it sounded good. By the time she left, the podcast producer had been eating out of her hand. Tranquillity smiled the cat-like grin she kept for moments when she was alone.

She went into the conservatory and said to Lorna, 'Well, I don't think there'll be any more interference from her. Now we have a bit more time to get your story straight and decide what to do. You'd better listen to me.'

* * *

Outside, Suzy walked to her car feeling worse than ever. She was confused. Despite what Robert had said about Tranquillity, the woman's openness was undeniable. And she clearly wasn't a fraud — she knew her stuff. Robert was shrewd and experienced, and Suzy trusted his judgement. But no one was right all the time. Could he be wrong about Tranquillity?

As she opened her car door, she felt she was being watched. She turned round to see Seth Beddoes, framed like a huge man mountain in the doorway of a small, lean-to type of garage. He raised his hand in a wave. But to Suzy it looked like a victory salute.

Had she been duped? If Robert was right — and it was a big if — Tranquillity Beddoes was a top-class manipulator and she, Suzy Spencer, was her latest patsy. It was a new feeling for her and one she didn't want to consider.

CHAPTER NINE

*I would lead you and bring you to my mother's house, she
who has taught me.*

Song of Songs 8:2

At around lunchtime that Sunday, Ro Watson and DS
Jed Jackson met at Workhaven police station on the West
Cumbrian coast. Workhaven was very different from
Norbridge. Whereas Norbridge had been there since the
Middle Ages and owed its success to agriculture, Workhaven
was more working class and owed its success to sea trade and
the industrial revolution. But it wasn't far between the two
towns. Since the cuts DS Jackson found he was driving as
often to Norbridge as to his office in Workhaven.

Ro had spent the last ten minutes telling Jed everything
she had learned from Suzy Spencer about the gardening
group. Jed had listened carefully. He respected Suzy, whom
he had known for years, and he knew that Ro was completely dedicated to her patch and picked up all the local
gossip. From what he had gathered so far, the Norbridge
police hadn't bothered to check out the gardening group or
the Friary. They were hardly suspicious characters. The dead
woman hadn't belonged to Cumbria and had been killed

not far from the layby where the murderer, presumably an outsider with a car, had dumped her.

'The handbag will need to go to Forensics,' Jed said. 'There must be something that could establish that it belonged to the dead woman. But, otherwise there's nothing in it.'

Ro was wearing her plastic gloves. 'Maybe I should check. There are usually loads of little pockets inside for phones and make-up, that sort of thing.'

The bag had an exotic label, which Ro didn't recognize, but she knew it was expensive. She lightly stroked the main compartment and put her fingers into the pouch for the phone, and then the pocket next to it. On the outside, sealed with a fancy brass zip, there was another section, maybe for papers or a Kindle. Nothing in that either. But then Ro felt something slightly stiff under the soft pink leather.

'What is it?' Jed asked.

'There's something in here.' Ro slipped her hand into the compartment. 'There's a zip. Not one of the fancy exterior ones.' She peered into the bag. 'Yes!' she said. 'There's another inner compartment.'

She unzipped it. Very carefully, Ro extracted a rectangular piece of card, about four inches by three. 'Good Lord!' she said. 'I don't believe it!'

'What is it?'

'It's a photograph, one of those publicity photos you used to get of stars or TV personalities. I had one of the Bay City Rollers in my school bus pass for years.'

'The Bay City Rollers?'

'I had the hots for Stuart Woody Wood.' Ro looked mildly embarrassed.

'And you scoff at me because Jesus is my hero,' Jed said. 'Anyway, who's the bloke in this picture? Fancies himself, doesn't he?'

'I recognize him, even if you don't, Jed. You weren't born when this guy was on the scene.'

'I haven't a clue.'

Ro said, 'It's Sol Temple. I haven't heard of him for, well, about forty years, I would think. Very good-looking singer and guitarist. Morphed from being Billy Fury into Bob Dylan. Dunno what happened to him. This looks like an early pic. Maybe he autographed it for her, and she's kept it all this time.'

'There's writing on the back. Faded but readable. Let's see what it says.'

Ro put the publicity shot face down on the desk, on top of the plastic bags they had at the ready. Jed read out loud: '*To our little sister. "Come away, my love. The flowers appear on the earth, the time of the singing of birds is come, and the sound of the dove is heard in our land . . ."*'

Ro said, 'That beats the usual "To Ro with love", doesn't it? Is it poetry?'

'This is from the Bible!'

'Well, you would know.' Jed Jackson was a churchgoer and had to put up with a lot of banter from his colleagues. Ro was an atheist and a cynic, and she occasionally joked about Jed's commitment, but she had learned to respect his integrity. 'So which bit of the Bible? There's a lot of it.'

'It's from the Song of Songs. Supposedly by King Solomon.'

'Oh, I've heard of that. Erotic stuff, isn't it?'

'It's a very beautiful love poem, possibly two lovers speaking to each other. Right, get this picture bagged separately and we'll send the lot off and see if the bag matches up with the victim's DNA.'

'It will,' Ro said grimly. 'If we're finished, can I go home? It's Sunday, remember.'

'Of course, I remember. And before you ask, I've already been to church this morning.'

'First things first,' Ro joked. Her own Sunday morning had been very different and had been interrupted by the phone call from the gardening volunteers. Now she wanted to get away. Her lover hadn't been in touch since she left. But maybe they could still grab some of the day back . . .

'OK, Ro, you go. I'm just going to google Sol Temple.'
Jed was staring at the picture.

'Didn't Solomon build the Temple in Jerusalem?' Ro
asked with a sudden flash of memory. 'Is that where Sol
Temple got his stage name, do you think?'

Jed thought about it. 'Yes, Sol Temple would have been
a catchy name back then. There was a lot of religious reviv-
alism in the sixties. Billy Graham and all that. Sol Temple
would be a name a lot of people would recognize. Before the
days of Barclay James Harvest and Pink Floyd.'

'I'm surprised you've even heard of them. Or Billy
Graham. I remember him. Some older girls from school went
to huge evangelical rallies. They were a big thing in Liverpool.
Could you keep me updated if there's any response to the
press appeal? I'm interested in this dead woman. Why would
she treasure a publicity pic of Sol Temple all this time?'

'Well, I know someone who kept a picture of the Bay
City Rollers in her bus pass.'

'Not for forty years,' said Ro. 'I never forgave Stuart
Wood for marrying someone else.'

'Maybe you both had a lucky escape.'

'Oh, get lost!' Ro left, laughing.

* * *

Jonty McFadden sidled up the path to his mother's house on
the council estate in Pelliter. He was on a flying visit to see her
and had mixed feelings about being back. When he was eleven
he'd got a scholarship to Dodsworth House private school. It
was all thanks to his godmother. She had been a teacher at his
primary school while his mam was a teaching assistant.

His godmother had retired to Spain and Jonty had
spent most of the school holidays with her at the condo on
the newly developed complex outside Malaga. Then he was
expelled from Dodsworth House when a drug-dealing episode had ended in knife crime, and he had made Spain his
full-time base.

But his mam was still his mam, and he was the apple of her eye. His older brother and sister were chavs as far as he was concerned, but his mam was tough and had taken no nonsense at the school, where she'd bullied the other staff. The powers-that-be had eased her out in the end. But she had trousered a full year's pay, and had soon found herself another job at the supermarket. Now she'd been replaced by a machine, though no machine could be as shrewd and sharp, with an eye to the main chance, as Callie McFadden.

That was before Covid, however. The lockdowns had driven Callie crazy, with no workplace to dominate and no opportunities for tormenting her neighbours other than playing loud music by herself.

So, Callie had tried dating sites, looking for someone who didn't give a stuff for the rules. She didn't want a toothless old gadgie so she'd found a site called 'Fair, Fat and Forty', which described her perfectly — if forty was the measurement around each thigh. Callie was a big lass these days. She wanted a younger man, and Noddy's profile had soon popped up. She'd thought he was in his late forties, though he looked older. She wasn't sure whether he was divorced, but who cared? He had driven up the motorway in an old banger and moved in.

They'd called themselves a 'bubble' and begun a life of booze, coke, weed, and had streamed sitcoms, which they snored through. Then Jonty had turned up out of the blue one night, after dark. Callie wasn't sure how he'd managed to evade the restrictions but there he was, larger than life and twice as appealing, grinning on her doorstep.

For a few days he'd stayed in his old bedroom, talking on Zoom and listening to Callie and Noddy through the walls at night. He didn't say much to Noddy, but you could tell the two didn't get on. Then he'd disappeared again. With his usual luck, Jonty had landed a cushy job. Callie was under strict instructions not to mention it to anyone, especially Noddy, and she knew better than to cross Jonty. Mind you, when she'd had a few, it was hard not to brag about her awesome son.

When Jonty had arrived back home on Saturday night, the house was a mess. Callie and Noddy had downed a bottle of vodka and done a couple of spliffs. Noddy had been sprawled on the filthy sofa in his sleeveless shirt and stained trackie bottoms, while Callie was in her dressing gown — as she had been all day.

Jonty had not been impressed. He'd stormed out and gone into Norbridge for the first time since coming back to Cumbria. He wasn't picking up with the old gang, though. He was a cut above, and had a new life now. But he'd seen his old schoolmate Becky Dixon through the window of the Crown and Thistle with her barmy mates. On Sunday morning, waiting for his Sunday dinner, he thought it might be sport to track her down and have some fun with her. She was petrified of him, he knew that.

He had gone round the Norbridge pubs and coffee shops looking for her and her group. Where else could they go on a Sunday? But he'd had no luck finding her and felt hacked off. He'd wondered about going out to the farm where she lived, but her grandad would be there, and Phil Dixon was one of the few people Jonty was wary of. He'd driven back out to Pelliter from the town centre feeling irritated and disrespected. Few people had recognized him in Norbridge and there were none of the shocked glances and scared looks he had expected as the local bad lad.

When he got to his mother's street, he walked quietly up the path and pushed open the front door. Noddy was lying on the sofa again, out of his head, but he opened his piggy little eyes. Callie was sprawled on a chair opposite him, snoring, her enormous thighs showing under the dirty robe. There was no smell of cooking.

Noddy called, 'Apologies, my lord, dinner will be a bit late. But you've got enough gravy already, ain't you, on the gravy train?'

Jonty ignored him and went into the little back kitchen. There was a packet of defrosting supermarket Yorkshire puddings on the counter and a piece of raw beef coagulating in a roasting tin. Callie had obviously stopped in the middle of peeling spuds, and the dried dirty rings of peel blocked the greasy sink. Jonty looked at his designer watch. It was quarter to three.

He strode back into the living room, picked Noddy up by the shoulders and hurled him at the wall. The man stayed stuck there like a squashed moth as Jonty advanced on him, cat-skinner knife in hand. He pointed the knife a millimetre away from Noddy's neck, then brought it up to nick the skin of his turkey wattles.

Noddy yelped in shock and pain as a globule of blood dripped onto his dirty singlet.

Jonty hissed in his best public-school tones, 'Get out of this house, scum. Now. Pack your bags.' He carefully made a small incision in the man's upper chest, and this time Noddy screamed.

Jonty twisted the knife. Noddy squirmed and whimpered.

'And don't bleed on the carpet,' Jonty hissed. 'Not that you can tell, in this pigsty. And if you ever come back here, I'll kill you. You know I mean that, don't you?'

Snivelling and clutching at his chest, Noddy stumbled to the stairs.

Jonty went over to his mother, who had woken up and was watching, wide-eyed.

'Sober up, Mam. And soon. If you ever tell anyone *any-thing* about my job — *anything*, you understand — I will make sure you never speak again.'

His face was right up to hers. They shared the same blue eyes and pointed nose, but whereas Callie was flabby-jawed and had a mess of greasy grey hair hanging down her back, Jonty was black-haired and neat as a pin.

He said with fake charm, his eyes an inch away from hers, 'And now, Mother dear, I want my Sunday dinner. And not with those plastic Yorkshire puddings either. I want the real thing. You know how to make them, don't you?'

Callie could just about nod.

'And you can call a taxi for your ratty shag-buddy. You disgust me. And you know what happens to people who disgust me.'

Callie knew. She scrambled to her feet and made for the kitchen.

CHAPTER TEN

Eat, O friends, and drink; drink your fill, O lovers!
Song of Songs 5:1

Suzy parked her car outside The Briars and walked into Tarnfield to meet Robert at The Plough for Sunday lunch. He'd already ordered a big roast despite the warm day. Suzy chose the vegetarian pasta and went to sit with him at the socially distanced tables. The Plough was still being cautious. Suzy quite liked the new arrangement. It meant they couldn't be overheard.

'So, how did it go?' Robert asked.

'Not like I expected, I'm afraid. Tranquillity Beddoes guessed I wanted to check up on Lorna.'

'That must have been embarrassing.'

'Yes, but she let me see Lorna without any problem, and we all had a chat. Lorna was much better, though she looked very tired. And she certainly seemed to be happy with the Beddoes.'

'And she was there voluntarily?'

'Absolutely. In fact, Tranquillity was encouraging her to phone Pat, and maybe go home with her later today.'

'And what did you make of the spiritual therapist? Did she do a laying on of hands or something?'

'Oh, Robert! If it hadn't been for you, I would have quite liked her. She was very upfront about how she needed to recruit clients post-pandemic, for their good as well as hers, and her credentials seemed impeccable. Jungian overlaid with modern ethical philosophy.'

'Wow. I can see that she impressed you.'

'And she's very well in with St Michael's. The vicar was going to see Lorna this morning. Bill Gibson? Isn't he the one you went to see yesterday, who's been accused of—'

'Don't say it out loud. Even if no one can hear you.'

'Whoops. Sorry. Anyway, sounds like the Reverend Bill Gibson's got a lot on. Dead body, distraught parishioner, horrible accusations . . .'

'Yes.' Robert stared at his roast beef. He thought about the priest, who was prepared to admit to something heinous to avert discovery of something even worse. He had been on Robert's mind overnight. Should he be trying to find out what that worse thing was? And how could he do that?

'Eat up, Robert,' Suzy said. 'This is delicious. I'm so glad you suggested we come out for lunch. I'd like to do a bit of work on *Lockdown Life Change* this afternoon. I have big doubts about it. Something Tranquillity said about the lockdowns being too serious to take lightly. And I want to call Molly.' Suzy frowned. It irked her that her daughter wasn't coming home for reading week. But Suzy was also pleased that Molly was happy enough in York to want to stay there. She sighed. Parenting became more complicated as they grew older. 'I want to ring Rachel as well. We haven't spoken for a few days, and she's having problems with her teeth. Implants.'

Robert nodded. Rachel was Suzy's closest friend. She was a London-based TV producer, specializing in politics and investigations, very different programmes from Suzy's lifestyle productions. But they had met years before and the friendship had stuck. Suzy usually phoned Rachel every week, depending on their work.

Suzy's other close friend was the PCSO Ro Watson, but while she and Rachel were total confidantes, Robert sensed that Ro sometimes held back, and that Suzy didn't ask. There was something reserved about Ro. Robert suspected she was in a relationship, but he hadn't asked Suzy if she knew.

'And what about the podcast?' he asked. 'Aren't you due to produce some more *Neighbourhood Norbridge*?'

Suzy sighed. She derived a small income from the national sponsors of the *Neighbourhood* franchise, who sent her advertisements to splice into the beginning, middle and end of her recordings. They had a format, but Suzy had adapted it to her own inimitable style. Her podcast had a high take-up in Norbridge, and the sponsors were pleased. But the *Neighbourhood* franchise liked her to put out fresh episodes regularly to reach listeners.

'I could maybe get away without having a new one straight away, seeing as the graveyard gardening episode will have to be ditched for now, but I need to get going on another. I did wonder about trying to get hold of Hiram King. He's a pro so it would be an easy recording and he could talk about his new rewilding grants for local communities.'

'That sounds good.'

'And after that I might do Norbridge's alternative medicine scene. I've a feeling we have more than our share of therapists and healers. Tranquillity could feature in that. I think she'd be good.'

'Really? Well, you've met her, Suzy, and I've only heard about her. But I don't like what I hear. On the other hand, maybe I should examine my unconscious prejudice.' He looked at the end of his fork.

'That's not a prejudice, it's a potato.'

They laughed. When she was with Robert, things always seemed better, though she felt she had made a fool of herself at Camomile Cottage that morning. But at least Pat Jones would be reassured that Lorna was in good hands.

Unless Robert was right . . .

* * *

Hiram King was fed up. He normally enjoyed Sundays when he usually organized a big mock family lunch with the workers. Lord of the Manor!

His choice of staff had been good, but he had needed a right-hand man, someone he could really trust. He'd interviewed dozens of people, anonymously on Zoom, ostensibly to work as a driver, but no one was right. The man he'd wanted needed to be young and fit, active, ruthless, interested in Hiram's embryonic and outrageous, controversial rewilding projects, and most of all, capable of complete devotion.

One day, chatting to one of his gardeners, who commuted from Norbridge, the conversation had turned to low life. The gardener fancied himself as a bit of a Jack the Lad — dope dealer, car seller, purveyor of questionable electrical goods. He had mentioned a name, and some exploits. 'Bit of a wide boy. He left the district after a nasty incident a few years ago. Said he was fitted up. He went to Spain. A smooth operator, charm itself. Good with animals.'

Hiram had a think. It wouldn't be hard to trace this boyo. It was a long shot, but he could Zoom him for interview and get him over here without too much difficulty — Hiram always knew the breaks — then suss him out. And he could give him the brush if it didn't work.

After that bit of inspiration, all he'd had to do was get Maggie to use her amazing research skills to track down this boy, then sack the gardener who had a big mouth. And that's how Hiram King had come to employ Jonty McFadden, knife wielder, petty criminal and Becky Dixon's nemesis.

Hiram had the contradictory personality of a lot of celebrities. He longed for recognition and to hobnob with the great and good, but he also flirted with the darker side of life. To get things done, he believed you had to take chances and bend the rules. Everyone who succeeded did that. Sometimes incidents from his past came back to haunt him, but he had his therapy for that. All great men needed fixers. Jonty would be his.

And Jonty wasn't just a thug. He had his soft side, Hiram thought. Look how he had asked for time off to go and see his mum. Sweet! Hiram was missing him already. Hiram liked the idea of being a hero to a younger man. Jonty had told him he was twenty-one, but Hiram guessed he was only nineteen. So, he'd lied, so what? And Jonty's driving licence might be a bit suspect. But if it was a forgery, it was good. Hiram liked a lad who would take risks and cut corners. Jonty had all the qualities Hiram was looking for to implement his big project.

Hiram had walked around the grounds that morning and his thoughts, as always, reverted to what he wanted to do. Sod wildflowers and roadside verges and deciduous woodland and all that crap. It was nice to be giving out grants for the softer stuff, to suck people into his plans. But that wasn't the sort of rewilding he really had in mind. Hiram was wedded to the project and, thanks to Jonty and his fast work, there would be no going back now.

Wolves. Hiram King was going to reintroduce the wolf to the Borders.

* * *

After PCSO Ro Watson had retrieved the pink handbag and taken it away, the gardening group trudged to the Friary. On the way up the path, Pat took a quick call from Suzy Spencer, who said she had seen Lorna for herself at the Beddoes' that morning. Lorna was still fragile but recovering, and Suzy had been surprised she hadn't yet called Pat.

'I'm sure there'll be a message somewhere,' she insisted. 'It might be on your landline. Tranquillity told Lorna she should phone you.'

Why would Lorna need Tranquillity's permission, Pat thought, but all she said was, 'Well, thank you for going round. That's reassuring.'

But it wasn't. The Lorna whom Pat knew would have hated to be seen as one of Tranquillity's lame ducks. Tim had picked up on that. He had insight. It was a pity he looked so fed up and miserable most of the time, making you wary of speaking to him. He probably had interesting views on a lot of things, and he had certainly done a challenging job as an ambulance driver.

Becky yelped with pleasure. 'These really are the missing secateurs!' She picked them up from beside the clump of marguerites.

'Good!' said Pat. 'That's all the tools accounted for.'

She pushed open the Lesser Friary door, and the group spent a satisfying time inside, wiping the tools clean and tidying up.

'How long do you think Lorna will be out of action?' Tim asked.

'I don't know,' said Pat. 'I spoke to Suzy Spencer as we were walking up. She said Lorna was going to call me, but she hasn't.'

'You look worried,' said Tim.

'Yes. It's not like Lorna not to ring. I really don't understand it. But then Lorna hasn't behaved like Lorna from the moment she opened that bin.'

'We don't have to try and second-guess Lorna Duxford all the time,' said Becky, her voice suddenly sounding loud, young and assertive. 'We could get quite a lot done ourselves.'

'I agree,' said Tim. But they both looked at Pat.

'Well — why not?' Pat felt unusually decisive. It was better to think about something practical than to worry. 'The three of us could get some more of that ivy ripped out today. Let's work for an hour, and then why don't you come to my cottage for tea, and we can talk about how we proceed.'

The idea had come to her out of the blue. It meant she didn't have to sit there alone waiting for Lorna to call. But would the others want to come to her cottage on a Sunday afternoon? They must have lives of their own.

To her surprise, Becky looked a lot cheerier. 'Ta. That would be good. My grandad is out today.'

'Your grandfather?' Tim asked.

'Yep. I live with him. There's just the two of us now. My gran died a couple of years ago. Cancer.'

'Oh, how terrible,' said Pat. 'That's how my husband died. You must miss her.'

Becky shrugged. 'Grandad and I manage.'

'He'll be sad when you go away to Cambridge.'

'Mebbe he will. Mebbe, he won't,' said Becky, and her face creased. But it cleared at the thought that she could go to Pat's for tea and not be alone at the farmhouse. Becky knew it was stupid, but she was frightened in case Jonty McFadden decided to turn up. If she went back now, she'd be home alone. Not a good thought.

'OK, let's get to work, and in an hour, we'll clear up and get away.' Pat looked at Tim. 'What about you, Tim?'

'Yes, thanks for the invite. I'd like that.'

Pat felt a rush of relief. Having guests for tea was something new. Perhaps they would enjoy the pizza and salad she had bought for herself and Lorna. The thought made her ache. Why hadn't Lorna been in touch?

But now there was something useful to do. Becky was brandishing the hoe again and Tim grabbed the shears and made chopping movements. He smiled at her. 'Let's give that ivy hell.'

* * *

At Workhaven police station, DS Jed Jackson was looking up Sol Temple on Wikipedia. Temple had been a London boy who shot to fame on the pop programme *Ready Steady Go*. He was a singer and guitarist, and his first hit, 'Better than Wine', was a haunting acoustic melody, with lyrics from the Song of Songs. It had earned him a lot of publicity. Sol Temple seemed to have made the erotic biblical book into his own brand.

Jed wasn't surprised at the biblical theme. As he had told Ro, churchgoing in the UK was at its highest ever in the 1950s, which always surprised people. After the Second World War the big revivalist rallies in UK cities had recruited thousands of young people. And there were lots of songs with biblical themes: 'All Along the Watchtower' by Dylan, covered by Hendrix, 'Rivers of Babylon' from Boney M, The Byrds with a rendition of Pete Seeger's 'Turn, Turn, Turn' from the book of Ecclesiastes. He had been surprised when Ro had made the Solomon's Temple connection, but it just showed how much residual biblical knowledge most people had.

He was musing about this when his phone rang. It was his chief, the DI from Norbridge.

'You still in the office?' the boss barked.

'Yeah, but I'm off shortly, sir. Any news on the handbag?'

'Yep, that's why I'm calling. Forensics worked today, which will mean a hell of an overtime bill, which is annoying, especially on an out-of-town case.'

'Out of town?'

'Yeah. The bag's hers all right but we'd identified her from fingerprints. It's a woman from Crosby. She was done for soliciting about thirty years ago, so her prints were on record. Merseyside police will be taking over now. I had a feeling this was a gangland thing from the very start.'

'How did she die?'

'That fits with gangland too. The pathologist says she was killed by a neat professional blow to the back of the head. Probably some sort of truncheon. No need to worry about the locals flailing around with their cheap gardening tools. There was grass on her body from the road end of the graveyard. The killer probably lured her onto the path, out of sight, then hit her from behind and heaved her into the bin.'

'But why choose the graveyard?'

'Well, the killer could have scoped the layby and known the bins were derelict. They hadn't been emptied for a decade. Normally it would have been months, years maybe, before she'd have been found. And it's a long way from Merseyside. It would be the perfect place to dump her.'

'But wouldn't gangsters have done something about the prints? Mutilated the fingers?'

'They were banking on the body decomposing, I suppose. But however you look at it, Jed, it's not our problem.

She was on the game and probably crossed some nasty characters.' The DI sighed gustily. 'Anyway, we've got this sheep-killer bloke causing chaos. I'm getting a lot of stick from the farming lobby. They're my problem. I don't need the Merseyside mafia on my watch.'

'OK,' said Jed, 'but there is one other thing. The PCSO, Ro Watson, said the bin was locked and must have been opened with a key. One was hanging in the church.'

'PCSO Watson at it again, is she? She takes her job a bit too seriously. She should be helping old folk cross the road, not interfering in a murder inquiry. Those keys are just bits of ironmongery. I expect you can get them anywhere.'

'And what about the publicity picture in the handbag?'

'What, the picture of that creep Sol Temple? He's been dead for forty years. She was carrying his picture about, so what? Leave it out, Jed. We don't want to have to deal with gangsters from the north-west. We've got our own rogues here. We'll do all we can to help, but it's not our problem.'

'OK, I'll be off home, then.'

'Yes. Enjoy your Sunday evening. What'll you get up to? Bit of God-bothering?'

'I did that this morning, sir. I'm giving the Big Man a rest tonight.'

The DI bellowed with laughter. 'Well, when you do have a word with Him Upstairs, ask for some help catching the phantom sheep killer.'

Jed smiled resignedly and rang off. The DI was a man of great self-confidence, five years from a well-earned and well-funded retirement. He knew Norbridge inside out. But he had automatically discounted the woman as the victim of a local crime because she was black and middle-aged, Jed thought. Black and young and unidentified, and the DI would have been in a state of acute anxiety — a student murder would have been a real crisis. But an older black woman — well, there were few of those in Norbridge, and all accounted for.

Jed wasn't happy. He felt the local angle shouldn't be discounted, however inconvenient. He thought about the info Ro had gleaned from Suzy about the gardening group — who they were, why they were in the graveyard, Lorna Duxford's obsession with rewilding the site, and the hope of a grant from Hiram King. Of course, Jed had heard of him. The gardening guru had his own range of wildflower seeds, sold in the sort of fancy shops Jed's wife liked. He had never thought about the name Hiram King before, but now it rang a bell he didn't expect. Though he couldn't put his finger on it . . . or could he?

Sol Temple. Hiram King. Maybe he should talk to Robert Clark, who was good on theology. Jed had known Robert Clark and Suzy Spencer for years. He could use Robert as a sounding board without fear of being laughed at.

Feeling better, Jed locked up the office and went home to his wife and family.

CHAPTER ELEVEN

Your teeth are like a flock of shorn ewes.

Song of Songs 4:2

Suzy sat at her desk in the attic office and reread the running order for the pilot of *Lockdown Life Change*. They were interviewing a woman in her seventies who'd had singing lessons on Zoom and been accepted at a prestigious college of music, a boy on a gap year who had been marooned in Ghana and fallen in love, and a delivery driver who'd had an affair with a shopaholic customer. All feel-good stuff. But now Suzy had a bad feeling about it.

She rose from her desk, walked to the new dormer window they'd had installed, and looked out at the rolling country at the back of The Briars. Somewhere over to her left, the hills dropped gently to the coast, and on the way was the town of Norbridge, with East Norbridge and the Lesser Friary punctuating the old road.

She couldn't settle to her work and, as always when she was feeling frustrated, she called Rachel, who lived in Islington. Rachel had been having a lot of problems with her teeth and had embarked on an expensive programme of implants. She hated taking time off work and had been irritable as a result.

'How's the gob?' Suzy said brightly.

'It's my lower mandible, if you don't mind. You don't have to be so cheerily crude. There seems to be a problem. I've got real pain in one of the so-called OK teeth. I'm going tomorrow for an early emergency appointment. In Harley Street.'

'Oh, get you!'

'Seriously, Suzy, my own dentist is snowed under post-pandemic and I need to get this fixed. We're midway through prepping that doc I told you about for the investigation strand on Channel 4. About assisted dying.'

'Sounds like fun.'

'It's fascinating, actually. It makes you think differently about pain, and I must say, my teeth are making me more sympathetic. It's agony! When I can talk without groaning, I'll go through the assisted dying controversy with you. I know you sold out to daytime TV, but I do trust your judgement. By the way, how's your own work going?'

'It's a mess. On both fronts.' Suzy briefly went through the issue of *Lockdown Life Change* hitting the wrong nerve, then how her podcast episode on the gardening volunteers had to be shelved because of the body in the bin.

'Sounds like bad luck. What are you going to do?'

'I was thinking of featuring the Hiram King grants instead,' Suzy said.

'Hiram King — that nutcase who believes we should all live in Sherwood Forest?'

'Not quite. He's into rewilding and giving out serious money locally. He's moved up here.'

'Well, he's a name. But when it comes to your other project, isn't the pandemic a bit too serious for this *Lockdown Life Change* idea? Or is this toothache making me negative about everything? Ouch, I'm going to have to go, Suzy. I need to lie down with a hot water bottle.'

'Oh, Rachel, I'm sorry. I'll call you tomorrow. OK?'

Rachel groaned. 'Speak then.'

Suzy said goodbye and stared out of the window again. If Rachel was thinking along the same lines as Tranquillity

Beddoes, then there was certainly a problem with *Lockdown Life Change*.

She was wondering what to do when she noticed a missed call from Ro Watson. Suzy called back.

Ro said grumpily, 'I had to go into work, and when I escaped it was too late for my date.'

Ro paused and Suzy clocked what she had said, but she knew Ro too well to push her for more information. She waited until Ro went on, 'The DI thinks this murder is a Merseyside issue. I'm a bit hacked off.'

'Join the club,' said Suzy. 'I'm hacked off all round. Why don't we meet for a drink? I can't get on with my work — it just isn't happening, and Robert is involved with some church business.'

Robert had phoned Bill Gibson earlier and agreed to go and see Bill and his wife Ruth, who was now back home. As priest in charge at the Friary, Bill Gibson was caught up in the finding of the woman's body, and that was adding to the pressure he was under.

But Suzy was thinking about Lorna Duxford. It was beginning to seem odder than ever that Lorna had been so traumatized about seeing the body in the bin. Everything about Lorna pointed to her being a coper.

'The thing is,' Ro said, echoing Suzy's thoughts, 'I'm not happy about this body-in-the-bin business being an out-of-town gangland murder. Why would they kill her in Cumbria? It might be the backwoods to Scouse gangsters, but it's not as if there aren't hundreds of places to hide a body down there.'

'I'm bothered about it as well,' said Suzy. 'There's another odd twist. You should know that Lorna Duxford has left her friend Pat's and is staying with the Beddoes.'

'Tranquillity Beddoes? The psychotherapist? Dolly Parton meets Carl Jung? That's interesting. I've met Tranquillity once or twice and, as far as I'm concerned, the jury's out.'

So, Ro shared Robert's disquiet. That was worth discussing.

'Why don't we meet at The Partridge in East Norbridge,' Suzy suggested. 'It would get us both out of the house and we could just have a pint of orange and soda each. It wouldn't do you any good to get pulled up by the cops!'

'Actually, Suzy—' Ro sounded serious — 'I think I'm out of favour with the cops anyway. The DI thinks I'm winding up Jed. But we're both convinced there's a local angle to this case. I feel it in my bones.'

* * *

Robert rang the bell at the vicarage for St Michael and All Angels. When he had phoned that afternoon, Bill had said nothing about the inappropriate touching allegations, but had volunteered that he would like advice on coping with the police over the murder in the graveyard. Robert had dealt with the local force several times before, on behalf of the Deanery Synod, so he was qualified to help.

'They say they want to find out who owns the graveyard and the bins,' Bill had said. 'There's a Norbridge officer plus a Merseyside officer coming to see me tomorrow. The dead woman came from Merseyside.'

'Yes, I know,' Robert had replied.

'Of course, you do. News travels fast. It's only human nature to enjoy the misfortune of others, so they say. *Only* human nature. But human nature is vicious. I'd appreciate it if you could come over, around five o'clock.'

It was a big concession for Bill to ask for help.

Ruth Gibson opened the vicarage door. 'Robert, how nice to see you, though in such awful circumstances.'

Robert wondered whether she knew just how awful.

'I came back as soon as Bill told me about this poor dead woman,' Ruth said. 'Horrendous. The study is here.'

Robert followed her along a crowded hallway. The vicarage was a large Victorian house, but the hall was cluttered with the stale residue of past family life. There was a mound of old coats of various styles, and an ancient hall stand piled with bags and hats.

'It's a mess, I know. The house is getting on top of me these days. And I haven't had time to deal with housework since I got back.' Ruth's pleasant, rather bird-like face showed no sign of deeper anxiety. 'Would you like a cup of tea or coffee, Robert? We've been eating in fits and starts today. One of Bill's parishioners, Lorna Duxford, found the body, as I expect you know. Lorna's staying with Tranquillity Beddoes, which is probably the best place for her. Bill went over there this morning.' Ruth pushed open a door into a front room on the right. 'Here's the study. Did you say tea or coffee?'

'Coffee would be nice.'

'I'll call Bill and tell him you're here.'

Bill's study was as untidy as Robert had expected. He peered at the bookcases. He always looked at the edges of people's bookshelves. It was often where they kept the books they treasured but didn't read. Bill had a set of the Sharpe books by Bernard Cornwell. He also had an old CD player with a shelf of discs. Bill obviously enjoyed gospel music — Aretha Franklin, Mahalia Jackson — but he also had some Christian pop artists: Cliff Richard, Paul Jones, the New Seekers and Sol Temple.

Bill came clumping into the study and closed the door. 'I haven't told Ruth anything about that letter,' he said bluntly. 'But if I did tell her, she would have complete faith in me. She knows I would never touch a teenage girl.'

'But you're still not going to contest it.'

'No, I'm not. Like I told you, it would mean going into things I don't want to discuss, raking up the past in a way that would do a lot of harm. The bishop needs to wait until this accuser comes back with more demands, if she ever does, and then negotiate.'

'It's not that straightforward, Bill. The bishop needs to act swiftly. You may say you're innocent, but the Church must consider the abused, not protect the abuser. Some terrible things have been coming to light.'

'But protecting me is the job of the new diocesan management,' Bill said bullishly. There's enough of them!

Nowadays, it's easier to put three country parishes under one overworked vicar and employ "Directors of Rural Mission" and heaven knows what, anything rather than parish priests. So let the bishop's *team* do some work for a change.' Bill Gibson's head came up, and his eyes met Robert's in confrontation. 'Anyway, I invited you here for advice about dealing with the police, not to go over the other matter.'

Robert paused, then thought better of reminding Bill that he was the one who had brought up the subject. 'OK. So, let's talk about the murdered woman found at the Lesser Friary.'

'She wasn't found at the Lesser Friary. She was in a bin on rough ground next to the layby. The layby belongs to the county council highways department.'

'But the woman was probably killed in your graveyard. And the bins are on your church's land.'

'It's not my church's land. The graveyard doesn't belong to the Lesser Friary anymore. There was an agreement about a hundred years ago when the Church made the graveyard over to the county to maintain. Of course, the county never did anything with it except mow round the path twice a year.'

'OK. But there's no need to bark at me, Bill. I'm only telling you what I think the police need to know.'

'But you can't blame me for being hacked off with the county council for doing nothing with the land until they decided to start one of those virtue-signalling community gardening efforts, when I said they could use the Lesser Friary for their tools.'

'So does the council own the bins as well?' Robert asked.

'Ah well, the bins *do* belong to the church. About fifteen years ago we ordered commercial waste bins from a company down in Manchester. At the time we were holding fundraising events for the hospice in the Lesser Friary and we needed big rubbish bins. We asked for them to be delivered to the car park, on the top road. But the company made a mistake and put them down by the layby.'

'Easily done, I suppose.'

Bill shrugged. 'We asked them to come and redeliver them. But they went bust and never moved them, and we just let it be. I'm to blame, of course. I should have had them removed years ago. You know, Robert, that's the job of a priest nowadays, sorting out bins and leaks and property problems. Drains matter more than souls.'

'Have you told the police all this?'

'About the bins? Won't there be trouble about me just leaving them there?'

'I doubt it. They have bigger fish to fry. But it's always best to tell them everything. You never know what will matter and what's irrelevant.'

The vicar shrugged again and then said suddenly, 'There's one thing which I *have* told Ruth, and you should know too. I'm going to take early retirement if I can. Once this murder inquiry is over, and once my so-called accuser has gone away, we're going to leave East Norbridge and seriously downsize.'

Robert wondered if it could all be sorted out as neatly as Bill Gibson hoped. Ruth came in with the coffee and they chatted about other things, including the surprise of Lorna Duxford breaking down after finding the dead woman. Bill was almost glowing about Tranquillity Beddoes' work.

'Tranquillity's a local girl,' said Ruth, 'not that I remember her. We've been here over thirty years, and I don't remember everyone.'

'And now it's time to move on,' Bill said. 'We both agree, don't we, Ruth?'

Ruth smiled. 'We've been very happy here, until recently anyway. But the house is too big. And I want to be nearer my granddaughter.'

'Well,' said Robert, 'times change. Let me know how it goes with the police.' He stood to leave.

On the doorstep he and Ruth looked out onto the evening darkness falling over the big, untidy garden. The smell of early night-scented stocks wafted towards them.

'It's all getting to be too much for Bill,' said Ruth. 'He's jaded, you know. It's not easy being a vicar these days.'

'That's true,' Robert agreed. 'But won't you miss Norbridge? Especially at this time of year. May is such a lovely month.'

'I suppose so . . .' Ruth sounded rather sad. 'I don't know. My mother died in May, just after we came back here to my hometown.'

'I hadn't realized you were local!' Robert said.

'Oh yes. My brother and I were brought up here. He's in Australia now. I haven't seen him for over thirty years, although we keep in close touch. He's been threatening to come and stay now the pandemic is over.'

And he'll walk right into a crisis, Robert thought.

Ruth was still talking, rather sadly. 'I loved this house from the start. My mother was going to leave her place in the town and live with us and help me with the babies. But she had cancer. She didn't last a year. I think her death was what made Bill take on the hospice work.'

'Bill has a lot of responsibilities.'

'Yes, and he's getting older. And crosser. To be honest, sometimes he gets so frustrated it worries me.'

Robert had guessed Bill was an angry man with a short fuse. He wouldn't be easy to live with.

Ruth said, 'I'm a realist, Robert. If we have to move, we have to move. And thank you for helping Bill. I know he needs it, but he would never say.'

Robert smiled his goodbyes and walked along the path to his car. The vicarage door shut behind him. It was a beautiful old house, but it needed more maintenance than the Gibsons could provide. The diocese would probably sell it to be redeveloped into flats. That would confirm Bill's disillusion.

And disillusioned he certainly was. Yet one thing struck Robert as inconsistent. Surely a cynic like Bill would have rubbished 'spiritual' psychotherapy? But Bill had made it clear that he thought Tranquillity Beddoes did great work. Still, if Tranquillity had got under Suzy's skin, anything was possible.

Bill was hiding something, though. He might not be guilty of sexual assault, but Robert was still sure that he was guilty of something else.

CHAPTER TWELVE

My heart began to pound for him.

Song of Songs 5:4

Pat and Tim waved goodbye to Becky as she set off into the dusk on her bike. She had opened up that afternoon, sitting in Pat's little courtyard garden eating pizza. She had talked about her unusual family life with her grandparents on their smallholding on the Solway coast. Pat had been deeply affected by Becky's attempt to be brave about her grandma's death. Pat got the impression Becky was much closer to her grandfather, but had still loved her gran, who had brought her up from a baby, after her mother died.

So much sadness in one short life, Pat thought. But Becky seemed resilient, and she was obviously thoughtful and intelligent. And there was a determined aspect to her, more than in the usual self-centred teenager. She was going to be a force to be reckoned with one day, but that afternoon they had seen her softer side.

Pat had talked about how her husband Derek had died from cancer too. Becky's grandma had had breast cancer, and Derek lung cancer.

Tim had said, 'It's the scourge of our time. I wonder if any of the medieval people who were buried in the graveyard had cancer?'

Becky had brightened up. 'It's fascinating the diseases they had. I've read this amazing book about old graveyards. Monks had what are called occupational diseases from having a rich diet and being sedentary. But in towns there was terrible air pollution, which caused lung disease. And there was leprosy, the tubercular kind mostly. And did you know there are examples of syphilis? We think that came from the Americas but we're wrong . . .'

'Goodness, you're very knowledgeable,' Pat had said.

'Yes,' Becky had agreed, 'I am. But there's no mention in the book of cancer. It was assumed cancer affected as few as one per cent of the medieval population. But there has been this amazing new research from Cambridge. They analyzed a hundred and forty-three skeletons from six medieval cemeteries and used CT scans to examine the bones.' Becky's eyes were bright with enthusiasm. 'The researchers think that between nine and fourteen per cent of medieval people suffered from cancer.'

'And no pain relief in those days,' Pat had said.

'Except alcohol and some herb drugs like henbane and hemlock, wormwood, mint and balm,' Becky had added. 'Grandma went into the hospice in the end. It was good because she was pain free thanks to them. Before that I just wanted her to die. Is that very terrible?'

'Of course not,' Tim had said. 'I can't tell you how often I've prayed for release for someone in pain. I saw a lot of agony in my job.'

'I felt the same way about Derek in the end,' Pat heard herself saying out loud for the first time.

Becky had looked at her. Usually, she protected herself from sad feelings, treating emotion analytically with her sharp brain. But Pat's tone got to her. 'Poor you,' she said and she meant it.

103

'It was a long time ago now,' Pat had said. 'And a very sad time. But it's so good to hear you talk with such enthusiasm, Becky. And it's great that Cambridge University made that fascinating discovery. It sounds like you're going to the right place.'

'I don't know. Academically, perhaps. But it's a different culture.'

Pat smiled. 'The culture comes second. Everyone talks about "uni" as an "experience" these days. But if you're a *real* student, it's the learning which matters. Whether you say dinner or lunch comes a long way behind having the chance to stretch your intellect.'

Becky looked surprised, then actually laughed. 'You're right. And for me Cambridge is absolutely the best place to learn. I've been worrying about it but maybe it will be all right.' Then the clear skin of her youthful forehead had furrowed over her eyes. 'And there are things to avoid in Norbridge.'

Talking to two oldies like Pat and Tim had helped clear things in Becky's mind. She desperately wanted to put behind her the torment Jonty McFadden had inflicted on her at primary school. She needed to escape — and where better than to Cambridge? Obviously, she needed a few months longer to get Grandad used to the idea. And to get the graveyard sorted. Becky really cared about the gardening project. Although she had said you couldn't reconstruct the past, you could still keep faith with it. The graveyard could be a fascinating place if properly tended. If Lorna Duxford and her clichéd ideas were out of the way, Becky, Pat and Tim could create something that celebrated those long-dead friars and their graveyard. As she pedalled off into the dusk, Becky felt much better.

Pat turned to Tim. 'She was rather sweet, wasn't she?'

'Yes, she was. And very interesting. Look, Pat, why don't I go round to the offy and get us a bottle of wine and we can carrying on chatting.'

Pat looked at him, astonished. It had never occurred to her that anything she said could interest a man like Tim. Maybe it was the evening light, but his face looked softer and kinder. 'Why not?'

'I suppose you like medium white?'

Pat would usually have answered, 'Oh yes, lovely' to any suggestion. But this time she thought, *No, I don't want medium white wine. Tim is only suggesting it because he thinks that's what all older women drink. Chardonnay, maybe. Zinfandel.* 'I'd really like a nice drop of New Zealand Shiraz. That would be lovely.'

'OK.' She could hear the surprise in Tim's voice. 'You're on.'

When Tim had gone out to buy the wine she thought again about Lorna. Still no call. Her hands twitched over her mobile. Why didn't she just ring her friend? Why was she waiting for Lorna to call her?

She pressed the number. It went to voicemail. Pat felt a rush of disappointment. And hurt.

When Tim came back, Pat said, 'I've made up my mind. I'm going to go round to the Beddoes' myself tomorrow morning and see Lorna. She's not responding to my texts or calls. I've been very friendly with her for six months, and we have a history. This is so odd.'

'You should do that. Take the initiative.' Tim didn't like to see Pat still fretting.

'I think I will. I'll try not to think about it until tomorrow.'

'Good. Let's sit in your courtyard with the candles lit and have a drink. And you can tell me all about Derek.'

* * *

Ro and Suzy sat in a corner of The Partridge.

'The dead woman has been identified as Deirdre Murphy, a prostitute from Merseyside,' Ro said. 'There'll be an appeal on Radio Cumbria tomorrow morning and it's online now.'

'So, the Merseyside police will be looking into her background?'

'Yes, but they already seem certain that she was on the wrong side of a drug deal or tried her hand at blackmailing one of the Lancashire mafia.'

'How do you know all this?'

'I talked to Jed on the phone this evening. He says our involvement will be reduced to tracing car number plates. Not that there are many cameras along the old road.'

'So you're back on the sheep-worrying case?'

'Not me. Tomorrow I've got to give a talk on drugs to the u3a and on Tuesday I'm manning — sorry, womaning — the information stall in the Norbridge marketplace, all part of community wellbeing.'

'Talking of wellbeing, what do you think about Tranquillity Beddoes?'

'Ah, well, when I was looking after the Help the Elderly campaign last year at the East Cumbria Show, I just happened to be chatting to the CEO of St Benedict's Hospice . . .'

'As you do.'

'She told me that Tranquillity Beddoes had befriended one of their carers and wormed some names out of him, and then she wrote to these people offering to "help" them. For a fee, of course. One of them complained to the management.'

'Nasty!'

'Well, it left a bad taste in my mouth. And she's pally with that weird dentist who does the hypnotherapy. One of his patients ended up in A & E a few years ago. I don't know, Suzy. Maybe I'm being unfair . . .'

'I went to see her this morning. I was quite suspicious, but she seemed to answer all my criticisms before I made them. I actually liked her.'

'Yes, well, that's how you get conned. I would be wary of her. Another orange and soda?'

Later, driving home, Suzy realized that neither of them had considered the reason why the Beddoes had taken Lorna Duxford to their home. Was it just altruism? Lorna was a key member of St Michael's congregation and, according to Pat, she had a smart flat in the Old Quarter of Norbridge. But she wasn't particularly prestigious or important. Were the Beddoes just being kind and helpful? Or could there be another reason they'd latched on to the woman?

But right now, Suzy had more pressing professional problems. She was going to have to decide about carrying on with *Lockdown Life Change*. And she also had to find another subject for her podcast episode. Hiram King would be ideal, but she needed to get to him. His agent might be in the contacts list at Living Productions. But she would also need some local vox pops. Some of the soundtrack Suzy had recorded in the graveyard might be useful, although a whole edition on the Lesser Friary would be somewhat insensitive at this point.

When she was back home, she put her recording kit on the kitchen table, took out the SD card, popped it into her laptop and put on her headphones. She listened to the interview with Lorna, complete with her panegyric about Hiram King. Then came the silly remarks from Seth Beddoes, then Becky's intelligent analysis, and Pat's common sense. At the section where the volunteers walked down to the bins, she heard Tim Markham saying, 'Lorna, don't!' and Lorna's chuntering, ignoring him, then the sound of the bin lid being lifted. And then she could hear clearly that Lorna wasn't just gasping. The recording had picked up more than the human ear. Suzy thought Lorna cried out 'Dear God!' Or 'Dear something', anyway.

Suzy dragged the playhead back along the track and hit play again. She heard Tim saying, 'Lorna, don't!' and Lorna expostulating, then the bin lid being opened . . .

Suzy slowed the playback to half-time and listened. What was she hearing?

She raised the volume and listened again. To Suzy, there was no doubt about it. Lorna hadn't said 'Dear God!'

She had said 'Deirdre.'

* * *

'I'm not so sure, Suzy,' said DS Jed Jackson. It was eight o'clock on Monday morning. He had responded to her early morning call by asking her to come over to the office straight away. Ro was there as well, for moral support.

'I think Suzy might be right,' Ro said. 'It sounds to me like she's saying "Deirdre".'

'If there's even a chance Lorna knew the woman in the bin, we should question her,' Ro said. 'Obviously we can get the track heard by sound engineers in Glasgow or Manchester. But wouldn't the simplest thing be to just go and ask her?'

'She's staying at the Beddoes' cottage in East Norbridge,' Suzy said.

'The DI has said this isn't our case,' Jed put in. 'He doesn't want any more resources spent on it. I'm supposed to be dealing with the sheep incidents.'

'Incidents plural?' asked Suzy.

'Yep. There was another one overnight, just this side of the Border. But Ro could go to the Beddoes'.'

'Yes, I could. My u3a talk isn't till lunchtime.'

'OK. Just see if you can get any steer on whether this Lorna knew the dead woman. After you've seen her, we can take it from there — if there is anything.'

'I'll get over there,' said Ro.

She and Suzy walked out to the car park together.

'Can I leave it with you, then?' Suzy asked. She had just looked at her phone. There were two new messages. One was from the senior producer on the *Lockdown Life Change* pilot. The seventy-year-old singer had pulled out, saying she didn't want her success in lockdown to minimize the suffering of other people. The second email was from the podcast sponsors asking when Suzy was going to deliver the next edition. Suzy sighed. 'I'm under a bit of pressure from work.'

'That's OK,' Ro replied. 'Get back to The Briars. I'll keep you posted on what happens. Maybe Lorna can explain everything. You never know your luck!'

'Thanks. I could do with a bit of luck now.'

* * *

Pat Jones arrived unannounced at Camomile Cottage. She felt nervous but determined, parked her car, and marched up to the front door. It was half past eight in the morning. She had hardly slept. She had been talking to Tim until ten o'clock last night, first in the courtyard and then over coffee in her cosy living room.

'Go over there early and catch Lorna off guard,' Tim had said. 'There must be a reason why she's avoiding you. It's inconsiderate, however upset she is.'

But as Pat lifted the ostentatious brass knocker on Tranquillity Beddoes' front door, she wondered what on earth she was going to say.

The weight of the door seemed almost too much for the slight woman who blinked out at her. Tranquillity was dressed in tight-fitting gym gear with her hair scraped back. Her huge dark eyes stared at Pat. Neither woman spoke.

While Pat was thinking what to say, she saw that Tranquillity's face was working, a frown rippling like the tide across her line-free forehead.

'Hello? Can I help you? You don't have an appointment, do you?'

'No. I don't. You must be Tranquillity Beddoes. I'm Pat Jones, Lorna's friend.'

Tranquillity blinked again. 'Pat? But what are you doing here? Is Lorna all right?'

'How should I know? She hasn't been in touch with me since Saturday night.'

'What? Well, she's not here. She left yesterday afternoon in a taxi. She said she was going to go back to your place.'

Pat was astounded. 'Could I come in?'

'Sure.'

Pat followed Tranquillity through to the kitchen. She was too shocked to take in her surroundings, but she saw that Seth was sitting at a huge marble breakfast bar with a large bowl of some sort of mush in front of him.

'Hey, Pat,' he said. 'How's Lorna? Did she forget something?'

'No . . . I mean, I don't know anything about this, Seth. Lorna isn't with me.'

'No?' Seth's mental processes seemed slower than his wife's. He turned away from Pat, shaking his big head before he looked back at her. 'You mean she didn't go back to your place yesterday?'

'No!'

Tranquillity was behind her. 'Seth was away most of yesterday. He needed to go over to a specialist plumber in Newcastle for a part for our septic tank pump. It's been playing up.'

'Correct,' mumbled Seth. 'When I came back your mate Lorna had gone. My wifey had put her back together again. That's what she does!' He smiled in a rather goofy way at Tranquillity.

'Yes, but I can't have been successful, can I, if Lorna was fibbing when she told me she was going to Pat's. I wouldn't have dreamed of letting her go home by herself.' Tranquillity turned to Pat. 'Have you tried her flat?'

'No, why should I? As far as I was concerned, she was here.' Pat rummaged in her bag, grabbed her phone and fumbled at the number. She was shaking. Lorna must have gone home. *Please let her be there*, she thought.

The phone went to voicemail. Again.

'She's not answering.'

'She might be in the loo. Or having a shower. Come and sit in the conservatory and have a cup of coffee.' Tranquillity gently prodded Pat through the glass doors.

'I don't understand it,' said Pat. Pointlessly she called Lorna again, as if she could magic her friend to answer. Still no reply.

CHAPTER THIRTEEN

Look! Here he comes, leaping across the mountains, bounding over the hills.

                              Song of Songs 2:8

Tranquillity put a cup of coffee in front of Pat and stroked her hand. The effect was strangely calming.

'Let me go over what happened yesterday,' she said. 'Lorna and I talked a lot on Saturday night, and I gave her some herbal sleeping tablets. We were up in the morning having coffee at about nine o'clock, isn't that right, Seth?'

'Yeah.' Seth had followed Pat and his wife into the conservatory. 'I got up late, did some stuff in the garage and went off to Jesmond to the plumber. We've got a problem with the septic tank. It's supposed to pump stuff into a soakaway, but the pump's duff.'

Tranquillity gave him a cold glance. 'Do shut up, Seth. No one's interested in our plumbing. Let's get back to what happened yesterday. Lorna and I went on chatting over coffee. And Suzy Spencer, the podcast woman, called by.'

'Yes,' Pat said. 'Suzy said Lorna was going to phone me, but she never did.'

'Are you sure? Lorna definitely wanted to get in touch with you. I think she felt bad about leaving you on Saturday night, but Seth went haring off to get her. You know what he's like. Impulsive.' She smiled brightly at her husband. 'And Lorna was happy to come here.'

'Yes, that's true,' Pat agreed rather weakly.

Tranquillity went on, 'By Sunday morning Lorna had managed to come to terms with what she had seen. And Father Bill popped in to see her after church.'

'So, she felt better by lunchtime?'

'Yes. And as a therapist, Pat, I know when to let go. She could always come to me for more sessions.'

'So why didn't she call me to come and get her?'

'I thought she did, and you weren't there. Anyway, we had a rather nice, comfy lunch, with a glass of wine. Of course, I couldn't drive after that, so Lorna called a cab. But she assured me she was going to your place, and she had a key if you were out. After she went, I had a snooze and then Seth was back.'

'And did Lorna call you later?'

'No. But I thought she would be with you, and you'd have a lot to talk about.'

Pat suddenly needed some action. 'OK. I'm going to Lorna's now. She has a key for my place, and I have one for hers. She must be there.' She stood up abruptly.

'It seems the most likely thing. Let me know as soon as you find her. Here's my card. Old-fashioned but effective.' Tranquillity slowly rose to her feet. 'I've got a couple of clients this morning, but I'll take your call, Pat, whenever it comes.' She leaned forward and, to Pat's surprise, embraced her. Tranquillity's small body was warm, and her hands made soothing strokes down Pat's back. It was slightly mesmerizing.

Dazed, Pat found herself hurrying through the hall, Tranquillity behind her. Then suddenly she was out, in the bright sunlight. She still felt the warmth of Tranquillity's hands on her back. The door closed.

* * *

Inside, Tranquillity turned to go upstairs and go through her morning exercise routine before her first client arrived.

'Teena?'

She turned round on the first tread of the stairs and looked back at her husband, one perfectly shaped eyebrow raised over her big dark eyes.

'I don't get it, darlin'. I mean, you weren't here yesterday when I came back from Geordieland. Where did you go?' He held her gaze. 'D'you know where the Duxford woman is?'

'Of course, I know where she is! She's gone somewhere where she can recover without all the local biddies all over her. She'll be perfectly safe.'

'But like, where is she?'

'You don't need to know. Really. It's got a bit complicated. Leave that side of things to me. Anyway, don't you think you'd better have another look at that septic tank? There's rather a strange smell out there.'

'Oh shit.' Seth roared with laughter at his own joke. 'But seriously, babes, where is she?' He looked hurt. 'We've always done everything together. Our blags and whatever. Can't you tell old Uncle Seth?'

'Not this time.' Tranquillity sighed noisily. 'This is really big. Now let me go and do my exercises. I need to work with the Indian clubs this morning.'

'OK, babe, you know best.' Seth watched his wife's taut figure sashay up the stairs. The thought of Tranquillity with the Indian clubs was really quite a turn-on. She was awesome.

* * *

At The Briars, Suzy emailed the Director of Programmes at Living Productions and asked for a Zoom meeting later that day to discuss *Lockdown Life Change*.

She needed to talk over the problem. The one colleague Suzy could trust about work issues was her best friend, Rachel. With luck Rachel would be back from the dentist in Harley Street.

'Suzy! I was just going to call you. I've got some fantastic new painkillers and a temporary filling. The dentist has done the root canal work already. Anyway, get this. Your luck's in.'

'Really? I don't think so.'

'Well, guess who I met at the dentist's. No, you'll never guess. Do you remember Margaret Chiltern from Granada?'

'Maggie Chiltern? The researcher? The woman who could find out anything in the days before Google?'

'Yes, but she's not in production anymore. She's a personal assistant. And guess who to? No, you'll never guess that either. It's Hiram King, the gardening guru you were talking about yesterday. She's looking for a new London dentist for him, in case your guy in the sticks screws up his pearly whites. Didn't you say you wanted to get in touch with him for your podcast? Well, Maggie remembers you with great affection, Suzy. I'll text you her number.'

'Rachel, you are a superstar.'

'I know. If you were here, I'd make you buy me a brunch of turmeric latte with blueberry syrup and strawberry churros.'

'If I was there, I'd vomit. But hey, thanks.'

'Maggie's in London until this afternoon, but she said she would be back tonight and was sure Hiram would do something for your podcast.'

'Rachel, you're amazing!'

'I agree. I'll have a rain check on the strawberry churros. Now I'm going to have to catch up on my own work. This assisted dying issue is coming alive again. Ouch, not very tasteful.'

'Like your choice of brunch. Speak soon!'

* * *

Pat inserted a key into the front door of Lorna's flat. She had rung the bell till her finger ached. Now she was terrified of what she might find.

As the door pushed open over the smooth parquet flooring, Pat could sense there was no one in. But she carefully

114

went through room by room. Lorna's flat was lovely, big, airy and modern, set in a small nineteenth-century mill in an area where Huguenot weavers had settled, starting the textile industry in the town. The block of flats was on a cobbled street leading to what had been the Ginnels, a network of old yards and alleys.

Pat suspected that Lorna's flat had been a shrewd investment. It was future-proofed, for the next ten years at least, with lifts to all floors, a maintenance contract, wheelchair-wide doors, and a reception area with a man in uniform on the desk. Lorna could be happy and safe here into her eighties and maybe beyond. It made Pat wonder about her own cottage with its low ceilings, steep stairs and tiny doorways.

All Lorna's stuff was neat and clean. Her laptop was still on her desk in the huge open-plan living room. There was nothing on the balcony except a few plants in pots attached to a watering system from the garden below, where the mill yard was now a neat strip of Nylograss. *Not very Hiram King*, Pat thought.

She tentatively opened Lorna's wardrobe. Lorna had a lot of outfits, but the wardrobe was full and her stylish, compact suitcase on wheels was still there.

Pat felt distraught. The sick feeling came in waves. How could Lorna do this to her? Where had she gone? And then Pat had another thought. She and Lorna were due to go to Liverpool for their old school reunion at Burnely House the next weekend. Now Lorna was missing, what on earth was Pat going to do?

Lorna had all the information about the reunion on her laptop and Pat had no idea of her password. But they had sent away for some memorial postcards showing the old building. Pat pulled open the drawer in Lorna's oak coffee table where she tended to keep random bits and bobs. No clutter on the surface for Lorna. In it were a few of the Burnely House postcards, still with a strip of wrapping around them. The postcards had a phone number for the chair of the Old Girls' Association. Pat put it into her phone.

Underneath was the sleeve of a Sol Temple CD. Lorna had always been a fan, and once, when they'd had a few drinks, she had subjected Pat to the sickly sound of Sol Temple crooning away.

Pat went over to the music centre on a shelf under the big TV and pressed eject. A Sol Temple disc was inside. Lorna must have been listening to it recently. It made Pat feel miserable, that she had ever secretly rubbished her friend's musical taste. She would do anything now to sit with Lorna and listen to that CD.

Where *was* she? Could Lorna have had some sort of physical breakdown and taken herself to hospital? Or could she have amnesia? Or be wandering about somewhere, confused after the shock of finding the body in the bin? Whatever she said about professional detachment, Tranquillity had been wrong to let Lorna leave.

Pat felt like crying but took a deep breath. She needed to talk to someone about this. She could call Tim. But maybe not. They'd had such a wonderful evening — at least Pat had. She had talked about Derek and his death, and it had been cathartic. There had been no one she could speak to so honestly before.

It helped that Tim was a medic, and that he didn't know Pat and Derek in their old life. They'd had many friends, but when Derek died, Pat's social life had already disappeared. Of course, she had a few personal friends, colleagues from her teaching days, and neighbours. But Derek had been ill for a very long time and Pat had slowly lost touch with them. Even so, she had been resilient — surprising both herself and those few friends who were left. Most of them were in couples and had expected her to go to pieces when her partner died. They were disappointed and even disapproving when she didn't. They acted as if she were being disloyal to Derek by coping.

Then when Pat's daughter Katie got pregnant with Bobby it had given her a lifeline. And from the moment Bobby was born Pat had loved him more intensely than she believed possible. Maybe it was because he had Derek's deep-blue eyes.

None of this reflecting was helping her find Lorna. There were a few more places in the flat where she could look, and there was something nagging at the back of her mind. But she couldn't take any more of it, not alone. Who could she talk to? She knew so few people in Norbridge. And no one other than Tim and Becky had seen what had happened to Lorna. Except Seth, and she couldn't possibly talk to him.

But there was Suzy Spencer. Pat left the flat and went out to the car park. She thought she would probably get Suzy's voicemail. If that were so, Pat could ring off without committing herself. But Suzy answered the phone straight away. 'Hi, Pat. You OK?'

'No, I'm not.' Pat said. 'Something terrible has happened. Lorna has disappeared.'

'What? Isn't she with the Beddoes?'

'No, Tranquillity says she went home. But she's not there.' Pat's voice was breaking. 'I need to talk to someone.'

'Come over to Tarnfield,' Suzy said, and told her how to get to The Briars.

After she'd finished, Pat texted Tim, the tone brief and cool. One night's conversation didn't mean they were bosom pals. She mustn't presume . . . She wrote:

> *Hi Tim, Lorna has left the Beddoes' and I can't find her. Very odd. I'm going to see Suzy Spencer now as she saw Lorna at the Beddoes' yesterday. Thanks for all your support. Pat.*

* * *

Within fifteen minutes of talking to Pat Jones, Suzy was standing in the attic looking out of the back window over the fields when she heard, two floors below, a knock at the door.

Robert was in the kitchen with the inevitable coffee, trying to read. They weren't expecting anyone. He wondered who was turning up out of the blue this time. He hoped the visitor wouldn't be put off by the front door's scabrous appearance. Suzy was right. He ought to paint it.

He opened the door to a tall, thin, black-haired man, whose sunburned face was etched with lines.

'Hi, does Suzy Spencer live here?' Tim Markham asked. 'I used to live in Tarn Acres, and I thought she lived at The Briars. Sorry to turn up on your doorstep, but I'm looking for a woman called Pat Jones.'

By this time Suzy had come downstairs. Over Robert's shoulder she said, 'Hello, Tim. You did a great job on Saturday. Pat is driving over here now. Come on in.'

'I'm sorry to barge in,' Tim said.

In the kitchen, Robert motioned Tim to sit down and pushed a mug at him, followed by the coffee jug. In the hall, Suzy was answering a call from Ro. Tim went on to tell Robert that Lorna had disappeared after going to stay with the Beddoes.

'Ah, Tranquillity Beddoes,' Robert said. 'I'm afraid I have my doubts about her.'

'Me too,' said Tim.

Suzy came to join them. 'I'm going to make some fresh coffee,' she said. 'Ro is on her way here and so is Pat. Ro went to see Lorna at the Beddoes' this morning too and was told she had gone home. But Lorna's not at her flat. I think we all need a confab.'

Ten minutes later, Suzy brought Pat through the hall and into the welcoming kitchen with its copper pans and big scrubbed table.

Pat looked surprised. 'Oh, Tim, you're here.'

'Of course, I'm here. I got your text and came straight away.'

Ro arrived last, in her uniform. It always made her look taller and gaunter next to Suzy. The scar on her face stood out, a souvenir of a difficult time in Ro's life. She sat down at the head of the table. Suzy shunted the coffee and a mug towards her.

Ro said, 'OK, according to Tranquillity, Lorna Duxford left at about three o'clock yesterday afternoon in a taxi. Tranquillity assumed Lorna was going to Pat's in Norbridge.'

'But Lorna never contacted me at all yesterday.' Pat was agitated. 'I've checked messages, emails, even spam and deleted ones, and all voicemails. I never answer the landline now — there are so many spammers out there using Covid as a reason to con you.'

'And there's something else I should tell Pat and Tim,' said Suzy. 'When I played my recording of the gardening group opening the bins, I thought I heard Lorna say "Deirdre".'

'The dead woman's name was Deirdre — Deirdre Murphy,' Ro added. 'She was a sex worker from Merseyside. There was a chance Lorna recognized the dead woman when she opened the bin. Maybe that has something to do with her disappearance.'

'Why don't we pool all our knowledge?' Suzy said. 'We know the local police aren't terribly interested in this murder. The dead woman was black, and she was a prostitute from Merseyside. Ro, you know more.'

'Yes. She was killed professionally by a blow to the back of the neck. She died instantly and her body was dragged through the grass of the old graveyard and deposited in a big commercial metal wheelie bin—'

'Which belongs to the church,' Robert contributed, 'according to the vicar, Bill Gibson.'

'And the bin was locked with a simple triangular key which could have come from the Lesser Friary, or which could have been bought in advance,' added Ro.

'Then we went down to clear the bins, at Lorna's prompting,' said Pat.

'And I sensed there was something in there,' said Tim. 'I warned Lorna against opening it. I'm sure she had no idea what was inside.'

'And it was a body,' Suzy finished up. 'Is there any more info?'

'Yes.' Ro addressed Pat and Tim. 'You guys found Deirdre's handbag thrown into some rhododendrons. You called me and I took it to the station.' She stopped for a second. 'It's probably completely irrelevant, but there was a publicity picture of a singer from the seventies called Sol Temple tucked in one of the inside pockets. He'd written a personal message to her. My boss, DS Jed Jackson, said it was something from the Song of Solomon in the Bible. Something about doves . . .'

Robert quoted, '*Come away, my love. The flowers appear on the earth, the time of the singing of birds is come, and the sound of the dove is heard in our land.*'

'Yes,' said Ro. 'It's rather beautiful, isn't it?'

'Lorna was a huge Sol Temple fan as well,' Pat said.

Robert thought for a moment. Where had he seen something to do with Sol Temple recently? He couldn't remember.

'I think we need to try to make a case for the police to search for Lorna,' Ro said. 'They won't want to. They're up to their eyes with a sheep-worrying nightmare and the DI is convinced this dead woman is the victim of a Merseyside gang killing.'

'But maybe we can make a start,' Pat said anxiously.

'Absolutely,' Ro agreed. 'I suggest Pat goes back to the flat and has another look. But don't disturb anything just in case.'

'In case of what?' asked Pat.

'In case someone else has been there and done something to Lorna.'

'What sort of something?'

'Well, there's been one murder,' Ro said grimly. 'And when that happens, there's sometimes another.'

CHAPTER FOURTEEN

We have a little sister, and she has no breasts. What shall
we do for our sister on the day when she is spoken for?
Song of Songs 8:8

After Pat, Tim and Ro had left The Briars that morning,
Robert Clark couldn't concentrate on reading. He thought
about the ad hoc meeting they'd just had and looked for
threads in the conversation.

The singer Sol Temple had featured a lot. The dead
woman had been a fan if the signed photo was anything to go
by. And so was Lorna Duxford. Robert had no recollection
of Sol Temple himself, but where had he recently seen the
singer's name? Somewhere unexpected but not completely
surprising. It nagged at him. What a weird thing memory
was. He could remember the atmosphere in which he had
seen the Sol Temple CD. But not exactly where.

He racked his brain. What a great phrase that was. He
wondered if people ever said 'racked' in any other context?
Pain maybe? Terminal pain? That reminded him of Bill
Gibson and his work at the hospice. He should call Bill again.

Suzy had disappeared upstairs to her office in the attic.
She was worried about *Lockdown Life Change* but there was

little Robert could do to help. She was imaginative and inventive, and usually had her finger on the pulse of popular feeling. It was a blow to her to have got this one wrong, but he was sure she would sort it out.

And then he remembered. It was the Bill Gibson thought which had jogged his memory. He had seen the Sol Temple CD on the shelf at the vicarage. Another fan.

The landline rang. Robert picked it up, not recognizing the mobile number on the display screen but still feeling he ought to answer. That was how the scammers got you, of course. Pat Jones had mentioned that this morning.

But this time it was someone he knew.

'Hi, Robert, it's DS Jed Jackson here.'

'Hello, Jed. How are you? Pretty busy I gather.'

'Yes. Look, Robert, something's come up which seems to have a Bible connection, and you know what the force is like. They'd be so busy laughing they wouldn't listen to me. But you will. The murder victim from the Lesser Friary had a signed photo in her handbag, in an inner compartment—'

'Yes, so Ro Watson told us. I've been thinking about that. Sol Temple seems to have suddenly resurfaced all over the place.'

'Yes. And on the face of it, this photo is just a stupid souvenir someone might carry around. But for forty years?'

'Wasn't it inscribed with a quote from the Song of Songs? That lovely verse about the flowers appearing on the land?'

'Yes, but it was dedicated to "our little sister". I don't know why, but that worried me. So I looked it up. It's the Song of Songs, chapter eight, verse eight. It says, "*We have a little sister, and she has no breasts. What shall we do for our sister on the day when she is spoken for?*"'

'Well, some of this stuff is uncomfortable for modern readers,' said Robert. 'But it's an odd reference for a pop singer to make in a dedication.'

'I'm glad you agree. But I can't take time out to fly a kite about the Bible. We've had another horrible incident of sheep slaughtering, and anyway, I'm not sure where to look. Could you try and see what this quotation might mean? That TV gardener, Hiram King, lives just across the Border. Wasn't Hiram something to do with Solomon? I don't know, I'm probably imagining it.'

'Leave it to me. I'll find out.'

As Robert rang off, he heard Suzy clattering down the stairs. 'What an afternoon!' she said. '*Lockdown Life Change* is being axed. I can't say I'm surprised but I don't like getting things wrong. And more important, on top of that, Becky Dixon has called me. She sounded scared stiff.'

* * *

Becky Dixon had woken up early on Monday morning in the big front bedroom at the farmhouse. It was a seventeenth-century building, but the Victorian gentry farmers had added bay windows at the front and Becky's room was one of the large first-floor rooms with a view out over the Solway.

She lay in bed looking at the sunlight coming through the floral curtains her grandma had made for her when she was a little girl. They weren't really to her taste now, but they reminded Becky of Gran. She hadn't had much in common with Judith Dixon, but Becky had been grateful for her fierce love.

Judith had been a good housekeeper. The farmhouse was still well decorated and smelled fresh. Phil Dixon used a cleaning company, which came once a week, and he and Becky both liked keeping the place neat. Becky had a PC and a laptop in her room and fitted bookshelves. It was a good place to do her revising, and since her success in the exams she had used the room for her research into medieval history. She had a sofa and chair as well and was able to ask her friends over.

But today she had no plans to go anywhere. She planned to spend the day looking at the details of the course and the college where she had a place. Then tonight she might talk to Grandad about making the break.

But today, like every day, the first thing she did after waking was to reach for her phone, charging by the bed, to contact her mates.

* * *

Phil Dixon was already up and about in the farmhouse kitchen. He had a busy day ahead.

He was a Pelliter lad made good and had moved back to Cumbria after making money down south in the City. The farmhouse near the coast had come up for sale when two farms amalgamated. Phil had bought the building and a few acres around it, where he bred sheep. It had started as an early retirement project, but he'd taken to it.

His daughter had died when her child was just a baby, and Phil and his wife had brought Becky up. It had been successful until Phil's wife Judith died of cancer. Now Phil and Becky had been alone together for nearly three years. But Phil was worried about Becky moving away. She had sailed through A levels and the Cambridge entrance process but had deferred her place because of the lockdowns. He sensed that she didn't want to leave him alone, nor did he want to lose her. Despite everything, her upbringing had been secure and close, perhaps too secure and close. She was ready to fly the nest, but she wouldn't make that final move. And he couldn't bring himself to nudge her.

He needed to take some late lambs to the sheep mart in Norbridge that morning and was hoping he might have time to meet up with a friend. Well, more than a friend. Phil's life was improving, and it wasn't just Becky who was having to think about change.

She had gone out as usual on Saturday night despite having been at the Lesser Friary graveyard that morning when the body was found. Phil put that down to the resilience of the young. But she had come home on Saturday night looking anxious and preoccupied, and he'd been quite worried about her. On Sunday she had gone out to the spontaneous gardening session cheerfully and had seemed much happier when she came home. He wondered how she was going to spend her Monday.

He fried some bacon and made some tea, the strong sort they both liked. He wasn't sure about Becky and bacon. She'd gone from voracious carnivore to vacillating vegan. He went into the hall and called upstairs. 'Becky? I've got bacon on if you want some.'

He heard her moving on the landing. Then she came down in her black onesie. Her face was white, and her short dark curly hair stood on end off her forehead. She had been scraping her fingers through it, a habit she had when she was stressed.

'What is it, love?'

'It's nothing, Grandad, really. You've got to go to Norbridge haven't you?'

'Yes.' Phil searched for something comforting but not patronizing to say. He asked, hoping she would turn him down, 'Would you like to come with me?'

'No!' Becky almost cried out. 'I'm staying here today.' But then she added anxiously, 'When will you be back?'

Phil's spirits plummeted. 'I'll come back as soon as I can once the sale's over.'

Becky saw the disappointment in his face. 'No, it's all right. I'll be OK.'

'Becky, love, what's up?'

'It's nothing, Grandad. Nothing. I'll have a cup of tea if one's in the pot.' She followed him into the kitchen. While Phil was at the Aga, she took her phone out of her pocket and looked again at her messages.

Hiya Bex, how's tricks? I'm fab and back in the boonies LOL. C U soon JONTY XX

How had Jonty McFadden got her phone number? And how come he was going to see her soon? Becky clutched the edge of the scrubbed table and shut her eyes. There was no way she could tell Grandad about this. He would go berserk and try to find Jonty, and there would be a fight, and Grandad might get hurt. Jonty was nineteen now, and when she had seen him in Norbridge he had looked muscular and strong. Grandad was getting old. It would be too much for him.

When Phil brought the mug of tea over, she tried to smile. 'Ta, and I'll have a bacon butty too.' It would make her gag, but it would reassure him if she ate it.

Phil smiled back, relieved. Maybe it was just her time of the month. But he would never mention such a thing to her. Phil was old-fashioned when it came to bodily functions. His marriage had not been entirely happy but there were moments when he really missed Judith — or longed for another woman in his life who could help him with his unusual granddaughter. He had recently hoped he had found someone, but now he wondered if this relationship would ever have space to develop.

Becky was nibbling at the sandwich but he could tell she wasn't keen on it. He sighed. Perhaps this murder at the Lesser Friary had upset her more than he'd realized.

Whatever it was, there was something up with his granddaughter.

CHAPTER FIFTEEN

Catch for us the foxes, the little foxes that ruin the vineyard.
Song of Songs 2:15

Pat and Tim left The Briars after the morning's discussion and stood in the lane outside the house. Neither seemed keen to go their separate ways.

'Interesting,' said Tim. 'Do you think that Lorna was really saying "Deirdre"?'

'I don't know. I can't see how she could possibly have known the murdered woman. I doubt she'd have anything to do with a prostitute and as far I know she always worked in the Midlands, but it's possible, I suppose.'

'Suzy Spencer seemed sure.'

'Yes, and she should know what was on the recording.'

'I was also interested in that vicar's involvement,' Tim said thoughtfully. 'I came across Bill Gibson a few times in my work. An ambulance is usually called when there's a death, and people sometimes call their vicar as well. He struck me as quite a good bloke. Quiet, a bit sombre and serious. Not one to offer cheap comfort. I'm surprised he's mixed up with the Beddoes.'

They stood looking at each other by their respective cars.

Tim cleared his throat. 'Pat, I'll go with you to Lorna's place if you like. It's not as if I have a lot to do these days. I was only going to the supermarket to stock up this morning.'

As if he really needed to stock up, he thought. It was a question of buying five ready meals and a couple of bottles of beer.

'Oh . . .' Pat was surprised. She was dreading going back to Lorna's flat, though she accepted that another look would be useful. Something was nagging at her. 'That would be kind, thanks.'

'Let's drive to your place and leave your car. I'll take you to the Old Quarter and maybe afterwards we can have a spot of lunch at The Partridge.' Tim wasn't sure why he was saying this. He was sure Pat would say she had to go and see her daughter or meet another friend.

Pat didn't know what to say. She knew she'd only fret about Lorna if she went home after going to the flat. She had eaten very little since Saturday and the thought of a lonely cheese sandwich for lunch was unappealing. And it wasn't as if Tim was interested in her as a person. Pat Jones, a boring old lady. It was the murder case which intrigued him, she was sure. The upside was that she wouldn't have to make bright conversation, or listen to him talking about himself, like she had with the other two men who had asked her to lunch since Derek died.

'Yes, Tim, that would be very nice. I have to say, I'm finding it hard to think about anything other than Lorna and it's hard to get other people to understand.' She'd had a quick conversation with her daughter, whom she'd phoned that morning. Katie had been mildly interested in the body in the bin, but not really engaged. She'd said, 'Well you know what Lorna's like, Mum, she's always in control. She must have a reason for going off somewhere. Maybe it's family.'

'I doubt it. She's not in touch with any family as far as I know.'

'Exactly. Maybe you don't know,' her daughter had said. 'I must dash — thanks for ringing. Remember you said I could use the car on Friday when Steve goes for this job interview in Doncaster.'

It isn't the *car, it's* my *car*, Pat had thought.

Katie went on, 'Oh, and can you have Bobby for a few days next week? It's half-term for him, but I need to go into school.'

'Yes of course.' Pat had felt a lurch in her stomach. It was lovely to be needed for Bobby again. If Steve was thinking of moving her beautiful grandson to Doncaster . . . *Don't*, she told herself. *It might never happen.*

'Penny for them?' Tim said. He wondered if Pat thought his invitation to lunch was a bit much after all the time they had spent together lately.

'Oh, I was just thinking about my daughter, Katie,' said Pat. 'She thought I was being ridiculous about Lorna.'

'You're definitely not,' Tim said.

At the cottage, Pat parked her car and then climbed into Tim's solid Range Rover. It was funny to be driven by a man other than Steve, who drove far too fast for Pat's liking, even with Bobby in the back. Steve never spoke to Pat when he had to take her anywhere. Tim was quiet too, but unlike Steve he didn't stare fixedly at the road ahead and swear at other drivers. And at Lorna's flat, Tim didn't wait tutting and offering to help as Pat fumbled with the keys. He followed her inside without saying anything about how posh it was or querying angrily where Lorna got her money. Pat suddenly realized that she didn't like the way Steve behaved. Perhaps she should stand up to him a bit more.

But she was thinking about Steve to avoid thinking about Lorna. She was worried that if she did, she might cry.

'Do you want to do the bedroom?' Tim said tactfully. 'Also, do you know if she has any rubber gloves? If you get them out, I'll put them on just in case I touch anything. Your fingerprints will be all over the flat already but mine might complicate things if . . .'

'If what? I'm not fragile, Tim. I want to know what you're thinking.'

'Well, it's not impossible that someone met Lorna here and took her away. Possibly even by force. If she really did know who the woman in the bin was, she might be a threat to the killer. I know it sounds ridiculous, but I've seen a few strange cases in my career.'

'Yes, I agree. We must face the possibility something bad has happened.'

Tim nodded. Pat had an inner strength which had been eclipsed by Lorna's more obvious forthrightness. He was coming to admire Pat's quiet persistence. She hadn't been fobbed off by Tranquillity Beddoes, for a start.

Pat went into Lorna's bedroom again. She had identified the nagging thought. There was a washing basket in the corner and Pat wondered if it might hold the answer, but when she opened it, there was just some underwear inside.

She went back into the sitting room, and said to Tim, 'I knew there was something odd. 'Lorna would have been in her gardening clothes. She went straight from my house to the Beddoes' with Seth, still in her scruffy jeans. I can't see her gone away in her gardening clothes. Even if Tranquillity had lent her some, she would have brought her dirty clothes back here.'

'Were they that bad?'

'You're a man, Tim. It's not so important to you. Lorna was a smart woman. If she came back here and went on somewhere else, she would have changed. We were all grimy after attacking the ivy, and Lorna had gone right up to those horrible bins. Her shoes would have been filthy. But they're not here.'

'So, what do you think that means?'

'Maybe she didn't come back here at all. And there's something else. We were supposed to be going to Liverpool to a school reunion this coming weekend. We needed to confirm today. Lorna was doing all the organizing.'

'Maybe she's still planning to be there?'

'But if she was going off somewhere in the meantime, surely she would have alerted me? My daughter is borrowing my car on Friday, so Lorna was going to drive us to Liverpool.'

'You could call and see if she'd been in touch with the school. Why not do it now?'

If Lorna had cancelled going to the school reunion without telling her, Pat would be devastated.

'Call the reunion people and find out,' Tim said. 'You're strong enough to cope. If Lorna is behaving hurtfully, it's because there's something wrong with her, not with you.'

Pat sat on the sofa and searched her phone for the number. The chair of the Old Girls' Association answered swiftly, and Pat asked if Lorna had confirmed.

'No, not today,' the woman said. 'But I had a chat with Lorna last Friday evening. She wanted to know what time we would finish on Saturday. She said she needed some time for a trip down memory lane.'

'Really?' Pat was astounded. 'She never mentioned that to me.'

'Didn't she? Maybe it was to be a surprise. She said she would book two rooms for two nights at a boutique hotel near the Philharmonic and you'd stay till Sunday.'

This was news to Pat.

'It's pretty pricey there but very good. Anyway, should I take this as formal confirmation for both of you?'

Pat paused. Then she said, 'Yes, please do. See you on Saturday morning.' After ringing off, she looked at Tim in puzzlement and repeated the conversation, adding, 'It's an expensive hotel. Lorna wouldn't book there if she wasn't serious.'

He asked, 'And what did she mean by memory lane?'

'I don't know. She never talked about her family or childhood much. We never socialized at school. I never went for tea at her house or anything like that. We lived at different ends of the city.'

'But you were friends?'

'No, not really. It was a small form, fewer than thirty girls. She wasn't my particular friend then. And since we've become close I've never heard her use an expression like "memory lane". She was quite scornful of nostalgia, especially about Liverpool. Now I'm not sure what to do.'

'Do you think she might be in Liverpool now?'

'I don't know. Why would she be?'

'Let's go to The Partridge and talk this through,' said Tim. A very odd idea had occurred to him. He would let it gestate over a half of bitter . . .

* * *

Hiram King had enjoyed his Monday morning prowling around his estate. When he had said to himself, sulkily, that he'd be all alone, he'd meant that Jonty and Maggie wouldn't be there. But the domestic staff were around — the house-keeper who cooked and kept the two cleaners in order, plus the gardeners.

Hiram had irritated the cook by going into the kitchen and pouring himself a big bowl of Choco Puffs for his break-fast, spilling the excess puffs on the floor, where her aged Labrador would hoover them up despite being on a strict diet. Hiram had also left the cream carton out of the fridge. Well, it was his house, wasn't it? His castle, in fact.

Then with the bowl and spoon he'd slouched around his land in the sunshine. The kitchen garden was great, with asparagus coming up, his own strain developed with a German producer, and broccoli too, plus his own heritage carrots and all the herbs you could think of. The mown grass sloped down to his meadow.

He had thought about the details of his plan as he'd walked around the big kitchen garden scattering breakfast cereal. For all the talk about growing your own veg and new plant-based food, Hiram was still the lad from Liverpool brought up on sugar butties. His gardener would sweep up the scattered Choco Puffs.

At the back of the house was an artificial rise that reminded Hiram of the earth-covered air-raid shelters that had still been around in the back gardens of Liverpool in the 1950s. But this was the icehouse. Icehouses had been pop-ular in the mid-nineteenth century, when Kirkaber Castle was built. The ice had been chipped from the nearby loch in winter and brought into this dark, cold, intense brick dome, where the insulation from a stone lining and straw kept it cold well into the summer.

Hiram had been fascinated by the icehouse. Most Scottish winters led to a freeze, and ice production was more dependable than in England. In the case of Kirkaber Castle the icehouse was much bigger than it looked from outside. It tunnelled underground for about ten yards and opened into what would have been a large dip where the ice would be deposited. There was a drain out of the pool and a door at the other end. The ice would be brought in at the front and out at the back. At least one researcher Hiram had read maintained that icehouses and the passages to them were the source of many of the legends about secret tunnels on Scottish estates.

Hiram liked the idea of secrets. Making sure the gardener was down on the path at the other side of the house, sweeping up bits of his breakfast, Hiram took a slim modern key out of his tracksuit pocket and slid it into the state-of-the-art lock on the new metal icehouse door. Inside he turned on the lights, now connected to the house by the underground wiring system he'd had installed.

Jonty had been working well. Where the pool had been, there was now a pile of half a dozen galvanized welded mesh panels. Jonty had sourced these on the internet, and they had been discreetly delivered after dark the week before. They were yet to be erected. There was also a heating system. Obviously, an icehouse could work in reverse and be kept warm. And Jonty had already installed two big fridge freezers for the meat the animals would need until they were set free.

Until he had talked to Jonty, bringing wolves back to Scotland had just been a dream. But now the dream was coming true. Jonty was on the track of sourcing a breeding pair. Of course, it was all a bit underhand. But that was what Hiram liked about Jonty. To get things done you had to bend the rules — Hiram knew that.

Later today both Jonty and Maggie would be back, and they would all start the second stage. They would need to get the cages built and the heating system absolutely right. Hiram also wanted to find a compliant vet who would ensure the animals were healthy and ready to be released into the countryside. They would feed on the deer, which had proliferated and were a local plague.

Once the wolves were out there and breeding, it would be too late for the wimps to make a fuss. There were so many experts now saying that wolves were good for the ecosystem. And Hiram was going to video every step of his rewilding project and catapult himself from folksy gardening guru to international champion of the ancient and glorious alpha predator, brought down by man and now set free again.

It was a wonderful ambition. And Jonty McFadden was the man to help it happen. Maggie, of course, had needed to be sweet-talked into it, but she was totally loyal and a trooper, and she knew everything there was to know about getting things done properly. With Jonty as chancer and Maggie as Mrs Organized, he had the perfect team.

But now they needed one more person. Someone who was a dab hand at construction. But not the last chap Hiram had employed. He'd been talked into getting the guy to build a wall in the kitchen garden and it was an eyesore. True, the bloke delivered, but Hiram liked neat work.

That was why he found Jonty so appealing. He was smart, neat, sharp — and also handsome.

* * *

At the farmhouse at Pelliter, Becky Dixon crawled back into bed. She heard Phil's Range Rover leaving the farmyard towing the trailer with lambs in. She hadn't offered to help but had scuttled back to her room after eating her bacon sandwich. Or half of it. She'd managed to get the other half into the bin when Phil wasn't looking. Normally she would have dressed and offered to help him load up the animals, but today she had just mumbled something about needing to call a mate.

In her room, with the duvet up round her chin despite the warmth, she found she was shaking. Jonty McFadden knew where she lived. He could turn up at any time. She closed her eyes and willed herself to go back to sleep. She wondered if she should have gone into Norbridge with Grandad, but say Jonty McFadden was cruising the town centre? Then she got up but didn't dress. She read some more about medieval churchgoing. It was good stuff, but her concentration faltered, which was unusual. She thought about calling her mates, but she wasn't sure what to say. Anyway, they usually called her.

It was odd not to hear from Roxy. They talked every morning. Becky tried Roxy's number, but it went to voicemail. Weird. They were normally very keen to chat. She thought she heard a car coming, but it was just her fear and imagination.

Suddenly she couldn't stand being here alone. Where could she go?

By noon, she felt shivery and cold, and scared of going out of her room. This was ridiculous. On impulse she called her friend Molly Spencer, at college in York. Molly had also been terrorized by Jonty in the past, but it was Becky he had really targeted.

Molly heard Becky out then said, 'Bex, call my mum. She'll come and get you in half an hour, I know she will. Tell her the truth. She knows all about Jonty. Go to The Briars till your grandad gets home.'

It was a good idea. Becky dialled Suzy's number. 'Suzy, it's Becky Dixon here. Molly said I should call you. Can I come to your house? I'm on my own at the farmhouse and I think I'm in danger.'

'What do you mean?' Suzy could hear the girl's quick breathing, her voice sounding high-pitched and panicky, not like the self-confident young woman Becky had become. She heard Becky take in a deep breath.

'I'm really scared, Suzy. Jonty McFadden is back.'

* * *

Jonty was back at Kirkaber Castle by 11.20 on Monday, forty minutes earlier than Hiram's deadline. It had been a hugely productive morning. *You make your own luck*, he thought, *or at least you give the devil the opportunities.*

He had left his mother's house at eight o'clock, making sure she got up to make his breakfast, which he'd hardly touched just to show her who was boss, then he had cruised the vicinity of the University of Mid Cumbria. He'd gone there on spec. Or perhaps by instinct. He had no idea where Becky Dixon would be, but he guessed she'd hang around the uni. She'd been at the back of his mind for years and he'd tracked her as much as he could.

Although he couldn't quite accept it, he had the vague sense she had bested him all those years ago. She had survived his bullying and threats, and now he'd heard she was going to a posh university. That would never do. She should have become a gibbering wreck, on pills, anorexic or obese — he didn't care which — too scared to leave the house. If anyone was a prime candidate for mental health problems, it was Becky after the way he had taunted her at school. They had both been caught up in the murder of one of their schoolteachers. Jonty had never been formally questioned, but he knew Becky had always suspected him of being more involved.

When Jonty had lived in Spain it had all seemed small beer, but now he was back, this was his manor and it mattered. No one should get the better of Jonty McFadden.

He had seen Becky through the window of the Crown and Thistle before she had seen him, and he had blanked her but had tagged her expression of terror. That was cool, the sort of reaction he wanted to see in Norbridge. There wasn't enough of it.

He'd thought of going to the farm to find her, but on Sunday he'd had bigger fish to fry with his mam and Noddy, her clown of a shag-buddy. On Monday morning he had found the college area of Norbridge strangely quiet till he remembered the students had some sort of half-term off for reading. What a joke! But some saddos with no mates would be wandering around and they were the sort that Becky palled up with. Making decent friends had never been her speciality. Who was that lardy girl she'd teamed up with in Year Six? Molly Spotty Spencer. What a GILF, not.

Then he had seen the other weirdo from the pub at the bus stop. Unmistakeable. Jonty had the devil's luck, like he always did. He'd pulled up and climbed out. Walking over to the creep, he'd said, 'Hey, mate, is this the right road for the town centre?'

Roxy had said, 'Oh, no, you're going the wrong way. This only goes into the campus area. You need to turn round—'

Swiftly, Jonty had walked right up to Roxy and with his body he'd hid what he was doing from the road. In his right hand was his cat-skinner knife, which had caught the morning sun. Jonty had snorted and said in a cruel, soft whisper, 'You can't tell me what road to take, you miserable tranny. You're all over the place yourself. Get your phone out.'

'You can have it.'

'I don't want your tat. Just give me a number.' With his left hand, Jonty had flicked his own phone out of his tight back pocket and expertly keyed into his contacts with one hand. He was brilliant with phones. 'I want a number for Becky Dixon. Now.'

Roxy had fumbled, finally found the number and read it out croakily. Jonty dialled it into his iPhone. Then for good measure he made a little nick on the white skin of Roxy's neck.

'Oh, you've got blood in your veins. I was just checking,' he'd said in a friendly, curious voice, which was even more chilling. 'I thought you might be a zombie. If you say anything, I'll know and come after you. You're not exactly inconspicuous round here. And here's a reminder.'

Jonty brought his knee up sharply between the legs of his victim, who gasped in pain and doubled over.

'Oh, wow, balls too!' Jonty had laughed out loud. 'What a surprise.'

Still laughing, he had gone back to the car. There was no one in sight. Obviously, they were all reading at home like good little scholars. Or in bed like the lazy twats these students were. Anyway, even if his pathetic victim could stand up, there was no fear of identification. Jonty always had mud or cow pats artfully smeared across the black Range Rover's number plates. You were supposed to be up for a grand in fines for obscuring car numbers, but mucky plates were all too common down country lanes in this shitty backwater. He laughed even louder.

But what he didn't know was that shag-buddy Noddy's only act of revenge on the return of the prodigal son, as he shambled out of Callie McFadden's house towards the waiting taxi, had been to pee on Jonty's car. The number plate had come up gleaming.

What Jonty also didn't know was that, far from being a loser, Roxy had a photographic memory and was tipped for a first-class degree in criminology. Even in the pain of straightening up, Roxy had seen the car number clearly and clocked it. They might have been in agony, but miserable and pathetic they were not.

CHAPTER SIXTEEN

So I looked for him but did not find him.
                                        Song of Songs 3:2

Suzy drove out to the farm near Pelliter to pick up Becky and take her back to The Briars. 'You have to call your grandad straight away, and tell him you've come over to our house,' she said.

'He's not picking up his phone,' said Becky. 'Actually,' she added, colouring, 'I think he might have a girlfriend. I hope so. I mean he hasn't said anything, and I know he's a bit old, but he's not bad looking.'

'What makes you think that?' Suzy asked.

'Oh, he goes out more. And this morning, he said he would come home early from Norbridge as I wasn't feeling great, but his face really dropped. I don't want to be a burden to him.' Her face crumpled.

Suzy decided not to question any further. But she said, 'Maybe you should stay for a few nights at our place, Bex. You can use Molly's room. If Jonty is back in the area, you're better away from the farm. Could you text your grandad and tell him I've invited you over? Molly might pop home for a few days if you're here.'

'Yes, great.' Becky immediately took out her phone and gasped. 'Hey, I've got a message here from one of my mates. It's only been sent a few minutes ago. It's awful. They were attacked this morning by someone who wanted my phone number.'

'Whoa!' said Suzy. 'Is your friend OK? I can't pull over on the dual carriageway, so you'll need to tell me that again slowly and carefully. You're saying one of your friends has been attacked? Or more?' Suzy still stumbled over pronouns, however hard she tried to keep up.

'They were kneed and cut on the neck. I'm going to call them now.'

Suzy had to concentrate on driving, but she heard Becky's side of the conversation. Her friend had been attacked at a bus stop that morning and had immediately packed a bag and gone home. Once on the train, the friend had messaged Becky. They were now safely out of the district.

'Roxy got the car number though,' said Becky. 'It must have been Jonty McFadden. That means we can report Jonty to the police for a transphobic attack. Yeah!' She punched the air.

Suzy was pulling into The Briars. 'Let's think about this. You need to stay here, and we need to get some advice. I'm going to call Ro Watson.'

When Suzy called, Ro had finished her u3a talk and was looking forward to an afternoon off and meeting a friend. But she immediately said, 'No probs, Suzy, I'll come over straight away. Don't let Becky do anything till we've talked this through.'

* * *

Ro arrived at The Briars at about four o'clock. Suzy was taking a prearranged vital Zoom call in the attic with the CEO of Living Productions. She had the germ of a new idea. It had come from something Pat Jones had said about never using her landline because Covid had given so many scammers an opportunity.

And Suzy was also hoping to hear from Maggie, Hiram King's PA. She'd left her a voice message, knowing her former colleague would be back at Kirkaber Castle that afternoon. If Suzy's friend Rachel had done the groundwork, hopefully Maggie would get back to Suzy straight away. Then, fingers crossed, both Suzy's work problems might be solved that afternoon.

Robert had gone out. He had nerved himself to go and visit Bill Gibson again for the second day running. If he turned up unannounced, it would be hard for Bill not to talk to him. So, it was Becky who opened the door of The Briars.

'Come in, Ro. Thanks for coming. It's nice to see you again.'

'Hi, Becky. Are you holding the fort?'

'Yeah. Suzy is upstairs doing a Zoom meeting. Would you like some tea?' Then with sudden inspiration, 'Or some wine?'

'Just tea, thanks, Becky.' Ro prowled around for a few minutes before taking a seat at the kitchen table. She was wearing an inconspicuous version of her uniform with no badges. Her dark trousers and white blouse were covered with a navy V-neck. She'd put a dash of lipstick on, and some mascara. She looked different, Becky thought.

'Tell me what happened to your friend,' Ro asked.

Becky repeated what Roxy had told her.

Ro pursed her lips. 'This attacker was more interested in getting your mobile number than in assaulting your mate. So it wasn't necessarily a hate crime.'

'He said some disgusting things to Roxy before the knifing and kneeing. Roxy's gone home to Nottingham but wants to come back when it's safe. The thing is, should we report this to the police? If we did, then Jonty would be brought in for questioning and he wouldn't be able to attack us, would he?'

'Well, the first thing we should do is try and identify Jonty. You say your friend clocked the car number?'

'Yes. I've written it down here, old school.' Becky produced a rather scruffy piece of paper. 'How long does it take to trace a number plate?'

About a nanosecond, Ro thought. 'I just need to make a call.'

While Ro used her phone, Becky looked around the cosy kitchen of The Briars. It was one of those rooms that were warm in winter, cool in summer. The back door was open and the fresh smell of the garden in late afternoon drifted through. It wasn't home, but it would do for a while. Maybe it would give Grandad a bit of space, and a taste of what it would be like without her . . .

Ro came off the phone, but her face was puzzled. 'I don't think we have any evidence against Jonty McFadden,' she said.

'How come?'

'The car is registered to Hiram King, the loveable TV gardener.'

'What?' Becky looked astounded.

'What's that about Hiram King?' Suzy had just appeared at the kitchen door, eyes bright. 'Because I've got an appointment to meet the man himself tomorrow morning — I'm going to be a VIP guest at Kirkaber Castle!'

'You might want to rethink that,' Ro said. 'It seems the car with the transphobic driver belonged to your gardening guru.'

Suzy plonked herself down at the table. 'You're joking.'

'No,' said Ro, 'I'm not. So, either the great rewilder was out this morning beating people up, or he'd lent his car to someone who was.'

'It has to be Jonty.' Becky was beside herself. 'It must be. The attacker asked Roxy for my number at 8.40. And Jonty texted me at 8.43.'

Suzy thought carefully. 'So Jonty McFadden is back, but he's only been seen in Norbridge twice. So where could he be staying, and have access to Hiram King's car? Maybe I can find out tomorrow at Kirkaber Castle. In the meantime, Becky you should stay here. Have you heard from your grandad?'

'No, not yet.'

'I have.' Ro's face reddened. 'I was meeting Phil for a drink this afternoon. I've asked him to come here instead.'

* * *

Robert knocked at the door of the vicarage of St Michael and All Angels, East Norbridge. It was four o'clock. Most traditional priests were at home or in their churches in the late afternoon. They were still expected to say evening prayer.

Ruth answered the door. Her little bird-like face was paler and more strained. 'Oh, hello, Robert . . . Bill isn't here.'

'Can I wait for him?'

Ruth looked confused and irritated at the same time. But then the habitual good manners of a vicar's wife took over. 'Of course. Come in.'

She offered no further information, and this time Robert followed her down the untidy hallway to the big family sitting room instead of into Bill's office.

'Would you like some tea?'

'Thank you, that would be very nice.'

Ruth looked as if she'd hoped he would say no. Making tea and talking to him would obviously be a strain. She was away for quite a while, but eventually reappeared carrying a tray with two mugs and a plate of digestive biscuits. It was all more slapdash this time.

'Do you think Bill will be long?' Robert asked.

Ruth looked down at her mug. She was thinking what to say. 'I don't know.' She paused. Honesty got the better of her. 'He's gone to see Tranquillity.'

'Oh. Really?' Robert was surprised. He knew Bill valued Tranquillity's work, but he hadn't imagined the vicar popping in on her. 'Is it to do with Lorna Duxford? But I hear she's left the Beddoes'.'

Ruth wouldn't lie, Robert thought. He was putting her under pressure, but there was something wrong here and he wanted to know what it was.

'No,' she said slowly. 'It's not that. To be honest, I don't know why he's gone to see her. He left rather abruptly. It's been a difficult day. My brother from Australia has emailed to say he's on his way to see us. He has some work in the UK. Typical of Malcolm to do what he likes and give us so little warning. Bill wasn't at all pleased. He started, well, stamping about as he does sometimes, and then said he was going to see Tranquillity.'

'Does your brother have a family in Australia?'

'It's just Malcolm. When Bill and I moved here, Mum and Malcolm were still living here. Malcolm was planning to emigrate and Mum was planning to live with us. After Mum died Malcolm left for Adelaide quite quickly. He and I kept in touch over the years, but Bill wasn't interested. He isn't pleased about Malcolm coming back.'

'Why's that, d'you think?'

'Oh, it seems to be the last straw. Bill has been very tense lately, ever since I got back from seeing our granddaughter in Skipton. Of course, he's had terrible pressures. The murder at the Lesser Friary for one.'

'And I know he's been thinking of early retirement. We talked about that, didn't we?'

'Yes. That should have been such a relief to him! But I don't think Bill has done anything about it. He's been so odd lately, Robert, shrunken and weary. I'm so worried. And he has these awful bouts of rage.'

Robert finished his tea and put his mug down. 'Ruth, is there someone you could talk to? A female friend, or someone in the Church? Neil Clifford's wife?'

'I couldn't do that. It would be disloyal. I'm talking to you because you're here, and you care. And, to be honest, because you're not a church professional. I wouldn't want anyone in the Church to know there was something wrong with Bill.'

Bit late for that, Robert thought. 'You can always talk to me, Ruth. Call me any time. It's not disloyal to try and get help for someone you love. Tell Bill I was here.'

Ruth seemed relieved that Robert was going. She followed him down the hall with an agitated, bustling walk, as if hurrying him out, and shut the door the moment he was over the doorstep.

It was Ruth's anxiety which decided him. On a whim, instead of turning his car towards Tarnfield, he drove to numbers 4 and 6 Lower Farm Lane, aka Camomile Cottage. If Bill was there, he would catch him.

It didn't take long. What was now Camomile Cottage was at the end of a long narrow lane with one other pair of houses a few yards away. It was a secluded spot. The cottage was wreathed in budding climbing roses at the front, but the English country garden scene was spoiled by three cars blocking the short gravel drive: a black Range Rover, which was one of the most popular cars in the area; a neat Mini convertible, which Robert guessed belonged to Tranquillity; and a huge Mitsubishi pickup truck at least fifteen years old, which Robert guessed was driven by the infamous Seth Beddoes. It was about thirty yards further before Robert found somewhere he could park. He walked back towards the so-called cottage.

He could hear angry voices as he approached. He stopped. Then he moved nearer. He could hear clearly, but he could see no one, and no one could see him.

'I'm leaving now,' came Bill's voice. 'I've done everything I can to help you, but this situation has to be cleared up.'

A sharp woman's voice said, 'It's just another few days. And I've told you, I'm not going to pursue the other matter now. If we work together, we can both do well out of this.'

'It's not about doing well. It's about doing the right thing. You had me over a barrel and I've helped you. You can't squeeze me anymore. You've tangled me up in too much. It's making Ruth ill and it's killing me. D'you hear, killing me!'

The woman said something sharp and angry. Robert was distracted by the sound of heavy steps on the gravel and a man's indistinct voice braying, 'Hey, you guys, what's the beef?'

'Oh, it's nothing, Seth.' The woman sounded vexed.

'Yay, I'm glad to hear it, folks.' The second man spoke in a deep, mumbling way, then laughed. It was hard to make out his words. Robert wondered if he was drunk or doped. But he did hear him say, 'Are you off then, Billy Boy? Will we see you soon?'

'I don't know.'

Bill Gibson's car door slammed, and within seconds the Range Rover backed out of the Beddoes' drive. Robert heard the woman say irritably, 'I do wish you wouldn't stick your nose in, Seth. I told you I was dealing with this.'

'Oops. My bad.' The man laughed.

'Yes. Now, can you move this mountain of rust from outside the front door? I've got a client coming.'

Robert backed into the privet bushes. They were all that was left of the neat red-brick houses, which had morphed into the rustic eyesore renamed Camomile Cottage. Both the man and woman crunched up the gravel drive towards the house. Embarrassed at having accidentally heard them, Robert turned and walked quickly back up the lane, keeping to the shadowy side of the road.

What had all that been about? And what had that final exchange meant? Bill Gibson had said, 'It's killing me,' and, now he had time to think about it, Robert was sure the woman had replied, 'Well, you should know about killing, Bill.'

CHAPTER SEVENTEEN

Depart . . . from the dens of lions, from the mountains of leopards.

Song of Songs 4:8

Pat and Tim sat at one of the window tables in The Partridge. She had given in to the dangerous temptation of a glass of red wine at lunchtime, but Tim was drinking apple juice. They both had sandwiches.

After a few bites Tim said, 'Lorna's flat is pretty impersonal, isn't it?'

'Yes, but whenever I went there, we mostly sat in the kitchen bit and there was always stuff out on the counters. It never seemed austere. Just modern.'

'What did you do?'

Pat laughed. She thought that Tim probably hadn't had a very convivial social life. 'We talked! Or we'd watch TV together, or loll about and gossip in the lounge, and it was very nice. Lorna herself was a big presence. She filled the place. But this morning, with no Lorna there, I agree it looked rather bleak.'

'Yes — no books or papers, or family photos.'

'That's what makes this Liverpool trip so odd. And why did she want me to go with her if she was revisiting her past? And odder still, why didn't she tell me? We talk about everything.'

Except family, Pat thought suddenly. She'd assumed it was because Lorna didn't have any. So Pat rarely mentioned Katie or Bobby. Lorna had once said she had never wanted children, but Pat didn't ask why. She assumed Lorna was an only child, with parents long dead, just not interested in family life. But Lorna had confided that, since meeting Pat, she had thought more about their old school. They both had memories in common — the crazy cookery lessons, the French teacher with the cloche hat who smoked upstairs on the bus, the camp in North Wales, the terrible smell of the school dinners . . .

The memories were a bond, but there was so much else to talk about now they'd met again — the failings of Lorna's lovers, her triumphs at work, the flats she had rented, the property she had bought, the cats she'd had for thirteen years, and they both discussed their health endlessly. There was also the Norbridge gossip, including the stories of Tranquillity Beddoes' remarkable success with those in need of her brand of therapy.

'You don't think Lorna might be dead, do you?' For the first time Pat mentioned her fears out loud, and her voice broke.

'Well . . .' Tim said, 'it had occurred to me. But there's no body, to put it bluntly.'

'But if she'd had an accident, a heart attack perhaps—'

'Pat, believe me, she would have been found. She left Tranquillity Beddoes' house feeling much better. She only had to take a taxi to her own place. There wasn't much scope for an accident. She's more likely to have gone away.'

'Yes. You're right. But where's her gardening clobber? Oh, Tim, I really don't know.'

Tim took a deep breath. He'd been wondering when to voice his suggestion. 'Look, I know this seems like a strange idea, but why don't you and I go ahead with the trip to Liverpool? Maybe Lorna's already gone there, and something has happened to her.'

'What, in Liverpool?'

'She might have suddenly decided, after what happened, that she wanted to go home.'

'She didn't think of Liverpool as home.'

'OK, I might be jumping the gun and she might still get in touch. But if she doesn't, why don't I drive you down there on Friday, seeing as your daughter needs your car? You could maybe find out Lorna's old home address from other girls at the school. Then we can do her memory lane trip without her and see what it throws up.'

Tim was desperately keen for Pat to agree. He knew that much of the reason for his suggestion was the emptiness of his life. It would be worse that weekend without any gardening group. And he was happy in Pat's company. He liked her quiet competence and lack of complication. His ex-wife was the sort of woman who had wanted to be 'understood' and set all sorts of traps for him to fall into. One of her favourite ploys was to say, 'Well, if you can't see what's wrong, there's no point me telling you.' Pat took responsibility for explaining herself, and everything about her seemed straightforward. Not only that, but she was also distressed, and it upset him. Of course, she was older than him, though probably not by as much as she thought, but it wasn't as if there was anything romantic going on. He just liked her.

She said after a few seconds, 'It's a bit, well, intense, isn't it? Going away with an elderly woman you hardly know? I mean, why are you so interested, Tim?'

'You're not so very much older than me. But that's not the point. My life is boring and sour, and I spend too much time in the pub.' He swallowed. 'And I want to work out what's happened. With you. It's interesting. You're interesting.'

Pat was surprised. She worked hard at being uninteresting because she never wanted to rock the boat. But maybe

Tim had sensed something deeper. She had a sudden, piercing memory of taking off with Derek to the Alps and trying to ski. Derek had said sadly one winter Sunday, reading the travel sections of the paper, 'I always used to fancy skiing.' The words 'used to' had galvanized Pat. The next month they had left on a package holiday. They were middle-aged, and had no idea what they were doing. It left Pat with a twisted ankle and a determination not to try skiing again. But they had never laughed so much.

And on a practical level, there was this expensive hotel booking in Liverpool. If she went to the reunion, she couldn't take her own car since her daughter needed it. She could go by train, but she was unfamiliar with rail bookings, and it all seemed too complicated. Tim was a sensible driver. He obviously wasn't after her money, which would have been laughable, or her body, which would have been even more laughable.

'That might work,' she said.

For the first time she saw Tim Markham grin.

* * *

Jonty returned to Kirkaber Castle on Monday morning and went straight to report to Hiram. Maggie wouldn't be back till the afternoon, and that gave Jonty an opportunity he couldn't miss.

'Hi, Mr King.'

'Jonty, hello. Welcome back. And it's Hiram — you know that.'

Jonty smiled ingratiatingly. 'Hiram. Wow, I can't believe I'm talking to the great man on first-name terms!'

'We're working together, aren't we? How did the weekend go?'

'Oh fine, thanks to you giving me the time off. Poor Mum. She needed help. You know what it's like when you're the only boy.' This wasn't true, but it pressed Hiram's buttons.

'I do, my son, I do. Well done you. Maybe your mum would like to come up to Kirkaber and meet me sometime?'

'Oh hey, that would be fantastic.' *And it's never going to happen*, Jonty thought.

'Sit down, la.' Hiram used his Liverpool accent judiciously when he wanted to seem approachable. But he never did the professional Scouser act.

Jonty sat down gingerly on the edge of one of Hiram's wing-backed leather chairs. Ahead in the bay window was his huge desk. The mullioned windows were at the front. The castle was a design mess, Jonty thought. But it rocked Hiram's boat. Hiram was great on gardens but knew nothing about architecture. These celebs were all the same. Jonty had come across a few in Spain. Excellent at one thing, but thought they were experts on everything.

This rewilding of wolves, for example. It was complete rubbish. Hiram knew all about flora, but sod all about fauna. Jonty, on the other hand, had kept a pair of Rottweilers in Malaga and had investigated getting a couple of Boerboels. He had contacts in the dangerous animal community in Spain, which were coming in very useful. When he'd been interviewed for the job, Jonty had raved about Hiram's rewilding ideas and talked about the wolf initiative on the Iberian Peninsula. There were more than 2,500 wolves roaming there now. True, farmers had caused a stink when their stock was attacked. But they could be placated. That wouldn't be an issue here, at least not for a time.

Jonty had seen Hiram's face light up. At last, a way of activating his plans. And so doable! The grounds of Kirkaber, for all the sense of wildness, were well fenced at the perimeters and the derelict ice store could be a subterranean wolf cave.

As they'd talked together over several nights, the project was fleshed out. They would start with putting the wolves in the converted icehouse. In a few months, in the early autumn, when their prey was plentiful — hares, rabbits, injured birds, even salmon — they would be encouraged to come out of their run into the estate. And of course, the proliferating roe deer, a scourge in themselves, would be at their most numerous, with plenty of young born in June, just weaned and at their most vulnerable when the wolves would be set free to roam the grounds in late September.

Then at some point, the wolves would 'accidentally' jump the Kirkaber perimeter fence, but by then, Hiram's project would have traction. He had the funds to pay off any farmers who lost stock. He would have masses of local support, helped by his hefty rewilding grants, and he would have started drip-feeding his videos onto the web, sanitized for general consumption.

Jonty was smart. He had latched on to the idea of the project almost before Hiram spoke. And it was he who had focused Hiram on wolves, not lynxes or polecats, which other rewilding heroes were talking about.

That Monday morning, Hiram looked at Jonty with approval. Nice of him to care for his mum. Jonty reminded Hiram a bit of Sol Temple before things went bad. Dedicated. Self-assured. Adventurous, misunderstood, but basically decent. Hiram prided himself on his knowledge of human nature. 'I had a look around the icehouse while you were away,' he said. 'You've done a great job sourcing the cage panels. Now we must get them erected.'

'What about getting that chap to do it? The one who did the kitchen garden wall? He seemed to work very quickly.'

'Speed isn't everything, as you will find out in life, my son. We need the cages to be well built. I want Maggie to find me some reliable builders. Maybe up in Glasgow. And we also need to get a vet organized.'

'A vet?' That was a surprise. Jonty hadn't realized that Hiram meant to be so thorough. 'Why do we need a vet?'

'Well, I trust you, my lad, and I know you have the contacts. But we need to be sure that the animals are healthy and can breed. Rewilding can't be done overnight.'

Oh yeah? thought Jonty. He had to tread carefully now. He had a perfect opportunity coming up, but if Hiram was going to drag his feet and go all goody-goody, then his plans would be kiboshed.

'Yes, we do need a good vet,' he agreed. 'And discreet, of course. But the news is that my chap in Spain has managed to get a fantastic breeding pair already. Iberian wolves. Spain is so much further advanced than we are with wolf rewilding.'

'Yeah. I've been thinking about contacting the Life Wolflux programme. It was brilliant that you alerted me to them. But I don't want to rush things. We've still got a lot of prelim work to do.'

'If we're going to get this pair, we need to work fast,' Jonty pressed. 'My mate can have them here by the weekend. They'll come in a container ship at Seaforth on the Mersey, and I can take the van and get them. We don't need to rewild yet. We can keep them in the icehouse. And there's no way of doing this without doping them, so they'll need to get that out of their system. And start eating the right stuff. Believe me, Hiram, I've done this before with my Rottweilers. Same supplier. We need to have an outdoor enclosure as well to start with. Maggie needs to get the builders here this week if we're going to take advantage of this. Unless you use that other bloke.'

Hiram looked doubtful, sipping at his glass of scotch.

Jonty jumped up from his seat. 'Hiram, we might never have another chance of a breeding pair like this. I think we need to go with it now. Summer is a bad time for wild animals, contrary to popular belief, so we can use these months to get them acclimatized. We can use the hot season to bed them in and get used to the diet and release them in September. If we wait till the autumn to get the animals, we might have to winter them here and then they'll lose the will to live in the wild.'

Jonty was aware he might be talking rubbish, but he hadn't anticipated Hiram wanting to do things properly. In their excited late-night talks over Hiram's best scotch, Jonty had been able to fire up his boss easily. But all this talk of vets and contacting the Spanish Life Wolflux project was new.

153

He'd just thrown the name out when talking to Hiram, to sound good. He hadn't a clue who they were and, frankly, he didn't want any contact with any official Spanish rewilding group. He guessed that pain-in-the-arse Maggie had been getting in on the act and cooling Hiram down.

But Jonty had a bigger plan than either of them, and he wasn't going to be thwarted.

* * *

'This is getting to be a habit,' Robert said when he reached home to find Ro and Becky in the kitchen.

'Yeah,' said Becky, completely unembarrassed. 'That's what these big kitchens are for. In the Middle Ages they had animals in here as well.'

'Becky, this house was built in the nineteenth century.'

'I know that! But it's probably on the site of an older dwelling!' Becky's face lit up. 'I've read all about it. Tarnfield's quite ancient, you know.'

'And so am I,' Robert said. 'Excuse me while I go upstairs and freshen up.'

Becky laughed. She liked Robert. He had encouraged her to go for Cambridge. And he'd been right.

'Phil's on his way too,' said Suzy to Robert as soon as they were alone together in the bedroom. She needed to change. She'd spent the rest of the afternoon in the attic and was now hot and sweaty. She had a lot to tell him, but there was one thing he needed to know before he put his foot in it. She waited to get his attention. 'Ro and Phil Dixon. They're an item!'

'Oh yes. I did wonder about that,' Robert said absently, stripping off his sweaty shirt.

'Oh, for goodness' sake! Are you suggesting that you guessed?'

'Not exactly.' Robert was searching for a clean shirt. He still looked quite good, Suzy thought. And he wasn't that much younger than Phil. Maybe Ro and Phil weren't such a strange combination. Phil was a bit taller than Robert but also a little more stooped and his hair was slightly thinner. But he had a healthy farmer's tan. Robert was paler and had that distracted academic look most of the time. His hair still flopped over his forehead.

He pulled a clean polo shirt over his head and waved his arms around, before re-emerging. 'Come on, Suzy, we both thought Ro was seeing someone and being a bit evasive about it. At first, I thought it might be another woman, but that was unlikely given the way she flirts with Jed Jackson. And then when I thought about it, how many new people do you get to meet in this area? Not that many.'

'True.'

'Anyway, Ro seemed to get on well with Phil all those years ago. Oh, just call it male intuition.'

'Argh!' Suzy pummelled his chest but laughed. She felt better in a fresh T-shirt. The weather really was getting quite clammy. Rain was forecast for the weekend.

They went downstairs just as Phil arrived. Any embarrassment was forgotten in the general brouhaha about drinks and whether everyone wanted a takeaway from Tarnfield's only fast-food outlet, the Star of Bengal, owned by the parents of Molly's first boyfriend, Rafi Hossein.

Funnily enough, Becky seemed the least perturbed of any of them about Phil's arrival and Ro's revelation. She said suddenly, 'Shall we get some curry for Molly as well? She's on the train from York.'

'What?!' said Suzy. Robert kicked her under the table.

'Molls says she'll get the bus from Norbridge and be here by about seven. She decided to come home this afternoon when I told her I was here. She'll need meeting at the bus stop of course. Grandad can go out for her now. He's not drinking 'cos he's driving.'

So that's all organized then. No need to ask me, Suzy thought, both furious and delighted.

As it happened, Phil returned from picking up Molly at the bus stop at the same time as the food arrived. It was a lovely, busy, gossipy catch-up evening. No one mentioned Jonty McFadden until Phil and Ro prepared to leave. Together.

'We'll both stay at the farm,' Phil said. 'Then if Jonty McFadden comes visiting, he'll get more than he bargained for.'

'Don't provoke him, Grandad,' said Becky, suddenly worried.

'Don't worry, I won't. But if he provokes me . . .'

Becky looked panicked. 'Please, Grandad, don't go there. He's more evil than you think.'

There was a silence while the remark sank in.

Then Molly said, 'Come on, Becky. Leave them to it. I'll sleep in Jake's room, you stay in mine. Let's go upstairs and talk.'

Suzy looked at her daughter. She seemed to have grown a few inches and lost a few pounds since going to university. She still had her crazy clothes style and was wearing black lace-up boots, orange tights and a floral smock with a black leather jacket on top. Well, it was a look, Suzy thought. But Molly was already more confident and grown up. And independent, deciding just to show up at The Briars when she wanted to. Suzy had always said The Briars was home to all of them, and Jake tended just to arrive on the doorstep. So now Molly was doing the same thing. It was encouraging and upsetting at the same time. But where did it leave Suzy? Not exactly central to her daughter's life. She felt the first prickle of a panicky hot flush.

Later, when the visitors had gone and the girls were upstairs locked in a chat about what Molly called 'the wrinklies' romance', Suzy and Robert found themselves alone with the dirty plates and glasses. Over the washing up Robert told Suzy about what he had heard outside Camomile Cottage.

'Bill said Tranquillity had him over a barrel.'

'Really? That sounds nasty. It looks like you were right about her, and I was wrong.'

'It gets worse,' said Robert. 'I heard her say that Bill knew all about killing.'

Suzy looked at him, horrified. 'You don't think Bill had anything to do with the body in the bin, do you?'

CHAPTER EIGHTEEN

My vineyard, my very own, is for myself; you, O Solomon, may have the thousand, and the keepers of the fruit two hundred.
Song of Songs 8:12

Robert paused. 'Well, it had occurred to me. Bill is frightened and ashamed about something. It must be something bad. Say Bill had been seeing a prostitute? Thirty years ago, Deirdre Murphy would have been in her late teens and possibly already a sex worker. She might have threatened him with a historic sex abuse case for money. Bill is one of the few people who knew all about the status of the bins. And I also think Bill is one of those people who could kill, in a rage.'

'But if he'd killed his blackmailer and put her body in a bin, he would have just told the Area Dean that the trouble had gone away.'

'But he didn't kill her until after the Area Dean got the letter and wrong-footed him! It would be his bad luck that the body was found, but then the police decided not to investigate locally. Maybe he reckoned he could bluster his way out of the allegations.'

'I don't know, Robert. It's not only Bill in the frame. There's also Jonty McFadden. It can't be a coincidence that the local psychopath reappears the day a woman's body is found. I'm not sure what the connection is, but Jonty is just as likely to be a killer as Bill Gibson. More so!'

'But the police still insist it's a gangland killing, according to Ro. And that makes sense.'

'It's also the easy way out. It means they can ignore Lorna's disappearance, but that must be part of this. She knew the dead woman, I'm sure of it. She definitely said "Deirdre". Maybe Lorna killed her and set it all up so the body would be found in a way that would never implicate her.'

'Or maybe Tranquillity killed the woman for some reason and had to stop Lorna identifying Deirdre, so she spirited her away.'

'Oh, this all seems like madness,' said Suzy. 'We're just speculating.'

'But you're right. The fact that Jonty's back and Lorna's missing means that something is rotten in the state of Denmark.'

'And I'm off to the Borders version of Elsinore tomorrow morning. I'm looking forward to meeting Hiram King in person and finding out why he lent Jonty McFadden a car to go round beating people up.'

'Well, don't fall for him like you did for Tranquillity. I told you she was a bad 'un.'

Suzy jabbed him in the ribs. 'Don't be such a smart aleck. You've still got Bill Gibson to sort out.'

Robert sighed. Suzy switched off the light and snuggled up to him. She was glad Becky and Molly were safe under the roof of The Briars. But she was aware that, despite the joking, both she and Robert were wide awake, worrying.

* * *

Suzy woke after a restless night, with that same sense that all wasn't well. She paused outside Jake's bedroom door and peeped inside. Her daughter was fast asleep, looking ten years younger. Rather warily, Suzy did the same outside Becky's door and met the same sight. So, both young women were

sleeping peacefully. The night had passed. She felt irration-
ally relieved.

She couldn't say exactly what she was worried about.
She knew all about Jonty McFadden and his treatment of
Becky at school. He had bullied Molly too back in Year Six.
But whereas he had treated Suzy's daughter with contempt
there had been something more visceral, evil and *dedicated*, if
that was the right word, about his behaviour to Becky. Suzy
had woken in the night imagining him prowling around the
house with a knife. But he didn't know Becky was at The
Briars, and he didn't know where Molly lived. She told herself she was overreacting.

The sunlight suddenly broke through the dusty landing
window. Normality shining in. *I must get that window cleaned*,
Suzy thought.

Robert came up behind her and put his arms around
her. '"New every morning is the love",' he said. 'The girls are
all right, aren't they?'

'Yes. But I'm still worried, Rob.'

'Me too.'

She was so glad he hadn't tried to jolly her along or dis-
miss her feelings. 'I've got to go out soon,' she said. 'Maggie
said to be at Kirkaber for nine thirty for coffee. Apparently,
the great man has some sort of wellbeing session on Tuesdays
at nine. He'll see me at ten.'

She padded downstairs, had a quick cup of tea, and then
went upstairs to dress. Within half an hour she was on the
road to Kirkaber Castle.

Robert mooched around, and then went into the small
single bedroom which he used for all his theological and academic books. He needed to do that bit of research Jed had
asked for.

Books were piled around and cluttering up a whole wall
of built-in bookshelves. He had a battered chair and a tiny
desk he had used for decades. He and Suzy had reorganized
this room as his study — now it looked as if it had been
like this for generations. But it was where he used to do the

ironing in that other life. He suddenly remembered being here years ago, looking out of the window at the lane outside, watching Suzy crash her car into his front garden fence and thinking, *Oh no, it's the local flake*. How wrong he had been. But it still sometimes seemed amazing that they were together. They'd called themselves 'the odd couple'. Suzy, the quirky single parent, and Robert Clark, the staid childless widower.

The thought made him feel vaguely romantic. Maybe on this peerless summer morning he should start with the Song of Songs. He sat down and read. He had forgotten how beautiful it was, though in places it was also rather strange. He wasn't sure how he would feel about his teeth being compared to a flock of sheep, some with twins. Maybe a mouthful of teeth was rare in the fourth century BC, perhaps the earliest date for the book.

It was supposedly written by Solomon, though that had long been questioned. In the poem there were several references to that Hebrew king, son of David and fount of wisdom. That accounted for the Song being kept in the Bible despite its obvious eroticism — and lack of God. But one of the earlier Jewish scholars had accepted it as an allegory of the historic love between God and his people, and in the Middle Ages it had been an inspiration to Bernard of Clairvaux, Theresa of Avila, and Bede of Jarrow in the north-east. Some even saw it as a vindication of human sexual love after the debacle of the garden of Eden.

But even if Solomon hadn't written it, there was something about the vivacity and sensuality which accorded with Solomon's lavish life and loves. For example, there was the way the building of the temple was described in the first book of Kings. Such a treasure trove! Robert turned to it. The first thing that leaped out at him was the line, 'And Hiram, king of Tyre, sent his servants to Solomon . . .'

Robert snapped out of his reverie about love and sensuality, fabulous buildings and cedars of Lebanon. Hiram King. Solomon's Temple. Was it a coincidence? Robert thought not. He should have spotted it earlier.

So, if Hiram King the rewilding champion had a link to Sol Temple, the seventies singer, whose picture was in the handbag of the dead woman, was that another piece of the strange jigsaw?

I am black but comely . . . That was made very clear in the Song of Songs. The dead woman was black. And comely.

It was the sort of idea that would have Jed Jackson's boss bellowing 'Rubbish' down the phone. It was tenuous, of course, but there was something compelling about it. The beautiful black woman, the quote from the Song of Songs on the photograph . . .

But what about the reference to the little sister? Where did that come in?

There was no rush to get back to Jed. Robert would wait till Suzy came home from Kirkaber Castle. She would have met the man himself, named after the king of Tyre, who supplied King Solomon with what he needed for his temple. King Solomon was a key figure in the Bible. But without Hiram, Solomon couldn't have succeeded.

Robert wondered what Suzy would make of his namesake.

* * *

At Kirkaber Castle, Suzy parked in the imposing drive and went around to the huge front door at the top of steps, which led to a crenelated battlement. It obviously owed its conception to Scottish baronial architecture, but this was no mini-Balmoral or Abbotsford. It was too much of a mishmash. The door, for example, was a pointed Gothic shape, in dark wood, pockmarked with what looked like random brass studs.

Maggie Chiltern came to the door and held out her arms. 'Oh, Suzy, it's good to see you after all this time. You haven't changed a bit!'

'And what about you?' Suzy said. 'You look positively glamorous!'

Maggie laughed. 'I've got Hiram to thank for that. Best hairdresser in town and a little nip and tuck a few years ago.

I've got new eyes as well, lens replacements. The specs have gone! And we must all stay fit to keep up with Hiram. We have a gym here. And a cinema.'

'It's amazing.' Suzy followed Maggie into a hall complete with stuffed animal heads and coats of arms. All it lacked was a suit of armour. It really *was* amazing. So was Maggie's transformation. She was much more talkative as well as more gorgeous. Suzy wondered if it was because she was stuck here, deprived of company.

Maggie leaned forward and whispered, 'The place is certainly impressive but it's not really my cup of tea. I prefer the Conran Shop for decor, and I miss Kensington High Street. But Hiram loves it here.'

'In the middle of nowhere?'

'Yes, he's thrilled to bits with it. Of course, it helps that he's able to buy in everything he needs. You can source a surprising number of things up here. Hawick is a lovely town. And Norbridge is quite near for people to commute.'

'So, some of your staff come from Cumbria?'

'Yes, Hiram's found a good counsellor after a lot of disastrous quacks in London. He's very choosy about therapy. A local woman with quite a reputation has helped him turn a corner. She tells him to find his "inner saint". It hits the spot. She's with him now.'

It had to be Tranquillity Beddoes.

Suzy hid her surprise. 'That's good,' she said neutrally. It was a turn-up. But hadn't Tranquillity hinted at something like this? A local VIP client? Suzy had suspected it was the MP, or the bishop, or some other regional bigwig. Not Hiram King!

Maggie said, 'By the way, don't mention the therapy to anyone. Hiram's quite open about it, with me and Jonty, but he doesn't want it widely known.'

'Jonty?'

'Yes, Jonty McFadden. He's from the Norbridge area as well. He's Hiram's driver.'

Another turn-up. So Jonty had a proper job, with access to Hiram's cars. And could Tranquillity and Jonty be connected? They must know each other. They were both the types to try and leech off a new local celebrity.

Suzy followed Maggie into a small but beautifully furnished and very neat office. Maggie sat on a sofa and indicated that Suzy should take an attractive modern chair opposite.

'Hiram let me furnish this myself. He knew I was missing my old flat. Of course, he's done the rest himself, like something out of Downton Abbey.' Maggie rolled her eyes, but it was obvious she adored her boss.

As if by magic a woman in a smart black overall arrived with a tray and coffee cups.

'I've followed your career,' Maggie said. 'Very exciting. *Living Lies* was a great success!'

That was Suzy's award-winning show. 'Yes,' she replied, 'but I'm not sure I can come up with anything as good. My latest TV idea has hit the buffers.'

'But you want Hiram for your local podcast, don't you? He was easily persuaded. It matters a lot to him to be popular in the Borders. I think this is his forever home. And he has big plans, some of them very exciting. Of course, this isn't about him, though, it's about the local grants. Hiram is the means to the end with this rewilding money. He's very happy about that—'

Maggie froze. It didn't sound as though Hiram was happy now. Footsteps hurried down the corridor to Maggie's office, and Hiram's usual warm, friendly broadcasting voice was cold and hostile. He was shouting before he came through the door.

'We're going to have to get Seth Beddoes to do it, Maggie. She's got me over a barrel . . . but I can't cope with this. I've spoken to Jonty. He needs to move on this—'

'Hiram.' Maggie spoke like a patient nanny. 'We can talk about that later. You have a full day. You need to get to the dentist this afternoon. And now you have an interview to do. Remember? This is my old colleague, Suzy Spencer. I told you. From *Neighbourhood Norbridge*.'

The small, immaculately dressed man by the door swept his eyes over Suzy with that look of irritated disdain seen only on the faces of VIPs.

'Who?' he snapped at Maggie, as if Suzy weren't there.

'My friend. The local podcast producer.' Clearly, Maggie was acutely sensitive to these outbursts, but capable of riding them.

Hiram turned his small, unnaturally smooth, tanned face to Suzy. It was crowned with a sort of auburn quiff. He was wearing slimline cream trousers which ended above a shapely ankle, and what Suzy took to be crazily expensive mushroom-coloured loafers. He had on a loose taupe cashmere sweater, with a high V-neck and no shirt underneath.

But suddenly his face cracked open in one of the widest grins Suzy had ever seen. 'Of course,' he said. 'You must be Suzy Spencer. I've heard so much about you. Just give me a moment with the awesome Maggie.' He beamed at his assistant, radiating warmth and charm in an instant mood change. 'And then we'll go up to my office.'

* * *

Tranquillity Beddoes had already left Kirkaber Castle, and she drove angrily south. Everything had been going really well, and she had been sure she could persuade Hiram to give Seth some work. Seth had used that irritating wheedling voice this morning.

'Teen, pleeease, can you get me some work up there again? With the gardening group on hold an' all, I need something to do.'

It wasn't a bad idea. The last thing she needed now was her big bear of a husband trampling around Norbridge, trying to worm out of her where she was hiding Lorna Duxford and getting in the way of her plans.

She had hinted to Hiram that she knew some dangerous information about his past, and he'd bitten. It was too soon to let him know just how much she knew. He needed to stew. Getting the cage building work for Seth had been dipping her toe in the water and it had been indicative.

Only Hiram hadn't been quite as malleable as she'd hoped. That made her cross. Of course, he had that Maggie woman supporting him. And that evil little driver, Jonty McFadden, was sticking his snout in the trough. Jonty had come on the scene after Tranquillity, and he had been an unexpected threat. She'd had to push quite hard but in the end Hiram had capitulated. Seth had got the gig.

She told herself she shouldn't have worried. After all, she was the one who had really hooked the big fish. She thought with satisfaction about how she had landed him. As soon as she had heard that the famous Hiram King was moving to the Borders, she had been in there like a rat up a drainpipe, as Seth would say. On the grapevine she had heard about Hiram's need for counselling — he was well known for chopping and changing his London therapists.

When she and Seth had arrived in Norbridge, it hadn't taken Tranquillity long to suss out which health practitioners would be susceptible to her charms and her philosophy. The dentist who specialized in hypnotherapy had helped Tranquillity with referrals. It had been a godsend when he'd told her that Hiram was going to him for his dental treatment. All she'd had to do was wait for a tip-off and bump into Hiram accidentally on purpose in the dentist's car park. The dentist had been seeing the great man out. Tranquillity had made sure she appeared unfazed, and moved away after just a few words, putting her facemask in place and keeping her distance. She was good at playing hard to get. She'd left the explanations to the dentist, but she had dressed for the occasion in a slick designer suit with big gardening boots so she looked authentic, cute and unusual all at the same time. Hiram was bound to ask who she was.

And the next thing, there had been a summons from the celeb. She had delayed making an appointment, to keep him warm. Then she had driven up to Kirkaber Castle in her gardening gear. She'd made a few clever but deferential points about horticulture and had followed up with a hint of Hiram's inner saint. And she had been in, as his new and only therapist.

Then there had been the latest supreme bit of luck. That was one thing she really did have to thank Seth for. He had his uses. It was so fortunate he'd been at the gardening group that day and had heard what Lorna said. After that, it hadn't been hard to winkle the truth out of her either.

But the denouement of Tranquillity's plan was yet to come. OK, Hiram wasn't as soft as she thought. But when she confronted him with what she knew, he would cave, she was sure. And then all her Christmases would come at once, if Seth didn't mess things up.

After the work she'd put in today, she knew Hiram would have told Maggie that Seth was the man for the job, and to make that call.

Her mobile rang. One good reason for driving home on the back roads was that she could talk on her phone without being pulled over. The caller was Seth — no surprises there. He would tell her the good news.

'Hi, darlin', you done it, babe. I'm starting at the castle again. Tomorrow. Building some sort of internal cagey things. They must be getting guard dogs.' He laughed.

'Great. Now look, Seth, you have to keep your mouth shut while you're there. You leave the talking and the brainwork to me. D'you understand? Your job is to keep an eye on Jonty McFadden. But we'll talk about it when I get home.'

'Yeah. See ya soon. Love ya, babe.'

'Love you too, of course,' Tranquillity said snippily.

Great, Hiram had bitten and now Seth would be kept busy — and report back to her about everything at Kirkaber. She had a spy in the camp.

Tranquillity was a good driver and the back roads were usually deserted. She felt her irritation slacken as she picked up speed. Hiram was virtually in the bag. She just had to pick her moment.

Her Mini crested one of the many hills between Kirkaber and Camomile Cottage. It was a bit of a switchback, but she found herself laughing. They were going to be made for life. She might even have another face job, and get the boobs redone to please Seth.

She rarely bothered to look in her rearview mirror. She didn't need to look behind. She needed to look ahead, in case some dopey farm worker was reversing his tractor into the road.

So when the shunt came from alongside, she went rigid with shock. The car was so close and so big, she couldn't make out what it was. Anyway, there was no time. The car had moved out as if to overtake and she instinctively slowed down, but not nearly enough, as she felt the pressure of the other vehicle pushing her sideways.

She was being nudged off the road, at the only stretch where there was a ravine on the left. At seventy miles an hour she didn't stand a chance.

Her Mini was forced into a brutal ninety-degree turn. And then it plummeted down into the valley, turning over as it went.

The other driver didn't wait. The Range Rover sped off, even faster, on the road south.

CHAPTER NINETEEN

What is that coming up from the wilderness, like a column
of smoke? . . . Behold, it is the litter of Solomon!
                                   Song of Songs 3:6–7

When Seth Beddoes was pottering around in his man cave,
he lost all sense of time. He'd been sorting out the carcass of
an old Bush radiogram from the 1950s. He had needed to
transplant electrics from a later model, but who would know?
The insides were now fine, and both speakers were opera-
tional. With a bit of effort on the wood finish, he reckoned
it might fetch 200 quid if the buyer didn't look too closely
at the workings.

He glanced at his old Rolex watch, a real vintage piece. It
was past one o'clock. Tranquillity should have been home by
now. Seth mooched out of his lean-to and walked round the
back of the cottage through some muddy patches, still there
despite the warm weather. They looked as if they were caused
by the malfunctioning septic tank. That would need attention.

He went through the conservatory without wiping his
boots, which would have driven Tranquillity insane. Despite
everything, he suddenly missed her nagging voice, in her gorgeous little body.

He went to the kitchen cupboard, taking out a bottle of vodka to pour himself a big slug. Neat. That took the edge off things for a few minutes. Then he put the bottle away. He looked at his watch again. One fifteen. It should have taken Tranquillity about an hour to drive back from Kirkaber Castle. She had another client that afternoon, a woman recommended by Bill Gibson. The client would be here at two.

Seth found his phone, which was sitting on top of the microwave. He hadn't used it since calling Tranquillity that morning with the good news about the work at Kirkaber.

He thought he had better call Maggie, the woman who had phoned him only a few hours ago to ask for his services as a builder. She would know when Tranquillity had left the castle. Of course, Seth didn't want to make a big fuss. But on the other hand, he needed to let her know he was worried about his wife.

'Hi, Maggie. Seth here. Mr Tranquillity. You gorra minute?'

Maggie said something mildly irritable, which Seth didn't quite catch.

'Maggie, I'm sorry to, y'know, bother you an' all, but Tranq hasn't come back yet. Did she get delayed with his nibs this morning?' He heard the high-pitched anxiety in his own voice.

Maggie's voice was clearer now. 'No, Seth. In fact she left quickly. Hiram had another appointment at ten.'

'But she's not home yet and she's got a client coming at two. She's never late.'

'I'm sorry, Seth, I can't help.'

'OK. I'll try her mobile again. But it's not like her.'

By two o'clock Seth was pacing up and down outside Camomile Cottage. When Tranquillity's client arrived, he sent her away. At two thirty he went online to check the local traffic news. He knew Tranquillity drove home on the back roads, but the traffic alert system he used showed nothing unusual for the roads into Roxburgh.

At three o'clock Bill Gibson drove his Range Rover into the driveway up to Camomile Cottage. Seth was outside again. It seemed to be the right thing to do, coping with anxiety by walking up and down outdoors. Two neighbours had passed him. He'd told them Tranquillity wasn't back from a trip to a client in the Borders, and he was worried.

Bill got out and slammed the car door. 'You didn't pick up!'

'Oh sorry, mate. I'm going out of my mind with worry, waiting for Tranquillity to get in touch. I don't know where she's got to. I haven't taken any other calls.'

'Well that's irresponsible. One of my flock's just been on to me in a state. She said Tranquillity wasn't here for her session. What's going on?'

'Tranquillity's not back from the Borders,' said Seth. In his worried state he'd dropped the slang, speaking more simply and clearly.

'Could there have been an accident?' Bill said.

'I've looked on the traffic website and there's nothing. But she uses those back roads, and she drives like a bat out of hell . . .'

'Ring the police!' Bill snapped.

He didn't need to. A police car was cruising slowly up the lane.

* * *

Suzy had taken the conventional route back from Kirkaber Castle, joining the A7 at Langholm. Her interview with Hiram had gone well. He had been friendly and charming. She was used to dealing with celebrities and knew they could be brittle, so she didn't relax, and occasionally she had pushed him, but not too hard. She had, she hoped, gleaned a little bit about the real man as opposed to the image.

Interestingly, Hiram had been quite open about his Scouse background, his time in London as a session musician in the seventies, and his return home to Liverpool to work for the parks and gardens department in the days before the city had become deeply divided and politically paralyzed. Then he had hightailed it back to London and the big time.

But all that was just background. Like most celebs, Hiram was exhilarated when talking about himself. He also had a cause, and when he moved on to rewilding he'd become even more animated. Suzy found herself wondering what could be quite so exciting about buttercups and daisies, but his enthusiasm was compelling. She'd got the soundbite she wanted.

'It's a new dawn,' Hiram had said. 'Rewilding is about a whole new way of looking at our relationship with nature. And you can do it everywhere, if you try, from the parks to the prairies, balconies to the bush.' He'd stopped, thrilled with his own eloquence.

'So would you extend this to animal rewilding?' she had asked. It seemed an obvious question but Hiram had suddenly pulled himself up, his brow furrowed. Used to the sudden mood changes of stars, she had wondered about withdrawing her question in case he walked out of the interview, but had decided to take the risk, waiting to see what he said.

Hiram had seemed to be weighing it up. 'It's interesting that you should ask that. Yes and no,' he'd said eventually. 'But the grants are not for that purpose. They're for groups in this area who want to turn public land into rewilding projects. A lot of people are interested, but they can't afford to buy land, or even if they can, they find the land is already owned by farmers or corporations. Getting places rewilded isn't as easy as you might think.'

'So can you describe what your ideal project would be?'

Hiram had seemed to flounder a little when asked that.

'OK,' she'd tried again. 'Say we take a specific project, and you tell me whether it might qualify for one of your grants? It would just give me a better idea. I know one of the groups who'll be applying to you will be the Lesser Friary gardening volunteers in Norbridge.' *If they ever get going again*, she'd thought, but never mind, they were a good example.

'They're turning an old disused graveyard from the fourteenth century into a meadow. Is that what you have in mind?'

'Could be,' Hiram had said, more responsive now he had something to reference. 'Making a meadow isn't as easy as people expect. It's not just about letting things go to seed, or letting the wrong sort of vegetation take hold. They probably need to start with something like yellow rattle. And maybe flax would have nice historic connotations. They're beautiful, though not as showy as my sweet meadow mix. But maybe a bit more authentic for the sort of ground you describe. That's how you need to start.'

Suzy had thought about Lorna Duxford's vision of bright poppies and blue cornflowers. She was clearly on the wrong tack.

Hiram had caught her hesitation. 'Are they experienced gardeners?'

'No, they're just local volunteers. One of them said it was more about collecting litter and clearing overgrown foliage rather than real horticulture. It's led by another Scouser by the way. A woman called Lorna Duxford.'

Hiram had stared at her, the thoughts crossing his face like ripples. 'You know, the name rings a bell,' he'd said at last. 'I'll be interested to hear from her. But I think the best thing is if her group just fills in the form and then when we come to assess the applications, we can make a judgement.'

'And who will be on the judging panel?'

Hiram had relaxed. He liked talking about his local influence. 'There's our MP here in Roxburgh, and two nationally known Scottish gardeners, one from Ayrshire and one from Glasgow. And Maggie's getting together a couple of other local worthies.'

A good way of making friends and influencing people, Suzy had thought. She'd recorded a little more of Hiram talking about the project, then called it a day. It had been a useful morning.

Packing the car after saying a big thank you to Maggie and promising to keep in touch, Suzy had suddenly remembered Hiram's odd reaction to the name Lorna Duxford. Had he remembered it?

And there was the Jonty connection too. At some point she could ask Maggie more about that odd hiring of the local bad boy. Presumably he had a berth at Kirkaber Castle, which explained why he hadn't been seen much in Norbridge.

But Suzy needed to move on with her own issues. Now she had the bones of the podcast edition in place, she could concentrate on her other work problem, the replacement show for *Lockdown Life Change*. Thanks to a remark Pat Jones had made, Suzy had another idea to develop . . .

Tomorrow she would be back at the office in Manchester, but she was going there and back by train in one day. As Molly was at home, she didn't want to miss out on time with her, either. It was going to be a busy week.

Suzy had reached Tarnfield by one o'clock. It had been a beautiful drive. She and Robert sat down for a quick lunch and a review of their respective mornings.

He went first. 'I found that in the Bible, King Hiram of Tyre was right-hand man to King Solomon of Solomon's Temple. Hiram King and Sol Temple. Do those names mean anything to you?'

'Of course, they do. Hiram King was quite open with me about his musical background. I remember now, when he first started appearing on *Good Day*, that TV morning show in the eighties, he used to chat about music while potting his cuttings or whatever. It added to his popularity and made other TV gardeners look a bit pompous. He had — and still has — oodles of personality, though he's a bit grand now.'

'So he might have known Sol Temple. Or worked with him?'

'Yes, easily. You know, I think we should put Rachel on to this.'

'Your friend Rachel the producer? But she works on serious programmes.'

'Hey, daytime TV has its serious side. And Rachel knows her stuff, music-wise. Or, if she doesn't, she'll find someone who does.'

'And what else did you uncover, Miss Marple?'

'Well, Jonty McFadden is working for Hiram as a driver. Goodness knows how he got that gig. And my other *surprise du jour* was Tranquillity Beddoes. She has fingers in the pie too. She's discovered Hiram's inner saint! And as with all these big egos, that plays perfectly. She's his therapist, and she's probably told him he's the Messiah.'

'If his chosen name is Hiram King, he probably knows his Bible, especially if he worked with Sol Temple.'

Suzy nodded. 'Let's see what Rachel can dig up. And we still have to work out where Tranquillity is in all this. Maybe she's got Lorna in the dungeon at Kirkaber Castle. And that reminds me — I think Hiram recognized the name Lorna Duxford. It's an unusual one. It certainly seemed to chime with him.'

'So, the plot thickens.'

'It certainly does.'

They sat companionably eating the chunky sandwiches Robert had made.

Then Suzy said, 'Well, this afternoon I need to work on my new TV submission. 'It's called *Out of Order*. It was after something Pat said. I reckon there are thousands of people out there who've been conned by scammers or let down by services. It started with Covid and now because so much is at breaking point it's getting worse.'

'That sounds more like it might strike a chord.'

'Or a whole keyboard if I'm lucky.'

* * *

Later in the afternoon Suzy called Rachel, whose teeth were much better. 'Rache, can you find out something for me?'

'I'm really busy at the moment, Suzy. This assisted dying stuff is actually very serious. And it should interest you. Listen to this. In England, assisting a suicide is a crime, whatever your motive. You could get up to fourteen years in prison.'

'Really? Do people ever get prosecuted?'

'Yes — there were a hundred and seventy-four cases referred to the Crown Prosecution Service last year. That many! The police withdrew over thirty cases, and a hundred and fifty or so were dropped, but there are eight ongoing.'

'Has anyone ever been convicted?'

'Yes, four cases. These aren't cases of murder for gain, they're people who just helped others to die. Sometimes of course the case is escalated to murder, but that's different.'

'That's really interesting. Now I feel guilty for asking you to do something to help me, it's so flimsy and trite—'

'Try me.'

'I need to know about the relationship between Hiram King, Maggie Chiltern's boss, and a singer called Sol Temple.'

'Sol Temple? Well-known misfit of this parish. He had a bad rep for young girls. But didn't they all? The difference was that he was religious. It added to the spice.'

'OK, Rache, so can you find out all you can about the relationship between Hiram and Sol? We have a murdered woman on our patch with a signed photo of Sol Temple, just thirty miles from Hiram King's weird and wonderful castle. Of course, there may be nothing in it and the police are looking elsewhere. But if the two men are linked . . .'

'Yeah, I can see the biblical connection. There was a lot of that in seventies' pop. Like Bob Dylan, 'Highway 61'. Old Testament for obvious reasons but the OT has a lot darker potential than your love and forgiveness stuff.'

'Yep. And talking of dark, there's even a biblical quotation on the photo. From the Song of Solomon. It's addressed "to our little sister", and this seems to be an allusion to another quote from the same book — "We have a little sister and she has no breasts."'

'Yuk. I don't like the sound of that.'

'Me neither. But maybe it's just a coincidence.'

'Leave it to me. It'll make a change from euthanasia and toothache.'

* * *

The previous day, Pat Jones had gone home after lunch with Tim and thought carefully about their plans. Tim would pick her up Friday lunchtime, and they would drive to Liverpool and check in at the hotel. They would have a walk around town, popping back every so often to see if Lorna had turned up.

If Lorna hadn't arrived — and they agreed it was unlikely — Pat would get up next morning and go to the reunion. Tim would look round the tourist sites and Pat would try to find out from her other classmates if anyone knew where Lorna had lived. The chance of the house still being there was slim, but while a lot of the city had been demolished, some areas were still intact although changed in nature. Thousands of people had left Liverpool since the 1960s, but those who remained had often done so because of deep family roots in the same area for generations. If she and Tim could find out where Lorna had been brought up, there was a chance that neighbours might be around and know something about her. It was a mad plan but, as Tim said, anything they could find out would be of interest. And Pat would still have the pleasure of the reunion. She could ask former classmates whether Lorna had ever been in touch.

Pat didn't want to tell her daughter Katie what she was up to. She wasn't sure why — she had nothing to hide. She examined her own feelings. Maybe she was worried her daughter would laugh at her. Going away with a younger man! She could hear Katie saying, 'Mum, you must be mad, he must be after something.'

But what? If Tim was a gold digger, he'd find little precious metal in Pat's bank account. If he was a con man, then a flat in Norbridge, where everyone pitied or blamed him for a nasty divorce, was hardly a sensible cover. Lorna had told her that everyone had talked about the Markham break-up, not least because Tim's wife was such a looker.

Not that Pat didn't speculate about people. She had always had an interest in narrative, which is why she'd taught English literature for over twenty years. Lying in bed, she tried out crazy scenarios in her head. Could Tim have another motive for befriending her? Was he trying to *stop* Pat finding Lorna? A trip to Liverpool for two days would certainly keep her out of the way.

Then Pat's imagination ran wild. Say Tim had killed the woman himself and dumped her in the bin? He could have had access to the key. And he had been very keen that they didn't open it. And if it wasn't a gangland killing, what was it?

She was being ridiculous. If she was going to suspect local people rather than the Merseyside mafia, then horrible hairy Seth and his manipulative wife were more likely candidates than the demoralized Tim Markham, who hadn't the energy to do much more than go to the pub. The only gang he was in was the gardeners.

The trouble with this train of thought was that you ended up not trusting anyone, which her daughter would probably advise as the best policy. But Pat thought not. You had to trust someone, or you became bitter and reclusive yourself. The two people in this mix whom she trusted were Suzy Spencer and Tim Markham. There was no way Suzy had committed the murder. And it was probable that Tim was exactly what he appeared, a man who'd had a bad experience and was using this drama to distract him from himself.

It was an act of will, but she put the bad thoughts out of her mind. And once the suspicions were quelled, she found she was looking forward to the trip. She even started wondering about what to wear.

She turned over and went to sleep.

* * *

Tuesday dawned fine. Pat did her housework and shopping because Wednesday and Thursday were her Bobby days. In the late afternoon she ran out of washing-up liquid. She hadn't been as organized as usual this week. She thought she might as well go out and get some before the convenience store on the corner closed.

At the till, a few neighbours were chatting with that intense, rather greedy expression that people wore when they had something juicy to chew on.

'Hi, Pat,' said one. 'Did you know her?'

'Know who?'

'The psycho-whatsit woman. Tranquillizer or something.'

'Tranquillity Beddoes,' the other woman said contemptuously. 'Get it right.'

'What about her?' Pat knew it was something awful by the expectant looks on their faces. Delivering bad news was one of life's guilty pleasures.

'She's been killed in a car crash up in the Borders. Terrible accident—'

Pat felt as if her breath had been whipped away. She heard herself gasping and making squeaky little sounds. After she stumbled out of the shop, she straightened up. This was a terrible shock — but she had only met Tranquillity once. Why was she so poleaxed?

Then she realized. If Tranquillity was dead, that was the last link with Lorna. At the back of her mind Pat had always thought Tranquillity was the key to Lorna's whereabouts. After all, she was the last person who had spoken to her.

Pat needed to talk to someone. It had to be Tim.

CHAPTER TWENTY

I slept but my heart was awake.

Song of Songs 5:2

Suzy found out about Tranquillity's death on Wednesday morning, on Radio Cumbria's news bulletin. She had been busy making breakfast and only caught half of the item, but it made her stop what she was doing. 'What was that?'

Robert sat frozen at the kitchen table. 'Didn't you hear?' he said hoarsely. 'Tranquillity Beddoes has been killed in a road accident in the Borders.'

Suzy found she was leaning heavily against the sink. She felt physically ill, as if someone had hit her. 'Oh no! Really? Are you sure? Was it definitely her?'

'I just heard it. It happened yesterday. They're asking for anyone who might have seen her car come off the road.'

'How absolutely terrible.' Suzy sat down heavily opposite him. 'Oh, goodness, I wasn't far behind her, in the car. But there was no sign of any accident on the roads I took.'

'The newsreader said it happened on a back road.' Robert had been listening more closely than Suzy. 'It's impossible to take in. I must speak to Bill Gibson. He'll be devastated.' Robert thought for a moment. 'Unless . . . No, that's ridiculous . . .'

'You mean unless he's relieved,' Suzy said. 'Poor Seth. Does he have anyone to go to?'

'I suppose he has Bill and Ruth. I don't want to intrude but I'll go over this morning and see if there's anything I can do. You'd better get off to the train, Suzy. There's no reason why you shouldn't go to Manchester as planned.'

Suzy drove into Norbridge in the slight daze which always follows startling news. Over the last few days they had speculated about the dead woman in the bin, and about Lorna's disappearance, as well as about Jonty's attack on Roxy, but none of it had seemed *really* to do with them. Of course, they had wanted to help find Lorna, and Suzy had sympathized with Pat. But there had been no sudden painful personal involvement, like a punch in the solar plexus. It had been an interesting scenario, but that was all.

Now, though, Suzy felt physically pulled into the story. She had met Tranquillity and had been half convinced by her. And she had been at Kirkaber Castle just before Tranquillity had left to drive back to Norbridge.

And how would Maggie and Hiram take this? Tranquillity was Hiram's valued therapist and she had been killed on his doorstep.

Suzy had learned over the years that it was better to make an overture and be snubbed than to wish that you had spoken. Once she was on the train, alone in the coach, she called Maggie.

'I'm so sorry about Tranquillity,' she said. 'I only heard this morning. How are you?'

Maggie sounded strained but capable. Unsurprisingly her first concern was for her boss. 'Thanks for calling, Suzy. It's awful for Hiram. He was so angry with Tranquillity, as you heard, but he's devastated now she's dead. It's a relief to talk to someone like you. The staff here just seem to be revelling in all the drama. Of course, they all knew Hiram was furious with Tranquillity yesterday morning.'

'Yes.' Suzy remembered Hiram stamping along the corridor as angrily as his neat little feet would let him. 'I remember. But why was he so angry?'

'Oh, Tranquillity had put pressure on him to employ her husband, that big messy bloke. Hiram didn't want him, but you heard him say Tranquillity had him over a barrel. Just before he did the interview with you — and he really liked you, by the way — he asked me to get on to Seth and offer him the work. He's supposed to be starting tomorrow. Goodness knows what will happen now.'

'Poor Seth. I didn't get the impression that he had many friends. But Tranquillity was pally with one of the local vicars. Maybe he and his wife will look after Seth.' *As if Bill and Ruth Gibson didn't have enough troubles of their own*, she thought.

'Or maybe Hiram will do something for him, out of remorse. You know what he's like. Quick-tongued but so generous,' Maggie said. 'I have to go, but maybe we could talk tonight. I'd really appreciate it. It can be a bit lonely here and I always remember you and Rachel as the good guys back in the day.'

'Of course,' Suzy said. 'I'm travelling back on the five thirty from Manchester. It's usually quiet. Let's talk then.'

They said goodbye. Now she had to think about the working day ahead. It was make-or-break time for her new series pitch, with the working title *Out of Order*. The programme would cover the real stories of people who had been exploited or defrauded by those using the pandemic as an excuse not to deliver. There was still a sense held by so many that things just weren't working anymore. She hoped that this time she had the zeitgeist right. She remembered Tranquillity saying, *Many people will never get over the lockdowns. I think we're only just realizing how serious it's been.* Tranquillity had been right, and Suzy had been wrong. The spiritual therapist had been such an odd mix of the shrewd, the sincere and the self-seeking.

There had also been something ruthless about Tranquillity. She had played Suzy from the start and done so with skill. How many other people had she taken in? And what about Lorna's disappearance? Suzy had joked about Tranquillity having Lorna in a dungeon, but something not very different was a possibility. Or had Tranquillity killed her? In that case, was Tranquillity's death in turn just a coincidence? Suzy thought of Jonty McFadden driving around the Borders in Hiram's classy car, and shuddered. Like Robert, she had the feeling that all these odd threads were woven together into some strange pattern she couldn't unpick.

But as the train pulled into Manchester Piccadilly, she relocated herself mentally as well as physically. She had a busy day in store.

* * *

Wednesday morning meant the same routine as usual for Pat, despite any disruption she might be feeling. She had to get up and be over at Katie's in time to take Bobby to school. Then there were a million things to do at Katie's. She often did Bobby's washing and ironing or tried to achieve some order in the terrible mess that was Katie's kitchen.

On the car radio on the way to Katie's, Pat listened to a later news bulletin than the one Robert and Suzy had heard. There was the police report of Tranquillity's death along with a very short biography, which described her as a major figure in the mental health scene in Norbridge.

The night before, Pat had broken the news to Tim on the phone. For once he'd had something to do in the evening and was meeting a former colleague for supper. But his conversation with Pat had been instantly close and familiar as they'd shared the shock.

When she'd put the phone down, Pat had felt their friendship had moved to another level. They had agreed to meet the next evening, Wednesday, ahead of their planned trip to Liverpool on Friday. Pat would see Bobby into bed as always, leave him with Katie and drive to meet Tim at The Partridge.

* * *

Becky Dixon and Molly rose late, slouching around at The Briars. Becky had a long phone conversation with Roxy, encouraging her friend to come back to Norbridge to establish that Jonty McFadden was their attacker. Roxy could identify him if they had the nerve.

Then Becky talked with her grandad, who told her the news about Tranquillity.

'Seth Beddoes' wife's been killed in a car crash,' she told Molly in turn.

'Seth who?'

'Beddoes. He's one of the gardening volunteers. His wife was a therapist of some sort in Norbridge.'

'Oh, Norbridge, that well-known world centre for counselling ha ha. Talking of the centre of the universe, why don't we go in on the bus and meet up with some of the gang from school? I bet you don't keep up with anyone other than your activist mates. You should broaden your mind.'

'And see if anyone knows any more about Jonty and his dodge in the Borders?' Becky felt better because Molly was here, being cool about everything. And if Jonty had a proper job, thirty miles away, he couldn't be stalking her every move.

'Why not, kiddo?' said Molly. 'Remember Madison Turner? She's working in Shearers, that new hair, nail and beauty salon. I saw it on TikTok. We might get a free cut and treatments as models.'

'We'd come out looking like the Kardashians. Or at least you would. My bum's gone to nothing.'

'Too true. You've lost weight. You're too intense. You work too hard.'

'Well, you're supposed to be studying too, Molls. Didn't you say that you had an assignment on the Bauhaus movement?'

'Oh, I did that yesterday,' Molly said airily. 'C'mon, Bex, time to go.'

* * *

On Wednesday morning, Tim Markham got up and dressed with an invigorating sense of purpose. He had really enjoyed the meal with his former colleague. They'd met at the Crown and Thistle in Norbridge. Tim had made an effort, wearing smart chinos and a decent polo shirt now the weather was warmer, instead of the jeans and scruffy jumper he'd worn in the past to meet Mike. Mike was one of the few workmates he'd kept up with, but in the past he had felt that Mike was just being kind. They'd had several sessions when Tim had literally cried into his beer, and afterwards he had felt stupid. But Mike was a good mate and each time it happened, a few months later he would call Tim and suggest meeting up again. Mike had been his co-driver and in the past Tim had been the one to take the lead, but now it was Mike who took the driving seat in their friendship.

'You look a bit cheerier,' Mike had said as they'd sat over their fish and chips having gone through the usual list of who'd retired, had breakdowns or died. 'Have you been out in the sun?'

'I joined this group of gardening volunteers. But then we found the dead woman in the bin on the old road. You must have heard about it.'

'Blimey, yes. That was you, was it?'

'Yep. I felt as if I was back on the job. But it's intriguing. The cops think it was a gangland murder because she was a call girl, but there are some funny circumstances.' He had outlined the story for Mike, aware that Pat's name cropped up quite a lot. But Mike had reacted most to the mention of Bill Gibson.

'The vicar chap from St Michael's? Nice bloke, I always thought. Did a lot for Benny's, St Benedict's Hospice. My father died there a couple of years ago. They are good people.'

'Yes, I always admired what they did. Anyway, getting involved in a murder case from the other side is interesting after years of picking up the pieces, literally, like we did.'

'Not so many murders. Lots of bodies, though.' Mike attacked his haddock with enthusiasm. 'Looks like your voluntary work has been good for you. You know, Tim, you should think about doing more of it. The hospice is always looking for volunteers. Why don't you try that? It seems gruesome but it's good work and your experience would be useful.' Mike had seemed to be getting enthusiastic on Tim's behalf, his chips dangling midway between plate and mouth. 'Hey, I can email you the name of the person who runs the vollies at St Benedict's—'

'I don't know . . .' Tim had said. But being involved in his old work environment without the pressure had made him realize how much he had enjoyed it.

'Go for it!' Mike had said. 'There's life in the old dog yet. Talking of which, who's this Pat person? Anything doing there?'

'She's a pensioner, Mike.'

'Well, so are you!'

That was very true, Tim thought. He'd gone home feeling a lot brighter. He might take up Mike's suggestion. He wondered what Pat would say, and then wondered why he cared.

He realized it was because he valued her judgement and wanted her approval. It was a strange feeling.

Then Pat had called him with the news about Tranquillity and he had forgotten all about the volunteering idea. But when he woke on Wednesday morning he realized that, for the first time in ages, he had two things to look forward to. Sometime in the night, subconsciously, he had decided to approach St Benedict's Hospice. And he was looking forward to meeting Pat at The Partridge that evening.

* * *

Seth Beddoes had spent his first night as a widower staying with Bill and Ruth Gibson. A lot of time seemed to be taken up with organizational things. He would go up to Scotland to identify Tranquillity formally the next day. The police Family Liaison Officer had followed on from the first officers. The FLO had sat with Seth on the big slouchy sofa in Bill and Ruth's living room and outlined what they thought had happened.

'A tractor driver from the farm up the road was passing at about midday on his way back for his lunch. He saw tyre tracks off to the side of the road and pulled over. Your wife's car could only be seen when you looked down into the valley, and the tractor cab was high up enough. The farm worker was what we call the initial informant, and he got the police out to the scene, but it must have happened some hours earlier. It took time for the police to climb down to the car.'

'Was any other vehicle involved?' Seth had asked. He couldn't believe anyone would think Tranquillity had just lost control. She was a good driver and knew the route. Did they suspect someone else?

'We're making enquiries about any car that might have been on the road at that time. But it's more likely that she was been startled by an animal, or swerved to avoid one. The deer can be a nuisance in that valley.'

'Yes. Tranq was soft-hearted about little Bambis.' Seth started to cry again, putting his huge hands in front of his face and making harsh, dramatic sounds.

Ruth had called her own doctor and after a long wait and a negotiation, Bill had picked up a sedative from the late-night chemist. Seth had slept heavily.

In the morning Ruth and Bill could hear him sobbing in the spare room. He had left his phone in the kitchen. When it rang, Ruth answered for him, explaining who she was.

'Oh, I'm so glad Seth had someone to stay with,' the woman at the other end said. 'Tranquillity worked for my boss. I'm Hiram King's PA, Maggie Chiltern, from Kirkaber Castle near Hawick. We heard the terrible news last night.'

'Oh, right. Quite dreadful.'

'Mr Beddoes was supposed to be starting some work with us today. So Hiram wonders if he might like to come up here and stay at the castle. It might make some of the police formalities easier for Seth if he's nearby. And, of course, he might like to lay some flowers at the scene. We can organize all that. And when he needs something else to think about, there is work here for him. No pressure, of course.'

'Well, having something to do sometimes helps.' Ruth remembered how the work and distraction of two small children had made her mother's death easier to bear — in the short term, though, not for ever.

Hiram's PA went on, 'And Seth must be very alone now. I remember Tranquillity saying neither of them had any family.'

'That's very kind. I'm sure he'll be grateful. I'll put it to him when he comes downstairs.' She hated to admit it, but it would be a relief to see Seth taken care of elsewhere. She had her brother arriving from Australia any day now. That would cause enough tension without having Seth around.

And all this was having a strange effect on Bill. Ruth couldn't quite believe it, but she had heard her husband singing in the shower that morning. It had made her shudder and hurry to get dressed.

At midday a black Range Rover, just like Bill's own, drew up at the vicarage. Jonty McFadden escorted Seth Beddoes into the back seat, accompanied by his tatty kitbag.

The two men hardly spoke on the way to Kirkaber Castle. But Jonty didn't mind the silence. He had a lot to think about. He'd just had confirmation that the wolves would be arriving at Seaforth Docks on Saturday. However distraught Seth seemed to be, he needed to lash up the enclosures over the weekend. But he was a quick worker and they didn't have to be perfect.

And Tranquillity, Jonty's main rival, was out of the way. Great. All Jonty had to do now was talk Hiram out of wanting a vet. That shouldn't be too hard. His influence over the celebrity gardener was growing. And it wasn't just good fortune. Lady Luck had found a very capable partner in himself.

Things were going well. Even the weather was nice. OK, it wasn't the Costa Brava. But he could see himself being back in Spain, off and on, quite soon, as cock of the boardwalk.

But home, from now on, would be Kirkaber Castle.

CHAPTER TWENTY-ONE

My head is drenched with dew, my hair with the dampness of the night.

Song of Songs 5:2

Suzy had had a gruelling day. The management team at Living Productions had been jittery after her lack of confidence in the *Lockdown Life Change* proposal, and unsure whether *Out of Order* would work for commissioning editors.

'Why don't we put out feelers on social media and in the press, asking people to come forward who feel they've been taken advantage of?' Suzy had suggested. 'If there's no response in a week I'll go back to *Lockdown Life Change*, but I think the moment for that has passed. Relief isn't the same as feel-good. We're not ready for feel-good about Covid yet. People are still weighing up what happened and realizing that a lot of pain was caused.'

The team had agreed, but Suzy could tell they were uncertain. Her ideas had never met with scepticism before. It had to happen at some point, of course. No one had endless success. But it wasn't a nice feeling.

On the train home she called Maggie as promised. 'How are things at the castle now?'

'Jonty went down to Norbridge and picked up Seth, and he's here and settled in. Hiram wasn't very keen on Seth as you probably heard, but they've had a drink together and talked about Tranquillity. Seth says he feels better here than in Norbridge, where everyone would be looking at him.'

'Well he is quite conspicuous. And Tranquillity was very well known. It will be a big funeral.'

'Eventually, though that might be some time away. Anyway, Seth said he's happy to do some work tomorrow. It would take his mind off it. That's a relief for Hiram too. I shouldn't really mention it Suzy, but I know you won't say anything . . .'

'Absolutely. Go on.'

'Hiram has got a big project coming off soon. Just out of interest you don't know any reliable and discreet local vets, do you?'

'Vets? I have to say, Maggie, that's one area where I have absolutely no contacts. But I could ask for you. There's a farmer, Phil Dixon, who would know.'

There was silence at the other end of the line and Suzy heard muffled voices, as if Maggie had put the phone face down.

Then the PA came back on the line. 'Suzy, forget that.' Maggie's voice sounded strained. 'It's not going to be necessary. I shouldn't have mentioned it. Look I need to go. I've got someone with me. I'll keep in touch.'

'OK, I'm here if—'

But Maggie had ended the call.

Suzy felt rather put out. She had been looking forward to a good chinwag about Tranquillity's relationship with Hiram, and maybe finding out more about Jonty too. But obviously Maggie had been interrupted, and if she didn't want to talk, there was nothing Suzy could do about it. She leaned her head against the window, feeling her eyes prickle and close.

She woke up in Norbridge and scrambled to get off the train. The drive home to Tarnfield, usually short and pleasant along the bypass then up through the village, seemed tedious and punctuated by delays — roadworks, then getting stuck behind a tractor. She could feel her irritation growing. It had taken her longer than usual to get through the town centre as well, and instead of the usual delight at the green fields and darkening fells in the rosy sunset, she felt harassed.

When she pulled up at The Briars the hot flush came in waves. There was the initial tickle of panic and then the knowledge that the heat was going to well up from her tightening chest, whatever she did to try and stop it. She could fight to take off her jacket but what was the point? The sweat would erupt over her head from a hundred tiny fountains. Only after it had dripped down and into her eyes did she know it was over, but that phase was almost as bad, as her eyeballs stung, and fat gobbets of perspiration dripped into her lap.

It was unbelievable that this was happening to her. But what a relief it was happening now, and not at the production meeting in the office.

As she left the car, she felt suddenly cold as the sweat evaporated. What she wanted more than anything was a glass of red wine, although everything she had read said that made it worse. And she so wanted to be cool and calm for Molly.

She needn't have worried. Molly and Becky were still in Norbridge with no message about when they would be home, or if they would need to eat. Suzy raked through her soaking hair, dropped her bags, poured herself a glass of Merlot, and opened the freezer. Ten minutes ago she would have leaned into it for some relief but now she was shivering.

Robert came up behind her. 'You're home!'

'Well spotted,' Suzy snapped.

'OK, OK, it's just a way of saying it's wonderful to see you, I've missed you, I love you, you're gorgeous—'

'Oh, don't humour me, Robert, I've had a hell of a day. I need to sit down and have a drink.'

Robert backed off with his hands up in a gesture of surrender. Suzy smiled. 'I'm sorry, Robert. I know I'm not a barrel of laughs these days.'

He looked at her. 'A barrel . . .'

'Yes?' Suzy stared back at him.

'That's reminded me. What Bill Gibson said to Tranquillity. "You've got me over a barrel." And didn't you say that Hiram said the same thing?'

'It wouldn't surprise me if she had some hold over both of them, so it's convenient for them that's she's dead. It puts them both in the frame — except that she seems just to have had a car accident. Did you try to see Bill today?'

'I went over there, but Ruth said he was out. And she's got this imminent visit from her brother from Australia on her mind.'

'And have you heard from Neil? As Area Dean he must know what's happening on an official level. Did he see the bishop about it?'

'I haven't spoken to Neil. Bill seems to be riding it out. Maybe they're all just waiting for the accuser to take the next step.'

Suzy took another sip. 'Yep. It seems as if so much is happening, but so much has stalled. No news on Lorna's disappearance. I was hoping to get some information about Jonty McFadden out of Maggie, Hiram King's PA, but she put the phone down on me. It's all making my head spin.'

'And you've got your work issues.'

'Yep. I've left them to get on with it in Manchester. We have a week to find out if there's any mileage in *Out of Order*. I need to stop worrying about it. I'd better get the dinner on. I'm assuming Molly and Becky will come home for food.'

'Here they are now.'

The kitchen door swung open and Becky came in first. Suzy could see from the look on her face that something was up.

'Hi Suzy, Robert,' said Becky. Then she almost whispered, 'Please don't say anything. Molly's upset enough.'

She moved into the kitchen as Robert and Suzy stared at the open door. When Molly came in it was with a look of defiance which said, *Do not speak on pain of death.*

Her hair was peroxide blonde with fat purple streaks. It looked awful.

* * *

At the same time, Pat and Tim were meeting in The Partridge. 'Still nothing from Lorna?' Tim asked, but he knew the answer.

Pat shook her head. 'For some reason I'm banking on the visit to Liverpool now. At first I thought you were mad to suggest Lorna might be there but — well, I suppose I've run out of other possibilities. And she did seem so keen on the reunion trip. I checked with the hotel. The rooms haven't been cancelled.'

'Well, we'll see. In the meantime, I've got some news. I've started on the process of volunteering at the hospice.'

Tim described how he had called in at St Benedict's that morning. The head of volunteers had been delighted. Tim still had his blanket criminal records clearance and was up to date with first aid. Two references could be easily obtained — he'd called Mike and his ex-boss. It would take a while for all the paperwork to be done but he had been invited for a trip around by the head of volunteers the next day. Tim had been bowled over by the sense of colour and light in the foyer of the hospice.

'Do you know,' he said to Pat, 'fifty per cent of the patients go home in remission or having their symptoms and pain managed. It's not just where you go to die.'

'Though we all have to do that.'

'Yes, but not in pain and indignity.' Then he remembered about Derek, dying at home. 'I'm sorry if that was tactless.'

'It wasn't. I stood by Derek, and he was stubborn. He was mentally fine up to the end and he stuck to his guns about no institutions. I would have argued with him but I didn't know enough about hospices. I had the house completely reorganized. We had carers and the local GP was wonderful. But I felt I couldn't do enough for the pain. The nights were terrible.'

'It must have been distressing.'

'Yes, it was. The trouble with a long death is that people think they know in advance what it will be like, and they make strictures for themselves and everybody else, which become so hard to keep. I've thought a lot about assisted dying. I can't agree with it, although I longed for Derek to pass from his agony. Now I think a hospice would have been the best place for him.'

'Everyone should find out about them,' Tim said enthusiastically. 'It's an amazing set-up. St Benedict's even have a house for visiting families. The funding for that was started by Lorna's vicar, Bill Gibson. Patients who come from remote villages have a heck of a travel problem.'

Pat looked into the one glass of wine she had allowed herself. 'I'm glad you're so keen. And I have this trip to Liverpool on Friday to look forward to, and tomorrow I have another day with Bobby.'

'What's he like?'

'Oh, I think he's gorgeous. Of course, I do. But he was a bit grumpy this evening when I picked him up. His friend Noah had gone to sit on another coloured square on the mat, next to a little girl. Bobby was rather cross. But I read him a bit of *The Groovicorn*, and we watched some CBeebies, so he cheered up.' She smiled. Her face had lit up and looked ten years younger. She stopped, worried she had gone on too much. Doting grandparents could be a pain.

Tim smiled back. 'You obviously adore him.'

'Yes, I do. But I need other things in my life. The gardening has been good, but if Lorna doesn't come back—' In a second Pat's smile had collapsed.

'Maybe you'd like to volunteer at the hospice too?'

Pat looked surprised. 'I don't think I could go through that again.'

'But it's not the same there, Pat. Believe me, I know. In the ambulance service we often went to people's homes where someone was terminally ill. The hospice is quite different.'

'Well, maybe I'll think about it, if you're there. And it's interesting that you have good things to say about Lorna's vicar. I didn't really like the sound of him. But obviously he has a good side. Only . . .'

'What?'

'I know this sounds weird. And I could be barking up the wrong tree. We all think Tranquillity was the last person to talk to Lorna before she disappeared, but her priest, Bill Gibson, went to see her on Sunday morning. Has anyone asked him if he said or did anything that would make her go missing?'

* * *

At Kirkaber Castle, Maggie went into her bedroom and locked the door. She had just been through one of the most horrible experiences of her life.

A few hours earlier she had been on the phone to Suzy from her office. Like Hiram's, her office was an inner sanctum, where staff knocked before entering or hovered on the threshold waiting to be summoned if the door was ajar. Of course, Hiram's office was bigger and more heavily furnished, a version of the study of a Victorian paterfamilias, complete with huge desk, hunting prints and glass-fronted bookcases. It was one floor above.

Maggie had been sitting in the G-plan-style easy chair by the marble fireplace, now with a simple but tasteful flower arrangement in the hearth (dried flowers from Hiram's sweet meadow seed mix). She'd been looking towards her own svelte desk and ergonomic office chair in the bay window, so the door was behind her. But suddenly, as she was speaking to Suzy, Maggie had felt hot breath on the nape of her neck. Whoever it was had come into the office, unheard.

She had turned around. Jonty McFadden's face was inches away. He was leaning forward, his bright eyes peering into hers with a look of faux innocence that was more menacing than straightforward hostility.

She'd put the phone face down on the coffee table.

Jonty whispered, 'Oops-a-daisy, Maggie, I don't think Hiram would like to hear you telling someone about his Big Project.'

'What the hell are you doing in here?' Maggie was a brave woman. She had made to stand up but Jonty had pushed her from behind down into the chair.

'Kill the call.'

The three words had sounded more threatening than anything Maggie had ever heard. Her knees had trembled and her guts churned. She had picked up her mobile and said, 'Suzy, forget that,' and then shut her eyes, realizing she had been stupid. Jonty didn't need to know who she was calling.

With speed and grace he'd pivoted from behind to face her, kneeling down with his hands on her thighs, his face even closer. The nearness of his warm, lithe body had made Maggie shake. It was both reminiscent of a lover and completely terrifying. For a moment she had wondered if he was going to assault her, but the idea had seemed ludicrous.

'Well now, Maggie,' Jonty had said good-humouredly but not moving, 'you're not bad looking for your age.' He ran a finger down her jawbone. 'I don't mind 'em a bit older. Grateful. Know what I mean? But that's not what this is about, although maybe you should bear it in mind. No, I wanted to say that this business of a vet, well, it's not a good idea.'

'What do you mean? Hiram expressly asked me—'

'Yes, but Hiram sometimes misunderstands how things work in the big wide world.'

'Don't be ridiculous, Jonty. You're a kid. Hiram is a highly experienced professional. What are you talking about?'

'Oh he might be good at taming a few patches of grass but we're talking real animals here. He wants wolves and I'm going to get him wolves. But we don't need vets getting involved. These are wild animals, for God's sake.' He had laughed scornfully. 'Tell him you've spoken to someone and they've said we don't need a vet. I don't care how you get out of it, Maggie, but we're not having one. And as well as that, get Big Seth on to building those cages PDQ. It's good for grieving, working. Understand?'

'You can't bully me. I can tell Hiram exactly what you've been in here doing—'

'And he'll believe you? Really? That I would threaten you with a bit of slap and tickle? Isn't that what Generation Menopause call it? That sounds like the delusion of a crazy middle-aged bint to me. You can get sad, mad cow ideas at your age. Would Hiram really believe I threatened to rape you? Me? With you?' He'd put his hand on Maggie's breast. 'Not bad,' he said. 'Bit saggy. But I could cope.'

'You're sick'

'Maybe. But if you talk, I'll tell Hiram you tried it on with me. I know which of us he'll believe.'

'Don't be ridiculous. I've been Hiram's PA for ten years.'

'So he might be getting a bit fed up with you, don't you think? New blood, Maggie. And talking of blood . . .' Jonty suddenly had his cat-skinner knife in his hand. 'I like it a bit rough, you know. Not where it would show, of course. So you'd better do as I say. No vet, got that? And from now on, where the wolves are concerned, you take your orders from me.'

* * *

Molly and Becky were in Molly's bedroom. Molly had her head in her hands. 'I don't know what the hell I'm going to do, Bex,' she wailed.

'I told you Madison was just an apprentice. You said she could try anything on you, as long as it was awesome. But at least you didn't have to pay.'

'Pay! You're kidding. Who would pay to look like a psychedelic zebra? Did you see Mum's face? I couldn't stay down in the kitchen. I had to escape. What am I going to do? What about Saturday? I can't go out like this!'

There was a tap on the bedroom door.

'Oh sugar, that's Mum.'

'Well you can't ignore her.' Becky called out, 'Come in, Suzy.'

'Don't do that!' Molly yelled.

'Too late,' replied Becky.

Suzy came in very slowly and took in Molly lying on the bed with her head under the duvet and her face peeping out. 'Are you OK?' she said tentatively.

'What do you think?' Molly said gruffly. 'No, I'm not. Obviously. Madison Turner was working at Shearers on Scotchgate and she said she'd do my hair for nothing if I let her go free range.'

'Let's have another look.'

Molly pulled back the duvet. Suzy couldn't help herself. The laughter and the tears started in her stomach and gurgled up to her throat. She swallowed it. She had wondered whether there was something she could do for her grown-up self-reliant daughter. And this was it.

'Look,' said Suzy. 'It can be put right, and I'll pay. I can call my hairdresser in Norbridge and you can go there and get it sorted. It might be possible to bleach out the stripes and then give you a rinse of your natural colour.'

'I don't want my natural colour. That's the whole point. Can you get it done before Saturday?'

As Suzy looked down at her phone for the number, Molly looked sharply over at Becky. It was a warning not to say more about *why* before Saturday. Becky nodded.

Suzy looked up. 'Beggars can't be choosers. Have you got a better idea what to do?'

Molly sniffled and said no, sounding more like a disconsolate fourteen-year-old than an undergraduate. But it didn't last long. 'Anyway,' she said, perking up and looking critically at her mother, 'you look weird yourself. I don't want to end up like that. Your hair is all plastered down on one side and sticking up on the other. What happened to you?'

Suzy looked at herself in the mirror. She hadn't brushed her hair since the sweat attack. One side was stuck to her head while the other stuck up in a single spike.

'You're right. I've got a bad case of hot-flush hair. I look like a unicorn.'

Becky snorted. 'Purple zebras, unicorns — am I the only normal one round here?'

Molly emerged from the duvet and jumped off the bed in front of the mirror. 'Hey, thank you but no thanks Madison. You've turned me into Florrie Fimble. And my mum is the Unicorn Princess. Or the Unicorn Princess's grandma.'

The mention of the TV shows they had watched when Molly was little, wrung Suzy's heart. Her daughter was still that mix of adult and child. And still needed her help.'

'Molly, let me ring my hairdresser's now and get an appointment for you. In the meantime you can wear this.' Suzy had been holding a carrier bag. She pulled out a crocheted black hair net of the sort last seen around 1980. 'I kept this from my youth. It'll cover your head till we can get it sorted.' Molly grabbed it and put it on.

'Cushty!' she said. 'I like it! Thanks, Mum.'

* * *

On Thursday morning Pat took Bobby to school. He chanted the days of the week, months of the year and numbers one to fifty, three times, then chuntered away about what he and Noah were going to do at playtime.

'It's half-term next week,' Pat said. 'I'll be looking after you for a couple of days.'

'Can we go to the children's farm, Grandma?' They did this every holiday. He loved animals, especially dogs, and always wanted to give them a hug, which was not always welcome.

At the school gates, Pat stood behind the young mums while they waited for it to open. Reception children had to be escorted to the veranda area at the back of the classroom, where they left their jackets. But Bobby and his friends were getting older now and wanted to run off by themselves. His hand twisted in hers.

In the queue for the gates, Pat looked at some of the others. She rarely spoke to them, but there were two other grandmas in the group and sometimes they chatted. One of them looked quite different from usual. She shook a mop of shiny black hair from her shoulders.

'Hey, you've had your hair done. It looks fab,' said one of the younger women.

'Thanks. I was sick of lockdown locks. Long tatty hair tied up in a scrunchie. No, the time was ripe for a makeover.'

Pat caught sight of her own reflection in the classroom window as Bobby squirmed away and ran off without saying goodbye. Her mousey hair was way too long, thin and shapeless. She made a sudden decision to have a makeover herself, since she was about to face her former classmates. And if Lorna came back, a needy, dishevelled wreck would be the last thing she'd want to find.

If Lorna came back.

But she would. She had to. And Pat had to fill in the time somehow before they left for Liverpool. The visit to the hairdresser's was something to do. Displacement activity. And so was the whole trip if she was honest. Deep down it was wishful thinking that visiting Liverpool could reunite her with Lorna.

Then again, she thought, those hotel rooms hadn't been cancelled. Was that because Lorna was going to turn up? Or because she didn't care about the wasted money? Or because she'd been prevented from cancelling the booking? Or because she was dead?

CHAPTER TWENTY-TWO

I looked for him but did not find him. I called him but he did not answer.

Song of Songs 5:6

On Thursday, Suzy put all her efforts into editing her podcast with Hiram King. There was no doubt he could turn on the charm. His voice was light, warm and accessible, as if he were welcoming you into his greenhouse and giving you a personal tour, confiding in you alone about his rewilding dreams.

For the rest of the day, she tried not to worry about whether members of the public were responding to Living Productions reaching out to people who had been conned because of Covid. Nor did she want to think too much about Lorna Duxford being missing, or the attack on Roxy. Becky said her friend was coming back that weekend and would be prepared to identify Jonty, though Suzy was unsure how far the police could act on that. At some point over the weekend she thought she would call Maggie again and enlighten her about Jonty, despite her former colleague ringing off so sharply the night before.

That evening, she and Robert took Molly and Becky to the Plough for supper and talked about colleges, degrees and the future. Suzy felt better for looking forward.

But Robert couldn't stop thinking about Bill. On Thursday afternoon Neil Clifford had phoned to tell him how his meeting with the bishop had gone.

'She was very surprised and shocked, of course. Like me, this just isn't the Bill we know. But there are so many examples of the hierarchy supporting guilty clergy they genuinely believed in. These people can be so credible. Also, organizationally it's difficult now. The Independent Inquiry into Child Sex Abuse will come out later this year, but till then bishops are still the first port of call for these allegations, not the police. The Church is setting up a new body to deal with them as well, but right now it's up to her. The bishop must take this very seriously.'

'So, what is she going to do?'

'I'm meeting Bill tomorrow afternoon to tell him that the writing's on the wall. If the accuser turns up and maintains the allegations, then he's out, immediately, unless he's got something absolutely convincing to say in his defence — like, for example, proof he wasn't there that week. Even so he'll be suspended pending inquiries. If the accuser doesn't come forward, there'll still be an inquiry and it won't be good for Bill, especially if he can't provide a cast-iron defence. The Church has to be seen to be robust against these awful abusers. There have been hundreds of complaints that were mishandled, across the country.' Neil sighed, worn down. 'In the meantime, Robert, can you keep an eye on him? I'm worried about his mental health as well. He could be innocent. And he won't talk to me in anything other than a formal way — hence the meeting tomorrow.'

'He seems to be avoiding me too.'

'But he's more likely to speak to you. You got more out of him than I did.'

* * *

'I'm off to the vicarage again at East Norbridge,' Robert said to Suzy on Friday morning. 'Bill is meeting Neil Clifford this

201

afternoon, but I want to see him first. There's no doubt he's avoiding people. I'm going to try again.'

But when Robert turned up at the vicarage there was no sign of Bill, and Ruth was in a state.

'I don't know where he is, and my brother is going to be here any minute. He landed at Glasgow first thing this morning. It's so like Malcolm not to give us fair warning. I've got the spare room done and I'm going to make a meal, but I could do with knowing where Bill has gone. It's not like him to go off. I don't know what's got into him lately.'

'Could he be at the hospice?'

'I've phoned them, and they say they haven't seen him. I've called his mobile a dozen times. Look, Malcolm will be here any minute—'

'Yes, I know. I'll get out of your hair.'

But it was too late.

There was the sound of a car pulling into the drive and Ruth flew to the door. A tall, suntanned man was getting out of a black Range Rover, with a huge backpack.

'Malcolm!' Ruth rushed at him.

The man picked up his sister and spun her round as if she were light as a feather. 'Ruthie!'

Robert hung back in the hall. Since Malcolm and Ruth were blocking the drive, there was no way he could quietly disappear. This was embarrassing. Then, as Robert watched, he realized that the siblings had become as awkward as he was. They stared warily at each other.

'So where's Bill?' Malcolm asked.

'He . . . he's out on some parish business. We didn't really know what time you'd be here.'

Malcolm looked suspiciously over his sister's shoulder to the open front door and the hallway, where Robert was standing.

'Oh, this is Robert Clark, he's waiting for Bill. He's a church colleague.'

To try and make the situation easier, Robert said nothing and strode forward, offering his hand. Malcolm took it

in a firm shake. But he didn't smile. 'Good ta meet ya, mate.'
He went on, for Robert's benefit, 'Yep, I'm sorry it's all been
a bit hectic. I got some work in the UK so I've combined
business with pleasure. I'm here quicker than expected. I just
got in the hire car and belted down here. How long has it
been since we met in person?'

'Over thirty years,' said Ruth. 'Look, Malcolm, come in
and put your stuff in the spare room.'

'And I'm so sorry to have been in the way,' Robert said.
'I'll be off.'

'No!' Ruth's manner had changed after the awkwardness
between her and her brother. 'Stay and wait for Bill. You've
been trying to get hold of him for a few days. I'm sure he'll
be here just as soon as I let him know Malcolm has arrived.'

'OK.'

But it wasn't OK. There was a coolness now between
the siblings, not at all like their first exultant embrace. It was
to do with Bill's absence. Robert could see that Malcolm
was puzzled and a bit hurt. He had flown 10,000 miles after
thirty years and his brother-in-law had chosen to be out when
he arrived. Whatever his sister said or did to make up for it,
it wasn't the warmest of welcomes.

Ruth and Malcolm had disappeared upstairs to the spare
bedroom, so Robert stayed in the hall feeling like a spare part
that had suddenly been called into service.

Ruth came back first. 'Forgive me, Robert,' she said,
'but this is very awkward. Malcolm is upset that Bill isn't
here. Of course, Mal and I have kept in touch — we even
Zoomed in the lockdowns — so although I haven't seen him
in the flesh, he's not a stranger to me. But Malcolm hasn't
spoken to Bill since emigrating thirty-three years ago. I do
hope Bill comes home soon.'

'Yes. He must be somewhere in the parish.' But Robert
was beginning to wonder. 'I assume you've checked with
your churchwardens or anyone else he could be seeing?'

'I rang them both with some fib about him having left
a folder behind. Neither seemed to think there was anything

up with him. He's obviously showing a different face to them than to me. I'll make some coffee. Do stay for a few minutes, Robert. Bill might be back soon.'

There was the sound of heavy but agile footsteps on the stairs and Malcolm reappeared, saying with forced cheeriness, 'Coffee sounds like a good idea, Ruthie.'

When his sister disappeared into the kitchen, Malcolm's cheeriness evaporated and he turned aggressively to Robert. 'What's going on here? Where's Bill? Ruth's trying to cover for him, but it feels like he's avoiding me.'

'I'm not sure, Malcolm.'

'But all's not well, eh?'

Robert didn't deny it. His silence seemed to calm Malcolm, who said, 'It's a bit strange, after all these years.'

Robert said, 'Yes. I agree. 'But I don't know myself what the problem is.' That was technically true.

'I'm sorry. I didn't mean to bite your head off, mate.'

They sat down awkwardly. To try and lighten the atmosphere Robert asked, 'How does Cumbria look to you?'

'Different but the same. It looks as if everything's had a lick of paint. I was twenty-five when I left. It felt grey and cold and depressing here then. I went to Adelaide on a short-term contract and there was sun and light and colour — and optimism. It was like walking from black-and-white to colour telly. My mother had died, my sister was wrapped up in her kids, understandably, and I had nothing here.'

'So will you be meeting old friends?' Robert asked, though it sounded as if Malcolm had been glad to leave them behind.

'Nah, none of that stuff. Most of my friends had gone on to pastures new. It was the time of the Great Northern Diaspora. There were probably more young Cumbrians in Manchester or London. Well, maybe it wasn't that bad. But it felt like it. The old gang have all gone.'

'Were there a lot of you?'

'Yeah, there were a few. But we thought we were a cut above the rest, y'know? One joined the army, officer corps.

Two or three went to university and didn't come back. We were a bit of an elite. From the grammar school, y'know?'

Robert nodded in understanding and smiled, although he sensed Malcolm was talking too much to cover his concern. Ruth came in with the coffee and they chatted a little more, but as midday came and went and there was still no sign of Bill, Robert felt he needed to leave them to deal with the vicar's discourtesy in their own way.

But was it discourtesy or something more sinister? That afternoon, Bill was due to have his meeting with Neil Clifford. Would he turn up for it? If these allegations were getting to Bill again, and if he really had been mixed up in something deeply wrong in the past, could he have done what was euphemistically called 'something stupid'? Robert didn't want to wake up and hear on Radio Cumbria of another unexpected death.

He was better off out of the vicarage. Malcolm and Ruth would have to talk honestly, and if he had helped them get over the first awkward moments, he was glad. Now it was time to go.

In the car he called Neil Clifford, who answered at once. Robert said, 'What time is your meeting with Bill Gibson?'

'Two o'clock.'

'I have a feeling he might not turn up. Ruth says he disappeared early this morning and hasn't been in touch since.'

'I'll keep you posted,' said Neil.

Robert drove towards Norbridge. At two fifteen Neil Clifford called back. 'Bill hasn't appeared,' he said brusquely. 'Obviously I'll wait but I'm not optimistic.'

Me neither, thought Robert. But he would go home via the hospice, just in case they could tell him more about where Bill could possibly be.

* * *

In the early afternoon Tim popped in at St Benedict's. He needed to deliver his criminal records clearance certificate, thinking he would drop it off before he went to pick up Pat.

He was trying not to think about their trip too deeply. He suspected they were both using it as a cover for something else, but he wasn't sure what it was he really wanted. Pat, he knew, would do anything to try and find Lorna, and he hoped he wasn't using her concern to satisfy his own need to have something to do and someone who needed him.

He found Robert Clark in reception at the hospice asking for Bill Gibson. The receptionist hadn't seen Bill for several days. She said, 'Father Bill last called in the other day to see the man in the hospice house, the place for rural relatives of people here. He's got Covid, poor chap, and is isolating. Father Bill is vaccinated and doesn't mind taking the risk. He's very good and doesn't worry about himself.'

Robert wondered about that, but Tim said, 'Yes, Mr Gibson's a good bloke. Hey, it's good to bump into you, Robert. Fancy a cuppa? There's a nice café here.'

Robert followed Tim to the small café. He had never been into a hospice before and was interested in how it worked, and why Bill, and now Tim, were so committed to it.

At the table, Tim said, 'I'm taking Pat to Liverpool later this afternoon. There's a chance Lorna will turn up at their old school reunion. And we're going to try and find out where she lived, on the off-chance she's gone to ground at her childhood home. It's ridiculous, I know, but it seems Lorna was so looking forward to going back and revisiting her past. I think both Pat and I feel better for doing something. And we seem to have exhausted all the possibilities in Cumbria.'

'True. It's very odd. I hope you get somewhere.'

'Unlikely, let's be honest. Let me have your mobile number, Robert. If we discover anything, I'll let you know.'

They swapped numbers and Tim stood up to go. He looked quite different as he walked away. Purposeful. At least someone was getting something out of the strange mess they were uncovering. The dead woman in the bin, Lorna's disappearance, Tranquillity's death, and the way she was linked to the Reverend Bill Gibson — a vicar accused of child abuse and scared of meeting his own brother-in-law. And the attack on Roxy. Plus, that odd quote from the Song of Songs. *We have a little sister . . .*

Were these links or coincidences, or just part of the usual muddle of life? Robert didn't know but he didn't like it.

On the other hand, he did like the hospice. Fleetingly he wondered who the man with Covid was. And why Bill had been visiting him so solicitously.

* * *

Mid-afternoon on Friday, Tim arrived promptly at Pat's terraced cottage. When she answered the door, he stepped back in surprise. 'What have you done to your hair?'

'Just had a cut and colour. It was a mess. And if I'm meeting ex-classmates I want to look as if I've stood the test of time, not as if I'm past my sell-by date.'

Tim laughed. 'I didn't think of you as competitive.'

'It has been known. I saw myself reflected in a window at Bobby's school and thought I look more like his great-granny. And it filled in the time, so I wasn't worrying about Lorna.'

'Well, you look very nice,' Tim said awkwardly.

'Thanks. I thought of having Scouse brows done as well, seeing as I'm going back to Liverpool, but I drew the line at that.'

'But not on your brows. Good thing, too. My ex had her eyebrows tattooed. She looked like something from a Halloween party. But she thought it was very sexy. Anyway, the man next door liked it.'

Pat laughed. It was the first time she had heard Tim joke about his divorce. Her laughter made her look even younger. She was feeling cheerful today herself, wearing shoes with a slight heel rather than gardening sneakers, so she'd gained an inch in height, and she had bought new slightly flared trousers. It was almost impossible to find a shop assistant in a big store these days, but a young and sympathetic woman had materialized in M&S. When Pat had enquired about trousers, she'd suggested the bootcut look, plus a new top and a loose casual jacket. Pat couldn't believe the difference they had made.

She flung her overnight bag in the back of Tim's car and waved to one of her nosier neighbours, who had come out to water the geraniums by her front door.

'I was glad I went to the hairdresser's for another reason,' she said. Becky was there.'

'Becky? I thought she did her hair with a Flymo.'

Pat laughed. 'It was her friend Molly, Suzy Spencer's daughter, in the chair. She was having a damage limitation exercise. One of their mates had got a bit overenthusiastic with the bleach. Anyway, Becky asked me about the graveyard this weekend.' Pat stopped. 'I don't know if I did the right thing.'

'What do you mean?'

'Becky said Molly was going out with a boy tomorrow and didn't want Suzy to know, so Becky's covering for her. But Becky doesn't want to go home to the farm or around Norbridge. She asked me if there was any gardening she could get on with . . .' Pat tailed off.

'And?'

'I gave her the key to the Lesser Friary and suggested she might go and do some ivy blitzing. But now I'm not sure. Do you think the Lesser Friary is safe?'

'Well, we've never had any trouble there. And why should Becky be in any danger?'

'She'll be on her own. But on the top road there are plenty of passers-by and the ivy is all around the church, not deep into the graveyard. I wish I hadn't given her that key, though. Then again, she asked, and she's an adult.' But Pat was troubled.

Tim had reached the big roundabout before the spur road down to the M6. 'Don't think about Norbridge any-more, Pat. We're off to the big city.'

* * *

Ro hung up after a call from DS Jed Jackson, filling her in as he often did, and getting her local knowledge in return. The police had started the investigation into Tranquillity's fatal crash. There had been a few cars sighted on the back road to Hawick that day. Two belonged to local farmers, one to a woman driving down to Langholm to shop, and a black Range Rover had been seen by the tractor driver, but he had no idea what its number was and anyway, it was very dirty.

'Black Range Rovers are as common around here as bloody sheep,' Jed said moodily. 'Talking of sheep, I need to get on with the flock-worrying case. But it's gone quiet now. The latest incident was last weekend first thing. There's been nothing this week and I hope it stays that way.'

Ro spent Friday in an impatient daze. That night, Phil was going to come and stay at Burnside Cottage with her for the first time. Becky was safely at The Briars till Molly went back to college on Sunday afternoon and Ro was lying low, under the radar of the DI in Norbridge, who wasn't a fan of uppity PCSOs. The phone signal at the cottage was erratic but she and Phil weren't expecting any calls. And the thought that they would be having a secret tryst was quite exciting. They had been together for three months, but never for two nights with a whole day in the middle. She was looking forward to it, but as with any new romance there was a degree of trepidation. Romance, she scoffed to herself. She had thought she was hardened. Life hadn't treated Ro kindly. She was the same age as Suzy but knew she looked older. And there was well over a decade between her and her taciturn old Cumbrian.

But that was how it felt. Romantic.

* * *

Pat and Tim had both been quiet on the journey down to Liverpool. They had stopped at the services at Killington Lake. When Pat had emerged from the ladies, Tim was waiting outside and had hardly recognized her. From a distance, she thought he looked better too. He was nicely dressed and seemed more alert. Less grumpy and introspective.

Tim navigated the city well. They parked in the cathedral car park and went into reception at the boutique hotel in the centre of Liverpool. Pat felt her heart pounding as she went to check in.

'I'm meeting my friend here, the one who made the booking,' Pat said. 'Lorna Duxford. Has she left a message for me?'

'No, we haven't heard from her.'

'I booked a room here yesterday,' Tim said. 'Bugger the expense. Dump your stuff and let's go for a walk. I want to see this famous city. We'll do what we suggested, coming back here every hour. There's still time for Lorna to turn up.'

If Pat knew her friend, Lorna wouldn't leave anything until the last minute. Then again, the last week had proved Pat didn't know her at all.

* * *

At the vicarage in East Norbridge, Ruth watched Malcolm go out for a walk after lunch. Then she texted Bill furiously. There had been no reply and he hadn't answered his mobile. Then at five o'clock, weak with relief, she saw there was a text message from him.

But when she read it, she heard herself making a weird wailing noise, as if from a distance.

Ruth, I'm very sorry but I need to go away for a few days. I've booked myself into a retreat. Don't worry about me, but I need to do some serious thinking. I won't be answering my phone, but you must have complete faith in me. I wouldn't lie to you. I never have. Just be patient, Ruth. Bill x

The pathetic 'x' at the end made Ruth's heart turn over.

When Malcolm returned, she was sitting on the sofa, pale and tearful.

'You'd better tell me what's really going on, sis,' he said.

'Oh, Malcolm!' she said, crying again. 'I would if I could. I really would.'

CHAPTER TWENTY-THREE

I will get up now and go about the city, through its streets and squares.

Song of Songs 3:2

On Friday evening, Pat and Tim faced each other across the restaurant table in Liverpool's Chinatown. The meal had been delicious and Tim talked about his walk round the sights.

'How long since you were last here?' Tim asked.

'Oh, I used to come back quite a lot with Derek to see my mum and dad. My parents died about twenty years ago now. Then I came to see elderly relatives, but less often. Funerals mostly.'

'Did you have a big family?'

'Not particularly. I have one sister who lives in Crewe. My mum was one of four and my dad of three. I only thought of this recently, but both sides of my family lived within the same square mile, I suppose, for about five generations. I still know neighbours from my childhood. Families in Liverpool go back a long way. So maybe we will find someone who remembers Lorna.'

Tim nodded.

'But to answer your question,' Pat went on, 'I think the last time I was here was for another school reunion about ten years ago. Lorna wasn't there. I don't recall anyone asking after her and I didn't miss her. She was a bit of a mouse at school but obviously something happened to bring her out.'

'Yes, she's not a mouse now. More of a tiger.'

'Absolutely. You said earlier we should "grab" some food. Lorna would have torn a strip off you for that. She would have said, "Does no one just obtain something, or, perish the thought, say please?"' Pat laughed.

Tim smiled too. 'And do you remember when that chap from the council was "running late"?' Tim did a good impersonation of Lorna's outraged tones. '"Running late? What do you mean, running late? Have you been hosting a string of international conference calls?"'

Pat added, 'And all those young men you see playing the guitar on the streets. "What right have they to pollute the streets with their whining versions of Bob Dylan? I don't know why councils allow it. They have no idea of what a good musician sounds like. You wouldn't find Sol Temple wailing on a street corner!"'

'Sol Temple again,' said Tim. 'I googled him. Apparently, he drowned in the Thames in the late seventies. Drugs and booze. Drowning when under the influence is fairly common. We hauled bodies out of the river in Norbridge from time to time.'

'Sad.' Pat shuddered. Suddenly she didn't want to make conversation. She had never wasted time with Tim in chit-chat. 'I'm very tired,' she said.

'It's coming up to ten o'clock. Time for one last enquiry at the reception desk. But I don't think she's coming.'

They walked back through the narrow Georgian streets leading up to the cathedral. Pat's heart raced again when they arrived at the hotel. But reception confirmed that Ms Duxford hadn't checked in and there were no messages. Pat felt the final physical deflation of hope gone. She was winded. She wanted to be alone with her disappointment.

Tim said, 'I won't persuade you to have a nightcap. 'I expect you've got a lot of thinking to do.'

Surprised at his sensitivity, Pat just nodded.

'I'm not one for meeting at breakfast,' Tim went on. 'Your reunion finishes at four o'clock, doesn't it? I'll see you in reception here afterwards. Maybe you'll get some info about Lorna's old home. You never know.'

'No, you don't,' Pat said. But she thought she did. It was all completely hopeless.

* * *

Molly padded across the landing to her old bedroom, where Becky was sleeping. It was eight o'clock, unprecedentedly early for a Saturday morning. She could hear her mum and Robert in the kitchen, talking and banging around with pans and kettles, and the smell of burned toast drifted up the stairs, mum's signature dish.

'Wake up, it's Saturday!' Molly bounced over to the window and opened the curtains. 'It's a beautiful day!'

'Oh, for God's sake, Molly . . .' Becky pushed her head out from under the duvet. They had spent the evening in a pub in Norbridge with a mix of their old school friends. Becky was a more experienced drinker than Molly, but that morning it was she who was feeling the pain.

Molly flopped onto the bed. 'Let's cuddle up like we did when we were ten. I want to talk to you!'

'Ugh, you are so effing cheerful.' Becky pulled a pillow over her face.

'Yes,' squeaked Molly, 'I am. I am sooo excited. Today's the day.'

'Oh for goodness' sake, you're just going to Glasgow with Rafi Hossein.'

'Correction, Miss Snots, I'm going to the School of Arts with the future Dr Rafi Hossein, formerly of the Star of Bengal takeaway in Tarnfield. Now at Glasgow University doing medicine and home for the weekend to see guess who

— me! But it's our secret.' Molly pressed her face close to Becky's ear and said 'Shhh' in a gurgling, whisper, which made Becky's ear reverberate.

'That's disgusting, Molls. Anyway, what time is he coming for you?'

'You plonker, he's not. We are *not*, I repeat *not*, letting my mum know about this.'

'So you've said a million times. But frankly I still don't see why. For a start, you're lucky to have a mum.'

'Oh, don't start that again. I know. It's terrible for you. You lost your mum when you were a baby and now you've lost your gran. I get it. I do, really. But that doesn't mean I have to treat *my* mum as if . . . as if—' Molly fumbled for the words — 'as if she was my *friend* or something.'

'But I don't see why you can't just tell her that Rafi is indulging you in your arty tastes and driving you to Glasgow in his clapped-out Fiat because he's in *luuurve*.'

'Becky! That is not the case. He's not in love . . .' Molly went pink. 'And that piece of fake news just proves my point. I don't want speculation and interrogation. Although my mum is the best, yadda yadda yawn yawn, she wouldn't be able to stop herself going for the full investigative journalism approach.' Molly imitated her mother's voice. '*Did you have a nice day, sweetie? How's Rafi? How are things with Rafi? Is it still on with Rafi? Are you using contraception? What shall I wear for the wedding?* I just want it to be private. The main thing is that you and I leave this morning as if we were just going into Norbridge.'

'Well, I'll need to take my bike because I want to go to the farm to pick up my gardening gear. But I'm not staying there. You know why.'

Jonty. Molly nodded.

'I'm going to have a go at clearing some ivy from the abandoned graves near the church at the Lesser Friary. Where should I meet you this evening?'

'We'll be back by six. I told Rafi I needed to be with family tonight. I'm playing hard to get.'

That made Becky laugh. 'Yeah, right.'

'Seriously, Becky, I want to spend Saturday evening with you. Our last night together before I go back to York.'

Becky felt touched.

'Keep in contact, Bex. We'll meet back here.'

Becky reached out and picked up her phone from the bedside table. 'Oh pants. The charger cable is loose. It's only on eighteen per cent.'

Molly couldn't leave Becky on her own for a day with a dying phone. 'Hang on.' She went back into Jake's room and returned a few minutes later.

'I thought so,' she said. 'Jake left a phone here last time he came home. He's always upgrading. When he gets a new phone he puts his old SIM in it, then puts his new SIM in the old phone so he has a back-up. He keeps it here as a spare. Yep. Put your SIM in this one. We'll explain to Jake later. Easier to get forgiveness than permission though both are tough with my big brother.'

'But my SIM is Android and this is an iPhone, and a different carrier. I don't think it'll work, Molls.'

'Well then, I'll just put my number in Jake's phone and you can call me. All I need to know is when you're going to be back.'

'Brill. And this one is fully charged?'

'One hundred per cent!'

Becky thought for a minute. 'Have you got Roxy's number?'

'No — why would I have that? I've never even met them.'

Becky smiled. Molly had got the pronoun spot on. 'I'd just like you to have it. I don't know why. Maybe because any friend of mine has to be a friend of Roxy's. I'll send it to you. And yours to them.'

'OK, cool.'

When the two girls left The Briars at nine thirty, Molly was on foot and Becky was pushing her bike — which Suzy thought was a bit odd, but she decided not to mention it. Maybe Becky had to ride home to the farm for something.

'We'll be back around six thirty,' Molly said, in a tone that said, *No questions.*

They walked up the track in the sunshine. Molly was tense with excitement. Becky understood. This wasn't a teenage date, this was a proper outing. She and Rafi would talk intelligently about the Glasgow School of Art. It was a trip with a purpose other than having sex in the car.

Molly was dressed differently, too, in a floral skirt that reached her knees, and huge white trainers. She had an orange denim jacket and had pinned crocheted flowers in her hair, which was now a rich all-over mahogany — not the boring brown Suzy had wanted, but something that might at a distance pass for natural.

Becky understood too about privacy. Suzy was a great mum, but all daughters needed a bit of distance. She wondered what it would be like to have Ro for a stepmother. Step-granny! It made her smile.

Molly grinned at her as if she knew her thoughts. The sun was shining. The world was good, after all.

Becky felt in that moment that she and Molly would always be friends. They were at that time in their lives where they'd move in and out of friendships with no knowing what the future would bring. But after this week, they would always be close, she was sure of it. Warmth tingled through her. She had Roxy and she had Molly. She felt protected. She was all right.

Her own phone was in her backpack. But without really knowing why, she took Jake's phone out of her bag and put it in her deep tracksuit pocket. It bumped next to her leg in a comforting way. There was something special about that phone with just one number on it. It was her emergency hotline to Molly. It was precious.

* * *

Saturday was sultry. Temperatures were in the high twenties by mid-morning and the sky had a metallic quality. Robert had spent the early part of the morning doing some gardening, and Suzy had worked on finishing the Hiram King podcast edition. Around eleven, Robert made himself some coffee and sat at the kitchen table, thinking.

After leaving the hospice, Robert had gone to the university and picked up some marking that needed to be done by Monday. He had a seminar to prepare. He was lucky, because his work could completely absorb him when he was stymied over other problems, and it wasn't until two hours later that he thought again about the mystery of Bill Gibson. He called Ruth.

'Yes, thanks, Robert, I should have let you know. I heard from Bill about an hour ago. He's fine.'

She sounded anything but fine herself, but Robert breathed a sigh of relief. 'So, is he home?'

'No.' Ruth offered nothing more.

'Is Malcolm still annoyed?'

'I've asked him to be patient. Bill says he will come back soon.'

'Do you know where he is?'

She paused. 'He says he's booked himself into a retreat for a few days, but he promised me faithfully he will be home soon. Robert, is there something you haven't told me?'

Robert had thought for a moment. 'Yes, there is something. It's complicated and difficult. You have to hear about it from Bill.'

'Oh dear God, I knew it.' Ruth had sounded near to breaking down.

'Listen, it's not great but it's something that can be sorted out if Bill is honest with us all. I expect that is what he is thinking about. All I can say is that as long as you know he's safe and well, then you — we, all of us — just have to wait. You have Malcolm with you, don't you?'

'Yes. And the children are coming tomorrow to meet him. It's not as if I'm not very busy.'

'Try to stay that way. And I'll ask the Area Dean to pop over—'

'No! Don't do that. Whatever this is, Bill and I will sort it out for ourselves. I need to go now, but I'll pass on what you've said to Malcolm. He's been an absolute rock since I heard from Bill.'

That was good news. Ruth had her brother, and Bill was licking his wounds somewhere. At least he'd messaged his wife.

Robert had put the Gibsons out of his mind for his Friday evening meal with Suzy. He'd listened instead to her worries about *Out of Order*. And now on Saturday morning after Molly and Bex had left for Norbridge and Suzy had gone back to work in the attic, he was sitting at the kitchen table wondering what more he could or should do about Bill. That was when his mobile rang and a strong Australian voice said, 'G'day, cobber.'

'Malcolm. How are you?'

'Ah, you guessed it was me. The word "cobber" never fails.' He laughed.

Robert smiled. Malcolm had a sense of humour. 'What can I do for you?' He felt relieved and somehow cheered by the Australian's call.

'Look, mate,' Malcolm said, 'I'm not a very high-principled person, so I nicked your number out of Bill's old-fashioned contact book in his office. Ruth is up to her neck in making lunch with vegan options and puréed organic vegetable food for the golden grandkid. So she's busy and she's OK, and her daughter's giving her an earful in the kitchen about the stress on their dad. I need to escape. And I wanna talk to you if I can.'

'Me?'

'Yeah. You. I know what you told Ruth about there being some bloody secret about Bill. I'm not asking you to tell me anything you shouldn't. I just want to get a feel for what's going on with the bloke. And maybe add my three ha'porth. There's a nice pub near here called The Partridge. Know it?'

'As a matter of fact, I do. Shall we meet?'

'Good idea. I can walk there. See you in half an hour?'

'Yes, why not?'

Robert called to Suzy that he would be out for an hour or so, and drove over to East Norbridge.

Malcolm was already there. At noon the pub was pleasantly buzzing but not too busy. Tables outside were occupied, but inside it was private in the window nook where Malcolm was nursing a pint. Robert sat down with a half.

'So,' Malcolm said, 'what's Bill been like for the last thirty years?'

'Bill's been a very good, dedicated clergyman. He still is, as far as I can tell. But he's having a crisis now about something which happened in the past. He's a man of strong emotions, I think.'

'You're right there. Bill was, and is, I suppose, very highly principled. Not like me. He was just right for Ruth, she was always like that too. She met him when she was training as a secretary in Manchester. Love at first sight, across the floor at the Christian Students Union.'

'So, they married . . .'

'And they were pleased as Punch when he eventually got the job at St Michael's. She came back home, and Bill and I palled up. Bit of an odd couple as friends — I was more free 'n' easy and he was Mr Conventional.'

'But you were close.'

'I would say that we were. I admit that once Mum died and I could get to Oz, I was so caught up in making arrangements that we didn't talk much, but for some reason Bill had gone cold on me anyway. I've never understood why, and I wondered if you might cast any light. I mean, it's been compounded by him doing a bunk now I'm here. Maybe he thought I was being insensitive over Mum's death.'

'Why would that be?'

'Well, I'd been offered a contract to go and work in Adelaide. I really wanted to go but I had to get over there soon as before my rival. And Mum was on her last legs. She was in a bad state. I wanted it to be all over. If she had lasted a few more weeks I would have missed out on the job. I was broken-hearted that she was dying, but I'd said my goodbyes.'

Robert nodded. He understood.

'Mind you, Bill was in the same boat, only he wouldn't admit it. They were so hard up, him and Ruth, and she was pregnant again so soon. I know he felt the same way. If Mum was going to die it would be better for both of us if she went sooner rather than later. And she was suffering. So, thirty-three years ago this month, she obliged us and passed away. And I could get to pastures new. Sounds heartless, but that's how it was.'

'It's not a crime to want someone's suffering to end. And we're all going to die sometime.'

'Quite right. And at our age, as they say in the outback, we're all in the holding pen!' Malcolm laughed.

But Robert had been thinking about what Malcolm had said. 'Can I just ask you to clarify something? You said your mother died thirty-three years ago this month?'

'Yeah. The fifteenth, to be precise.'

'I don't suppose you can remember what day of the week that was?'

'Yeah I can — it was a Tuesday. Why do you want to know?'

'And was Bill around at the time she died?'

'He gave her Communion early that evening. Not last rites or anything Roman Catholic. Just home Communion. He did it every week, after tea on a Tuesday. She popped her clogs a few hours later.'

'Malcolm, I can't tell you why, but this is really important. Was there anyone else around?'

'I had some friends round. We didn't think Mum was going to go that night. It was a bit of a surprise. Maybe it was the heat that finished her off. It was the hottest day of the year, unusually hot for May. Like now. Anyway, we were drinking in the garden, me and my mates — I think I told you about them.'

'Two who went to uni, one who joined the army?'

'Well, there was Simon Bewdley, for one. Funny chap with one of those hyena-type laughs. And there was Chris. Chris and I went in to the home Communion service with Mum. I wasn't a big believer, but I felt Mum knew I was there, and Chris was into religion.'

'So, they were friends with you and Bill?'

'Not Bill. Bill wasn't one for palling up with the youth. Not like your vicars today. He joined us for a quick glass of wine in the garden. Mum died a few hours after he left.'

Malcolm was wrapped up in his memories. Robert nodded. He didn't want to push too hard. But he was going over it in his head, when Malcom added: 'And I asked Ruthie what sort of rig Bill was driving these days. He always liked wheels, you know. They were his only weakness, and now he's got a Range Rover, eh? Well, Mum's money got him started with nice motors. Yes, Mum going when she did was good for both of us . . . Don't be shocked. I'm just telling it like it is.'

Robert had that odd feeling you get when a wonky lid that won't fit suddenly closes with a couple of smooth twists onto the jar. People talked about pieces of a jigsaw falling into place, but they didn't fall, they slotted — but you had to guide them yourself, and sometimes push a little. This was what was happening now. It wasn't all there, but he felt for the first time that he had the corner pieces of the picture. He needed to go home and think. 'I hope I've helped,' he said.

'Yes, mate, I've appreciated your time. And it got me out of the house. I think after Ruth's family lunch I might take a drive. They say Hiram King the Pommy rewilder has a place near here.'

'Yes, Kirkaber Castle just beyond Langholm on the way to Hawick. He apparently has a beautiful wildflower meadow there. You can see it from the road. He has a lovely estate with one of those small Scottish fake castles. A bit twee but very pretty, I've heard. My wife has been up there.'

'Well I may go up there later and take a look. Thanks again, mate. I can't say I understand Bill much better but at

221

least I know he hasn't been cooking the books or worshipping Satan for thirty years.'

'No, not that.'

'And I feel better about Mum, after talking to you. But neither of us will mention this in the meantime, to anyone, eh?'

'Of course not.' *But we might need to mention it to quite a few people in the long run, if my theory is right*, Robert thought. He wondered how long Malcolm would be around. 'And this is a working holiday for you? How long are you here?'

'I go back in three weeks. Until then, no rest for the wicked.'

Malcolm wasn't wicked, Robert thought. Just painfully, terrifyingly honest.

CHAPTER TWENTY-FOUR

While the king was on his couch, my nard gave forth its fragrance.

Song of Songs 1:12

The school reunion had got off to a better start than Pat could have hoped for. It was well organized, so people who had started school in the same year were put together at tables for coffee when they arrived. The catering was in the basement where the kitchens had been for the chaotic cookery classes. Pat was surprised that only five people from her year had turned up. Some classes had fifteen or twenty old girls. But in a way, having just five alums was better. Pat remembered all of them. One had been a teacher like Pat, one had become a professor, one had been a GP, and one a senior nurse. They all looked good and Pat was glad she'd had her mini makeover.

After they had broken the ice, she asked if anyone had heard from Lorna Duxford.

'Who?' the nurse asked.

'Oh, I remember Lorna,' said the professor. 'Very quiet. Too quiet, I always thought.'

'It's usually the home life,' said the GP. 'Looking back, I think there were one or two in our year who would have been safeguarding cases these days.'

'But not Lorna?' Pat asked, curious.

'Oh, Lorna was well cared for, no doubt about it. But there was something wrong. She was fostered, you know. I don't know what her home life was like originally.'

Pat was stunned. 'Where did she live? I don't think it was in the north end near me.' Pat had been brought up in the leafier Edwardian terraces of Walton Vale.

'I don't know,' the GP said. 'But you could ask Marion from the year below us. I think she was in the same foster home.'

Pat let the conversation swirl around her, smiling and nodding as people and their careers were picked over. There was a tour round the refurbished building, a talk from a prominent former cabinet minister, a buffet working lunch with talks about the school's history, and the inevitable rallying cry to fundraise. There was a quick tea break before the final session, which was going to be an attempt to revive and sing the old school song, long abandoned by modern educators.

At teatime, Pat left her group and went to find Marion from the year below. It was difficult to know what to say.

'Hi, I'm Pat Jones from the year above you. I've been told you might be able to help me trace Lorna — Lorna Duxford.'

The small, red-headed woman turned reluctantly away from her noisy classmates, who were shrieking over memories of playing hockey and having showers in wooden cubicles that were 'alive with verrucas'.

'Oh yes. Poor Lorna. I thought she might be here. I haven't seen her for over forty years.' Marion smiled and looked questioningly at Pat. She wanted to get back to the laughter.

Pat said hesitatingly, 'I understand you were brought up together for a while?'

'Oh yes, just for six months or so. My dad went through a bad patch after my mum died. We didn't have any other relatives so I was short-term fostered. Lovely people. They lived on Princess Lane in Toxteth, in one of those big houses. Lorna lived there for years.'

'I don't suppose you know if she's made any attempt to get in touch — with her foster family, I mean?' It seemed so funny to be saying these words. Throughout the morning and the lunch, so interesting and distracting, Pat had clung on to this new information. She had joined in with the laughter, the reminiscences, had taken in all the information and cheered the former cabinet minister. But all the time, she had been aching to try and pin down Marion, the woman who might know more. Why had Lorna never told her she was fostered?

But it sort of fitted. All that silence and evasion about the past, the love–hate relationship with their hometown. And yet she had been the one to suggest the reunion.

Marion smiled. 'I've never been in touch with Lorna. I wasn't in the foster home long. My dad remarried and I'm one of those lucky people who got on with their stepmum. She was Breda's aunty — Breda's the woman in your year who became a doctor.'

The GP. So that was how she knew Lorna was fostered — because one of her own relatives had been fostered too. Liverpool, a big city, but these days with so many cross-connections. That was what happened when a place became depopulated. The people left behind were the ones with the closest connections and the deepest roots. Pat's own family weren't so different. There had been a network of great-aunts and uncles, then aunts and uncles, who had slowly died off. But there had been strong bonds between them.

'You can't remember which house number on Princess Lane, can you?' Pat asked.

'Number 23. It's still there. No idea who lives there now. It's very smart.'

'Thanks.' Pat was worried that her questions would seem nosy. How could she explain?

There was no need. Marion had turned away and plunged into a lively discussion about whether navy-blue knickers had been compulsory for the sixth form.

Pat didn't wait for the old school song, which was erupting in gales of laughter and conflicting rhythms, and went out through the elegant entrance hall with its curving staircase and scholarship nameboards in gold and black.

She was early at the hotel and used the time to ask reception for a printout of the local area. If she was right, Princess Lane was within walking distance, just outside the Georgian Quarter on the way to Sefton Park.

Her spirits had lifted. It had been a stimulating day, but the important thing was that she no longer felt hopeless about Lorna. She had no illusions about finding her friend at her foster home but she wanted to see it for herself and get a feeling for the sort of childhood Lorna had had. From what Breda, the doctor, had said, the foster home had been good. Marion certainly seemed to have done well there. But why had Lorna been sent there? In the fifties, when Lorna and Pat were children, illegitimate or orphaned children were usually adopted. Fostered children had more complicated lives.

But the fact that there was already one mystery in Lorna's life somehow made the current mystery easier to cope with. Tim arrived early and Pat fell on him with her news. He had news too, of a sort, but he could see this wasn't the time.

'I want to go over there now,' Pat said breathlessly. 'Princess Lane. It's only half a mile away.'

'OK, no problem.'

Pat set off walking briskly past the cathedral on their right, and on into what had once been the area of elegant Victorian villas. Liverpool had been Britain's second most important port when they were built and it was still a grand area, though many of the houses were shabby now.

She didn't want to talk to Tim — what was there to say? But she was glad he was behind her as he tried to keep up. It was a wild goose chase but she just wanted to see . . .

Princess Lane was a broad street lined with plane trees, off the main road. Many of its white stuccoed houses had been converted into flats. Pat easily found number 23, a huge four-storeyed terraced house with a portico and large

226

floor-to-ceiling windows. It hadn't been subdivided. Without allowing herself to think about who might answer it, Pat rang the bell.

The door was answered by one of the most beautiful women Pat had ever seen. She was black, six foot tall, slim as a wand, dressed in blue-and-gold African clothing with a turban. She smiled. 'Hello?'

'Oh.' Pat was taken aback. She was aware of Tim lurking behind, feeling embarrassed. 'I'm so sorry to bother you — this is a completely crazy question, do forgive me — but you don't know anything about a woman who lived here more than forty years ago? Lorna Duxford?'

The woman's smile dissolved into confusion. 'But you're not Lorna?'

'No,' said Pat, suddenly puzzled. 'No, I'm her friend Pat.'

'Pat. Pat Jones?'

'Yes.'

The woman seemed to release inner tension and stood away from the doorway as if to welcome them. 'Oh, thank goodness. I haven't heard from Lorna for over a week. You'd better come in.'

* * *

Becky waved goodbye to Molly, who had been so keen to get into Rafi's car that she had hardly said goodbye. The Fiat spluttered off towards the bypass and the motorway to Glasgow.

Becky mounted her bike and pedalled along the old road past the Lesser Friary and into East Norbridge. She avoided the centre and in ten minutes was out on the other side of the town, heading towards the west coast. In half an hour she had cycled to Pelliter and then on to where her grandad's farm stood on the brow of a hill that sloped down and crumbled into a soft bramble-and-bracken-covered escarpment above the long gritty beaches of the stunning Solway Firth.

Becky didn't want to linger at the farm. Grandad would be out on a Saturday morning, probably getting feed or tackle, or doing the weekly shop. She parked her bike and dashed inside the farmhouse to fetch her gardening shoes and her trowel, which was bigger and heavier than the cheap ones Pat and Lorna had bought with the start-up money from the council. Becky had her own secateurs as well, larger and sharper than the pink ones that Lorna insisted on using so they could be found easily in the ivy. Using Mickey Mouse tools was idiotic and condescending. Sometimes she thought Lorna was idiotic and condescending altogether. But, since their bossy leader had disappeared, Becky missed her. Lorna had been a pain but she got things done.

She stuck her tools in her tote bag and, remembering that it might rain later, she took a parka off a peg in the porch and stuffed it into a bigger backpack. She reorganized her stuff but left Jake's phone bumping away in her baggy tracksuit bottoms.

She slammed the front door, got on her bike and started back down the farm track inland to the road. It would be five minutes to Pelliter, thirty minutes to Norbridge, ten minutes across town and another ten out on the old road. It was a route she knew well, with enough traffic around to make her feel she wasn't alone. In an hour she would be at the Friary, and at the top of the graveyard there were always dog walkers or passers-by. There was also a little convenience store with a coffee machine on the more suburban upper road. She would get herself a cappuccino and enjoy it while she tackled some ivy. It was a nice morning and cool when you were on the bike. She could buy herself a sarnie for lunch as well. This afternoon, if Roxy was back, she might brave it into Norbridge. If they were together, she wouldn't be scared of meeting Jonty McFadden in the town.

Perhaps she should be less scared of him altogether. She would never be free of him unless she tackled her fear of him. She was glad to be out on her own, independent. Being on the bike was like flying.

As Becky turned onto the main road and pedalled along the familiar, comfortably busy road towards Pelliter, with none of the flash cars Jonty favoured anywhere in sight, she was unaware of a black van with filthy number plates which had caught up with her where the farm track met the main road, and was now slowly following her.

* * *

Three hours earlier, at seven in the morning, Jonty had break-fasted with a tired and fractious Hiram. Today was the big day when they would pick up the wolves. The night before, they had sat until three in the morning in Hiram's study, drinking his expensive whisky, and Jonty had slowly turned Hiram from being vexed, apprehensive and wrong-footed, into an exultant, triumphant crusader.

Hiram was easy to twist. He was pathetic. He wanted this rewilding project so much he would believe anything, even though, when Jonty wasn't there, his common sense told him they were taking huge risks. Jonty thought with due satisfaction that his threats to Maggie had paid off, too.

Hiram had surprised him with last-minute doubts. He liked his team to eat together, but it had been rather a fraught communal supper, with Maggie white-faced and thin-lipped.

'Jonty, you know I'm not entirely happy about your trip to Seaforth,' Hiram had said. 'Maggie can't find a vet and I don't really want to go ahead without one.'

'But that would be so cruel. The animals are on their way here. What will happen to the poor creatures if we don't pick them up? It would be tragic to both sides to lose this pair of wolves. And, you know, there's no urgency about a vet, is there? We can get someone next week, can't we? They'll be OK till then. They're going to be in the safe enclosure.'

Jonty had kept his exposure to Hiram to a minimum since the beginning of the week. He had spent a lot of time preparing the icehouse with Seth Beddoes, or servicing the van for the pick-up. He knew that if he let Hiram chat to him, the older man would start talking himself out of the venture. He'd also reckoned that if Hiram had to make the first move, had to find Jonty to tell him to back out of the deal, his pride wouldn't let him. Jonty was a shrewd operator.

Hiram had visibly relaxed. 'Yeah. Good point. We'll get the vet next week.'

'Mind you, it's not like Maggie to fail to deliver,' Jonty had said. 'There must be dozens of vets around here. I'm only sorry I couldn't find someone for you myself, Hiram. I know just about everyone who's anyone in Norbridge, but I wasn't into animals till I went to Spain. I've got someone over there who can do a Zoom next week . . .'

He had a mate all set up to say the right things to Hiram, though of course that wasn't the same as a real vet physically inspecting the animals. But it might keep Hiram happy until the plan worked itself out.

He repeated his criticism of Maggie to make sure the point went home. 'No, it's not like Maggie. She's a brilliant fixer. Usually . . .' He let the word drip out like poison.

'So, what time will you be leaving tomorrow?' Hiram had said irritably. 'I assume the van is all set up?'

'Oh absolutely. I've adapted it inside and there's a very efficient aircon system. The wolves will be drugged when we load them, and I'll get back as fast as I can and get them into the icehouse before they come round. I'll stay with them all night tomorrow. Seth has turned out to be a very good workman. I know you had your doubts, but I'm impressed.'

'How much does he know?'

This was another danger point, but Jonty could effort-lessly defuse it. 'He doesn't know much. He's not very switched on. I think he thinks we're expecting a couple of Dobermans. He doesn't ask many questions. He's still griev-ing, obviously.'

'Hum . . . yeah.'

Better change the subject. Jonty had assumed his wide-eyed role of admiring, perhaps overwhelmed, acolyte. He'd said in an innocent voice full of boyish enthusiasm, 'It's going to be a wonderful day for wildlife in the Borders tomorrow.'

He had waited, wishing Hiram would ask him to sit down and then turn to the decanter. Jonty would know, then, that he'd won him round.

'Oh, Mr King, just think of it,' he continued. 'Our wolves, safely brought to Kirkaber. Once they've started to acclimatize, and of course after the vet has seen them, then we can let them out into the wider enclosure.'

'I don't want the staff seeing them and gossiping to the neighbourhood.' Hiram was still in grumpy A-lister mode, a well-known minefield for those who relied on celebrities for their living. It could go either way.

'But Seth and I have put foliage all over the exterior fencing. Just as you specified, Mr King. Nobody will be able to see what's in the run. We can take as long as we like to get it right. But don't you see?' Jonty had taken a risk and come up to Hiram to put his hand on the older man's sleeve. It was a light, slightly caressing touch, executed by Jonty as if he was totally unaware of its effect, and the shiver that ran through Hiram. 'Our own wolves will be here tomorrow. And then our project will have started. Our project . . .' He'd turned his large, piercing pale blue eyes on to Hiram's small hazel ones. Then just in case he had overdone it, he stepped back. 'Perhaps I'd better get an early night.'

'No!' Hiram had been snared by the touch on the arm. 'No, let's have a drink, Jonty la. And call me Hiram. You're right, I need to man up. No, I know you didn't say that, but that's what you're thinking and you're right. You know, Jonty, sometimes you remind me of my old mate. The one and only late, great Sol Temple. I still miss him, you know.'

Jonty had smiled with childlike charm. 'Crikey, no one has ever said I remind them of Sol Temple!' Although dotty old Hiram had done so at least twice before. And who the hell was Sol Temple anyway? Some dated singer. Prehistoric. A guy Hiram had the hots for, obviously. But the mention of Sol Temple was good news. It meant the danger was over, and Hiram was back on side. 'OK, Hiram,' Jonty had said. 'Just a little snifter. I've got a big drive to do tomorrow.'

'Sit down, meladdo. I was just going over everything, that's all. You've got to be sure in this game.'

'Oh yes, of course,' Jonty had murmured as he'd sat in another huge leather winged chair. As if this were Hiram's game! Daft old git. But if that was what he needed to believe, so be it. Now was time for the bonding blarney. Jonty needed to make sure there was no way out for Hiram King.

They had sat up talking and drinking more and more excitedly until the early hours. When Jonty had come down to breakfast on Saturday morning, Hiram was crabby again, but his irritation seemed to mask excitement and anxiety about the delivery rather than any deeper misgivings.

But Jonty felt like shit. The night's drinking had left him tired and dehydrated, and he wasn't totally confident Hiram wouldn't crack at the last minute. As belt and braces, the day before, Jonty had cornered Maggie in the corridor and given her a little reminder with the cat-skinner knife. If she spoke out of turn to Hiram when Jonty was off in the van, he would do for her.

But he reminded himself that in any case, once he had the wolves and was on the way back, it didn't matter what Maggie said or did. Unless Hiram was going to shop himself to the authorities, he was up to his neck in the project. They were his wolves, paid for by him, picked up in his van. There would be no going back.

Jonty had minimized his contact with anyone else that morning, eaten only a piece of toast, no time for the contents of the great metal chafing dishes in the breakfast room. He left without saying goodbye, about an hour earlier than he needed to.

He needed to warm himself up for action. The guys he was dealing with were serious people and he had to be sharp. He had a few snorts of coke at the ready, in the glove compartment, from Noddy's old stash. After a quick fix, Jonty instantly felt better. A few miles further on he did the same again and felt it racing through his body. But what really put him on his mettle was the thought of having another go at snotty little Becky Dixon. It was six days since he'd intimidated Roxy and he had no idea whether his tactics had affected his uppity little schoolyard pal. He wanted to see her shake till she wet herself.

He was drawn to her in a way he couldn't explain. She was a one-off like he was, but he was jealous of her strength and ability to be unconventional. He should be the special one, the one who broke the mould, not her with her pervy ideas.

It was hardly out of his way to overshoot the motorway turnoff and bowl down the coast to Pelliter. He would park up by the farm. If her bike was there, he might be lucky and could do a little bit of Becky-menacing. That would make him feel good. After that he'd be pumped up for anything and could set off to Liverpool and Seaforth container docks.

CHAPTER TWENTY-FIVE

Dark am I, yet lovely.

Song of Songs 1:5

Robert went over the new facts at his disposal as he drove home to The Briars from the pub. The letter from the person accusing Bill Gibson of sex abuse had been very specific: it had happened on a Tuesday night in May, thirty-three years ago, and the letter writer had included the detail about it being the hottest day of the year so far. They had wanted to pinpoint that one definite night. And what had Malcolm said? That it had been very hot the night his mother had died. Very hot days in May were rare and hot spells did not last as they did in July or August. So, Bill had been accused of inappropriate touching on the same night as he had been giving home Communion to his dying mother-in-law.

He just wouldn't have had time, to put it bluntly. Malcolm had said Bill went to give the sacrament to his mother-in-law every Tuesday after tea. If he had also gone over to the church and tried touching someone up in the vestry, that would take at least an hour out of the timeline.

So why didn't Bill say to Neil Clifford that he had been administering home Communion, and ask his brother-in-law to verify that he had stayed for a chat with Malcolm and his friends? It was a perfect alibi.

What was Bill guilty of? Had Bill been involved in some sort of assisted dying scenario? Was he in league with Malcolm? Malcolm had made it clear that his mother's dying sooner rather than later had been convenient for them both. Was this the crime that was worse than inappropriate touching? But if that touching had never happened, why had the accuser made the allegations?

Robert sat with Suzy over lunch. Neither felt hungry. They talked through what Malcolm had said and what it could mean, until Suzy felt as confused as he was.

'Let's go through this step by step,' she said. 'Someone has accused Bill of something he couldn't possibly have done, and has asked for compensation? Right?'

'Yes.'

'Well, say that person knows what Bill was really up to. Assisted dying, maybe, with or without Malcolm's help. Though I can't see that Malcolm was involved, because why would he talk so openly about it to you? But say one of the friends — this Simon Bewdley with the funny laugh, or the religious one, Chris — was also involved in the assisted dying, but didn't want to be implicated . . .'

'Go on.'

'. . . and now, for whatever reason, that person needs money and wants to blackmail Bill. So, they accuse Bill of something else on that very specific evening, which Bill has to say he did, and the Church, which is richer than Bill, has to pay up. Historic sex abuse in the Church is all over the papers and the Church is doing everything it can now to address it. So maybe the accuser wants free therapy? Or maybe it was Tranquillity doing the blackmailing?'

'But how would she know? The people at the house the night Malcolm's mother died were his two school friends, Simon and Chris.'

'Well, maybe they've been using Tranquillity as a channel. The Church pays for therapy and she passes the money on. Therapy is much more credible than just cash.'

'Yes.' Robert thought about it. 'That fits. But then why did Bill ever say he was innocent? Why didn't he go along with the accuser from the start?'

'Because he didn't put two and two together. The Area Dean throws this accusation at him and his first reaction is "No way, José" — or Hosea, to be a bit more biblical. He denies it and then he's trapped.'

'True. But it looks bad for Bill either way. Inappropriate touching is a terrible mistake. And assisted dying is a crime. Did Bill do it to relieve his mother-in-law of terrible pain? Or to get a car? Surely if it is the latter it's murder. That's the problem, isn't it? The motive?'

'Exactly. Rachel is making a documentary about it. It's a very complicated issue. Is there any sign of Bill?'

'No. Neil Clifford has left me a message to say he's contacted all known retreats in the North trying to find Bill. No luck.'

Suzy toyed with some limp salad. 'By the way, I spoke to Rachel this morning.' She went over the conversation she'd had with her best friend.

'I'd asked her to find out about Sol Temple and Hiram King. Hiram played keyboard in Sol's band when he branched out into a more rock style. It never really worked. Sol was overtaken by events. His soulful acoustic singing from the Bible couldn't compete with Hare Krishna. Lennon had won. Sol had a few minor hits but nothing as big as "Better than Wine". He went downhill, and there were rumours, the usual stuff about blow jobs in the backs of motors and schoolgirls lining up for him, though his star was on the wane. Rachel said Sol Temple was always looking for the love of his life, the woman from the Song of Songs.'

'Our little sister. Beautiful and black.'

'Yes, something like that. Sad really.'

They both sat and felt the warmth from the kitchen window, which overlooked their garden. It was facing north-west and the sun had come round. It really was very hot. Dust motes floated on the air. It was a bit late for a spring clean,

Suzy thought, but she needed to tackle the grimy woodwork. She didn't want to think about it. 'What are you going to do about Bill?' she asked.

'We can only wait. He promised his wife he'd come back. When he does, I'll go and see him. Maybe if he, Malcolm and I talk, we can find out the truth about what happened that night.'

'Good luck with that.' Suzy sighed. It seemed they were getting nowhere. Lorna had gone, and now Bill. Would they ever find out what all this was about? 'I'm going back upstairs to do some more work on this *Out of Order* thing. Then, shall we open a bottle of wine and sit outside? It might be our last chance for a time, if the weather breaks.'

'Good idea.' As he said it, Robert's mobile rang. He picked it up and walked to the window. Suzy heard his side of the conversation, but it meant little.

Robert came back to the table looking thoughtful. 'That was Tim Markham, in Liverpool. He's still waiting for Pat's school reunion to finish and then they're going to try and find where Lorna lived. But he's had an idea and he wants us to follow up on it. It's a bit tricky and I'd like your help.'

'Of course. I'm getting a bit stale sitting upstairs anyway.'

'We need to go out. I'll explain in the car. Get your bag.'

'Where are we going?'

'St Benedict's Hospice.'

* * *

Becky had bought a coffee and walked with her bike to the Lesser Friary. She chained her bike to the railings, grabbed her backpack and gardening bag and, carrying everything at once, struggled down to the church. The big iron key that used to be Lorna's badge of office, and had now passed to Pat, was also in the tote, which banged against her knees. She was making slow progress with the bulky backpack as well, so she took out the big unwieldy parka and put it on, then repacked her tote bag of tools into the backpack. Despite the heat the old parka felt quite good. It smelled of the farm and, although the temperature was now in the high twenties, she liked the feel of the tatty faux fur round the hood. It came down to mid-thigh. She couldn't remember when she had last worn it.

She stood slurping the coffee outside the shady porch of the church and put the empty cup in the small litter bin by the church car park. Some dogwalkers had parked their Prius, and there was a black van with filthy number plates. The local bus went by and stopped outside, letting people off. The top road to the Lesser Friary was a busy spot, with passers-by, unlike the old road at the bottom of the hill, which just had east–west traffic and no pavement, only the grimy layby where the dead woman had been found in the bin.

She slipped the big key into the lock of the church door. She wanted to get inside to pick up the garden waste bag for the ivy she was hoping to uproot.

It didn't unlock — it had been bolted on the inside. Either that or it had been fastened some other way, maybe nailed by the police or the church officials, worried that publicity about the murder might attract vandals. But as she tried again she was sure she heard footsteps ringing on the stone-flagged floor inside.

She backed out of the porch and went around the far side, away from the road. It was much quieter there. There was a rarely used park bench facing the graveyard, under one of the long, narrow arched Gothic windows. She stood on the bench and craned up to try and see in, but the unstained glass was too dusty.

Suddenly someone pulled her off the bench from behind and pressed a knee in her back. A hot hand slapped over her mouth and a rough arm pulled her backwards into the shade of the horrible Tree of Heaven they had planned to uproot. *Ailanthus altissima*. Native of China. Suckers. Grew to thirty feet. Becky said it over again to make her brain work clearly.

She knew it was Jonty, even before he said, 'Hello there, Becky. I told you I'd be back.' He must have followed her.

Maybe he had been hiding out at the farm in Pelliter, waiting for her. She could smell the sweet, almost floral, smell from his runny nostrils. And his voice was slurred. Becky had lived with the fear of Jonty for over six years. She had experienced his strength and brutality before. This time was different, though.

Jonty was clearly on cocaine, but he'd taken too much and instead of making him sharper it was making him sloppy. She had always known this day would come and she had been prepared for a fight, to the death if she had to. But Jonty was overestimating his strength. She could hear his laboured breathing and smell his sweat. Jonty was too high.

Becky moved her jaws against his hand as if squirming, locating the fleshy pads at the base of his fingers, and plunged her teeth in, biting as hard as she could.

Jonty yelped, then laughed and snarled, 'Pathetic. You'll have to try harder.'

She bit again and his grip relaxed, if only slightly. She bucked her back and bottom into his groin and brought her elbows up and out. The movement gained her about two seconds, but she had squirmed slightly to the left and had felt him stumble.

Ahead she could see the two dogwalkers coming up the path. They stopped, unsure what they were seeing. Some rough sex going on? They moved in unspoken agreement that this was something they didn't want to acknowledge.

Things weren't going the way Jonty had expected. He guessed that Becky must weigh less than eight stone and be under five foot three. He had never expected her to be so strong and brave. And he certainly hadn't expected her to know anything about self-defence. The effing internet had a lot to answer for. And now these stupid old codgers were approaching with their cockapoo.

But it didn't matter what they'd seen. He took his hand from her mouth and put his arm around her in a cast-iron embrace. She started to scream so he moved in to kiss her and she bit his lip. There was nothing for it but to bash her face into his shoulder and cart her off to the van. 'Walk!' he yelled.

The dogwalkers were watching them warily. Jonty propelled Becky to the passenger door of the van and threw her inside, slammed the door and raced round to the driver's side. As he tried to get in, Becky flew at him, screaming, scratching and kicking. He flailed her with his arm and strapped the seat belt on as tight as it would go. Then he pulled off his leather belt and fought with Becky to get it round her arms. All the time she screamed incoherently. It was unnerving. He pulled the buckle tight. She was yelling but no one could hear.

The dogwalkers were coming up to their parked Prius, trying not to look at what was going on. Jonty leaped out of the van and hailed them. 'Lovely day, isn't it?' he said. He stooped down and fussed the cockapoo, pulling its ears. The dogwalkers looked suspiciously at him. All this overdone bonhomie was alarming. But Jonty was bursting with hail-fellow-well-met geniality. He knew how charming he could be. No one could suspect a man like him of abducting a girl in his van, especially if he stopped to chat. Masterstroke!

Jonty had no idea how his sweaty face and erratic behaviour came across to the elderly dog owners. But they were swiftly forgotten the moment he returned to the van. Inside Becky was fumbling with her bag for her phone. Jonty flung the door open and reached to grab it. Out came his cat-skinner knife. 'OK, clever arse. I know what you're doing. D'you think I'm stupid? Here you are.' He fished in the bag and pulled out her phone. There was still ten per cent of the charge left.

'So you wanted to text someone? Fat lump Molly Spencer? Great idea. Go ahead.' He flapped his lower arms and laughed raucously. 'Go on. Say this: *I'm fine, Molly, but won't be back till tomorrow.*' He experienced a moment of exhilaration. 'I know what you should add. Say you're meeting your nutter friend in a frock and you're having a sleepover. That sounds nice and girly, doesn't it. Go on, do it.'

With the knife at her throat and Jonty's back blocking the view from the dogwalkers, Becky had no option. She keyed in: *Hi Molls. I'm having a great day and have met up with Roxy. I'm going to stay over with him for a few days. See you soon.*

'Let's see.' Jonty read the message. 'Perfect. Press send.'

He revved the engine. It stalled.

He swore and the repeated F-word calmed him. The van moved off. This would be fun, remember? He had no time now to sort out Becky Dixon, but there would be opportunities later.

He pulled up a few yards down the road, opened his window and threw Becky's phone and backpack into the graveyard. Jonty laughed wildly. He was glad he'd snorted the coke. His confidence was supreme.

Becky sat back. She could see that Jonty was looking wild, his eyes huge and rolling, sweat pouring down his face. His breathing was ragged. She knew what had happened. Jonty had got bad coke, cut with something else. She was surprised. She would have thought he'd have his own top supplier.

Beside her, Jonty was unaware that his pulse was racing and that his eyesight was getting blurred. His driving was erratic, but when they hit the bypass he seemed calmer. He talked to himself, burbling in a random way, not to Becky.

If he stayed on a crazy high, maybe from cut cocaine, Becky suspected he would do something even more stupid than chucking her phone and backpack out of the window, and she could take advantage of that. The trouble was that cocaine left the body quickly. In an hour or two Jonty would come down and then he would feel awful, but he wouldn't make mistakes.

But his sloppiness this time meant that Becky still had Jake's phone in her tracksuit pocket, protected by the long, thick parka. Thank goodness. She could still make contact, if only with Molly. Jonty hadn't even frisked her and obviously hadn't realized she had two phones with her.

She stared out of the window. This time Jonty McFadden had overplayed his hand. She felt a cold, strong strength building inside her. This was going to be Jonty's last go at intimidation. She would get him this time, even if she died trying.

* * *

Tim and Pat sat on the sofa drinking lemon and ginger tea in Maya's spacious, calm, under-furnished drawing room. Maya, now a lawyer, was the daughter of Sid and Joyce Williams, born to them when Joyce was in her mid-forties. Before Maya's birth they had fostered — black, white and mixed-race children. Lorna had been fostered when she was nine, and was sixteen when Maya was born.

Lorna had babysat Maya several times, and had adored her, but left the foster home two years later when she was eighteen and finished school. She'd had no option and neither had Sid and Joyce. Those were the rules.

'It was a difficult system,' Maya told them. 'Children could stay in their foster homes till eighteen but then they had to leave and be self-sufficient. Remember, most teenagers those days went to work at fifteen or sixteen if they were lucky, and paid their mothers rent. Young people today resent the boomers for having it all, but that's a myth. For most working-class kids then it was factories at fifteen or offices or typing pools at sixteen if they were a cut above. And their wages went on their keep. Lorna had nothing to keep her in Liverpool. She left for London, and Sid and Joyce lost touch with her. But a few months ago she made contact with me.'

'How did Lorna find you?' Pat asked.

'I have quite a high profile around here,' Maya said. 'Lorna read about me in the online *Echo*. I think she was quite bitter about having to leave our home when she was eighteen. She said she went to London to do secretarial training. Perhaps got a local authority grant. It was interesting to hear all about living here in the sixties.'

'But why did she get in touch?' Pat prompted, anxious to find out where they stood now.

242

Maya was unhurried. 'She wanted to know if I knew anything about another of Mum and Dad's foster children, Deirdre Murphy. I didn't remember Deirdre at all till she reminded me.'

Pat gasped. 'Deirdre was found dead in Cumbria.'

Maya nodded. 'I know that now. It was covered in the press here. But Lorna contacted me some weeks before Deirdre was found. When I said I couldn't remember her, Lorna went quiet on me. Then two weeks ago she emailed again and said she wanted to come and see me and to introduce me to her friend Pat. You would both be at the Burnely House reunion. I can't tell you, by the way, how proud Sid and Joyce were that Lorna passed the scholarship and got in. They supported her through the sixth form, you know. Not many foster children stayed on at school. Most left their foster homes at sixteen and went into hostels.'

'Lorna must have been lucky.' It was the first time Tim had spoken.

Maya looked at him in surprise. 'You're right. In Liverpool in the sixties only one per cent of women went on to have further education, never mind higher education. Astonishing, isn't it?'

Pat was getting impatient. 'Do you know why Lorna suddenly decided to introduce me to you and talk about her background?'

Maya frowned. 'She said she wanted me and her friend Pat to witness a document. I was hoping to find out more tonight. There was no further communication from her. When you turned up, I thought you must be her! And you say she's gone missing?'

'Yes. We haven't seen her since last Saturday and we have no idea where she is,' said Pat.

Tim stood up. 'Actually we do have an idea. But only an idea. I haven't shared it with Pat yet. But I think that rather than stay in Liverpool tonight, we ought to get back to Norbridge. Time might be of the essence. It's four thirty now. If we get our skates on we can be in Norbridge by about seven. I might be barking up the wrong tree, but I'm expecting a call.'

Maya took their empty cups. 'Well, you must keep me informed. When you find Lorna safe and well, please do come back.'

'I'm sure we will,' said Pat. 'One other thing — what did the foster children call one another? I mean, did they behave as siblings?'

'Oh yes,' said Maya. 'Brothers and sisters. Deirdre was Lorna's little sister.'

Tim and Pat exchanged a glance, thanked Maya and left. She waved to them gracefully from the portico.

'We need to get our bags, check out and get going,' Tim said. 'Even if I'm wrong, with all the information we have now, we need to be back in Cumbria trying to make sense of this.'

'I agree. I think we've got somewhere, but I don't know how it all fits. Suzy Spencer's recording was right. Lorna did recognize the woman in the bin, obviously. It was her little sister.' Pat ran to keep up with Tim's strides. She stumbled and he put out his hand to steady her.

'Oh,' he said. 'You're lighter than I thought!'

'And you're more tactless—' But Pat was breathless and couldn't keep up the argument.

A few seconds later she realized Tim was still holding her hand. He seemed to have forgotten. She gently detached herself. She'd had enough surprises for one afternoon.

CHAPTER TWENTY-SIX

They beat me, they bruised me, they took away my cloak.
                                            Song of Songs 5:7

Molly and Rafi sat in his car where the slip road to Tarnfield
came off the bypass and swiftly dwindled to a quiet country
road. Molly had had an awesome day and hadn't even looked
at her phone. She couldn't wait to tell Becky all about it. The
art tour in itself had been wonderful, then she and Rafi had had
tea and cocktails in a fantastic little bar in Finnieston. She'd
gone to sleep on the way home and when Rafi had slowed
down to come off the motorway she had jumped awake and
asked him anxiously if she'd been dribbling. He had laughed
and said no, she looked as cool as ever. They both knew without saying that they had enjoyed the day equally.

But now she was coming down from cloud nine. She
was supposed to meet Becky on this corner at six o'clock but
it was now quarter past.

She pulled her phone from the bottom of her patchwork
cloth bag, where it had sunk beneath the leaflets, sweets, stupid souvenirs, and arty bits and bobs she had accumulated
during the day. She'd liked the Rennie Macintosh stuff. The
scarf Rafi had bought her was divine.

And she saw a text message from Bex. That was weird — she and Molly always used WhatsApp. She stared at it and read it again. Becky had said she might meet up with Roxy in Norbridge if they were back, and maybe it fitted that Becky might want to stay over. But Molly had been looking forward to spending the evening with her best mate and felt a bit hurt that she had decided to do something else.

On the other hand, it gave her more time with Rafi and that was an intoxicating thought. Molly had an idea. She called Suzy's phone but it went to voicemail. She tried Robert, but he didn't answer either. Maybe both of them were out. She felt the prickle of excitement.

'Raf,' she said, 'I think I might be home alone for a while. Why don't you come down to mine? It would be a lot more comfortable than the car . . .'

Rafi smiled and started the engine.

This was thrilling, Molly thought. Even if Suzy did come back, maybe it was time her mother realized she was an adult and could entertain who she liked in her bedroom. Anyway, the chances were that Suzy would have left a note, old school, saying where she was and when she would be back, and Molly would have at least an hour without maternal interference. She could rely on Robert to leave her to it, if he was around.

But despite it all, she was miffed with Becky and that took the shine off things a little bit. And when she thought about it, there was something odd about that message, something that started to preoccupy her as they drove through the village. Becky might well have met up with Roxy, might even be going to stay overnight, even though Molly had come back especially to be with Becky before she went back to college.

One thing was very confusing, however. Her friend was super pronoun conscious. What on earth had made Becky call Roxy *him*?

* * *

Tim and Pat loaded their cases into the car and drove without speaking through the city centre to the M62, en route to the M6 North.

'OK, we've escaped,' Pat said when they reached the motorway. 'I hope this isn't a stunt to get you out of another evening in my hometown.' *Or my company*, she thought.

'Of course not. I loved it. Especially the Albert Dock. No, we need to be back home. Can you keep my mobile with you? It's in my jacket pocket in the back.'

It felt strangely intimate probing the inside pocket of Tim's jacket for his phone. 'I've got it.'

'When it rings, just press the green symbol. It's a touchscreen.'

'That's very trusting of you.'

'I don't get many calls and none I'd not want you to know about.'

'Oh . . .' Pat was flattered. And a little wary. 'What's all this about, Tim?'

'I'm expecting a call that could tell us where Lorna is.'

'What?'

'Don't say anything, Pat, and don't get your hopes up. I might be totally wrong. Today when I was at the Maritime Museum I saw pictures of hospital ships and I started thinking about quarantine. There was a padre in one picture. And then I thought about something you said — that the Reverend Bill Gibson had been to see Lorna at the Beddoes' last Sunday before she disappeared, but no one had asked him about it.'

'That's right.'

'Yesterday I met Robert Clark by chance at the hospice. He was looking for Bill Gibson. The receptionist said the last time they had seen him was on Thursday, when he'd been to visit someone in a house the hospice uses to put up relatives of sick people who live a long distance away.'

'Where's this going, Tim?'

'Well, the receptionist implied it was a man. But how would they know? It could have been a woman.'

'And you think it might be Lorna?'

'It's a thought, isn't it?' But Tim suddenly felt rather silly. 'Anyway,' he said, 'I thought it might be worth Robert popping over and asking.'

'But wouldn't the hospice know exactly who was staying in their accommodation?'

'Not necessarily. The accommodation is run separately by the Friends of Benny's. It's a different organization. And guess who is Chair of the Friends?'

'Bill Gibson?'

'Correct. I have to say, though—' Tim sounded disappointed — 'I would have thought Robert would have called me back by now. What time is it?'

'Just gone six.'

'Hopefully we'll hear from him soon. I might just be imagining things. If so, I'm sorry about dragging you away.'

'No. It was the right thing to do. Lorna isn't in Liverpool. If she was, she would either have been at the hotel or at Maya's. Cumbria is the most likely place. We still need to get home and find someone who will listen when we tell them that Deirdre was Lorna's sister. Now Deirdre is dead and Lorna is missing, that must mean something.'

'Yes. We need to talk to that PCSO friend of Suzy's. She'll advise us. Anyway, at least we're on our way. I'll just pull in for a pit stop at the services at Burton-in-Kendal. That OK?'

'Fine.' Pat needed a loo break. 'That won't slow us down too much. And maybe Robert will call soon. You know, it's not such a mad idea about Bill taking Lorna to the hospice house. Lorna would trust Bill Gibson with her life.'

* * *

A few hours earlier, slumped against the window of the black van, her arms still constricted by Jonty's leather belt, Becky had realized that Jonty was starting to come down. He'd stopped singing and talking to himself and she could tell he was very cold. Without saying anything he had pulled

248

off the motorway onto a back road near Carnforth and had rummaged behind his seat for a jumper. Then he'd got out of the van and started retching.

Jonty was furious. He was never angry with himself. He was furious with Noddy. How could that fuckwit have had his stash cut with something that didn't agree with people? What the fuck was it?

Jonty could hardly remember the day's events. He felt sick and exhausted. Somewhere around Shap Fell he had begun to think rationally again and realized that he had made a stupid mistake abducting Becky. He could turf her out of the van, but she'd find someone to take pity on her. He could put her out of her misery, but then what? He had no time to deal with a body and anyway, ham-fisted tactics like that weren't his style. And something visceral stopped him from just disposing of Becky. They had a history that needed to be played out and a swift blow to the back of the head wasn't the endgame this time.

He looked at his watch. He was behind schedule now. He'd been driving erratically as sleep had nearly overpowered him. He hadn't averaged the eighty miles an hour on the motorway that he'd planned. He was going to miss the pick-up if he didn't move fast.

When he was back in the van, Becky said, 'I need to pee.'

He said nothing but got out again, came round to her side, heaved her out of the van by the tail of the leather belt and pushed her into the bushes. 'I'm not looking. Go here. And don't tell me to undo the belt. You've got the use of your arms below your elbow. You can manage.'

She did. He pulled her back into the van. He didn't want to speak to her. It was her own effing fault she was here. She should have collapsed in a quivering heap back at that old graveyard. She would just have to stay in the van till the pick-up was done. When he was back at Kirkaber he would truss her up and leave her in the back while he introduced Hiram to his new pets. After that he'd have some fun with her.

He needed to concentrate, though his head was hammering and he had the shakes. But after another ninety minutes he turned onto the M58 West towards Litherland and the Seaforth container depot. He looked at his Rolex. Two o'clock in the afternoon.

Pulling into the superstore car park, he said nothing to Becky and got out and went into the store. He needed to buy some things to get a car parking ticket.

He'd been told exactly where to park. His confederates had said there were no CCTV cameras. The store used detector vans to monitor for non-payers, so if you had a ticket you were OK. No one would see the handover. And even if they did, so what? This wasn't a drugs deal.

When the driver's door slammed behind Jonty, Becky wriggled and braced her feet against the dashboard, but the leather belt didn't slacken and the seat belt kept her constrained. If she could just get to Jake's phone . . .

She had no idea what Jonty was doing or where he was going, but she had seen the signs to the docks and was terrified he might be taking her away on a ferry. She told herself to think logically. There was no luggage in the van. And how would Jonty get her onto a boat without her being discovered? It was a container dock, in any case. The way he was driving against the clock, and the things he had been muttering when high, suggested he was picking something up. She had noticed the fuel gauge — the tank seemed fairly full. She had a feeling this was a round trip.

Jonty came back and went round to the rear of the van. The back doors opened and she felt a rush of air. Jonty was talking in a language she thought was Spanish but there were guttural elements. She had the impression that the two other men, with harsh voices, were the ones in control. Money changed hands and she heard one of the men spit with a great slurping noise.

She lurched sideways and saw in the driving mirror a huge crate being lifted on what must have been a forklift truck into the back of the van. Her first thought was that the crate was very cold, and then that an unpleasant feral smell was emanating from it. The doors slammed.

Jonty sat in the driver's seat, ate a sandwich and drank a can of Red Bull, then gunned the engine and pulled out of the car park, driving far too fast towards the M6 junction back to Cumbria.

Once Becky realized they were going north, she relaxed just enough to lay her head against the window and fall into a fitful, shallow sleep.

She lurched awake with the sound of rain on the window. The weather had changed. The van was cold. Jonty was swearing. Lorries were throwing up sheets of dirty water onto the windscreen. Jonty was using the wipers but they were useless against the mud from the tyres all around them. He kept pressing the washer function but after the first gush, which cleared the windscreen for a few seconds, it dwindled to nothing. It was impossible to see through the driving rain. From the clock on the dashboard, they had made slow progress.

Suddenly Jonty pulled into the inside lane and signalled. They were drawing in to the services at Burton-in-Kendal.

* * *

The rain hadn't reached North Cumbria yet. It was still hot. Everywhere was looking tired. The fresh greenery of May was drooping, and dust rose in little clouds on the edges of the country roads. On the way to St Benedict's, Robert outlined Tim's theory to Suzy.

'But that's ridiculous,' Suzy said. 'A place like St Benedict's would never let a woman be held against her will in a visitors' flat.'

'But it might not be against her will.'

'In which case, why are we going to Norbridge? To spring someone who doesn't want to be sprung?'

'Because Tim asked me to suss it out. And say Lorna *is* there? What's to stop us seeing her and asking if she knows where Bill is? Or what's going on generally?'

'Because the person in that flat has Covid, Robert. If it's Lorna she may be infectious. We won't be able to just pop in.'

'But say the Covid is a cover? OK, I know. Everything you say is right. But in the past you've barked up a lot of wrong trees. Just indulge me.'

Suzy turned tetchily to the window. The glass was baking in the afternoon sun and she felt another hot flush coming on. 'It's so warm in here.'

Robert laughed. 'Yes, I think I'll need to adjust my temperature control, never mind the car's.'

'Oh great, thanks, Robert.' Suzy's face was unnaturally red and sweat was prickling along her hairline. 'How wonderful for you to be able to adjust your thermostat. You know it's impossible for me when I'm having a hot flush! How thoughtless can you be?!'

Robert grimaced. 'Sorry. I know it sounded insensitive.'

'It didn't *sound* insensitive, it *was* insensitive! One day when you're old and immobile I'll prance up and down and tell you how I'm enjoying using my legs.'

Suzy glared out of the window and waited for the horrible tight breathing and the intense internal heat to subside. She felt as if her organs were cooking. This was a ridiculous venture. How on earth could they persuade anyone at the hospice to tell them anything? She took out her phone and put it on mute. She knew nothing about hospices but she imagined they would be hushed, possibly dark or quiet places where you wouldn't want your phone to ring out, particularly one with Suzy's cheery ringtone.

She and Robert didn't speak to each other again until they were inside St Benedict's. She was still cross. But once inside, she instantly felt calmer. The hospice was quite different from what she had expected. There was something about the light and the colour scheme that relaxed her. She reminded herself she was suffering from the menopause, not a fatal illness, and she had a lot to be grateful for. But Robert should think sometimes before he spoke. It was so hard to explain how debilitating hot flushes were. No one could really understand till it happened to them. She could think of nothing comparable for men.

Robert approached the friendly woman on reception, who sat masked up behind a Perspex screen. It wasn't the same person as the day before.

'Hi. I came yesterday looking for Bill Gibson. Is he here today?'

'No, I'm afraid not. He often pops in on a Saturday but not today.'

'I see. I need to find him. I understand you have someone staying in the Friends of Benny's accommodation? Mr Gibson has been visiting them. Could he be there now?'

'Oh, I wouldn't know. Father Bill doesn't have to inform us when he goes there, though I know he's been in and out a lot lately.'

'Do you know who's staying there?'

'No,' the woman said in a voice that implied that if she did, she wouldn't be telling other people. 'Relatives apply to the Friends to stay there. It's not the hospice's property. If it were it would have to be under NHS rules. It's offsite so it's much better if it's organized separately.'

'I see. But when I was here the other day the receptionist referred to a man staying there who has Covid? Or was it a woman?'

The receptionist looked rather wary. 'We really don't get involved. I wouldn't know for sure if it's a man or woman or who it is. But I believe one of the flats in the house is taken at the moment. That's all I can tell you.'

There was nothing more he could ask. He turned rather desperately to Suzy, who was still angry with him, waiting a few feet behind. She came up to the desk. 'I'm so sorry we're pestering you about this,' she said. 'I can see it's not your wheelhouse. It's just that we think a friend of ours may be staying in the flat, marooned with Covid, and we want to contact Mr Gibson to find out.'

The woman nodded, more reassured.

'We'll try another way, but there is one small thing you could do to help us, just so as we don't have to start googling,' Suzy said. 'Do you have a list of who else might be on the committee of the Friends? Then we can go to them . . .'

The receptionist looked relieved. 'Of course. There's Father Bill, our Anglican chaplain as Chair, as you know, and the Deputy Chair is the Area Dean, Neil Clifford—'

'That's fine, no need to go any further.' Suzy beamed at her. 'We know Neil well. We'll talk to him. Thank you so much for your help. You have a lovely manner, dealing with nuisances like us.'

The receptionist smiled. 'There are worse, but I never said that!'

'Thank you so much. And this is such an amazing place.'

Suzy nudged Robert in the back to move. 'We should call Neil,' she said as soon as they were outside.

'Of course. Thanks so much, Suzy. That was a brainwave.'

'Yes. Well, it was luck too. I was sure we would know someone on the board of Friends of Benny's. But it's great that it's Neil.' She paused. 'You know what? It's gone cooler. It's not just me.'

They stood together in the hospice garden and watched the breeze shiver through the purple clematis flowers on the trellises. Robert grasped Suzy's hand. There was a sense of peace. And not only in the garden.

'I'm sorry,' said Robert.

'I know. Now call Neil. He may even have keys to the house. And maybe you're right and we'll find Lorna and Bill having tea together and all will be well. But somehow, I don't think so.'

CHAPTER TWENTY-SEVEN

Let me see your face, let me hear your voice, for your voice is sweet, and your face is comely.

Song of Songs 2:14

At Burton-in-Kendal services Pat and Tim bought some tea. It had started to rain and it became heavier as they queued at the café. It had that unrestrained force of pouring down after a hot spell. It sluiced over the plate-glass windows.

'I'll get some more petrol while we're here,' Tim said.

But Pat wasn't listening. Her phone was ringing and with an anguished voice she said, 'I'd better take this, it's my daughter. I have no idea what it can be about.'

When Tim came back from the till, Pat was looking both furious and stricken. 'I'm so sorry, Tim. I know you want to rush back and try to pull all these threads together, and I appreciate you might have the right theory about Lorna. There's nothing I want more than to see her safe. But Katie has called in a real panic. Steve has had a bad accident with a hedge trimmer. They're at the hospital and she wants me to look after Bobby.'

Tim bit back his disappointment. 'Of course. That comes first. Do you want me to drop you at the Infirmary?'

'No, Katie is bringing my car back to my house, then going back to the hospital in a taxi. I need my car with a child's seat if I'm going to look after Bobby for any length of time. He needs to go to junior football tomorrow morning. There are all these complicated chauffeuring arrangements when you have small children. I'm so sorry this has happened, Tim, just when we were getting near to working out some answers.'

'No problem. I'll drop you off at home. But I'll go to see Robert after that. It's odd that he hasn't phoned.' Tim brightened. 'And maybe we can meet up later when Bobby is in bed?'

'No,' Pat said. Steve's foot injury was nasty and he had lost a lot of blood. 'Let's get in touch tomorrow. You might have found out more by then. I'm desperate to find Lorna, but Bobby needs me. I know you'll do your best. I would have loved to carry on doing this with you tonight. I would have really loved it.' There were tears in her voice.

It's true, thought Tim, *she really has enjoyed being with me. She's torn and she's chosen her daughter and grandson, but that's only right. We can start again tomorrow.*

They ran out to the car under Tim's anorak, another strangely close moment.

'I'll just gas up.' Tim pulled into the petrol station under the garage awning out of the rain. A black van was parked ahead of them outside the shop. While he was filling up and paying, the driver of the van was doing something under the bonnet. When he came out of the shop, the van driver emerged and turfed an empty bottle of windscreen washer fluid into the rubbish bins. He was very young and pale, and looked anxious.

Tim was feeling good for the first time in months or even years. It made him want to say something to lighten the face of the wretched young man. 'Good thought,' Tim said to him pleasantly. 'I must check my washer bottle too. I've forgotten all about it lately, with the heatwave.'

The young man scowled. 'Yeah.' He turned away.

Tim didn't like it when people were boorish, and so he went on, 'Does the rain clear further north, d'you know?'

256

'No I don't. I'm going all the way up to the Borders and this weather is shit. I'm in a hurry.' The lad strode round to the driver's seat.

When Tim got into the car, Pat said, 'That van driver, what did he say?'

'Just that he was going up to the Borders.'

'That's crazy . . . Tim, you'll think I'm mad but I'm sure Becky Dixon was in that van, her face was right up against the window. She was mouthing something.'

'Becky? What would she be doing in a van at Burton-in-Kendal?'

'I don't know. Look, I've got Suzy's number. I'm going to call her. Don't tell me I'm overreacting. I'm sure it was Becky.' Pat punched the number. There was no reply. Pat sat looking at her phone. 'I've got her landline number too,' she said after a minute. 'I got both numbers when we first met up.'

She got through to Suzy's landline voicemail.

'Suzy, it's Pat Jones here. I'm on my way back from Liverpool with Tim. I know this is very odd, but I think I've just seen Becky. She's staying with you, isn't she? I met her and your daughter in the hairdresser's on Friday. But this is very strange, Suzy. I'm sure I've just seen Becky at a service station on the M6. She was in a black van being driven by a rather edgy young man. He's making for the Borders. I hope you don't think I'm fussing, but it didn't look right to me. I've called Becky's phone and it just goes to voicemail. Does Molly know about this? Should Becky be in this van?'

At The Briars, the sound of the landline pealed through the house.

'That's a blast from the past.' Rafi rolled away from Molly's embrace. 'It gave me a quite a shock.'

'Me too.' Molly sat up. 'Bloody hell, Rafi, someone's leaving a message. Listen.'

They sat up, dishevelled on the bed as Pat Jones' dis-embodied voice floated across the landing from the landline phone. Molly shot out of the bedroom door.

'That was a message about Becky. How do you get this bloody thing to play back?'

'My gran uses this all the time,' Rafi said. 'She calls it an ansaphone. Look, you have to press this button.' There was an endless wait as the machine clicked and paused. Then a robot voice said there was one new message. The clicks started again.

'Not exactly intuitive, is it?' Molly snapped.

They listened.

'Oh shit,' Molly groaned. 'Becky said she was going to Roxy's but she used the wrong pronoun. Becky would never do that. I think she did it to tell me something was going wrong. I think Jonty's got her in that van.'

'Well, can you get hold of this Roxy and find out?'

'Yes!' Molly punched the air. Of course. She had Roxy's number.

Roxy answered straight away. 'Who is this, because if it's a spam call, get lost!'

'No way! I'm Becky Dixon's mate Molly. I got your number off her, is she with you?'

'Bex? Nah. I was hopin' to catch up wiv 'er but 'eard nuttin.'

'Oh shit.' Molly's heart lurched. 'She's missing, Roxy.'

'OMG, is it that creep who attacked me?'

'I don't know,' Molly wailed. But she did. Of course, it was that psychopath, Jonty McFadden. And what was he capable of doing to Becky, if he could do what he did to Roxy?

Roxy said in a less affected, more ordinary tone. 'We need to join forces. I'll get a cab over to you — safer than the bus after what happened last time I was waiting at a bus stop. Where d'you live?'

Molly spelled out the address of The Briars.

'Neither of us should be alone on this,' Roxy said. 'Becky is the best friend I've got and you're the best friend she's got. We'll work together and find her before that creep can harm her.'

'Absolutely. And the good news is my boyfriend's here, and he's got a car.'

* * *

Neil Clifford met Suzy and Robert half an hour later in the hospice coffee shop, which was still dispensing good stuff — albeit from a machine — on a Saturday night.

Robert said, 'I think either Bill himself or someone who might help us locate him is staying in the Friends of Benny's house. They've allegedly got Covid, which would keep everyone else away. Can we go and find out?'

Neil had the keys, and they walked there through the rain. Suzy's jeans were soaked round the hem and she was aware her hair was messier than ever, but at least it was cooler.

The Friends of Benny's had raised funds about twenty years earlier to buy a terraced house. It was at the end of the suburban road where the hospice had been the substantial family home of a mill factory manager. Suzy had been reading its history on the boards in the reception area as she waited. The terraced house had been subdivided into two flats for short-term stays for people from the far-flung reaches of North Cumbria and the southern Borders. There was a chunk of information about the Friends and the amazing work they had done, including providing the accommodation.

Neil went through into a hall with stairs up to the second flat and a front door to the right for the ground-floor flat. He knocked on it. There was no answer and when Neil opened the door it was empty. He closed it and went upstairs.

Robert and Suzy followed. He knocked on the door of the first-floor flat. He, Robert and Suzy were all wearing masks, and when the door flew open they instinctively stepped back.

Lorna Duxford said loudly, 'Suzy Spencer, is that you behind that mask? And who the hell is with you? Is Pat there? Where's Father Bill? Things are getting really urgent. We can't go on waiting. I'll get my bag. We've got to get moving.'

'Hold on . . . What do you mean?' Suzy asked.

'What do I mean? Don't you know? Hasn't Bill sent you?'

'No,' Robert said. 'We just guessed you might be here. Should we come in?'

'Come in? I don't think we've got time for that.' Lorna's voice, always carrying, now had the incessant tone of incipient panic. 'I haven't seen anyone since Father Bill's last visit on Thursday morning. I've only had my gardening kit, and thank goodness they have a tumble drier here because I've been reduced to wandering around in my undies while I wash my only set of clothes. I've had two sleepless nights going over everything. Now I need to get to Kevin's as soon as I possibly can. He's in serious danger.'

'Kevin?'

Lorna shook her head pityingly. 'Don't you know? That's the old name for Hiram King.'

'Lorna, I'm sorry, but we're completely at sea here.'

For the second time that afternoon Suzy heard the words 'I'll explain in the car'. Lorna added, 'I assume you've got transport?'

'Well yes, but—'

'There really isn't time to waste. I've had six days in this flat, the last two with no outside contact, and I've figured it all out. I've been waiting for Father Bill, but you will do. Please don't argue. Just take me to wherever it is, Cupcake Castle or whatever.'

Lorna had a packed bag at the ready in the narrow hallway and turned back to grab her gardening anorak off the peg.

Robert turned to Neil. 'You go. You've got to find Bill.'

'Bill? Is he missing too?' Lorna asked. 'I thought he was on the edge of something stupid when I saw him last. But all you need to know is that there's evil on the loose and a lot of people are in danger.'

* * *

In the van, Becky closed her eyes and prayed. Her family had never been churchgoers, but as a teenager Becky had had odd feelings about spirituality. Once before when she had been in danger she had prayed, desperately and sincerely. Of course, she reasoned, people all over the world in terrible circumstances must call on God and get no respite. Why should she be different? Yet at the same time, she had nothing better to do on this long, wet journey to hell, other than to talk to something, anything, outside herself.

She found her prayer wasn't for safety but for strength. When Jonty had turned off the road to the service station she'd thought that if he would only park somewhere with other vehicles, she could mouth out of the window. These days people were much more sensitive to the idea of tricked or trafficked women. She'd thought they might take notice of a desperate girl screaming wordlessly through a van window. She closed her eyes and prayed much more fervently.

When Jonty had parked outside the shop and gone in for the washer fluid, she had plastered her face to the glass. She'd had no idea if anyone could see her with the rain and the height of the van, but she'd yelled, 'Help me! Help me!' The sound of her own screeching voice had frightened her more than anything.

Then Jonty was back in the cab and silently driving on, eating a pasty with messy flaky pastry spraying around the driver's seat. The crumbs annoyed him and he kept dusting himself down. Becky guessed he had the munchies and had grabbed the first food he could find at the shop. He was normally so fastidious in that picky, creepy way.

After a few miles of silent prayer, Becky said, 'I need to pee again.'

Jonty was beyond talking to her. He was driving head down, into the rain. He took the next turning and hardly yards from the motorway drove onto the verge, got out of the van and swung round to her side. It was the same procedure with the end of the belt.

As he turned away from Becky, his phone rang. He swore and jammed the end of the belt into a cleft in the scrawny branches of a stunted shrub. 'Just get on with it!'

Becky tried to listen at the same time as working her tracksuit trousers down, feeling for Jake's phone. Jonty's usual cool, arrogant tone had become fraught and angry. 'I'm on my effin' way back, I tell you,' he snarled — twice. Then he walked a few yards off.

She grabbed the opportunity. She was as quick with mobiles as he was. She found Molly's number, texted: *Kirkaber Castle* and pressed send. As Jonty turned back she dropped Jake's phone and kicked it away into the bushes. Jonty mustn't find it, so it was better abandoned. He wasn't going to start scrabbling around in the undergrowth where she'd peed, just to check.

It had been her one chance and she had taken it.

* * *

When Roxy had turned up at The Briars, Molly was waiting and ready to go, in her floral retro catsuit, but with her huge plastic mac over it and giant sparkly trainers. So practical for a wild goose chase.

'I've had a message from someone who's seen Becky in a van going up to the Borders, one of her gardening group. I know Jonty is working up there for that TV gardening bloke, but I don't know where it is.'

'Bummer,' said Roxy. 'Look, let's get on the road and you can google that gardening celeb. His website might say where he's based. Or you can try and get in touch with someone who might know. Ring that woman back who called you.'

But at that moment, Molly's phone lit up. So did her face.

'It's from Becky. It just says Kirkaber Castle — so Jonty's taking her there.'

* * *

Pat arrived at her cottage in Norbridge at almost the same time as her daughter.

'There you are, Mum. Where have you been?'

'Liverpool, I told you, my school reunion. I wasn't supposed to be coming home till tomorrow but we left early—'

'Mum, I haven't time to talk. Bobby's in the car. He knows about Steve, and he's upset but it's his bedtime in an hour or so. I don't know if he'll settle. He's wide awake. Look, Mum, I need to get back to the hospital. I've ordered a cab and it's already here at the end of the road. I'll keep you posted — remember it's junior football tomorrow morning.'

Pat opened the car and smiled at Bobby.

'I don't want to go to football!' came a high-pitched voice from the back of the car.

'Oh, I can't handle this!' said Katie. 'Steve's having an operation. He's not in a good place. I have to go. Bobby will be fine with you.' She turned and ran through the rain towards her waiting cab.

Pat poked her head through her car's open window. 'Hello, Bobby! You need to come into Grandma's house, out of the rain.'

'I don't want to. I want to see the doggies.'

'Not tonight,' Pat said. 'Do you need the toilet? Have you had your tea?'

'I've got my meal deal bag. And I don't need the toilet. I want to go and see the dogs. My daddy's had an accident but he's going to be OK and I've been very good indeed and Mummy promised me a treat.'

'Yes, but not now.'

'Now!'

Tim had been watching. 'Pat, leave him in the car. He's had a shock and a bad afternoon. I've had to deal with kids who've had this sort of fright a thousand times. I'll get in the back with him and you can drive us to Kirkaber Castle. At least it will probably get Bobby off to sleep. And we might be able to help Becky. Why not?'

Pat thought of the option. Trying to placate a disturbed and frightened child with the self-will of Napoleon was a worrying thought.

'OK,' she said. 'I'll drive. You navigate, watch the phone and keep Bobby happy.'

Tim climbed into the back of the car. 'Hello, young man. Gran is going to drive you to see a castle and then we'll come home, safe and cosy. My name's Tim and I was a paramedic. I used to drive an ambulance. So I know your daddy's going to be fine.'

'Mummy said he was stupid to cut his foot with the hedge trimmer.'

'Well, accidents happen. Look, here's my ambulance.' Tim showed Bobby an image on his phone.

'Daddy went in one like that,' Bobby said. 'Do you drive one?'

'I certainly did,' said Tim. 'Very fast with a blue light on.'

Bobby thought about it. 'How many ambulances are there? One, two . . .'

They had reached 100 by the time Pat was out of Norbridge and on the road north.

CHAPTER TWENTY-EIGHT

Whither has your beloved turned, that we may seek him with you?

Song of Songs 6:1

Lorna sat in the back of Robert's car with her eyes closed as they wound out of Norbridge and north towards Langholm.

'Well, she's got her mojo back,' Robert whispered.

'I wonder if she knows about Tranquillity's death?' Suzy said.

'I heard that,' said Lorna. 'I have excellent hearing. I do have my mojo back, thank you. And I do know about Tranquillity. I was very shocked. But when I came to think things through, it was inevitable. Whoever killed Deirdre probably needed to get rid of Tranquillity too.'

'So you think Tranquillity was murdered?' Suzy asked.

'Absolutely. But the first thing I want to do is apologize for going to pieces. It's not like me, at least not like me as I am now. I had a very difficult early childhood with alcoholic parents, and I lived under constant strain. In later life I managed to come to terms with it, but I'm afraid on rare occasions I do suffer from panic and a sort of catatonia.

Anyway, it never lasts and now I'm back to normal. Poor Pat. She must have been going crazy with worry.'

'She was. But Tranquillity told her you'd gone home, and you seemed to have disappeared without trace.'

'Ah.' Lorna nodded. 'Tranquillity promised to contact Pat for me. Ha bloody ha. I'm afraid that like a lot of people I was taken in by our spiritual psychotherapist.'

'You and me both,' Suzy said. 'But can you tell us why we're driving hell for leather to Hiram King's castle through a torrential rainstorm?'

'Because someone wants to hurt Hiram by blackmailing him. The blackmailer killed Tranquillity, and would have killed me if I hadn't been in hiding. And Hiram's still in danger, I'm sure of it. I'll explain once we've made sure Hiram is safe.'

Lorna put her head back on the car seat and her jaw went slack with instant sleep. She was deeply exhausted.

'Did you hear that?' Suzy said.

Robert nodded. 'I must say, it's a hell of a story. Who could the blackmailer be? They would need to be of a certain age.'

'Not necessarily. They might just have had access to Hiram's past. It could well be Jonty McFadden. He's probably wormed his way well in.'

'Or Maggie Chiltern? She knows everything about Hiram, or so you say.'

'What about Seth Beddoes? Right age group, but his brains are shot to hell. And would he kill his own wife?' She paused. 'Or Father Bill? I hate to say it, but he fits the picture in every way and he's gone to ground. He could easily have been stringing Lorna along.'

'Well then, what about Malcolm, Bill's brother-in-law? Suddenly turning up from Oz? And he's shown a lot of interest in visiting Kirkaber Castle. Today, in fact. And there's the black Range Rover seen on the road where Tranquillity died. Everyone has one. Father Bill, though it's a classy car for a priest. Malcolm had hired one. Jonty drove Hiram's. Phil Dixon has one. And Tim Markham . . .'

'True. But what shall we do when we get to Elsinore?'

'What any visitor would do. Knock at the door and ask for Hiram.'

* * *

Pat and Tim were ahead of Suzy and Robert on the A7. It was still raining heavily. Bobby had eaten some of his meal deal and nodded off holding Tim's hand. Tim had made up a story about Amber the Ambulance, which had Bobby giggling. Once the child was asleep Tim used the satnav on his phone. The A7 was very quiet and the country roads were less alarming than Pat had feared. By seven thirty they had reached the imposing metal gates to Kirkaber Castle, and they were open.

Pat realized why. Up ahead, just parking, was the black van they had seen on the M6. It had made slower progress than their car. Pat turned in straight away, then hung back for a minute as a man got out of the van and another man met him.

'What do we do now?' Pat said.

'When they move away, we'll go up the drive, park and I'll see if Becky's still in the van. If not, I'll go and bang on the castle door.'

'What about Bobby?'

'He's absolutely out of it. The best thing is to let him sleep. I'll loosen his car seat straps so he's more comfortable. You should stay with him while I do the looking around.'

There was a vast amount of space in the car park in front of the castle. Pat felt as if her little car would hardly be noticed parked next to the other Volkswagens and Renaults, presumably belonging to the staff. Tim climbed out and went to look at the van.

He came back. 'It's too dark to see clearly inside but I think there's some massive box in the back. I can't see Becky, but there's what looks like bags on the front seat. She could be slumped there or she could have been taken out—'

'Get in the car, Tim, someone's coming.'

Pat opened the passenger door silently and Tim slipped inside. It was hard to see in the dusk, through the rain, but the two men had come round from behind the castle carrying a ramp and wheeling a flat trolley. They approached the van, opened the back doors and put the ramp in place. Between them they slid the weight of the crate down

One of the figures went to the passenger door of the van, pulled it open and dragged out a bundle. When he flung it over his shoulder they could see it might be Becky's slight figure. They started to move off, slowly pulling the trolley.

'I'm going after them,' Tim said.

As he opened the car door, Pat could smell the cold, clean smell of freshly soaked vegetation. If it hadn't been such a sinister scene, the smell of wet woodland would have been intoxicating.

Suddenly there was a pounding shower of rain like a timpani crescendo on the car roof. Pat glanced at the sleeping child and grabbed the anorak Tim had left on the front seat. He would be drenched.

She left the car and ran towards Tim. Her own anorak hood kept slipping down and she stumbled in the wet. She was just yards behind Tim, but when she caught up with him he had turned the corner towards the back of the castle.

She needed to get back to Bobby. 'Tim! Your anorak!'

He held his hand out and the path lit up in a brilliant beam.

He pushed her into the undergrowth. 'Security lighting. Get into this shed doorway.'

Pat was wet through herself now and needed to go back to the car. She followed Tim into what looked like an old Anderson shelter, presumably a garden shed. She needed to get her breath back, fix her hood, and go. If Bobby woke and found himself alone in a dark car, all the good work Tim had done reassuring him would be wasted.

She stumbled over a bag at the door of the shed. The bag groaned.

'Becky!' Tim pulled her to her feet.

She was gagged with a rough piece of cloth. In the eerie silence Pat realized they were in a low-lighted passageway leading to a large domed building. Beneath the dome was a cage of metal mesh fences. The crate from the van was on its side, and in the middle of the cage were two huge animals. One staggered drunkenly to its feet.

'Wolves?' Pat mouthed in astonishment.

Becky nodded again. Her arms were constrained by a leather belt pulled around her shoulders. Pat started to work at the buckle.

The belt slipped off. Becky flexed her shoulders but left the gag in place. Her wide eyes warned Pat and Tim not to speak.

They could hear the two men talking. But there was a third voice too. It was the unmistakeable sound of Hiram King, national treasure. His voice was high-pitched with vexation. 'But this isn't right, Jonty.'

'No, it isn't. You've fucked up, Jonty, mate.' The other voice was deep, authoritative, with a twang Pat couldn't place. 'First of all you bring a girl along for the ride and then you get the wrong sort of wolves—'

'You wanted wolves and I've got you wolves.' For the first time Becky heard nervousness. She knew at once that this was the person Jonty had been talking to on the phone. The real boss.

The strong voice said, 'You were supposed to get a healthy pair of Iberian wolves. These are Mackenzie Valley wolves from the US. Bigger, fiercer. More dangerous.'

'I thought that was what you wanted! It was your scheme. Get wolves that would attack Hiram. I went for the most aggressive I could get.'

'What?' Hiram shrieked.

The bigger wolf followed the noise with its snout. The unknown man said, 'We didn't need gigantic beasts from the Arctic Circle. I suppose they're hungry?'

'Fucking starvin', mate.' Jonty sounded more confident.

'What are you talking about?' Hiram's voice was an octave higher.

'It's all part of the boss's plan,' Jonty said, triumphantly. 'We're going to feed you to the wolves. Literally. You're no use to us dead. But tragically injured and dependent on your faithful servants . . . well, now we're talking. And if you don't pay out, we've got all sorts we can pin on you. Trafficking girls for your old mate. Very topical, eh? Murder? Why not? So long as you do what the boss says . . .'

'But you don't remember me, do you Hiram?' said the other man. 'There were so many hangers-on, fawning on you and your bestie sickly Sol that you didn't have time for the workers. I was your roadie for a couple of months but to you I didn't even exist. How times change! Now you'll be managed like never before.'

Jonty cackled. 'And we'll manage your money too. That's for us. Right, boss?'

'Wrong,' said the other voice. 'There is no us.'

There was a yelp from Jonty and a sickening crack. Something heavy fell to the floor.

'Oh my God!' Hiram was screaming. 'You've killed him!'

'Yep.' The voice sounded perfectly calm. 'He'd become a liability and I've had to improvise a bit tonight. Fortunately, I can kill when I need to. I'm trained for it. I killed Dee Dee first. Stupid cow was going to let you off the hook and wreck my dodge. Then I killed the gorgeous Tranquillity. She was a cow as well. She thought she could get one over on me and she treated me like dirt. The next big-headed bitch to cop it will be Lorna Duxford when I find her. So be warned, Hiram. And don't worry about the bodies. I have plans. Now it's your turn. Just a smear of sheep's blood to whet their appetites.'

'Oh no, please . . .'

'It's going to hurt a bit. But like Jonty said, bless his cotton socks, we don't need you dead. Just dead scared. So, talking of socks, I'm going to stick your legs through the netting, so the wolves only get to nibble your toes.'

Hiram screams turned into whimpers.

270

The calm, authoritative voice went on, 'Good job Jonty got some butchering done with his sheep-worrying lark. You never guessed, did you? We've a freezer full of this stuff. The smell should get them going. Now, the noise is rousing the beasts, Hiram, and they're going to come and start sniffing around you. Don't worry, you'll just be injured through your own stupidity. No doubt Maggie will have a doctor on call for you.'

Pat was aware of what he was saying but it was a jumble in her head. She had to get back to Bobby. Hiram was alternately whimpering and screaming at the other end of the building, beyond the dome. Tim was a few feet ahead of her and must have heard everything too. Becky had slumped when Jonty's body had fallen to the ground.

While Hiram and the boss man moved towards the door at the rear of the icehouse, Pat stumbled through the front into the open. At that moment a yell sounded from the other end of the building. Hiram was screaming, 'You fool! They're out! These bloody useless cages won't hold big animals like this. They're getting out!'

Pat didn't care about the security lights. She raced back around the castle towards her car. It was raining more softly now, and for a moment she smelled the potent tang of the wet pine trees. But then something, perhaps the overwhelming sense of the looming forest and the wild fells, made her stop and turn round.

The wolves were out in the grounds. She had a confused idea they were supposed to attack Hiram but that hadn't happened. They must have passed him and made for the smell of the forest and freedom.

Up ahead her car door was open. Bobby's tiny figure in his pyjamas and slippers was standing by the car door.

'Doggies!' he shouted joyfully. 'Hello, big doggies!'

Pat stood stock still. The wolves looked at Bobby curiously. The smaller one lifted its muzzle and bayed softly into the trees. To Pat, the animals still seemed dazed. She had to get to Bobby before they did.

A shot cracked through the air. The bigger wolf jumped and skittered away from the little boy. It lurched towards a dark figure standing on the other side of the car park, holding what looked like a rifle. The smaller wolf followed. It stopped, confused.

Pat had a sense the wolves were more frightened than she was. Behind them, she moved very slowly to Bobby, who was watching, transfixed. Within seconds she had his small, damp body in her arms and threw him into the back seat of the car.

'Grandma!' Bobby was outraged.

'The doggies need to go to bed, darling.'

'They were big, really big. I loved them, Gran. Thank you!' Bobby's eyes were round and wide in the darkness. 'Can I have my juice?'

Crack. The big wolf had collapsed and now its mate fell too.

The shooter strode down the path towards Tim and Becky, who'd followed Pat from the icehouse to the car park. Two men appeared from around the back, heading for the van. One was dragging the stumbling form of the other. The weaker man was obviously Hiram, in his designer over trousers, boots and chic outdoor jacket. The man behind him was massive.

The shooter came towards them. 'Simon!' he yelled at the big man shoving Hiram along. 'Stop, Simon! Let go of him!'

'Malcolm!' said the big guy. 'Well, fuck me. After all these years.'

Tim realized dimly in the chaos that the man who had Hiram King in his grasp had to be Seth Beddoes — but a different Seth, taut, fit, strong. Still huge but not shambling. Focused.

The whole scene was surreal. It was being played out not only under the security lights, Tim noticed, but the lights of a car in the drive. An old Fiat had stopped, blocking the exit, the engine still running, while the people got out to see what was going on.

There were three people, looking phantasmagorical in the gloom. One was a slight figure with long curls, and a floppy hat with an oversized brim. Then there was a girl in chunky trainers, a crazy catsuit and a great shining raincoat, with flowers in her hair. And there was a slim, dark figure, who put his arm protectively around the girl. Molly, Roxy and Rafi had arrived. They were walking up the drive, bemused. Molly suddenly shouted, 'Becky! Becky, we're here!'

There was the sound of a shot and a roar from Seth Beddoes. He dropped Hiram like a bag of rubbish and ran for the drive, brandishing what looked like a club and shrieking like a banshee. The shooter was taking aim again. The three figures pressed back into the verge as Seth ran past, into the open door of Rafi's car.

'Hey!' Rafi made to run after him but it was too late. Seth accelerated, swung the car around and drove off into the night.

'You'd better phone the police,' said an Australian voice to Tim. 'If I use my phone, it all goes via Oz. Oh, Maggie! What took you so long?'

Maggie Chiltern had emerged from the front door of the castle, wearing a dressing gown. She ran down the steps under a massive golf umbrella.

'I was staying out of your way as agreed,' she said. 'What's happened?'

'It's OK now, but you were right. Those animals shouldn't be here. I brought the stun dart and managed to sedate them. They won't come to any harm. But I'd like to get them back into shelter and look them over. I wasted one dart on that piece of shit who was trying to hold your boss hostage and I haven't another so we need to get them properly caged now. And by the way, your man isn't feeling too great either.'

'Hiram!' Maggie ran up to the staggering figure. 'Are you all right?'

'Yeah. No. I don't know. Oh, Maggie, it's been horrendous. Oh my God, what did I unleash? I've been through hell. And Jonty McFadden, treacherous little creep, is dead in the icehouse.'

'What? Has someone rung the police?'

'Me,' said Tim.

'And who are you?' asked Maggie. 'Oh, never mind. You'd better all come in, don't you think, Hiram? You too, Malcolm, as soon as you've got the animals safe.'

Pat had ventured out of the car with Bobby in her arms.

'And there's a little boy here too,' said Maggie. 'I can see we've all got some talking to do. Come into the castle and our housekeeper will make hot drinks. We'd better all stay put till the police come. Hiram, you're in a state.' She put her arms round her boss's slim figure and lurched along with him back towards the castle.

CHAPTER TWENTY-NINE

No wonder the maidens love you!

Song of Songs 1:3

Robert and Suzy were nearly in Kirkaber when an old Fiat passed them in the opposite direction. It was going so fast and so erratically that they pulled over to give it clearance. It veered off onto one of the back roads.

'If I didn't know better I would say that looked like Rafi Hossein's old banger,' said Robert.

'I know!' Suzy smiled. 'I wouldn't have thought there'd be two like that in a fifty-mile radius! That reminds me, I must call Molly and tell her we'll be home late. At least it's good to know she's with Becky and they're both safe at The Briars.'

'I'm not so sure about that.' Robert had turned into the open gates of Kirkaber Castle, his headlights catching Molly, Rafi, Roxy and Becky in a stumbling, crying group hug. Molly broke away and waved their car down.

She thrust her head through Robert's open window. 'Mum! Robert! Why are you here? You won't believe what's been going on. We're all going up to the castle.'

In the back of the car, Lorna Duxford suddenly woke. 'We have to see Hiram King,' she shouted to Molly.

'The telly bloke? Join the queue.'

* * *

In the castle, after a quick slurp of Lagavulin, Hiram was recovering. He had been shaking uncontrollably, but was never more alert than when in a drama, especially when it revolved around him. Maggie had provided him with his thick tartan dressing gown and moccasins as he prepared to meet his unexpected guests.

In the baronial drawing room, Pat sat with Bobby on her knee and the housekeeper's gentle old Labrador at their feet. Bobby was entranced. 'He thinks he's in the castle from *Frozen*,' Pat murmured to Tim.

Lorna appeared at the door and rushed over to them.

'Lorna! Oh, thank God you're OK!' Pat cried.

'Yes, now I am. Oh, Pat, where have you been?' The two women embraced, and Pat felt the tears come.

'Is Hiram safe?' Lorna asked.

Hiram chose that moment for his grand entrance. 'Yes, I'm safe.' He walked over to her. He was paper white and his eyes shone unnaturally, but he was keeping himself calm. 'You don't look any older,' he said. 'Please don't say the same to me. I have been through a day like no other. I have aged twenty years. I don't know if I will ever get over it.' He rolled his eyes dramatically while sinking into a winged chair, nursing his glass of whisky.

'Oh, Kevin—'

'Hiram, please.'

Suzy Spencer suddenly went into media-producer mode. 'Hey, listen up everyone. Can we all explain one by one why we're here?'

'Starting with me,' said a voice from the doorway.

They all stared at Malcolm in his jeans, stockinged feet and army-surplus sweater.

He took the floor. 'The most important thing is that the animals are OK.'

'Well, thank you,' said Hiram waspishly, but the Australian ignored him.

'You need to know, everyone, that I'm a vet. That's why I'm here,' Malcolm said.

'What's that got to do with anything?' Lorna snapped. 'Hiram needs to know he's in danger from a vicious blackmailer.'

'Hold your horses,' said Malcolm. 'You need to hear the whole story. My name is Malcolm Scott. I'm back in Britain on a work project and to visit my sister and brother-in-law, Ruth and Bill Gibson. By the way, he's also gone missing—'

'I know where Bill is.' Becky's voice sounded cracked and hoarse. 'I'm pretty sure he's in the Lesser Friary. There was someone in there when I went over this afternoon.' It seemed like a year ago rather than a few hours.

'I'll call Neil Clifford,' Robert said. 'He needs to know this. He'll go and check.'

'Now let me explain what I'm doing here,' said Malcolm. 'I'm from Norbridge but emigrated to Australia over thirty years ago. I'm a vet and a wallaby expert. They have feral wallabies on Loch Lomond, surprisingly. I'm doing some work for the Scottish Wild Animals Trust, and I needed to get hold of a wallaby to test for disease.'

'So that's why you had the dart gun?' said Tim.

'Yes. Medetomidine. I fired a dart at Simon when he was holding Hiram hostage, and he realized he was cornered, panicked and ran. He literally didn't know what had hit him. He must have thought it was a bullet. But it wouldn't have had too great an effect — it was meant for the wallabies.'

'I think you'd better explain the whole story,' said Suzy. 'If you were in Scotland to check out feral wallabies, how come you ended up sedating wolves in the Borders?'

'It's straightforward really,' Malcolm said. 'I set out for Loch Lomond today but I'd read about Hiram King, so I thought I'd take a look at his place on the way. I turned up, met Ms Chiltern and told her I was a vet.'

'A visiting vet who knew about wild animals was a gift!' said Maggie. 'I was unhappy about the whole wolf venture. Sorry for going behind your back, Hiram, but I asked Malcolm to look around at the provision for the animals.'

'I could see it was a terrible set-up,' Malcolm said. 'The cages were very sloppily built. They would be hard put to hold Iberian wolves never mind the Mackenzie Valley species.'

Maggie huffed. 'Seth was always a useless workman.'

'But while I was here in the afternoon, something strange happened,' Malcolm went on. 'The man you called Seth was sitting on a stone on the hill, having a break. He had his hair swept back, and he looked fit and tough. And he laughed. So pleased with himself. It was the laugh that made me realize I knew him, even with the extra beef. It was Simon Bewdley, my one-time friend, who joined the army and went to the bad. I made up my mind then to come back in the evening to see the animals.'

'Seth Beddoes,' said Lorna. 'Of course. It was Seth, wasn't it, who was blackmailing Hiram? That's where I come in.'

'And we know how,' said Pat. 'We met Maya in Liverpool. The dead woman at the graveyard was your little sister.'

'What? How could that be?' asked Suzy.

'I know,' said Lorna. 'She was black and I'm white. But Maya's parents were my lovely foster parents. Mine and Deirdre's. Yes, Deirdre and I were brought up as sisters. I'd met Kevin McMurran, Hiram King, at a coffee bar in town. He was up from London where he worked in the music scene. We palled up — just friends, you know — and when the fostering rules meant I had to leave Sid and Joyce, he invited me to go back with him. I was just a mousey thing till I met Hiram.'

'And you went to London and found your feet?' Suzy said.

'Absolutely. But Deirdre was only fourteen. She begged to go with me. I said no, but she followed me. We were both Sol Temple groupies. But I'm afraid he was like a moth to a candle with her. He was obsessed with her and called her his little sister, like I did. It chimed with all that Song of Songs stuff he liked so much. But he never touched her. Then the drink and drugs got to him and he died in that drowning accident. After that, Hiram just disappeared from our lives and the next time I saw him was on TV as a gardener! And eventually Deirdre and I lost touch. She'd been seduced by the music scene, literally, and she only knew one way to support her lifestyle . . . I didn't hear from her for years.'

'Until a few months ago,' said Pat.

'Yes! Deirdre wrote to me saying someone from the old days had been in touch. She wouldn't tell me who. At that stage they were in it together. Everyone was talking about MeToo and sex abuse. It was rife in the pop business. I realize now that this person must have been Seth. He suggested to Deirdre that she should accuse Hiram of pimping her to Sol Temple. Then Hiram could be blackmailed. I was horrified.'

'What did you do?'

'I persuaded her not to. I said there was no evidence and it was a wicked scheme. Deirdre went quiet on me, and then about six weeks ago she called me to say she had thought things over, and she agreed with me. Despite the rumours, Sol Temple never touched her. Other people, later, but not Sol. She told me who the man behind their blackmailing scam was, but the name Simon Bewdley meant nothing to me. Anyway, I suggested that she sign a statement saying Hiram and Sol were innocent of wrongdoing. I would arrange to witness it when Pat and I were in Liverpool for the school reunion, and I'd get a copy to Kevin just in case the man who was putting Deirdre up to it tried again. I wanted two witnesses and I thought of Pat and Maya, my foster parents' biological daughter.'

'So it was a horrific shock when you saw Deirdre was dead.'

'Unbelievable. I was stupid enough to call her name out, and Seth Beddoes heard me. He came to Pat's that night and suggested I went to stay with him and Tranquillity. He said he had heard me call out Deirdre's name and that could mean I was in danger from the killer. I didn't think it through, I just went. I told Tranquillity everything. She is — was — so compelling.'

'You can say that again,' Suzy said. 'So what was Tranquillity up to?'

'It was all my fault. After I told Tranquillity everything, I think she saw a chance to blackmail Hiram herself. I'm sure she had no idea that Seth was already up to the same thing. I think, looking back at the way Tranquillity behaved to Seth, he was probably seething at being treated like a big toddler. He'd got hold of Deirdre independently and thought up his scam for blackmailing Hiram, but that was his own game and he didn't want Tranquillity muscling in, especially as she treated him like an idiot and didn't tell him. But I spoiled it all. I told Tranquillity that, far from accusing Hiram, Deirdre was going to exonerate him, but Tranquillity didn't want to hear that. Tranquillity never knew who had killed Deirdre, but she could put Hiram in the frame and get paid to keep quiet. But for that to work, she needed me out of the way until she'd extorted a hefty blackmail payment. So, she got Father Bill to give her the keys to the hospice house, saying a murderer was after me. And she locked me in with a supply of ready meals and washing powder. I thought she was saving my life!'

'Well, she saved you from Seth,' Suzy said. 'And you went off happily into hiding.'

'Yes. Tranquillity told me she would explain it all to Pat. But, of course, she didn't. When I got to the flat I realized I didn't have my phone — now I think Tranquillity must have taken it.'

Suzy turned to Hiram. 'So, both Tranquillity and Seth were going to blackmail you separately? Great minds thinking alike, but she didn't know it?'

Hiram shut his eyes. 'I didn't know about Seth,' he murmured. 'Simon as was. But Tranquillity had already started. She said she knew something from my past and everyone would believe her, not me. She made me employ Seth, ironically, which got him back to Kirkaber again with his horrible little accomplice, Jonty McFadden. They were thick as thieves already. They must have first met when Seth was building the kitchen garden wall and identified each other as psychopathic blackmailing bastards.'

'But if Seth Beddoes knew you from your past, Hiram, how come you didn't recognize him?' asked Suzy.

'Yes,' said Tim. 'He said he'd been your manager.'

'It was forty years ago.' said Hiram. 'And on reflection I do remember a weirdo bloke called Simon. Very square. Ex-army. Bit of a pain. Up himself. He was a roadie for a while.'

Lorna sat back, exhausted. 'When I was at the hospice house I worked it out, especially after Tranquillity was killed. An accident was too much of a coincidence. Why would anyone want Tranquillity out of the way unless she was treading on their toes? I also thought it was odd that Tranquillity didn't tell Seth where I was. But I never thought they were rival blackmailers. And I have to say, during the long nights I did start to wonder about Father Bill, especially when he didn't come back to see me.'

'We'll be able to ask Bill himself where he fits in,' said Robert, who had been on his phone. 'Becky was right. Neil Clifford, the Area Dean, has found Bill in the Lesser Friary. He's taken him home. I've said we'll go and talk to him when we've got this part of the story straight.'

'And it's quite a story,' said Hiram, with a touch of hysteria in his voice. 'I feel a feature film coming on. I wonder who will play me!'

Everyone started to talk at once, but the excitement at piecing together the story was eclipsed by a reality check. Flashing blue lights appeared outside the mullioned windows. There was still a body to be removed and a murderer to be found. The group were hushed, waiting for a rap from the police on the big studded door. They saw flashlights going around the castle and then the knock came.

Maggie went to answer. They waited in near silence. She came back before the officers.

'The police will be here in a minute to speak to all of you. A mortuary van is on its way for Jonty.' She went over to Hiram and knelt at his feet as he sat curled in the winged chair.

'You don't have to be brave anymore, Hiram,' she said. 'It's all over now. The police told me that Seth drove that car over the edge of the ravine where Tranquillity was killed. He's dead too. You're safe now.'

Hiram's facade crumbled as he sobbed into his PA's shoulder.

Maggie too felt a surge of relief. Jonty McFadden was dead. She and Hiram were both survivors.

And maybe living in the Borders might be OK after all. She flashed a smile at Suzy. She had a friend.

* * *

The police formalities took a few hours. But it was clear that three people had heard Seth Beddoes kill Jonty with a blow to his head. Thinking about it, Suzy realized Seth had probably started his own blackmail idea before he'd met Jonty when working on Hiram's kitchen garden wall, and then, once Deirdre reneged on their deal, Jonty's wolves project had presented the perfect opportunity to get Hiram under their control.

It seemed, according to Lorna, that Seth had originally contacted Deirdre, whom he remembered from their joint past in the music business, with the bright idea of putting her up to blackmailing Hiram. They had agreed to meet and he must have gone to Liverpool to pick her up. But she told him she wasn't going through with it and wanted to be mates with Hiram again. She must have told him that she planned to exonerate Hiram of trafficking rather than accuse him, so Seth had probably killed her to save his plot. Then he'd needed to get his hands on Lorna, because when he heard her call out Deirdre's name in the graveyard, he'd realized she knew the dead woman.

He had lured Lorna away from Pat's to Camomile Cottage by saying she was in danger. But he hadn't reckoned with Tranquillity prising Deirdre's story out of Lorna and planning her own blackmail scam. Seth had planned to kill Lorna too but Tranquillity had inadvertently saved her life by getting Bill Gibson to take her to the hospice house. But Tranquillity had put herself in the firing line.

Once Seth suspected that his infuriating wife was also going to try and blackmail Hiram, his cash cow, he needed to dispose of her. What he had said in the icehouse showed how deeply he resented his wife's treatment of him. As far as he was concerned their marriage was a humiliating sham and he wanted out of it. But he needed funds. Hiram's money was his lifeboat. He needed to get rid of Tranquillity and set the ball rolling with Hiram. He would find and deal with Lorna later.

For Suzy, the only mystery now was the car Seth had used to edge Tranquillity's Mini into the ravine. His old pickup would have been far too rickety, and identifiable. So where did he get a black Range Rover, Suzy wondered?

Malcolm eventually re-joined them all in the drawing room after examining the wolves and contacting the nearest sanctuary. They would fetch the animals the following day. Hiram had disappeared upstairs for a soothing bath, but would come back to the drawing room later. Hot drinks and food were constantly provided by the housekeeper and her Labrador, helped by Bobby, now thoroughly overexcited at having a late night and talking ten to the dozen about different breeds of dog. He was up to twenty and still counting.

The gathering broke into groups. Molly, Becky, Roxy and Rafi sat at one end of the room, constantly texting and scrolling. Phil Dixon still could not be traced.

'Maybe he and Ro are spending the weekend together?' Rafi suggested. 'The signal is terrible around Burnside.'

'Is your grandad having an affair?' Roxy was astonished.

'Gross, isn't it?' said Becky.

Molly hooted with laughter. 'Well, however disgusting, you should be tolerant of pensioner passion, Roxy.'

They were already making plans to meet up before Becky went to Cambridge. She still wanted to see the gardening plan through, so she would be in Norbridge all summer. It had taken a while, but Becky realized at last that Jonty was gone. She was free of him. Her big eyes glazed a little.

'It's funny to think Jonty is dead,' Molly said perceptively, and put her arm round Becky. 'He was part of our lives, wasn't he?'

Becky nodded. She felt in her bones that Jonty was even more to her than her friends understood. He was her own demon. And now he'd been exorcized. She felt light and liberated but also dizzy and anchorless.

Roxy took her hand. 'Forget him, Bex. You've got a big future ahead.'

Lorna sat next to Pat on the sofa while Tim huddled in the overstuffed armchair beside them. 'So, you've been making a fool of yourself with a younger man while I've been incarcerated,' Lorna said. 'I'm not surprised. I could tell you'd be easy pickings for the first man that came along once you'd managed to extricate yourself from your daughter. Honestly, Pat, you've just been a doormat for that girl!'

'Lorna! That's not fair!'

'Yes it is. But at least it's Tim you've teamed up with and not some idiot from the internet. I sincerely hope this isn't going to spoil our friendship.'

Tim laughed. 'Don't worry about that. Pat is devoted to you, and I should know. But you have your own interests, like the church.'

'I certainly do. I suspect Father Bill is going to need a lot of help. We still don't know where he fits in to all this.'

'But you'll find out, I'm sure,' said Tim drily.

At the other side of the room, Malcolm finally sat down with Suzy and Robert.

'What really made you recognize Seth, or Simon as we should call him?' Robert asked. 'He's been bumbling around Norbridge for the last few years and no one else remembered him.'

'Well, three of those years were the pandemic. If I remember rightly, Simon was from a small hamlet out west so he wouldn't have been that well known in Norbridge as a young man. And he left for the army at eighteen, when he was clean-shaven and thin as a rake, with a short back and sides. When I saw him on the hill he'd been sweating and had pushed all his hair back. There was no one around, or so he thought.' Malcolm paused. 'And there was something about the arrogant way he held his head. I guess in Norbridge he mostly shambled around. I've been wondering about his wife, too. Apparently, she was local as well.'

'Tranquillity? Yes.' Suzy thought for a moment. 'You know, she didn't seem to have any old friends from the past. And she had definitely had plastic surgery. Maybe no one recognized her either.'

* * *

By midnight, they were given leave to go home. A little earlier, Pat's phone had rung out with a sudden piercing sound. She had moved to the window to answer it.

'Mum, it's me. Steve's had an emergency op but he's OK. Can I have the car? I'm going to need it to get to and from the hospital. I can come and fetch Bobby from your house now.'

'That's great news, Katie. But I've had a very odd day. I need to tell you—'

'Oh give me a break, Mum, I haven't got time to hear about your old school reunion. I'll get a cab and be on my way.'

'Don't hurry. We won't be home for an hour.'

'What? It's nearly midnight! Where are you? You're out with that man, aren't you? Mum, you're making an absolute fool of yourself and it's pretty irresponsible to have taken Bobby with you.'

As usual, Pat had been about to say, 'I'm sorry, darling', but she had caught Tim's eye.

'Katherine,' she'd said firmly. 'I have other obligations besides you. Tim has been a great support to me lately and if I'm making a fool of myself, that's my own concern. Bobby is absolutely fine. I will bring him to your house in an hour. I may or may not let you have my car tomorrow, depending on whether I can get lifts from Tim. Is that understood?'

She hadn't waited for an answer, but carried on more gently, 'And I'm glad Steve's foot is OK. By the way, did he get that job in Doncaster?'

'Yes he did.' Katie had sounded chastened.

'So you'll be moving?' Pat's spurt of independence melted away.

'Moving? Don't be ridiculous, Mum. Everyone in IT works from home these days. Steve will go down to the office once a week at most. Mind you, when he does, we're going to need you . . . Mum, Steve's calling me. I have to go. See you in an hour.'

Pat had smiled, and Tim had winked at her. Lorna had sniffed and said, 'That's more like it. You needed to get that girl under control.'

Hiram came back to talk to everyone and see them off the premises, with a promise to invite everyone back to Kirkaber 'in more propitious circumstances'. He looked exhausted. Maggie supported his elbow and escorted him back to his four-poster bed.

* * *

Pat drove Lorna, Tim and Bobby home via Katie's, where Bobby woke up and said to his mother, 'It was awesomeful,' before lolling back to sleep on her shoulder. At Pat's cottage, Pat, Tim and Lorna had a drink and talked till dawn.

Suzy took Molly, Rafi, Roxy and Becky back to stay at The Briars. Robert travelled with Malcolm, who was going back to the Gibsons'. Although it was after midnight, Robert was hoping they could get to talk to Bill. Suzy would join them to pick Robert up, after dropping off the four kids.

In the vicarage at East Norbridge there was a stilted welcome for Malcolm from Bill. They shook hands awkwardly at the front door, and it was Ruth who bustled them all, including Robert, into the living room.

Malcolm was buzzing. 'Jet lag,' he explained. 'I haven't travelled out of Australia much. My body clock is all over the place. Now we're home, Bill, how about offering us a drink?'

'Yes . . . yes.' Bill looked smaller, dressed in a thick jumper and baggy jeans. He'd obviously bathed and shaved since his night at the Lesser Friary. Ruth seemed much better. Her face was smoother and she had a look of peace. When Suzy knocked at the door, Ruth welcomed her and she joined them all in the living room.

It was Malcolm who grasped the nettle. 'So you've been camping in some church, I understand, Bill, rather than face me?'

'You could say that. I needed to think,' Bill Gibson growled. 'I've gone over and over it in my mind, Malcolm. But now it's you who have to come clean.'

'Me?' Malcolm looked astonished. 'What on earth do you mean?'

Bill was almost shouting as he thrust his face towards his brother-in-law. 'I've lived with this for over thirty years, Malcolm, while you swanned off to sunny Adelaide. Now you're back here and I'm amazed you can show your face after what you did.'

'What did I do?' said Malcolm, angry but bemused.

'Assisted dying. That's what you did. To your own mother.'

CHAPTER THIRTY

Daughters of Jerusalem, I charge you: do not arouse or awaken love until it so desires.

Song of Songs 8:4

Malcolm leaped from his chair and stood over Bill. 'That's a horrible thing to say, Bill. And it's bollocks. My mother died naturally that night, after you had given her Communion. Maybe it's you who hurried her on her way.'

Bill stood up in turn, levering himself awkwardly to his feet. 'How dare you accuse me! I knew you would. I've lived in fear of a prison sentence for thirty years because of you.'

'Stop it,' Ruth said. 'This is madness. Mum was in pain. We all saw her suffer and I think we all wanted it to be over. But neither of you would have done such a terrible thing. Explain, Bill.'

'Chris told me you had administered some drug you had as a vet. Ketamine. There'd be no post-mortem because your mother was so ill you could get away with it. Then you could escape and get that job in Australia. Chris knew it all.'

'Chris? When did you hear this rubbish?'

'The next day. Chris came over to the vicarage and said I ought to know that Malcolm had administered a fatal dose of animal sedative. I tried to get hold of you, Malcolm, but you were so busy preparing to go to Australia you had no time for me.'

'But that's bull,' said Malcolm. 'Why did you believe Chris?'

Suzy said quietly, 'Chris — he was one of your friends too?'

'No.' Malcolm looked at her, puzzled. 'Chris was a girl. She hung around Simon and me for a few weeks. She was just a kid.'

Bill held his head in his hands. 'Christina was Tranquillity Beddoes,' he said between his fingers. 'She sowed the seed of Malcolm's guilt, and my guilt by association, in my mind, but she did nothing about it for thirty years. When she came back to Norbridge she wormed her way into my congregation and wanted referrals. But when my help ran out she wanted more, and that's why she dreamed up the inappropriate touching.'

'Was Seth in on this?'

Bill shook his head. 'This was Tranquillity's own little earner. She was so clever. She knew I had seen the ketamine in the house and the syringe. Suggesting Malcolm had killed his mother and that I knew about it was insurance for her for the future. She was always manipulating people. She went to London and let me sweat. Sometimes I managed to forget about it. But it was always there, a sickening doubt. And a guilt.'

'Bill, you damned fool, that ketamine was for my job.'

'Yes, but you could have done it. Chris would have dragged it all up again if I hadn't gone along with her abuse allegations. You would have had to face a police inquiry, Malcolm, and think what that would have done to Ruth.'

'So Tranquillity accused you of historic sex abuse, but you knew if you tried to prove your innocence, she would accuse you and Malcolm of assisted dying?' Robert said.

'But exposing either you or Malcolm as complicit in that wouldn't make her any cash,' Suzy added. 'She had to monetize her hold over you and that was where the Church came in, and the false abuse claim. Potentially much more lucrative.'

'Yes.' Bill had covered his face completely. 'That would have been her plan. But the Church doesn't do private deals anymore. There would have been a big inquiry. It took me a while to realize how serious it really was. When Tranquillity died, at first, I was so relieved. Then I thought of the implications — and who else had she lied to about the assisted dying.'

'There was no assisted dying. Mum died naturally,' Malcolm said again. 'Yes, it was a bit sooner than expected, but only a matter of weeks. And yes, it was convenient. I got the job in Oz, you got a nice set of wheels. Maybe she knew.'

Bill almost sobbed. 'I didn't care about a car, you fool! But when you went off so quickly, I took it as a sign of your guilt. And Chris was so credible. You know that.'

Suzy sighed. 'Don't we all. Did Tranquillity and Seth, aka Christina and Simon, meet again in London?'

'Yes,' said Bill. 'She was always mad about him.'

'How much did you know about the blackmail attempts on Hiram King, Bill?' Robert asked.

'Not much. Tranquillity knew all about Deirdre from Lorna, and she told me the woman in the bin was probably murdered by someone who wanted a secret from the past hushed up. Tranquillity had no idea the murderer was Seth but she guessed that because Lorna knew the same secret, she too was in danger and needed sanctuary. So, I put Lorna in the hospice house just for a few nights. Then Malcolm turned up. I even wondered if he had arrived earlier than we thought and killed Christina to shut her up about his mother's death. Maybe that was the secret from the past, and Christina had told Lorna. I was petrified of inadvertently leading Malcolm to Lorna. I've been in hell over this. I just had to get away.'

'But just think, Bill, of all the good work you've done as a result of all this,' Ruth said. 'You wouldn't betray my brother and it was Mum's death that made you get involved with the hospice. I think you've paid your dues.'

'And I think you've been a drongo, mate.' Malcolm drained his glass and shut his eyes. When he opened them, he was almost amused. 'A sort of noble drongo, though. Typical Bill. And you're right. I might have done it. But I didn't.'

* * *

Suzy slept well. No night sweats. She had a great sense of security. All four of her chickens were safe under her wing. But she felt a little differently after she peeped into Molly's room. Becky and Roxy were asleep in the big double bed. She could see the edge of Becky's red pyjamas. Roxy, lush curls falling across the pillow, seemed to be wearing one of Molly's nighties. It was a chaste, if bizarre, scene. But it meant Rafi and Molly were together in bed in Jake's room.

Oh well . . . who was she to judge? But were they using contraception? Was this serious? How could she ask?

Robert had got up and gone to church, but Suzy sat in the quiet kitchen, nursing a cup of tea. Then she remembered about Ro. And Phil. She was wondering what to do when Ro called.

'Are you around this morning, Suzy? Phil and I thought we might pop over and get Becky. Phil can put her bike in the Range Rover. We want to talk to her about something.'

'Yes, that would be a good idea. I'm sure she wants to talk to you too. We've had quite a night . . .'

Suzy gave a very brief outline of what had happened. Becky could supply the details of her trip to Seaforth with Jonty McFadden later. No point in going into that on the phone.

Ro was silent. 'Well, I suppose that blows our news out of the window. We were just going to tell Becky we were thinking of getting married. Or a civil partnership. Something, anyway.'

'That's fantastic news!' Suzy punched the air. 'Get over here straight away, I'll put some bubbles in the fridge.'

* * *

Later, driving home from The Briars, Becky told Phil and Ro all the details of what had happened.

Becky found that she was crying a lot. She was relieved that Jonty was dead, but she confided to her grandad that she also felt strange, as if a bit of her was missing. She drifted off to sleep as Phil drove the Range Rover back to the Solway.

'It's odd,' Phil said to Ro. 'Remember all those years ago, after their teacher was killed, how we thought that Becky and Jonty might have the same father?'

'I remember,' Ro said. 'When I worked on that case, I always thought Jonty was both drawn to Becky and repelled by her, even at school. She had the good genes and he had the bad ones. I always rather thought he knew and resented that. Did you ever tell her?'

'I mentioned it at the time but there was such a cloud hanging over Jonty, and within weeks he'd been spirited off to a different school, so I never laboured the point.'

'From what she said today, she had some sort of sense of a deeper, scarier relationship than just bully and victim.'

'I think she must have blanked it, but they always seemed to be linked somehow. There's often an attraction between separated siblings, though in this case it was something more sinister. And now she's free of him and we never need to talk about it again.'

Ro wasn't so sure. At some point, she thought, there would have to be a longer conversation with Becky. But in one sense, Phil was right.

'It's all over, Ro. There's only us who can remember Jonty's connection with the teacher's death.'

'Do you think it's closure?' Ro asked.

Phil thought for a moment. 'No, it's not. Closure is the end of something. This is the start of something else.'

He took her right hand in his left for a minute, then put his hand back on the steering wheel, driving his family safely home.

* * *

It was a few days before DS Jed Jackson called in at The Briars with more information. 'The Scottish Police found an Indian club in the Fiat that Seth Beddoes crashed. It had Jonty's blood and Deirdre Murphy's DNA on it.'

'So, pretty conclusive,' said Robert.

'Yep.'

Suzy looked puzzled. 'But Seth didn't have a black Range Rover, and that was the only strange car seen the day Tranquillity was pushed off the road.'

'That's where you're wrong. We searched Camomile Cottage. Seth's lean-to had a false back wall and there was a garage inside with big barn doors at the rear. There was a Range Rover there. We also found Deirdre Murphy's diary, along with other stuff from her handbag. Seth must have used his Range Rover to pick her up in Merseyside first thing in the morning. I think Deirdre believed Seth was taking her to see Hiram.'

'Where she wasn't going to accuse him,' said Suzy. 'She was going to vindicate him. Being a confident person, she told all this to Seth. And that wouldn't suit Seth's plans.'

Jed nodded. 'He probably killed her in anger in the graveyard. He knew about the bins and had probably seen the key in the church and snaffled a copy for good measure in advance. We're going to look for Deirdre's DNA in his car. His secret Range Rover was damaged on the left side, with traces of the Mini's paint, so it was almost certainly him who derailed Tranquillity.'

'Tranquillity told me that shortly after they moved to Cumbria, she went back to London for a few weeks to try and drum up clients,' said Suzy. 'Seth must have created the fake garage then.'

'And he also had the biggest septic tank you've ever seen. It was always muddy at the back of his garage because the tank never drained properly. Jonty's body was destined for it. And maybe Tranquillity's as well if the road accident hadn't been successful.'

'So obviously Seth and Tranquillity weren't partners in crime,' Robert said. 'But Bill felt that Seth was genuinely worried when Tranquillity didn't come home.'

'Worried about his crime being discovered, more like.'

'And he did have feelings for Tranquillity,' Suzy put in. 'The way he looked at her . . . There was definitely something there. I think they were sort of symbiotic competitors.' Suzy shuddered. 'His doting affection and fake uselessness were obviously some sort of inverted resentment. Yet he killed himself at the place where she died. Maybe they needed each other.'

Jed looked a little sceptical. But Suzy had no time to persuade him. She needed to move on from the weird world of the Beddoes. Her new idea to replace *Lockdown Life Change* with *Out of Order* looked like it was taking off. The researchers at Living Productions had received over 1,000 responses from people who felt they had been conned as a result of Covid malpractices or let down by subsequent inefficiency and lack of care. The show had developed into championship of the consumer, and all they needed now was a friendly, credible, trustworthy anchor. And Suzy had had a brainwave. She was going to ask Hiram King to present the programme.

She was also going to take Lorna Duxford's typically sharp advice to stop flapping around in a heat rage trying to cope with the menopause. They had met in The Pantry. 'HRT worked wonders for me and Pat,' Lorna had told her. 'Pat's even got a new lover. Personally, I think that's going too far. A toy boy!'

'Tim is only seven years younger than me,' Pat had said. 'And I'm wearing very well, thank you.'

Pat had winked at Suzy. She was hurrying off later to meet Tim, whose son was coming back to Norbridge that day to introduce his fiancée to his dad. She was expecting a baby in the autumn.

'Another fan for Amber the Ambulance,' Pat had said, thinking of Tim's stories for Bobby in the car that terrible night. 'You'll be a fantastic grandad, Tim.'

* * *

Hiram sat in his monumental drawing room, looking at his visitor slyly to see how he was reacting. The other man seemed slightly fazed by the grandeur, but recovered and sat down opposite him.

'Thank you so much for coming,' Hiram said. 'I invited you here because you and I have never met.'

There was silence.

'So, what do you really want?' Bill Gibson said.

Hiram squirmed and leaned forward. 'I want absolution — now, if possible.'

'Absolution? Good heavens, man! What for? I thought that you were innocent of pimping for Sol Temple.'

'Yes, I was. Innocent of that. And you were innocent too.'

'Of inappropriate touching? I may well have been innocent but there are probably dozens of churchmen, at least, who were guilty. It's ghastly what went on, particularly in the sixties and seventies, when repression was seen by liberal society as the real problem. It was horrific that so many men were protected by the cloth and then the Church.'

'I know. Believe me, Father Bill, it was rife in the entertainment industry too. There were plenty using youngsters for their own gratification. It's easy to condemn the Church because it's an institution. But the pop business has a lot to answer for as well. Some of those abusers are household names, still venerated. But that's not what this is about.'

'So?'

'For fifty years I've been haunted by something. I've never told anyone . . .'

'Go on.'

'I knew Sol Temple never touched Deirdre Murphy. After Sol, there were others who took advantage of her, I'm sure of that. But not him. I know because I was there the night he finally cracked. The three of us were down by the Thames, near the famous Eel Pie Island, you know — where all the big groups played. We were drinking and smoking a bit of dope.

The river was full. It's tidal there. Dee Dee was looking gorgeous. And Sol grabbed her. I could see things were going to end badly. So I — well, I wouldn't say I attacked him exactly. But there was a scuffle. And Sol went into the river.'

'Did you push him?'

Hiram wailed. 'I don't know. I honestly don't know. And the only other person who was there is dead. Was that what Deirdre was really going to accuse me of? Killing Sol? I'll never know. And was I guilty? I don't know that either. I can't live with it anymore.'

Bill thought for a moment. 'If Deirdre was going to accuse you of killing Sol, that would have been music to Seth Beddoes' ear. Juicy stuff to blackmail you with. He would never have killed her.'

'Oh, yes . . . that's true.' Hiram frowned. 'But it doesn't mean I didn't kill him.'

'Oh, for heaven's sake, man. Of course, you didn't kill him. Not intentionally. If you had, you would know. Look, everyone can have absolution if they are genuinely sorry. But what are you sorry for? You tried to protect a young woman. Sol Temple was all over the place on drugs and drink, everyone knew that from the post-mortem. It was in the news.'

Hiram looked at him, transfixed.

'There was a fight of sorts and Sol lost his balance and fell into the river,' Bill went on. 'If you want my advice, come to terms with this. You could tell the police, but I very much doubt they'd pursue it. They'll think all this business has unhinged you. You'd be better off talking to God, as a starter. I can help you with that.'

'Is that what you did in the Lesser Friary? Talk to God?'

'Yes. But I should have talked to Ruth too.'

'But there's no one from my past I can talk to. Maggie has only been with me as my PA for ten years. I love her to bits in my own way, you know. But do you mean that I should tell her?'

'Well, maybe . . . She might not have been there that night, but I'm sure she knows what you're capable of. Or not.

And you could do something in memory of Sol and Deirdre. Then come to church like other poor sinners, for forgiveness. Don't demand instant absolution in your huge private drawing room. It's not a magic spell. Comprehension. Contrition. Forgiveness. You need all three. It takes time. Meanwhile, get out there and do some good.'

Bill's sharp advice soothed Hiram more than any idea that he might have an inner saint.

* * *

That summer, a large anonymous donation was made to restore the grounds of the Lesser Friary to a monastic garden. Given that she suspected Hiram was the donor, Lorna Duxford was very happy to drop her idea of a sweet wildflower meadow. Becky was able to see the project started before she went to Cambridge. And a new organist joined the music group at St Michael and All Angels, Norbridge.

He was good. The other parishioners were a little over-awed at first. But he put them at their ease.

'Just call me Kevin,' he said.

THE END

THE SONG OF SONGS

This short book of the Old Testament is part of the 'wisdom literature' of the Hebrew Bible (including Proverbs and Ecclesiastes). The full Hebrew title is Solomon's Song of Songs, which could mean it is by, for, or about King Solomon, or written in the tradition of Solomon's famous wisdom. In some bibles it is called the Song of Solomon. But whereas Solomon died in 931 BC, most scholars agree that the language is that of a much later date, perhaps between 400 and 200 BC. No one knows who wrote the song, or whether it has a single author.

Calling the book Song of Songs means it is the greatest of songs. It is a series of thirty-one lyrical poems describing a passionate relationship between a woman and a man — love in all its beauty and power, including moments of tension and ecstasy. There is no mention of God, or of the nation of Israel, though there are echoes of other Old Testament books, especially Psalms.

So why is the Song included in sacred scripture? Compilers of the Hebrew Bible understood it as an allegory of love between God and his people, the Jewish nation. It is still sung at Jewish festivals. Later, Christians read the text as an allegory of love between Christ and his church or individual believers. For both faiths, the Song brings out the passionate nature of that love, and the passion appropriate in the human response. But on the face of it, the Song is about intense love between a woman and a man. Extracts from it are popular readings at weddings.

There is no overall story, no narrative plot. Rather, the Song is a collection of love poems. But some of them are like mini stories. For example, in chapter 5, the woman at first refuses to let her lover into the house, so he goes away. She goes out to look for him, without success. The city guards beat her, she asks the 'daughters of Jerusalem' to help find him, and gives a detailed description. They agree to look, but by then the lovers are reunited.

Most of the songs are alternating contributions from the two lovers. The female voice predominates, taking up about two-thirds of the text. She is lovesick, searching for him. Each gives vivid head-to-toe descriptions of the other, with much use of simile and metaphor: 'His eyes are doves'; 'Your breasts are like young twin gazelles'. Mothers are mentioned frequently, fathers never.

There is much sensuous imagery drawn from nature. The poetry is mostly set in habitable countryside — pastures, groves, hills and gardens. This provides the idyllic setting for young, romantic love. Urban settings can spring unpleasant surprises, making the couple feel unsafe.

They are not married, at least not yet. But their love is exclusive, consuming them with overwhelming power, burning with the intensity of a blazing fire. The Song is interpreted as singing of the beauty of love as a gift of God, part of his good creation, even if we distort and abuse it.

ACKNOWLEDGEMENTS

I would like to thank St Joseph's Hospice, Hackney, London, for showing me round and being so very welcoming and informative.

I would like to thank Richard Baynes, Phoebe Adler-Ryan of *The Media Podcast*, Simon Massey, Nicki Cloutman, Brian Parsons, Avril Gardner and Jo Murray for their expertise. Any mistakes are mine, not theirs.

Burnely House is loosely based on Blackburne House, the Liverpool Institute for Girls, my old school and the first state girls' grammar school in the country. A fantastic reunion was organized in April 2022.

I would also like to thank the volunteer gardeners in the grounds around St Andrew's Church, Thornhill Square, Islington, London. Avril, Carol and Debbi are an inspiration, but not for the characters in this book!

A feral colony of wallabies really does exist on an island in Loch Lomond.

I would like to thank Lesley Beames for her advice on the manuscript as always.

I would also like to thank Richard, who has learned over the years not to refer to his 'inner thermostat' if he wants to stay alive.

Many thanks to St Joseph's Hospice for the information provided about hospice care.

Founded in 1905 by the Sisters of Charity, St Joseph's Hospice is one of the oldest and largest hospices in the UK. We provide high-quality, specialist palliative care and support to people in our local community, who have a life-limiting illness. All our services are free of charge. Our patients are at the heart of everything we do. Our care is inspired by love and a commitment to supporting patients in their preferred environment, whether in the Hospice, at home, in the community, or by caring for others who give care.

Our five Core Values are fundamental to how we live and work at the Hospice. We constantly strive to improve by using our Values for guidance, ensuring those values of quality, justice, compassion, advocacy and respect for all in relation to our patients and each other.

St Joseph's Hospice is a registered charity. A little over half of our income comes from the NHS. We need to raise an additional £7 million a year to run the Hospice. This additional income is raised from legacies, donations and other fundraising initiatives that we undertake. We owe our longevity to the generosity and goodwill of our local communities, to whom we offer a sincere thank you for the many ways they support us and raise vital funds.

Find out more about St Joseph's Hospice at www.stjh.org.uk

THE JOFFE BOOKS STORY

We began in 2014 when Jasper agreed to publish his mum's much-rejected romance novel and it became a bestseller.

Since then we've grown into the largest independent publisher in the UK. We're extremely proud to publish some of the very best writers in the world, including Joy Ellis, Faith Martin, Caro Ramsay, Helen Forrester, Simon Brett and Robert Goddard. Everyone at Joffe Books loves reading and we never forget that it all begins with the magic of an author telling a story.

We are proud to publish talented first-time authors, as well as established writers whose books we love introducing to a new generation of readers.

We have been shortlisted for Independent Publisher of the Year at the British Book Awards three times, in 2020, 2021 and 2022, and for the Diversity and Inclusivity Award at the Independent Publishing Awards in 2022.

We built this company with your help, and we love to hear from you, so please email us about absolutely anything bookish at: feedback@joffebooks.com.

If you want to receive free books every Friday and hear about all our new releases, join our mailing list: www.joffebooks.com/contact

And when you tell your friends about us, just remember: it's pronounced Joffe as in coffee or toffee!

ALSO BY LIS HOWELL

SUZY SPENCER MYSTERY SERIES
Book 1: THE FLOWER ARRANGER AT ALL SAINTS
Book 2: THE CHORISTER AT THE ABBEY
Book 3: THE DEATH OF A TEACHER
Book 4: THE JUDGE AT ST JANE'S
Book 5: THE GARDENER IN THE GRAVEYARD

www.ingramcontent.com/pod-product-compliance
Lightning Source LLC
Chambersburg PA
CBHW032153190626
46814CB00005BA/1966

* 9 7 8 1 8 3 5 2 6 1 4 6 0 *